C00 44730918

EDINBURG

D1491754

Praise for Pierre Pevel and *The Cardinal's Blades*:

'This is a swashbuckling novel packed with rooftop chases, back-alley swordfights, epic tavern brawls, clandestine roadside meetings in coaches and cool diplomatic exchanges between men of power where what is left unsaid can be as important as what is voiced . . . Overall, *The Cardinal's Blades* is a rollicking good book, full of action, adventure, mystery and some quite delicious intrigue'
The Wertzone

'If you are looking for a swashbuckler, you won't be disappointed with *The Cardinal's Blades*, especially if you like your swashbuckling with a smattering of history'
Interzone

'If I had to sum up *The Cardinal's Blades* in two words, they would be: great fun. This is the France of Alexandre Dumas and Fanfan la Tulipe: a land of flashing blades and break-neck chases, beautiful women and gallant warriors, of masquerades and midnight plots and sword play'
Strange Horizons

'A fantasy novel of depth and style . . . Thanks to Pevel's eye for detail, swashbuckling action and characterisation this is something quite original'
SciFi Now

'An enormously thigh-slapping, cheering, toasting, roaring, puking, bawling, galloping, adventuring hearty piece of fiction'
Adam Roberts

'A fast-moving fantasy of sword play, disguise and deception in the Paris of *The Three Musketeers*, with the blood of dragons splashed across the unforeseen consequences of follies and tragedies past. Dumas would surely approve and I loved it'
Juliet E. McKenna

Also by Pierre Pevel from Gollancz:

The Cardinal's Blades
The Alchemist in the Shadows

The Dragon Arcana

PIERRE PEVEL

Translated by Tom Clegg

GOLLANCZ
LONDON

Original text copyright © Pierre Pevel/Editions Bragelonne 2011
English translation copyright © Tom Clegg/Editions Bragelonne 2011
Map copyright © Pierre Pevel/Editions Bragelonne 2009

The right of Pierre Pevel to be identified as the author of this work
and of Tom Clegg to be identified as the translator of this work has
been asserted by them in accordance with the
Copyright, Designs and Patents Act 1988.

First published in Great Britain in 2011 by Gollancz
An imprint of the Orion Publishing Group
Orion House, 5 Upper St Martin's Lane, London WC2H 9EA
An Hachette UK Company

A CIP catalogue record for this book is available
from the British Library.

ISBN 978 0 575 10792 2 (Cased)
ISBN 978 0 575 10793 9 (Trade Paperback)

1 3 5 7 9 10 8 6 4 2

Typeset at The Spartan Press Ltd,
Lymington, Hants

Printed and bound in Great Britain by
Clays Ltd, St Ives plc

The Orion Publishing Group's policy is to use papers that
are natural, renewable and recyclable products and made
from wood grown in sustainable forests. The logging and
manufacturing processes are expected to conform to the
environmental regulations of the country of origin.

www.orionbooks.co.uk

This book is dedicated to my father

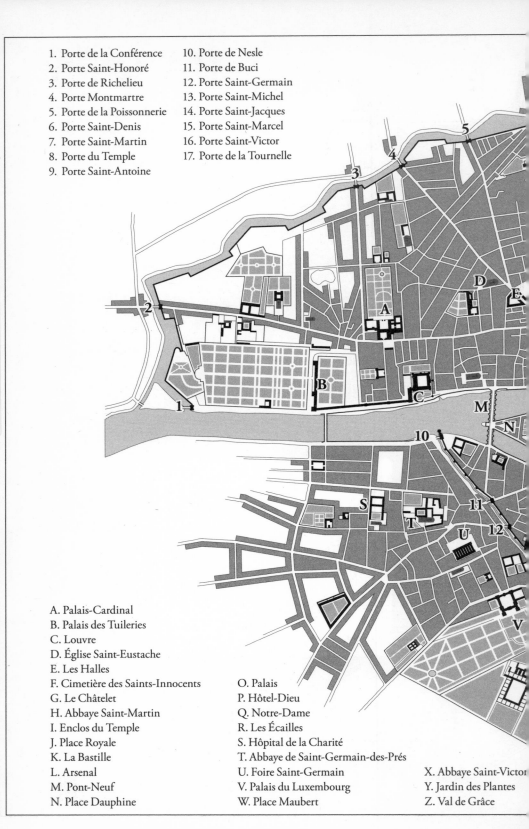

1. Porte de la Conférence
2. Porte Saint-Honoré
3. Porte de Richelieu
4. Porte Montmartre
5. Porte de la Poissonnerie
6. Porte Saint-Denis
7. Porte Saint-Martin
8. Porte du Temple
9. Porte Saint-Antoine
10. Porte de Nesle
11. Porte de Buci
12. Porte Saint-Germain
13. Porte Saint-Michel
14. Porte Saint-Jacques
15. Porte Saint-Marcel
16. Porte Saint-Victor
17. Porte de la Tournelle

A. Palais-Cardinal
B. Palais des Tuileries
C. Louvre
D. Église Saint-Eustache
E. Les Halles
F. Cimetière des Saints-Innocents
G. Le Châtelet
H. Abbaye Saint-Martin
I. Enclos du Temple
J. Place Royale
K. La Bastille
L. Arsenal
M. Pont-Neuf
N. Place Dauphine
O. Palais
P. Hôtel-Dieu
Q. Notre-Dame
R. Les Écailles
S. Hôpital de la Charité
T. Abbaye de Saint-Germain-des-Prés
U. Foire Saint-Germain
V. Palais du Luxembourg
W. Place Maubert
X. Abbaye Saint-Victor
Y. Jardin des Plantes
Z. Val de Grâce

PARIS

THE YEAR OF OUR LORD
1633

July 1633

Night coiled itself around Mont-Saint-Michel.

Forbidding but elegant, the abbey built on the summit over-looked the immense bay that stretched out below it, still damp from the last tide and crossed by short-lived streams. A thin crescent moon floated in an ink-black sky. Just above the sands, dragonnets dove and twirled in the banks of mist, their wings tearing it away in tatters that immediately dissipated in the air.

A rider came to halt on the shore. She was young and beautiful, slender in build, with a pale complexion, green eyes and full, dark lips. Her heavy black curls were gathered into a braid that had started to come undone during her long jour-ney on horseback. She wore thigh boots, breeches and a white shirt beneath a thick red leather corset, and carried a sword at her hip. She was no ordinary rider. She was a baronne, bore the name of Agnès de Vaudreuil, and belonged to an elite unit serving at the command of Cardinal Richelieu: the Cardinal's Blades. But her past concealed other secrets, most of them painful.

One of them had brought her here.

Agnès considered the abbey for a moment, its Gothic spire and tall shadowy buildings, and the village that slumbered beneath its walls, sheltered behind solid ramparts. Having undergone various changes over the centuries, the site now belonged to the Sisters of Saint Georges, the famous Chate-laines. The mission assigned to this religious order was to protect the French throne from the threat of dragons, waging a veritable war against them. And no war could be won without possessing a strong citadel. The abbey of Mont-Saint-Michel had become the Chatelaines' citadel, and they had

proceeded to enlarge and embellish it, hollowing out mysterious underground chambers beneath it and covering its
roofs above with draconite – a rare alchemical stone as black
and shiny as obsidian. Pilgrims ceased to visit. These days, the
abbey was more often referred to as 'Mont-des-Chatelaines'
than as Mont-Saint-Michel.

Referred to with a certain hint of fear . . .

Sitting straight, her hands on the pommel of her saddle,
Agnès eased her shoulders slightly forward and closed her
eyes. Perhaps to catch the caress of the sea breeze. Or perhaps
to collect her thoughts and summon her courage. She only
opened them when she heard another rider arrive behind her.
She didn't turn to look. She knew who it was.

Ballardieu drew up by her side. Squat and heavily built, the
old soldier presented the ruddy face of a man who had no fear
of indulging in wine and good food. He had put on weight
over the years and no doubt he walked with a slower step now
than in his youth. But it would be a mistake to be taken in by
that, for he remained a force to be reckoned with.

'No one followed us,' he announced.

Agnès glanced at him.

'Good,' she said with a nod.

With Ballardieu watching her out of the corner of his eye,
she looked up at the abbey again. Her beautiful face was grave,
and a curl of black hair fluttered at her cheek.

'Let's get on with it.'

She urged her horse forward.

Mont-Saint-Michel was a craggy island, surrounded by water
at high tide. It was crowned by the imposing and mysterious
Chatelaine abbey, while the village occupied its two more
accessible sides – so accessible, in fact, that ramparts had been
built to defend them. In contrast, even at low tide the western
and northern sides of the island were impregnable. Here there
were no walls, towers, or gates, just steep, rocky slopes that
were hidden by dense trees, condemning any attackers to
attempt an impossible climb.

Agnès and Ballardieu made a wide detour before

approaching the mount again from the north. They stopped in the shelter of a spur of rock on which stood an ancient chapel dedicated to Saint Aubert. They dismounted and, handing her reins to the old soldier, Agnès observed the night sky before saying:

'I must hurry . . .'

'Are you sure you would not rather—'

'Stay here and mind you keep the horses out of sight. I'll be back soon.'

'Be careful, girl. Don't make me come and get you.'

Ballardieu watched with a worried gaze as the young woman moved quickly towards an old tower that stood below the first of the rocky cliffs. This tower housed a spring that had once provided Mont-Saint-Michel with fresh water. Originally it had been accessible via a narrow stairway between high walls that descended directly from the abbey. The stairs were no longer maintained, but they were still passable. Following her instructions, Agnès knocked at the door that guarded their entry and waited.

The door opened slightly and a sister of the Order of Saint Georges peeped out warily. She was young. No doubt she had only taken her vows in the past year.

'I am Agnès de Vaudreuil.'

The sister nodded and hastily let Agnès pass. She was wearing an ample black cloak and hood over her white robe and veil. She held a similar cloak out to the baronne de Vaudreuil, and said:

'This is for you. I am Sœur Marie-Bénédicte.'

'Please don't lock the door, sister,' Agnès requested as she pulled on the loose-fitting garment.

'But I—'

'If I must make my escape on my own, I would prefer not to break my neck running into it.'

'Escape?'

'You never know, sister . . .'

Worried, and visibly pressed for time, the young Chatelaine conceded the point.

As she followed the sister up the steps, Agnès recalled her

own novitiate in the religious order. Had she really been so young, when she was forced to make the choices that would decide her future? She could scarcely believe it. And yet she had come very close to taking the veil.

The stairway was so steep it couldn't be climbed without growing short of breath. When they reached the top, a second door was unlocked and opened onto a narrow terrace looking out at the tall façade of a Gothic building that was impressive both in its size and its beauty: the church known as 'La Merveille'. The terrace served as a defensive walkway. Agnès and the Chatelaine quickly crossed it, and the baronne allowed herself to be led into the secret heart of the abbey.

Happily, there were few sentries about.

As a result, and despite her fears, Sœur Marie-Bénédicte was able to deliver Agnès to her destination without mishap. The sister opened the door at the end of a narrow archway, and followed the baronne inside after giving a last nervous glance around. They found themselves in a dark vestibule, where a burning oil lamp cast only a dim glow. The young Chatelaine lit a torch before leading them into a blind corridor.

'Here we are,' she said, halting before a door.

She looked furtively to left and right before pushing it open and then moving aside.

'Be quick,' she murmured. 'They could discover I took the keys at any moment.'

The baronne de Vaudreuil nodded and, unaccompanied, entered the austere, windowless convent cell. A woman lay sleeping on the narrow bed. Agnès had trouble recognising the beautiful face in the shadows, its pale features marked by fatigue. But it was Sœur Béatrice d'Aussaint. What ordeal could have affected her so deeply?

Béatrice and Agnès had first met and been friends during their novitiate. But Sœur Béatrice had taken the veil and even gone on to become a 'louve', or a she-wolf, as the young baronne had originally hoped to do herself. Forming an exclusive band within the Sisters of Saint Georges, the *Louves*

4

blanches, or White Wolves, took their name from the Saint-Loup convent where they were based, as well as from their military calling and their tendency to hunt in packs. Both nuns and warriors, the White Wolves rode on horseback and tracked down dragons, often armed with no more than a draconite blade and the shield of their faith. Agnès had little doubt that Sœur Béatrice d'Aussaint was one of the best.

Removing her black cloak, the baronne sat on the bed by the sleeping woman and touched her hand. Sœur Béatrice immediately opened her eyes, and Agnès was forced to bite back a gasp of surprise when she saw their glassy whiteness and realised her friend was blind.

'Agnès? Is that you, Agnès?'

'Yes, Béatrice. It's me.'

'Lord be praised! My prayers are answered!'

'My God, Béatrice, your eyes! What happened?' asked Agnès in a soft voice.

'It's nothing. Just the price of . . . It won't last, I believe.'

'The price of what?'

'You must know, Agnès. You must see what I have seen!'

The louve tried to sit up in her bed, but Agnès prevented her, gently pressing down on her shoulders and saying:

'Calm yourself, Béatrice. You need to rest. I can come back later.'

'No!' cried the other woman. 'Now! It can't wait! Give me your hands, Agnès.' The sister's fingers gripped those of the baronne. 'And now, see . . . See,' she repeated in a weaker tone. 'You must . . . see.'

Her milky white eyes darkened as if injected with a black liquid, and suddenly Agnès' awareness plunged into their abysmal depths.

And she *saw*.

It was night. Panicked crowds ran through streets lit by flames to the sound of a deafening, crackling roar. Fire rained from the sky in brief but powerful gouts, belched out by a great black dragon. Incandescent blasts struck the rooftops; the dazzling columns produced explosions of tiles and red-hot sprays of particles fell to the ground below. The city's bells were pealing in alarm. The terrorised residents jostled, fought and trampled one another in their desire to flee. Fear and panic were killing as many people as the fires and the collapsing buildings. Some soldiers were firing their muskets futilely into the air. Human torches wriggled and thrashed horribly. The blazes consumed entire neighbourhoods and the whole immense conflagration was reflected in the dark waters of the Seine as it flowed past the Louvre. The royal palace, too, had been set alight.

Paris burned, helplessly exposed to the rage of a dragon whose onyx scales glowed red and gold. It roared, spat and exulted. A single crafted jewel shone flamboyantly upon its brow. Its fire lashed out as it descended from on high to skim over the rooftops. Then it rose again with a few beats of its wings, leaving a swathe of destruction in its wake. The creature was immense and powerful, its anger bestial. It lingered for a moment in the black skies, contemplating its work, no doubt searching for another spot to continue its ravages. Then, having found its goal, it dove back towards the flames and the horror . . .

Suddenly, the bells of Notre-Dame began to toll.

Agnès came back to her senses with a jolt.

Her eyes filled with tears and she was stunned for a moment by this shared vision which had seemed so powerful, so vivid, so real. Then the full realisation of what she had seen struck her with all its terror.

Sœur Béatrice had relinquished her grip on the baronne's hands. Her eyes had turned milky again and, having fainted, her face now expressed a measure of peaceful release: finally freed of a burden she had borne to the very limits of her strength.

'No . . . no!' Agnès exclaimed. 'Béatrice! You must explain this to me! You must!'

She took hold of the Chatelaine by the shoulders, sat her up and shook her, forcing her to respond:

'Tell me, Béatrice! What did I see? What did you show me?'

'This . . . this will come to pass,' the louve murmured.

'Who is that dragon? Where does it come from?'

'No . . . No name . . . The Primordial . . . The Primordial of the Arcana . . .'

'What? I don't understand, Béatrice. Speak sense, I beg of you!'

Struggling against exhaustion, Sœur Béatrice replied:

'The Arcana . . . Beware of the Arcana . . . and of the Heir . . . There are many of them . . . The Alchemist . . .'

'The Alchemist?'

Just then, Sœur Marie-Bénédicte opened the door from the corridor and announced:

'It's time, madame.'

'One moment,' said Agnès, without turning round. Still holding Sœur Béatrice by the shoulders, she asked her, 'This alchemist, it's the Alchemist of the Shadows, isn't it?'

'The Alchemist . . . of the Shadows.'

'It's time to leave, madame!' the young Chatelaine insisted.

'Then leave!' Agnès snapped sharply.

Turning back to the louve, who was beginning to nod off, she said, 'Béatrice, the Alchemist has been taken care of. You haven't heard, but we defeated him. He can no longer harm any—'

'The Alchemist . . . The queen . . . in danger . . .'

'No, Béatrice. Calm down. The queen is safe, I assure you. You must tell me about the black dragon. I need know what—'

'The queen . . . The Heir . . .'

'The dragon, Béatrice! The dragon!'

But Sœur Béatrice had lost consciousness again, and Agnès laid her head on the pillow before turning back to the doorway . . .

. . . to find that the young Chatelaine was no longer there.

The baronne swore and went out into corridor. It was empty: Sœur Marie-Bénédicte hadn't waited for her. Swearing even more roundly, she swept her black cloak about her and set forth. Would she be able to find the way out on her own? She reached the vestibule where the Chatelaine had lit her torch and almost ran into someone. It was the sister returning.

'Some louves have arrived,' she announced. 'Three of them. On wyverns.'

'So?'

'They were not expected,' the young Chatelaine explained anxiously. 'One went to wake the mother superior. The other two have summoned the guards and—'

She did not finish, for just then the bells began to ring.

Nagged by worry, and spurred on by his instincts, Ballardieu became convinced something had gone wrong when he saw three wyverns in white harness arrive. He was nearly halfway up the stairs leading to the abbey when he heard the bells start to toll. The old soldier picked up his pace, swearing under his breath as he climbed.

'Leave me,' said Agnès in a low voice.

Her tone brooked no argument.

She and Sœur Marie-Bénédicte had paused at the corner of a building. The bells were still ringing and the abbey was beginning to stir.

'I beg your pardon?' responded the young Chatelaine.

'Leave me here, and go back . . . Go to wherever you should be.'

'Madame, I promised Mère de Cernay—'

Interrupting her, Agnès took the nun by the shoulders and looked her straight in the eyes.

'Listen to me, sister. You have done all you can. Soon, this place will be swarming with guards. I am used to these situations and I can outwit the sentries more easily if I am on my own. Off with you!'

'Will you be able to find your way?'

'Of course,' the baronne de Vaudreuil lied. 'Now, go! Run! And thank you.'

At first reluctantly, then with a swifter step, the young Chatelaine moved away and disappeared beneath an arch.

Still hoping to leave the abbey by the route she came in, Agnès headed for the long narrow terrace at the top of the abandoned old stairway. From there, she intended to go back

8

down to the bay and rejoin Ballardieu by the Saint-Aubert chapel as quickly as possible. The old soldier must have heard the bells and she knew him well enough to know that he would not sit still for long . . .

Avoiding a patrol that hurried past, Agnès made her way by guesswork through the maze of buildings forming the abbey. She had almost reached her goal when she made an error and climbed a flight of stairs. Her blunder allowed her to evade a second patrol which was investigating more slowly and thoroughly than the first, but it brought her to a sort of balcony from where she could only gaze helplessly at the terrace she was trying to reach. The detour saved her from worse trouble than the patrol, however, when she saw guards moving back and forth along the terrace while a figure in white – one of the louves, no doubt – gave them their orders. Armed men were already making their way down the stairway that led to the old spring.

And to freedom.

'Merde!' Agnès muttered between her teeth, thinking of Ballardieu.

Would he be able to escape? If he did, he would take the horses with him.

Determined to find her own way out, the baronne de Vaudreuil drew away from the parapet, turned around, and froze: three men had crept up behind her and now advanced in a threatening manner. Dressed in black, they belonged to the redoubtable Guards of Saint Georges, better known as the Black Guards. They were all gentlemen, all skilled swordsmen, and they protected and served the Chatelaines with absolute devotion.

The three guards drew their weapons.

'Surrender, madame,' said one, as the other two moved out to his right and left.

Sure of themselves, they had not called for reinforcements. That stung the impetuous baronne de Vaudreuil's pride, and she wondered if they knew with whom they were dealing. But their excessive confidence could be useful. Spreading open the front of her cape, she unsheathed her rapier, with a blade made of the finest Toledo steel.

She placed herself *en garde*, but her wrist trembled and her eyes darted about nervously.

'Come now, madame. Give us your sword, I beg of you.'

'If you insist.'

Taking advantage of the narrowness of the balcony, Agnès attacked with a feint. She slammed a sharp elbow beneath the chin of one guard, parried the blade of the next, and fell back before the third, who lunged too far. She doubled him over with a vicious knee to his belly. The two men she had struck collapsed, one of them knocked out cold and the other not much better off. The last man standing believed he still had time to act. But the young woman turned and pressed up against him, seizing his collar. There was a click and a metallic hiss. With her thumb, Agnès had released the stiletto blade concealed in the grip of her sword. The sharpened steel sprang from the pommel and its edge now tickled at the astonished guard's throat.

'One word, one murmur, and you die. Understood?'

The man nodded.

Unfortunately, the guard she had felled with her knee was now getting up. Staggering to his feet, he took hold of the parapet and shouted:

'HELP!'

All eyes on the long terrace, including the louve's, lifted to the balcony. Reacting immediately, Agnès spun on her heels and used her momentum to push the man she held toward the parapet. Surprised, he tripped and fell out into the air. He screamed briefly, clearly believing his death was at hand, but landed without too much injury on a roof two metres below.

A black cloaked figure, Agnès took flight.

The obsessive steady tolling of the bells was now mixed with the voices of the guards calling out and guiding one another. Rapier in her fist, she ran. Mont-Saint-Michel had become a net from which she had to escape at all costs. For it was not simply a matter of her freedom. She had to alert people of the terrible danger that threatened Paris. But the abbey, greatly enlarged by the Chatelaines' building and digging into the rock, was a labyrinth of passages, galleries, and narrow stairways often hemmed in by high walls. Despite her fear of becoming lost and constant dread she would run into a sentry, Agnès could not afford to slow her pace.

Bursting out of a small courtyard, she was suddenly forced to halt. A patrol was coming toward her. She turned back, re-entered the courtyard, and heard more pursuers approaching from the opposite direction. The guards would be on her in less than a minute. She dashed beneath an arch only to run into a locked door, and grimaced. She pressed her back to the wood. Was there any chance that the soldiers would pass by without seeing her? Probably not. She was cornered. There was only one question left in her mind:

Surrender or fight?

A movement caught her attention. Agnès was astonished to see Ballardieu behind the parapet of a roofed gallery over-looking the courtyard. She gave him a sign which he answered. He understood the situation and would act. She also understood and nodded reluctantly, reminding herself that it was essential she got word of her discovery out.

The patrols arrived in the courtyard from either side at the same moment. They were not solely made up of Black Guards. There were also halberdiers and several harque-busiers drawn from the village garrison. Ballardieu let the guard of his sheathed rapier scrape against the stone wall as he rubbed past it. The sound seemed involuntary and im-mediately alerted the armed men below to his presence.

'Up here! Up There! The intruder!'

The old soldier pretended to be startled before taking to his heels. Shots were fired and the hunt took a new course that drew the guards away from Agnès. Nevertheless, she waited a moment before abandoning her hiding-place. She listened intently, watching the shadows, and then sped away.

An idea came to her.

Her cloak flapping in the dark shadows, Agnès ran with long silent strides. Twice she had to conceal herself in a corner or recess as guards approached her, their weapons clanking and hobnailed boots clattering on the flagstones. They passed by without bothering to search, however.

Ballardieu had attracted the pack's attention and artfully kept them busy, but he could only offer the baronne a brief respite. She knew time was working against her and that the guards would soon be on her trail again, but there was still no question of descending the old stairway to the spring. Nor of going down to the village with any hope of successfully scaling its defensive wall. And even supposing she managed to escape the mount, what would she do next? Regain the mainland on foot? She was sure to be spotted and captured on the bay's immense tidal flats, especially now that all the sentries were on alert. Or be drowned in the next high tide that would come sweeping in at dawn. Its speed here at Mont-Saint-Michel was notorious. Not to mention the dangers posed by quicksand and wild sand dragonnets.

That left only the air.

That left the louves' wyverns.

The winged steeds should still be waiting on the abbey's flight platform. Supported by a solid framework, its floor jutted out from the north-eastern corner of La Merveille. It could be reached from the upper floor of the church, but also by means of a series of stairways and landings forming a permanent wooden structure that climbed the outer wall of the building.

As she expected, Agnès found a sentry at the bottom of the first flight of stairs. She quickly knocked him out and began her ascent to the platform. She took the steps two at a time, then slowed down and cautiously unsheathed her sword as she approached the top. A strong wind was howling in the night. The place seemed to be deserted, but the wyverns were there, under shelters that extended from the slate roof.

She set one foot down on the floor which, although it appeared solid, creaked like a ship's deck at sea. Suddenly, she heard the echo of distant shots. They weren't shooting at her, so they could only be aimed at Ballardieu. She hurried forward, crossing the platform, and looked down from the other side.

The view was dizzying. La Merveille's height was added to that of the mount, so the platform was perched nearly a hundred and fifty metres above sea level and overlooked the long terrace which guarded the north side of the rock, serving as a walkway for its defenders. That was where Agnès had arrived, and it was where she now saw Ballardieu running, closely pursued, with shots whistling past his ears. No doubt he had hoped to escape by the stairway leading down to the spring. But he couldn't. Cornered, he unsheathed his sword and turned, his back against the parapet. Another shot grazed him. He realised that he was finished and raised his arms wide in surrender. A Black Guard ordered the arquebusiers to cease shooting, but too late. They had already knelt to take aim and opened fire. The shots cracked out in a cloud of smoke. Hit square on, Ballardieu toppled over the wall and out into empty space.

Agnès' eyes opened wide in disbelief, a cry held prisoner in her knotted throat. Trembling, she stumbled away from the edge, back toward the centre of the flight platform.

She had just watched Ballardieu die.

Her face was livid and she fought for air, but the howling wind didn't stop her hearing:

'Now that was a useless death.'

She spun round and found herself in the presence of three Chatelaines, one of whom remained still while the other two carefully spread out to surround her. They were armed with draconite rapiers. Their heads were covered by veils and wimples, but they also wore boots and breeches beneath their white robes.

The louves.

'It's over,' said the one who had just spoken. 'Your sword.'

Her black cape flapping about her in the gusts of wind, Agnès de Vaudreuil placed herself *en garde* and, with a look full of hatred, indifferent to the outcome of a fight that she already knew to be lost, she issued her challenge:

'Come and fetch it.'

Above the abbey, three shapes had appeared in the night sky. Three white shapes, diaphanous spectres that held the glow of the thin crescent moon. Three great shapes that hovered in place, beating their wings, and seemed to waiting, watching something going on below.

The shape of three dragons.

The Chatelaines' Prisoner

Captain Étienne-Louis de La Fargue stood in silence before the grave. Legs slightly apart, he held his hat in both hands in front of him. He was staring down at the grey stone cross. But what did he actually see? A hint of pain flickered in his eye, like lightning in a slow-moving raincloud.

Perhaps he was praying.

Tall and broad-shouldered, he was a gentleman grown white-haired with years, but hardened by many ordeals survived, battles fought, and losses mourned. His coat and his breeches were black, as were his hat and boots. As for his shirt, it was the same dark crimson shade as his baldric and the sash about his waist, knotted over his right hip. His rapier was a long, heavy and quite sturdy Pappenheimer, a weapon which resembled this old soldier: driven by honour and duty, it was said he would rather break than surrender, and he had never broken. His patriarchal features – a grim mouth, handsome wrinkles, and a firm jaw with a closely trimmed beard – were marked by small cuts still in the process of healing, while a patch covered his left eye. His split lower lip was swollen and dark.

The captain lifted his head and his sad gaze seemed to lose itself among the rooftops of the magnificent Saint-Germain-des-Prés abbey. He was alone in the small, hushed cemetery in the faubourg of the same name. It was pleasant here, among the old stones, the ivy, and the silence. The weather was sunny, and although it promised to be another day of scorching heat, the air was still mild in Paris on this morning in July 1633.

It was a season meant for life to be relished, for laughter and for love.

Without ever appearing to, a young man kept watch over the entrance to the cemetery. Leaning against the wall by the gate, he seemed to be waiting for someone as he flipped a coin in the air, killing time. His name was Arnaud de Laincourt. He was not yet thirty years old and he had only worn the steel signet ring of the Cardinal's Blades for a short while.

A pretty young maid, who was walking jauntily past in the street clutching an empty basket, offered him a saucy glance and a cheeky little smile.

Dark and thin, Laincourt was dressed as a gentleman in a quietly elegant costume: a felt hat with the brim tilted up on one side, a slashed dark red doublet, matching breeches, a white linen shirt and top boots. With one heel placed flat upon the wall against which he slouched, he cut quite a dashing figure, his left hand resting on the pommel of a fine rapier. The crystalline blue of his eyes did not detract from his charm.

Laincourt politely saluted the young woman with a slight nod of his head.

You're good-looking, boy.

He made no response to the person who made the remark. Not just because Laincourt was the only one able to see and hear him, but because he didn't know what to reply. He, too, had noticed that women were looking at him differently.

But he was at a loss to explain why.

It's because you've gained confidence.

You think so?

To be sure! You cultivated the art of being invisible for far too long. It was becoming second nature to you. You were basking in it . . .

I was a spy.

But now, you accept the fact that people see you. And you happen to be a handsome lad. You're attractive. That's how it is.

Laincourt felt the tap of a friendly hand upon his shoulder. He glanced at the old man beside him. The old hurdy-gurdy player always appeared in this guise, dressed in rags. But his face was no longer bruised and bloody, as it had been the last time Laincourt had seen him alive. He was even smiling now, with a proud, affectionate expression that a father might bestow upon a son.

Could he be right?

Laincourt felt he had undergone a change since joining the Cardinal's Blades, the elite and secret band of five men and a woman, commanded by Captain La Fargue.

No, four men and one woman.

Or perhaps just three.

And what of that pretty young lady who occupies so many of your thoughts?

The old man pretended to be busy with his instrument.

Aude de Saint-Avold?

That's the one.

The young's man gaze grew distant.

She's gone home to Lorraine. And I doubt she will be able to return to France.

Lorraine isn't so far away.

Laincourt remained silent.

Lorraine was an independent duchy which France was preparing to invade. The French king's regiments would soon march on Nancy, the duchy's capital and a notorious hotbed of intrigue. No doubt Cardinal Richelieu would find some use for his Blades in the course of the operation. There were always opportunities for secret missions and cloak-and-dagger work in times of war.

Where is Maréchal? the hurdy-gurdy player suddenly asked.

Maréchal was the emaciated, one-eyed dragonnet that the old man used to take with him, attached to a leash, while he earned his pittance playing music in the streets. After his death, Laincourt had inherited the small winged reptile.

The young man smiled.

In his cage.

You know how he hates to be locked up—

I know. But it's the safest place for him, in these times.

Yes, the hurdy-gurdy player agreed sadly.

Then in an offhand tone he said:

Nice ring, boy. Goodbye for now.

Saint-Lucq was making his way over from the rue du Sépulcre.

Laincourt did not look, but he knew the hurdy-gurdy player had vanished.

Saint-Lucq gave Laincourt a nod as he entered the cemetery.

He was dressed entirely in black: breeches and doublet, boots and gloves, and a felt hat. Even the fine-looking basket guard of his rapier was black. A thin scarlet feather adorned his hat. It was the same colour as the lenses of the curious round spectacles that protected his reptilian eyes. For Saint-Lucq was a half-blood. Dragon blood ran in his veins, which accounted for the dark animal charm that emanated from him. Slender and supple, elegant but sinister, Saint-Lucq was a magnificent and deadly weapon.

He walked towards La Fargue and halted a few paces away, behind him and to the right. Certain that his captain had heard his approach and recognised him, he uttered no greeting but waited patiently in the sun. Almades should have been standing here, in the best spot to keep an eye on the surroundings and guard La Fargue without being intrusive. But Almades was not here. The Spaniard's tall, thin figure would never be seen again.

'He knocked three times,' La Fargue said, lowering his eyes to the grave.

Saint-Lucq did not reply.

'Just after he shut the door,' the captain continued. 'He knocked on it three times with his fist. Three times, the way he always did. In spite of the circumstances. In spite of the danger. In spite of—'

He broke off.

Almades had been his friend and his bodyguard. Exiled from Spain following some dark business, the former fencing master had already been at La Fargue's side when the Blades were formed. Silent and serious, not given to making confidences, and grim to the point of bleakness, Almades had possessed a sense of dignity that tolerated no exceptions. His only foible was that of repeating his gestures thrice. Was he saddling his horse? He tightened the strap three times. Dusting off his doublet? The brush tripled its movements back and forth. Sharpening his sword? He applied three strokes of the whetstone to one side of the blade, and then three to the other.

He couldn't help it.

'He knocked three times,' La Fargue repeated. 'He knocked three times, and then everything went up in flames.'

It had happened in broad daylight. A great black dragon had attacked Le Châtelet, the fortress in the middle of Paris whose central keep housed a prison. The bells of the French capital had pealed in alarm and those who had seen the creature passing over the city had been scarcely able to believe their eyes.

La Fargue and Almades were on the fourth floor of Le Châtelet, where the captain was visiting a prisoner in his cell. The prisoner in question was the Alchemist of the Shadows – a dragon, but one of those for whom the human form had become more natural than his true, monstrous shape. He had just masterminded a plot to abduct the queen during a ball organised by the duchesse de Chevreuse; a plot which the Cardinal's Blades had foiled. But if the queen had been saved, if scandal had been avoided, and if most of the guilty parties had been arrested or killed, numerous questions remained unanswered. And it was those questions La Fargue had intended to put to the Alchemist.

One after another, all the city's bells tolled as a great shadow passed with slow, powerful beats of its wings and settled on the keep of Le Châtelet. In a cell grown suddenly dark, La Fargue turned towards the window . . .

. . . and froze when he saw the enormous jaws opening to reveal the infernal glow deep within.

Almades reacted immediately.

With a single bound, he shoved a dazed La Fargue out of the cell and slammed the door shut behind him. The old captain nearly stumbled down the stairs before he caught himself.

'No!' he cried, spinning round as he heard Almades rap three times in quick succession on the closed door.

But the dragon was already belching its flames. The door exploded, blasted apart by a raging firestorm. A burning shockwave slammed into La Fargue, accompanied by a hail of wooden splinters. Propelled backwards, he rolled down the steps and lay stunned by a blow to the head. But the fall saved his life. Almades had known, in a fraction of a second, that there wasn't time for them both to leave the cell and still close the door.

Neither he nor the Alchemist survived.

Of their bodies, only scattered ashes and a few bones remained. Although the Alchemist was a dragon, in human form he had been no more resistant to the blast than any common mortal. With its task complete, the great black dragon had flown off, and one by one, the bells of Paris had ceased to toll . . .

As he always did, La Fargue made a rapid recovery, like a knotty old oak that only lightning could kill. He had suffered a few bruises and superficial wounds, and the doctors assured him that his eye would heal. But the pain he felt lay elsewhere, in his grief and anger, in the frustration born of impotence, and in the guilt of having survived through the sacrifice of another man.

Raising his head, La Fargue drew a deep breath.

He paused, and then turned to Saint-Lucq. His eye patch gave him an even greater air of a rough gentleman hardened by battle, but his gaze was weary.

'Still no news of Agnès?' he asked.

'None. Nor of Ballardieu.'

'I'm starting to worry.'

'Yes,' the half-blood agreed impassively.

The captain of the Blades looked down once more at Almades' grave. He remained lost in his thoughts, until his attention was drawn by a dragonnet speeding through the air above the cemetery. The little winged creatures were rarely seen at large now, as Parisians had recently begun to shoot them with slingshots, crossbows and arquebuses. Traps were set and people made sport of tormenting them, in lieu of their more distant, powerful cousins.

'We'd best be getting back,' said La Fargue, donning his hat.

The Hôtel de l'Épervier was a very austere and rather uncomfortable mansion which a Huguenot gentleman had commissioned after the Saint-Barthélemy massacre. It stood on rue Saint-Guillaume, in the faubourg Saint-Germain, not far from the large La Charité hospital. Built of grey stone, it had the unwelcoming look of a fortified manor. A high wall cut its courtyard off from the street. Flanked by a turret and a dovecote, the main building comprised a ground floor reached by a short flight of steps, two storeys with stone-mullioned windows, and an attic with a row of small dormer windows set in the slate roof. It was not an immense house, but it was efficiently arranged. The Blades had made it their headquarters, with a staff consisting of an old concierge, a young female cook and a former soldier who served as a groom.

Upon arriving at the Hôtel de l'Épervier, La Fargue, Saint-Lucq and Laincourt found the great carriage gate open and a coach standing in the courtyard. It had a superb team of horses and the coachman waiting on his seat was clean, freshly shaved and well dressed. Prestigious coats-of-arms were painted on the coach's doors.

'The marquis' carriage,' noted Saint-Lucq.

The captain nodded.

An old man was already descending the front steps as quickly as age and his wooden leg would permit. Small and thin, he had bushy eyebrows and a crown of long dirty blond hair circling his bald pate. It was Guibot, the concierge. He wore buckled shoes, a pair of dubious-looking stockings, breeches made of coarse cloth, and a shirt of yellowed linen beneath a long, sleeveless vest. Looking anxious, he tried to speak, but La Fargue cut him short.

'Give me a moment, would you?'

Just returning from the Palais-Cardinal, Marciac entered the courtyard on horseback. He leapt from the saddle and, holding the reins in one hand, he removed a sealed letter from his doublet with the other and brandished it in the air.

La Fargue seized it.

'Good news?' he asked.

'An audience,' the Gascon replied.

'At last!'

Marciac watched as the captain broke the wax seal and opened the letter. He wore a satisfied expression, but his features were drawn, his cheeks were unshaven and his hair was in disarray. His clothes were also rather unkempt, as was usually the case with him, although today he had the excuse of having spent part of the night up and about. He was dressed in a blood-red doublet, matching breeches covered in dust, a shirt with its collar hanging wide open, and a pair of worn boots. Blond, attractive, with the eye of a seducer and a roguish smile, he wore his sword with a casual grace.

'No doubt we owe this hearing to dear old Charpentier,' he explained. 'I think he took pity on us. That, or he's fed up with seeing one of us hanging about the Narrow Gallery, day and night.'

Within the Palais-Cardinal, the Narrow Gallery was a dimly lit corridor, furnished with a pair of benches facing one another between two doors, where those Cardinal Richelieu could not receive officially were forced to wait. Over the past few days Marciac, Laincourt and Saint-Lucq had each spent long hours sitting there.

'The Cardinal will receive me at ten o'clock,' La Fargue announced as he refolded the letter.

That did not leave him much time.

'Go and freshen up,' he said to Marciac. 'And get some rest.'

Then he turned towards Guibot.

'Where is he waiting for me?'

'In the main hall,' replied the concierge.

'Good. Thank you.'

'Captain?' ventured Laincourt as La Fargue was starting up the front steps.

'Yes?'

'Will you be needing me right away?'

La Fargue frowned for a moment.

'No,' he said. 'I don't think so.'

'I haven't been home for several days now, captain.'

It was true, but Laincourt really wanted to see his friend Bertaud and Bertaud's daughter, Clotilde. Jules Bertaud was a bookseller in his neighbourhood. Laincourt was always made welcome at his shop and, even if he remained oblivious to the feelings which sweet, young Clotilde had for him, he knew that both father and daughter worried if he went too long without paying a visit.

'Very well. But be here when I return from the Palais-Cardinal. God only knows what will come out of my interview with His Eminence. Is that understood?'

'Thank you, captain.'

As Laincourt went on his way and Marciac made a detour to the kitchen, La Fargue and Saint-Lucq entered the main building.

All residences of a certain social standing had at least one room large enough to hold a reception. It was called the hall, the other rooms being known as chambers and not having any specific purpose. The Hôtel de l'Épervier had such a hall, but the Blades had converted it into a fencing room where they trained, and as the place where they gathered together when they could not use the garden.

As Guibot had already informed them, the marquis d'Aubremont was waiting there. Like La Fargue, he was about sixty years of age, and was an elegant grey-haired gentleman with a dignified air, who still wielded a sword confidently and had an unwavering gaze.

When the Blades' captain entered, the two men exchanged greetings and, without further ado, La Fargue said:

'Welcome. I must tell you that the cardinal has just granted me an interview, for which I have been waiting some time now. I'm sincerely sorry about this, but I can only spare you a moment.'

He pointed his friend to an armchair, took another himself, and they sat facing one another in the sunlight from a window looking out over the garden.

'You needn't apologise,' replied the marquis. 'I did not take the trouble to warn you of my visit.'

La Fargue and d'Aubremont were not only friends, but also brothers-in arms. They had fought together during the civil and religious war that had ravaged France, and helped Henri IV seize his throne. They had since drifted apart. Unlike La Fargue, the marquis had a name, a title, lands and a fortune to look after. All the same, their friendship had remained intact.

In the large, silent fencing room, d'Aubremont leaned forward and La Fargue did likewise, as the marquis said in a low tone of voice:

'You will have guessed what has brought me here, Étienne. But before I say anything else, I would like to offer my condolences. I'm afraid I received your letter announcing Almades' death too late, and I regret not having attended his funeral.'

'Thank you.'

'He was a brave man. A man of integrity.'

'He saved my life. If not for him—'

'What happened, exactly? Is it true, what they are saying?'

The captain of the Blades nodded sadly.

'Le Châtelet was attacked by a great black dragon,' he explained.

'In broad daylight? Completely out of the blue?'

'Yes. It came to destroy the Alchemist. It was only by chance that Almades and I happened to be there.'

'So the Alchemist is to blame for this death as well?'

La Fargue understood what his friend was trying to say and met his sorrowful gaze.

'Yes. In a manner of speaking.'

The Alchemist of the Shadows. He had been the Black Claw's agent and an old adversary of the Blades. Five years earlier, in 1628, when the town of La Rochelle was besieged by the French royal armies, La Fargue had believed they were on the point of eliminating him, but the operation had become a terrible fiasco during which a Blade had lost his life. A young gentleman named Bretteville, the marquis' eldest son. D'Aubremont mourned him deeply but had never said a word of reproach to La Fargue who, for his part, was keenly aware of his responsibility for the young Blade's death.

There was a knock at the door and fair-haired Naïs, no doubt sent by Guibot, came in bearing a bottle and two glasses upon a tray. Sweet and self-effacing, she moved silently, her eyes lowered, as if she feared being noticed. She left almost immediately and La Fargue poured the wine. As brief and as discreet as it had been, the servant girl's interruption had brought the two men back to the present.

And to the reason for the marquis' visit.

'Have you discovered anything about François?' he asked.

Recently, d'Aubremont had requested the Blades' assistance in the matter of his second son, the chevalier d'Ombreuse. He served with the Black Guards of the Sisters of Saint Georges, the religious order that had defended France and the crown against the dragons for the past two centuries. The Black Guards were charged with protecting the Chatelaines whenever they weren't carrying out secret missions or military operations. But the chevalier d'Ombreuse seemed to have disappeared following a mysterious expedition to Alsace, and his father was desperate for news of him. So far all of his enquiries to the Chatelaines, as the Sisters of Saint Georges were commonly called, had been in vain.

'It's always the same closed doors, the same silences, and the same damned lies,' declared the marquis. 'I know they're lying to me. Or, at least, they're hiding something . . . But don't I have the right to know what has happened to François?'

La Fargue had agreed his friend had the right, as had Agnès. She was the one person who could help d'Aubremont, having once been on the point of taking her vows with the Chatelaines. She had reluctantly agreed to renew contact with the community which, except for a few friends, had left her with bitter memories.

'Agnès had a meeting with Mère Emmanuelle de Cernay,'

explained La Fargue as he poured another glass of wine for the marquis.

'The former Mother Superior General of the Sisters of Saint Georges,' d'Aubremont said in a hopeful tone. 'And so?'

'Mère Emmanuelle could shed little light on our affair. But as discreet as she was, the visit that Agnès paid her had an almost immediate effect: she provoked the interest and perhaps even some anxiety on the part of the present Mother Superior General, Mère Thérèse de Vaussambre.'

'And what happened?'

'You are aware that the queen detests the Chatelaines so much that she deliberately makes matters difficult for the sisters within her entourage, who are charged with ensuring her safety. Using this information, the Mother Superior General persuaded the Cardinal to assign Agnès to the queen's service: as Agnès had been initiated into certain secrets of the Order during her novitiate, she would be able to protect the queen. As she is not one of the Chatelaines, she could do so without arousing her mistrust. And in order to lend a note of urgency to the Superior General's argument, the head of the Chatelaines claimed there was an increased threat to the queen, justifying extra precautions.'

'But this threat was actually merely a means of preventing the baronne de Vaudreuil from investigating further.'

'No doubt,' said La Fargue.

Privately, he thought, however, that Mère Thérèse de Vaussambre may have been killing two birds with one stone. Of course, by assigning Agnès to the service of Anne d'Autriche, she could keep Agnès away from other sensitive matters. But subsequent events demonstrated that the queen had indeed been facing a grave threat. Had the Superior General got wind of the plot that the Blades had thwarted in the days that followed?

'Be that as it may,' resumed the captain of the Blades, 'Agnès was very speedily admitted into the regular household of Her Majesty. Later, however, at the end of a course of events about which I'm afraid I can say nothing, Agnès received a letter from Mère Emmanuelle. I don't know what the letter said, but Agnès left immediately, escorted by Ballardieu. That was a week ago, and we've had no news of them since.'

'What?' exclaimed d'Aubremont.

'After François, now Agnès and Ballardieu have disappeared. Given the circumstances, I can scarcely believe it is a coincidence.'

In the modest room that he rented on rue Cocatrix, Antoine Leprat, the chevalier d'Orgueil, examined his reflection in the cheval glass that the tailor and his apprentice had left, at Leprat's request, after his last fitting. The tailor had agreed politely, with a smile that failed to mask his unease.

So Leprat had hastened to reassure him:

'You can send someone to fetch your mirror in an hour. I simply want to make sure that no further alterations are needed.'

He was lying.

Leprat was not a vain man, and he had no doubts about the cut or about the quality of the clothes he had ordered: the doublet and breeches suited him perfectly, and the shade of grey the tailor had recommended was both elegant and discreet. But as soon as he was alone, he put on a cape that he kept in a chest. Then, not without some apprehension, he turned towards his own reflection.

It was an old blue cape, with a white cross and silver braiding, which had been carefully washed and pressed. The cape of the King's Musketeers.

Standing gloved and booted in this small room that was already growing quite warm, his famous white rapier at his side, Leprat needed to reassure himself that the musketeer's uniform did not look incongruous upon his shoulders.

Not in his eyes, at least.

For being one of the King's Musketeers was no small thing. Led by the comte de Tréville, the company formed part of the king's military household. They were an elite body of gentlemen, all of whom had proved their quality through some bold action or several years of service in another corps. One did not become a King's Musketeer through favouritism. It was an honour that was earned, and even then, one had to go on proving oneself worthy of wearing the coveted cape.

The chevalier d'Orgueil adjusted his.

Admitted to the Musketeers shortly after his twentieth birthday, he had distinguished himself in their ranks before he was recruited by La Fargue. But then the La Rochelle fiasco occurred, with the death of Bretteville and the inglorious disbanding of the Blades, sacrificed by Cardinal Richelieu on the altar of political expediency. Leprat had returned to the Musketeers and had served five more years there, until La Fargue re-formed the Blades and recalled him. He had accepted out of a sense of duty, but during his latest mission he had been forced to make intolerable moral compromises. And since Tréville had sworn, many times, that the door would always be open for him . . .

Leprat took a deep breath, straightened up and gave his reflection a determined look. After long deliberations he was left with one conviction, one which held no appeal for him: he had lost faith in La Fargue's methods and would never again be a Cardinal's Blade.

La Fargue accompanied the marquis d'Aubremont back to his coach, then watched as the team passed through the carriage gate and turned into the narrow rue Saint-Guillaume.

Saint-Lucq joined him.

'What did you tell him?' asked the half-blood.

'The truth,' replied La Fargue as he walked towards the stable.

Saint-Lucq followed him.

'And?'

'And then I had to dissuade him from appealing directly to the king.'

In the warm dimness of the stable, André was already saddling two horses for them. They waited for him to finish.

'The marquis has a name, a title and a fortune,' said the half-blood, cleaning the red lenses of his spectacles with a handkerchief. 'He is a knight of the Order of Saint-Michel and the king honours him with his trust. Since this concerns his son, why hasn't he appealed to His Majesty before now?'

'Precisely because it concerns his son. The marquis is one of those men who believe that rank does not confer privileges. Asking for aid concerning his son would have been like asking for aid for himself, as a reward for his past services. D'Aubremont has too much nobility for that.'

Saint-Lucq put on his spectacles and observed:

'But it is no longer just a question of his son.'

'Indeed. So now the marquis sees fit to make use of his rank. It's no longer a favour for himself, or for a noble of similar standing, but for another person. A woman, as it happens . . .'

'That is a tribute to his sense of honour. So why convince him to do nothing?'

'Because we aren't certain of anything and I would like to speak with His Eminence first. D'Aubremont will help us as best he can, if we request his assistance.'

André led out the two saddled mounts. La Fargue thanked the groom and mounted up, immediately imitated by Saint-Lucq. In the courtyard, the air was already baking under a high, bright sun. The Saint-Germain abbey bells, in the distance, were ringing half past the hour.

'God's blood, it's hot!' murmured La Fargue, before lightly spurring his horse forward.

The stone was cool in the deep shade.

There was a metallic rattling sound in the heavy lock before the door opened with a creak that sounded like a high-pitched scream in the heavy silence. As it slowly swung wide, torchlight from the corridor illuminated an irregular trapezoid patch that gradually extended across the floor, strewn with old straw, before lapping against the rear wall. Widening further, the light finally reached Agnès, sitting in a corner of the cell. She looked up, a lock of hair falling across her weary face, and squinted painfully in the brightness.

2

The hot weather had endured for too many long days and the brief nocturnal storm that had interrupted it the previous week had brought little respite. Paris was condemned to a prolonged ordeal under the scorching sun. Along with the heat came the smell and the filth. The still air stank, aggravated to the point of nausea by the acrid odour from the cesspits, the piles of manure in the courtyards, and the latrines where a mixture of urine and excrement fermented. And then there was the Parisian muck, a vile mud born of all the rubbish and droppings which proved impossible to remove from the streets of the capital. In the heat it formed a hard crust that crumbled beneath shoes, hooves, and iron-bound wheels, becoming a dust that got everywhere, sticking to damp skin, burning eyes, irritating throats and nostrils, and invading lungs. Even the most hardened individuals suffered sickness and headaches from this pollution, and one could only imagine the damage it did to those with weaker constitutions. Every year during this season, the dust drove the well-to-do out of the city and into the countryside in search of pure air. Today, as La Fargue and Saint-Lucq were crossing the Pont Neuf on their way to the Palais-Cardinal, the king himself was preparing to move his royal court to the Château de Saint-Germain.

But was his purpose solely to flee the foul air of Paris?

Sitting behind the desk in his splendid library, Cardinal Richelieu scratched Petit-Ami's scaly skull with one fingernail. Rolled into a ball on his lap, the scarlet dragonnet sighed happily, its eyelids half-closed, while its master meditated, absently gazing at the documents before him.

There was a knock. Then Charpentier, His Eminence's old and faithful secretary, appeared in the doorway.

'It's La Fargue, monseigneur.'

'Send him in.'

Bowing, Charpentier withdrew at the same time as the Blades' captain, his hat in hand, entered with a firm martial step, stood at attention in front of the desk, and waited, left fist gripping the pommel of his heavy Pappenheimer.

He didn't move when the cardinal rose to put Petit-Ami back in its suspended cage, the dragonnet allowing itself to be shut away with obvious reluctance. Having performed this task, Richelieu did not return to his seat. Instead, turning his back to the room and to his visitor, he looked out of the window for a moment. He had a view of the magnificent gardens and the fountain that were being laid out to the rear of his palace, but his eyes were lost in the distance beyond them.

'Paris is growling,' he said. 'I can hear her. Paris is growling with anger and this heat is not likely to help. But how can we blame her?'

The cardinal fell silent for a moment, then added:

'Paris was attacked by a dragon, captain. In broad daylight, and without our being able to determine why. Furthermore, and worse, it singled out Le Châtelet, one of the symbols of His Majesty's justice and authority. Do you know what people are saying? That before leaving, it circled the Louvre three times, roaring. A final challenge, as if to add insult to injury. It's untrue, of course. But the rumour itself is significant, don't you think?'

The cardinal sat back down at his desk. La Fargue thought he looked more tired than usual, his face gaunt, skin pale and lips dry. And there was a worried gleam in his eyes.

'The people of Paris are angry because they are afraid. And, since that anger has to be directed somewhere, I seem to be their target of choice.' Richelieu smothered a small laugh. 'As far as that goes, I am no more to blame than the poor dragonnets that are being exterminated in the streets . . . But that would be of no account if Parisians were not Parisians – by which I mean, if they were not so prompt to run riot. And these messieurs who sit in Parlement, and claim to speak on behalf of the kingdom, they have no qualms about demanding measures to calm the hotheads down. I have no doubt that the very first of such measures would be to remove me from power. Which is something neither you nor I wish to happen, is it?'

The question was perhaps not entirely rhetorical.

'It is being murmured that the Mother Superior General of the Chatelaines may be soon admitted to the king's Council,' said La Fargue.

Richelieu gave him an inscrutable look, and then invited him to present his business. La Fargue proceeded to explain that he had been without news of Agnès and Ballardieu for several days, that he was growing worried, and that he was asking for permission to investigate the Sisters of Saint Georges.

'Why?' asked the cardinal with a frown.

La Fargue mentioned the other disappearance; that of the chevalier d'Ombreuse, son of the marquis d'Aubremont.

'So, the son of monsieur d'Aubremont is with the Black Guards?' Richelieu interjected.

'Yes, monseigneur.'

'I didn't know that. Continue.'

La Fargue resumed his tale, recounting how Agnès had promised to do her utmost to discover, through her connections with the Chatelaines, what had become of François Reynault d'Ombreuse. This led to the letter from the former Mother Superior General, and the subsequent hurried departure of Agnès and Ballardieu.

'Since then,' he concluded, 'there has been no news.'

'Do you know the content of this letter?'

'No, monseigneur.'

His elbows on the arms of his chair, Richelieu gathered his bony fingers into a steeple before him, and asked in a calm voice:

'What is it that you want from me?'

'First, I am asking Your Eminence to let me search for Agnès de Vaudreuil and Ballardieu.'

'And why should I do that, rather than employ you to learn why a dragon attacked Le Châtelet and killed the Alchemist of the Shadows,' replied the cardinal, betraying a dry sense of irony. 'Or assign you to some secret mission in Lorraine, where the armies of His Majesty are preparing to invade—'

'Monseigneur—'

'And those are merely the first two ideas that spring to my mind, captain.'

'Monseigneur, Almades is dead and the chevalier d'Orgueil has rejoined the King's Musketeers for good. How can I carry out any mission without Agnès and Ballardieu? If it weren't for the timely arrival of Laincourt, I would be forced to rely on just two men!'

'Marciac and Saint-Lucq. There are captains who would give their right arms to have those two . . .'

'Nevertheless, they are only two, monseigneur.'

'Why don't you recruit more?'

'Time presses, monseigneur. And the present circumstances are not propitious.'

'That's true . . . So?'

'So I beseech Your Eminence to persuade the Chatelaines' Mother Superior General to receive me.'

Before replying, the cardinal gave himself a few seconds to think, during which his gaze remained locked with the captain's.

'How are you?' asked Tréville.

'I'm fine, captain.'

'Really? You're fully recovered?'

'Fully recovered, captain. Thank you,' said Leprat.

He was lying.

Although he felt fine at this particular instant he knew he was seriously ill, and so did everyone else, ever since he collapsed at the foot of the grand stairway in the Hôtel de Tréville, with black bile on his lips and his body shaken by terrible convulsions before the eyes of all those – musketeers and gentlemen, valets and servants, traders and petitioners – who had been present that day. He had been immediately attended to and carried to a bed, while the bells of Paris pealed in alarm around him. It had happened on the very day he had come to tell Tréville that he was leaving the Blades to rejoin the Musketeers. And it had been the very same hour when the great black dragon had attacked Le Châtelet.

Leprat had the ranse; the disease believed to be transmitted by the dragons, or brought on by the noxious effects of their magic. Western physicians maintained that good health depended on the balance of four humours that suffused the body's organs: blood, yellow bile, black bile and phlegm. To these four humours, some added a fifth, called obâtre, which was peculiar to the race of dragons. According to this school of thought, the ranse was caused by the abnormal production of obâtre by a human. But this theory mattered little to the unfortunate wretches who suffered from the disease. They knew they were condemned to a slow corruption of their flesh and an irremediable fall from social grace, because death would not release them from their fate until they had been reduced to deformed, pathetic creatures; quivering idiots afflicted by incomprehensible ravings, their bodies twisted and full of ulcers, their eyes crazed, their mouths drooling and muttering as they held out their begging bowl to seek a miserable pittance.

Leprat had resolved to kill himself before that happened. But he had not reached that stage yet. To be sure, the ranse had spread across his back in a scaly violet rash threaded with black veins, which seemed at times to palpitate with a will of its own. And to be sure, he felt less vigorous than he had previously and his wounds took longer to heal. But he had only been infected for two years and could still lead a normal existence, despite the alarming nature of the fit that had so publicly revealed his condition.

A normal life, yes. But the life of a musketeer?

It was precisely this point that worried monsieur de Tréville, without his feeling able to fully acknowledge the fact.

This was the day that Leprat resumed service in the uniform of the Musketeers, and his captain had summoned him to a private interview, as was the custom in such circumstances. The two men were in Tréville's office, on the first floor of his mansion on rue du Vieux-Colombier.

'I can assure you,' said Leprat, 'that I am perfectly fit to perform my tasks, and to do more if necessary.'

Tréville, who felt a deep affection for his musketeers but tolerated no failings where their duties were concerned, gave a sincere smile.

'Fine, fine . . . Let's drink to that, shall we?'

Without waiting for a reply, he filled two glasses from a silver ewer placed on a small table, between the two windows overlooking the courtyard. They clinked, Leprat smiling while maintaining a certain reserve and that severe military posture that was second nature to him. Even without his cape he was clearly an officer. Tall, athletic, with an even gaze and a determined air, he was left-handed and thus wore his white rapier on his right. The rapier which, from pommel to point, had been carved in a single piece from the tooth of a great dragon of high rank.

'I am truly delighted to welcome you back among us,' said Tréville.

'Thank you, captain.'

'You'll see that nothing has changed. D'Artagnan is still my lieutenant. Of course, after you left, the rank of ensign you were expecting went to another man . . .'

'I understand.'

'But there are two ensigns in my company, and although I can't promise you anything the other post may become vacant soon.'

Leprat nodded.

'Good!' exclaimed Tréville, rubbing his hands together. 'If you have any other matters to attend to, do so right away. The king will be leaving soon, for his château at Saint-Germain, and we will accompany him as is proper. We depart the day after tomorrow, fully equipped. Do you have a musket, a horse and a lackey?'

'I am only in need of a lackey.'

'You can borrow one.'

Leprat saluted and Tréville insisted on accompanying him to the door, before taking him by the shoulder and saying:

'Your ranse is still new, I believe.'

'Two years.'

'Then you should know that my doctor, to whom I made enquiries concerning you, thinks that your . . . that your weakness the other day, there, at the foot of the stairs, resulted not so much from the disease as from the combined effects of fatigue and the heat . . . So it may in fact be less serious than it seems . . .'

'Thank you, captain.'

As he descended the grand stairway, Leprat smiled as he thought of the kindness monsieur de Tréville had shown him. But he also knew that he should not have succumbed to the first serious fit of this kind for several more years, and that it had nothing to do with either fatigue or the heat. Several days before this sudden fit had struck he had visited a particularly powerful ritual chamber, where he had suffered an initial malaise. He did not know how or why it had occurred, but he was firmly convinced that the draconic magic which had impregnated that forbidding place had aggravated his disease.

He could lead a normal life, yes. And perhaps even the life of a musketeer.

But only for a few months.

After that, death would come. Leprat very much doubted he would see the next snowfall.

One of the rare amenities offered by the sombre and austere Hôtel de l'Épervier was a garden that had been left in a wild state, with weeds grown tall and brush climbing the walls. A chestnut tree stood in the grounds, providing shade for an old oak table. It was never brought inside, so it looked like driftwood, with bindweed entwined around its cabled legs.

When the weather permitted the Blades liked to assemble around this table, so it was here that La Fargue and Saint-Lucq found Marciac and Laincourt chatting over a jug of cool wine. The captain dropped into a chair with a weary expression, and it creaked ominously beneath him. Without saying a word, Saint-Lucq poured two more glasses and handed one to La Fargue. The latter gave him a glance of thanks, and then sipped gravely.

As Marciac and Laincourt waited expectantly, the half-blood explained:

'We have just returned from the Palais-Cardinal.'

'And?'

'And the cardinal granted my request for an audience with the head of the Chatelaines,' La Fargue announced. 'But he was half-hearted about it, to say the least. Plainly put, he forbids us nothing, but he does not support us in making this enquiry.'

'In spite of your worries concerning Agnès and Ballardieu?

'In spite of them.'

'Perhaps,' ventured Laincourt, 'the cardinal preferred to entrust you with another mission—'

'There was no question of that,' the Blades' captain interrupted bluntly.

A silence fell beneath the chestnut tree, where the shade was dappled with sunlight filtering through the branches. It was again Cardinal Richelieu's former spy who attempted to reopen the discussion. He did it prudently, however. For although he, like the other Blades, had been given a steel signet ring stamped with a Greek cross whose arms were capped by fleurs-de-lys, he had not worn it for very long.

'Captain,' he said, 'it has only been a few days without news of Agnès and Ballardieu . . .'

'And that's a few days too many,' interjected Marciac in a tone that made it clear that Laincourt was treading on dangerous ground.

'Certainly. But it's also less time than it would take to travel to Lyon and back. Perhaps the cardinal judged that it was too soon to become alarmed. And perhaps we should do the same . . .'

La Fargue directed a calm yet chilling glance at the young man, his expression revealing nothing of his thoughts.

Unperturbed by the growing tension, Saint-Lucq, impassive behind his red spectacles, waited for the conversation to unfold with a mixture of curiosity and amusement. Marciac dreaded the worst, however, and attempted to smooth things over.

'Arnaud,' he said to Laincourt, watching his captain from the corner of his eye, 'you've not known Agnès and Ballardieu as long as we have. Therefore you're not as attached to them as we are. Perhaps if you loved them as we do, you would share our worries.'

To which the young man replied in a steady tone:

'No doubt. But would I be right to be so worried?'

Silence fell once again, until Saint-Lucq finally made a suggestion:

'And what if the cardinal knows what lies behind all this? And what if he does not wish to give us an opportunity to discover it ourselves? Let's not forget that Mère Thérèse de Vaussambre is a relative of his, and that he helped her become the Mother Superior General.'

'No,' replied La Fargue. 'When I laid out the facts for him I mentioned the chevalier d'Ombreuse. From his reaction, I saw that His Eminence had not known that Reynault d'Ombreuse served with the Black Guards. And that is something that the cardinal would have been aware of, had he already been familiar with the affair.'

'What the cardinal knows,' confirmed Laincourt, 'he knows down to the smallest detail . . .'

The captain of the Blades reflected further and finally, reluctantly, admitted:

'Laincourt is right. The cardinal no doubt deemed it was still too soon to go to the Superior General with questions, and to risk incurring her displeasure by suggesting that the Chatelaines had anything to do with the disappearance of two Blades.'

'Well . . . presented in that light . . .' Marciac conceded. 'So when will La Vaussambre receive you?'

'Tomorrow. But I doubt that our interview will be fruitful.'

'Why is that?' asked Laincourt.

'La Vaussambre nurtures some resentment towards me. If

the cardinal supported me in this matter then perhaps I could obtain answers from her. But if we must depend on her good will alone . . .'

The door opened with a creak, and the gaoler holding the torch stayed in the doorway while the other man, always the same one, entered the cell. He was a tall man, strong and heavy, who spoke in a calm, even voice, and with a friendly tone intended to soothe. His gestures were equally gentle and careful, almost affectionate. He was one of those people who seemed to be sincerely kind, and so tended to instil in others a desire to please them in return.

Crouching down near Agnès, he discovered that she had not touched her meal and had drunk only a few drops of water. Yet he knew the stew was good, for he ate the same himself. And the water was cool and clean.

'Madame,' he said in kind reproach, 'you are still not eating. It is an unhappy thing to see you perishing in this fashion . . .'

He shook his head with a disconsolate air.

Seated on the ground in a corner, Agnès pointedly looked away from him. She was pale and thin, filthy from wearing the same clothes she had been captured in, and her long curls of black hair had almost all escaped from the remains of her braid. In her weakened state, her stomach ached and her blue eyes blazed with the sickly, savage glow of hunger. She had steadfastly refused to eat for several days. Partly because she had given in to despair, haunted by the image of Ballardieu falling backwards into thin air. But also because it was one of the few things she could still do, stuck in this cell without light or air.

'It serves no purpose to let yourself die in this manner, madame,' added the gaoler as he gathered up the full bowl and wooden spoon. 'But I will leave you the water.'

Hearing that, Agnès looked daggers at him as if he had insulted her and she kicked over the ewer standing on the floor. She couldn't bear the presence of this man, because of the kindness he showed her. She would have preferred some silent, pitiless custodian, one she could naturally hate, whose throat she could cut at the first opportunity.

And the worst thing was that, as far as circumstances allowed, he was looking after her much as Ballardieu would have done.

In a sorrowful voice, he asked:

'Come now, madame . . . Why do that?'

He did not wait for a reply, but stood up and walked to the door.

Then, in a tone betraying a certain discouragement, he said:

'We won't allow you to die, madame. I may very well receive orders to force you to eat. It would involve soup, a funnel and an oily leather tube. It's . . . It's extremely unpleasant.'

Resolute, Agnès turned her head towards the wall.

With a sigh, he went back into the corridor where his colleague had stood with the torch. He closed the door and turned the key in the lock twice, leaving his prisoner in the dark.

The night passed, and took the brief coolness with it.

The following morning, Paris woke up with the air already warm and a merciless sun blazing a path up to its zenith. A thousand hot stinks rose and, without any wind, remained there to bake all day beneath the vault of the dazzling sky.

Before noon, La Fargue and Laincourt asked André to saddle two horses. They left the faubourg Saint-Germain and crossed the Seine by way of the Pont Neuf, where, despite the heat, the traders, actors and charlatans managed to draw crowds which were almost as numerous as usual. Standing on a stool, a man was distributing pamphlets and haranguing his audience against the cardinal. It was imperative, he claimed, for the king to dismiss Richelieu and place power in the hands of the Sisters of Saint Georges, as they alone knew how to protect the kingdom from the dragons that had already begun their assault on Paris. And the man stretched his hand towards the massive silhouette of Le Châtelet where his audience could just make out, in the distance, the burnt-out remains of the central keep. La Fargue took a pamphlet which he read while continuing to ride. When he finished, he crumpled the paper without uttering a word and threw it away as they arrived at the Mégisserie quay on the Right Bank.

Travelling upstream alongside the river, the two Blades came to Place de Grève, passed in front of the Hôtel de Ville, and by way of the rue des Coquilles and then rue Barre-du-Bec, they entered the rue du Temple which they followed for its full length beneath the burning sun and slowed by the congestion of carriages and foot traffic, encroaching market stalls, deliveries, and the sporadic fights that were all common phenomena in the streets of Paris.

Finally they reached their destination, with dripping backs and damp brows under the brims of their hats. They crossed the drawbridge leading into the Enclos du Temple in silence, entering the former Templar headquarters in the heart of Paris, still surrounded by its crenelated wall, which now belonged to the Order of the Chatelaine Sisters.

Mère Thérèse de Vaussambre received La Fargue in the chapter hall, a vast high-ceilinged room, almost bare but luminous with the light streaming through the arched stained glass windows. A table stretched before the rear wall, covered in heavy white cloths that seemed to merge together and fell to the flagstone floor, beneath a large tapestry depicting Saint Georges in armour and on horseback, slaying the dragon with his spear. There was only one chair at this table, one made of black wood with a narrow seat and a tall back. And upon this chair, at the centre of the table, facing the room and the captain of the Blades as he entered, alone, sat the Mother Superior General of the Sisters of Saint Georges.

The heels of his boots ringing out in a heavy silence, La Fargue advanced with a firm step, bare-headed, his hat in his right hand and his left fist curled around the hilt of his sheathed Pappenheimer. He gave her a dignified salute, and then he waited. The cold setting for this audience failed to daunt him, but it did not augur well for the outcome of their meeting.

'It has been a long time since last we met, monsieur,' declared Mère de Vaussambre in a clear voice.

'It has.'

The Chatelaines' leader might have been forty-five or fifty years in age. Tall and slender, her expressionless face enclosed within the oval of her wimple, she wore the white robe and headdress of her Order. She was sitting very straight, her arms extended before her and slightly apart, her hands placed to either side of a letter whose broken wax seal lay scattered in scarlet pieces across the immaculate tablecloth.

'I was asked to meet with you,' she said without lowering her eyes to the missive sent to her by the cardinal. 'Speak then, I pray.'

This prayer sounded more like an order.

'I have come to request your help, mother superior.'

'My help?'

'I mean to say, the help of the Sisters of Saint Georges.'

'I'm listening.'

'Agnès de Vaudreuil is missing—' the captain of the Blades began.

But he did not finish, as he caught glimpse of the hint of a smile on the nun's harsh, thin lips.

'Do you not find it somewhat ludicrous, monsieur, that you of all people come here, asking none other than me for help, in an affair that concerns the young baronne de Vaudreuil?'

La Fargue remained silent.

'Because was it not you,' insisted Mère de Vaussambre in an even tone, 'who took her away just before she made her vows? If not for you, and if not for your Blades, Marie-Agnès would have taken the veil and today she would be sitting at my right-hand side.'

The old captain wisely chose to hold his tongue. If she continued along these lines, the conversation could only become acrimonious. And displeasing La Vaussambre was the last thing he wanted.

'If not for you,' continued the Superior General, 'Marie-Agnès would have followed her destiny. Do you have any idea of the consequences that her refusal to take her vows had? Do you know what it has cost us? And do you know what it will still cost if she does not come to reason?'

'By come to reason, you mean come to you,' La Fargue could not help himself from saying.

He immediately regretted it, seeing a flash of fury cross Mère de Vaussambre's hitherto icy gaze. But she quickly regained mastery of her emotions, aided by a welcome distraction. Having knocked, a Chatelaine entered by a small door and with muted steps in the deep silence, she slipped between the wall and the long table to whisper a few words into her superior's ear.

La Vaussambre listened before giving a nod.

Having recovered her self-control, she waited until she was alone again with La Fargue, and then said in the most formal of tones:

'So, captain, you find yourself without news of the baronne de Vaudreuil for a short while. Is there any serious reason to be worried by this?'

'I believe so.'

'You *believe*,' stressed the Superior General.

La Fargue clenched his fist around the hilt of his rapier.

'I suppose,' he conceded.

'Ah, now you *suppose*. Soon, you will *imagine* . . .'

And then, locking her eyes on the captain's, Mère de Vaussambre lifted the cardinal's letter from the table and, slowly, deliberately, she tore it in two.

La Fargue returned to the Hôtel de l'Épervier boiling with rage. He swept across the fencing room where Saint-Lucq and Marciac were waiting and vanished into the small office set aside for his personal use. Laincourt came in just as the captain slammed the door shut violently behind him.

'THAT BITCH!' they heard La Fargue yell.

In the large hall furnished with odds and ends, Marciac and Laincourt exchanged a glance, before the first man asked, 'As bad as that?' and the second replied, 'I fear so.' But the young man knew nothing more, as the Blades' captain had seethed with silent anger throughout their return trip. Sitting in profile in the deep recess of a window, Saint-Lucq turned his head towards the garden.

After a moment's hesitation, Marciac drew a deep breath, clapped his hands against his thighs, and then rose from his seat to knock on La Fargue's door.

'What?'

'It's Marciac, captain.'

'Come in.'

The Gascon obeyed.

After spending a while containing his urge to break something, La Fargue had finally removed his hat and hung up his baldric. He fell into his armchair, placed his crossed feet upon his desk, and sat there breathing heavily, his face grim and his fingers drumming an ominous beat upon the elbow rest.

'La Vaussambre made a fool out of me,' he said in a strained voice. The drumbeat abruptly ceased. 'She only received me to show me her contempt and demonstrate my impotence. She knows I can learn nothing from her unless she wants me to and she had no fear of letting me know it. It doesn't matter to her that I serve Cardinal Richelieu. Or the king. Or even if I served the Pope. Nor did it take her long to dismiss me, on the pretext that His Majesty urgently required her at the Louvre.'

'That is quite possibly true,' said Laincourt.

The young man had joined them, standing at the office's threshold while Marciac sat before the desk in the only other chair within the modest room. Saint-Lucq, whose senses were more acute than those of common mortals, could hear everything from his post in the fencing room. He had closed his eyes behind his red spectacles and looked as though he was napping.

'There is talk that Mère de Vaussambre will soon occupy a seat in the Council,' explained Laincourt.

'Truly?' said La Fargue, frowning.

'Nothing has been decided, but—'

'Then the situation is even more serious than I thought.'

'The people are afraid and the Parlement is demanding that

the Chatelaines be brought into government, as they were in the past. Some even believe they should be given the keys to the kingdom, if it would help them rid France of the dragons.'

'Right now,' interjected Marciac, 'I couldn't care less whether La Vaussambre becomes pope or sultan. What did she have to say about Agnès?'

'Nothing,' the captain of the Blades was forced to admit. 'Nor anything about Ballardieu . . . But she knows something, I'm convinced of it.'

In the adjoining room, Saint-Lucq opened his eyes a fraction of a second before Guibot came through the door to the main hall, hobbling on his wooden leg. He carried a letter which he hastened to hand over to the half-blood, who asked in return:

'From whom?'

'From a boy on a mule who just arrived,' replied the concierge. 'He said—'

'The mule spoke?' interrupted Saint-Lucq, without the slightest trace of a smile.

'No, the boy . . .' Flustered by the interruption, Guibot struggled to resume his train of thought. He looked at the half-blood with an astonished and fearful expression, and then stammered: 'He said . . . He said he was the stable boy at the *Reclining Lion* inn.'

'Never heard of it.'

'It's in Trappes.'

Trappes was a village outside Paris, where old Guibot had no doubt never set foot in his life. Saint-Lucq gave him an intrigued glance.

'It's what he told me,' the concierge explained. 'The boy, I mean,' he added, just in case.

The half-blood nodded and abandoned the game.

'Thank you.'

Realising he'd been dismissed, Guibot bowed, but then asked:

'And about the answer?'

'Thank you, Guibot.'

The old man departed, thinking to himself that the boy

could wait for a while, or go back to Trappes on his mule, just as he had come. After all, Guibot had other matters to attend to. And so he closed the door with a worried frown, wondering if Saint-Lucq had been jesting when he asked whether or not it was the mule who had spoken.

The letter was simply addressed to: *Hôtel de l'Épervier. Rue Saint-Guillaume. Faubourg Saint-Germain.* Saint-Lucq opened it and raised an eyebrow.

So, Ballardieu was alive.

They arrived covered in dust and drenched in sweat, on horses that were exhausted having kept up a fast trot all the way from Paris. La Fargue was the first to alight from his saddle in the *Reclining Lion*'s courtyard. Marciac, Laincourt and Saint-Lucq immediately did likewise and all of them entered the inn. If the din of their mounts' hooves had drawn the eyes of all those present to the windows, their sudden appearance brought conversation to a halt.

A man of about fifty, with a receding hairline and sagging cheeks, was wearing an apron over his full belly. Who else could he be, but the inn's proprietor?

'My name is La Fargue,' said the Blades' captain, holding up the letter that had arrived an hour earlier at the Hôtel de l'Épervier. 'Where is he?'

With a shaking finger, the innkeeper pointed to the staircase and, more generally, to the floor above where the guestrooms were no doubt located. The four men took the steps two at a time, with a clatter of spurs and a hammering of hobnailed boots that soon resounded across the ceiling. They found Ballardieu sitting in a bed behind the third door they pushed open. His head bandaged and his cheeks hidden by a villainous-looking beard, the old soldier flashed them a smile that erased the traces of fatigue from his rugged face.

They were forced to abbreviate the embraces that Ballardieu was keen to distribute all around. Then, since he was in as fine a shape as could be hoped for, despite a great weariness, a devil of a thirst, and a hunger worthy of Pantagruel himself, La

Fargue made him tell his story as he devoured an omelette, pâté, and ham, all the while emptying bottle after bottle. It was an impressive spectacle, Ballardieu having the appetite of an ogre even under normal circumstances. They finally resorted to driving away the servant girl who was bringing up more and more victuals. Softened by a smile from Laincourt, one look from Saint-Lucq put an end to her visits, and they closed the door to the room much to the regret of the curious onlookers who had crowded behind the innkeeper in the stairwell.

So: Agnès and Ballardieu had left for the abbey at Mont-Saint-Michel, acting upon a letter received from Mère de Cernay, the former Mother Superior General of the Sisters of Saint Georges. The young baronne de Vaudreuil was hoping to uncover information about a secret expedition to Alsace; the expedition that had included François Reynault d'Ombreuse, a lieutenant in the Black Guards and the missing son of the marquis d'Aubremont.

'Reynault stopped sending his father news when he embarked on this mysterious journey,' Ballardieu declared between mouthfuls.

'And this worried his father greatly,' said La Fargue. 'Especially when the Chatelaines refused to give him any explanation. Do you know who Agnès was going to meet at Mont-Saint-Michel?

'A Chatelaine she knew from her novitiate.'

'Her name?'

The old soldier thought for a moment, but then admitted:

'No, I've forgotten it.'

'Never mind. Continue.'

They had used the cover of night to carry out their operation. While Agnès secretly entered the abbey with help from an accomplice, Ballardieu had remained at the foot of the mount, in the bay, guarding their horses. But he had grown worried and finally climbed the same stairs the young woman had taken and had entered the abbey in turn.

'That was when the alarm was sounded.'

'Through your fault?' asked Marciac.

'No! But I quickly realised that the girl was in trouble.'

Ballardieu did not recount how he had deliberately diverted Agnès' pursuers towards himself, but rather jumped forward to the moment when he took a musket ball to the shoulder and had fallen into the void.

'I hope that Agnès did not witness it,' he said in a desolate tone. 'Or she will believe me dead, poor thing.'

'So you don't know what has become of Agnès?' commented La Fargue.

'Not for sure. But I believe she is being held prisoner in the abbey.' And seeing the worried glances being exchanged by his audience, he understood and protested, 'Hey now! None of that! Agnès is still alive! I would know if something had happened to her . . .'

'How?' Laincourt asked.

'I . . . would . . . know,' replied the old soldier, carefully articulating each word with a stubborn air.

'Very well,' intervened the Blades' captain. 'Let us assume that Agnès is alive and is being held prisoner at Mont-Saint-Michel. Now you, Ballardieu, what happened to you next?'

He took a great gulp of wine.

'Well, I can assure you that this abbey is very high, indeed. You simply don't realise how high it really is, until you topple over its walls.'

His fall had been painfully broken by the branches of the trees covering the north side of the mount. It was largely thanks to his bull-like constitution, and also, perhaps, to the proverbial luck of drunkards, that he did not suffer any broken bones. Nevertheless, his head had taken a brutal blow from landing on a stone. So, dazed and staggering, but also fearful that his adversaries would come after him to make sure he was truly dead, Ballardieu had continued his flight down the steep and rocky slope, braking himself against tree trunks with an unsteady hand, seizing hold of low branches, often stumbling and sometimes falling, but always rising again. Finally, he had emerged from the foliage and stepped out on the sandy bed of the bay.

'My head was spinning and my vision was blurred. But I

knew the sun had risen and that time was of essence. So I walked towards the mainland shore. Which was not an excellent idea.'

He had forgotten about the great tides. The sea water rushing back into the bay had caught up with him and the waves had first battered at his calves, and then around his waist, before overcoming his last remaining strength. Swept off his feet, he'd lost all consciousness.

'I was sure I was going to drown. But my hour had not yet struck and I was washed up on a beach, where I eventually came to my senses.'

As for what followed, Ballardieu had only scattered memories. Befuddled and almost delirious, his ears buzzing and the ground pitching beneath his leaden feet, he walked on, crushed by a terrible sun that blinded him, without any idea of where he was heading. How long did he wander?

He collapsed, only to wake in a bed.

'Some peasants found me in a ditch and brought me to their village priest. Their holy man bandaged my wounds and watched over me until I came round. I was weak and famished, but I was saved.'

Alone, he could do nothing for Agnès. Therefore he'd needed to return to Paris as quickly as possible, and without waiting to fully recover, he took to the road on the back of an old mule that the priest had kindly loaned him against the promise of future payment. For Ballardieu had lost everything during his escape: his weapons, his purse, and even his boots.

'As for my boots,' he commented, 'I do wonder if they are being worn at present by one of the peasants who carried me to the priest. But I suppose, as the saying goes, every deed deserves its reward.'

Since he had not spared it, the poor old mule had died near Trappes after an exhausting four-day journey, which Ballardieu endured on an almost empty stomach.

'And here I am. You can guess the rest . . . Now pray tell, where is that sad fellow, Almades? Did you leave him behind in Paris? And what of Leprat?

*

The Blades were soon on the road back to Paris, riding at a slow trot beneath a blazing sun. Ballardieu was on a rented horse. They remained silent, out of respect for the old soldier who had barely been able to contain his tears when he heard of Almades' death under such terrible circumstances.

'A dragon,' he muttered from time to time, with a mixture of grief and disbelief. 'Burnt alive by a dragon . . .'

At last, when they passed by the first houses in the faubourg Saint-Germain, Laincourt asked him:

'Why didn't you write to us earlier? A letter would have reached us faster than you would have . . .'

'But I did!'

'We never received anything,' La Fargue said over his shoulder.

'My first letter must have been lost . . .'

'Or else it will arrive eventually. No matter, now.'

Ballardieu urged his horse forward to draw level with La Fargue.

'We must rescue Agnès, captain. And when that's done, we must avenge Almades.'

'Believe me, Ballardieu, I will not rest until Agnès is free. But Mère de Vaussambre is hostile to us and I don't imagine we can take Mont-Saint-Michel by force.'

They were riding up rue du Cherche-Midi at a walk, towards Place de la Croix-Rouge.

'And Richelieu?' insisted Ballardieu.

'We can expect no help at all from the cardinal,' admitted La Fargue.

'What about Mère de Cernay! She feels affection for Agnès and has no fondness in her heart for La Vaussambre. Surely she will help us? She already has!'

'Do you know where to find her?'

The old soldier's expression clouded over.

'No,' he confessed. 'Only know that she cannot reside far from Paris. Agnès was not long in returning, last time she went to find her.'

'But it's simply not possible to go knocking on the doors of every convent, retreat and domain the Chatelaines possess in the region,' Marciac pointed out.

'It would take us more than a week,' said Saint-Lucq.

'And to what result, other than alarming La Vaussambre?' the Gascon added regretfully.

Upon hearing those words, a glow suddenly kindled in La Fargue's eyes.

The Gaget Messenger Service was located in rue de Gaillon, at the corner with rue des Moineaux, not far from the Saint-Roch hill and its picturesque windmills. The owner had been exercising his trade with a royal licence for several years now and was the sole agent authorised to employ trained dragonnets to carry letters to Reims or Rouen, Amiens or Orléans, and even as far as Lille, Rennes, or Dijon. The services his company provided were more expensive, but also quicker and more reliable, than ordinary post and couriers.

That evening, Urbain Gaget had a satisfied air as he stood in the shadow of the circular tower which, pierced with rows of half-moon openings, housed his carrier dragonnets. Slim and grey-haired, he was a fairly handsome man dressed in bourgeois fashion. Oblivious to the activity going on in his courtyard, he was observing the five wyverns he had recently acquired. Thanks to them he was about to expand the scope of his operations. To be sure, his business was flourishing and would continue to do so as long as he retained the royal licence protecting his monopoly, a privilege that he owed to the confidence Cardinal Richelieu had placed in him. But ministers came and went, and kings died. Moreover, Gaget was an entrepreneur at heart and his messenger business was starting to bore him, now that it had become prosperous. It was time to take on a new challenge.

Having given his instructions to the great reptiles' handlers, Gaget returned to his office, leaving word that he was not to be disturbed. But he had barely shut the door when a voice made him turn round with a start.

'Those wyverns, what are they for?' asked Saint-Lucq.

The half-blood was leaning against a wall, with his arms crossed, in a shadowy corner.

Recognising him, Gaget let out a sigh, and in a reproachful tone said:

'Good Lord! Why must you always slip in here like this? One day, you'll be the death of me!'

'I don't like knocking on doors. And do you really want people to see me knocking on yours?'

'No . . . No, of course not,' Gaget admitted grudgingly.

He sat down.

'So? What are they for, the wyverns?' insisted Saint-Lucq. 'They're new.'

'Well, since there are travellers who rent horses . . .'

The half-blood nodded: he already understood.

'But almost everyone knows how to ride a horse,' he objected. 'And even if they don't know, they can still hope that if they fall off they won't injure themselves too badly. Whereas if they find themselves on the back of a wyvern . . .'

'My beasts are the most placid to be found. They can also carry two, with my wyverneers guiding.'

'When will you start?'

'Soon. It's all in place.'

'That's good to know.'

Gaget preferred not to respond to this.

The royal licence that had made his fortune had come with certain strings attached, Richelieu having quickly seen how to make best use of this dragonnet messenger service. It sometimes involved transporting documents as a matter of urgency and with no questions asked. Or else arranging for certain items to make a quick detour by way of the Palais-Cardinal before being delivered to their final destination. Or receiving these visits from Saint-Lucq who, as he had continued to serve His Eminence after the disbanding of the Blades, had been discreetly coming here to pick up his orders.

Gaget had no doubt that sooner or later his rental wyverns would also be required to make a contribution. But he did not have leisure to dwell on this thought, as Saint-Lucq was asking him:

'How much to carry a message?'

'That depends. Where does it need to be delivered?'

'In the area around Paris.'

'The area around Paris? That's not a proper destination!'

'To be honest, there are several destinations, all of which I have listed here.'

Monsieur Urbain Gaget's eyes widened as they ran down the list that the half-blood unfolded under his nose.

'Really?' he asked, incredulous.

'Really.'

'As you wish. But my dragonnets will only travel at night. There have been too many imbeciles using them for target practice, of late.'

Gaget's first dragonnets took flight just after dusk, and numerous others followed until well after midnight. All of them reached their destinations and the next morning, in the Enclos du Temple, the comte d'Orsan requested an audience with the Chatelaines' Mother Superior General. Slender, with fine features and dark eyes, he wore the black uniform and breastplate of the company of the Saint Georges Guards, of which he was the captain at the age of thirty years. Mère de Vaussambre bade him enter immediately and was handed an unsealed letter that was not addressed to her and whose contents she read with a frown.

'Well?' she asked, raising her eyes to meet his.

'Other letters, identical to this one, were sent last night to all our convents, fiefdoms and domains throughout Ile-de-France.

The Mother Superior General read the letter a second time:

To mother superior de Cernay,
 Agnès is being held prisoner at Mt-St-Michel. Help us if you can.
La F.

'Captain La Fargue must be desperate to resort to such a manoeuvre,' she observed with a half-smile. 'It's not his style . . . It's disappointing, even.'

'It's a manoeuvre which might meet with a certain degree of success, mother superior.'

'Do you think so?' Mère Thérèse de Vaussambre asked in amusement. 'Let us suppose that one of these letters actually reaches Mère de Cernay. Or that the content is simply reported to her . . . What then? What can she do? Nothing. Absolutely nothing.'

'Mother superior de Cernay still exerts a certain influence.'

'But does she have the ear of the king, as I do? Does the Parlement wish to see her seated on the Council?'

D'Orsan made a bow in her direction.

'Certainly not, mother superior . . .'

Thoughtful for a moment, La Vaussambre toyed distractedly with the unsealed letter.

'There is one aspect of this message, however, that does bother me,' she said.

'And that is?'

'La Fargue knows that we are holding Marie-Agnès. He even knows where. That is a new development which is cause for concern. Who could have told him? And what will he do when this ridiculous appeal to Mère de Cernay leads him nowhere?'

Seeing that Mère de Vaussambre was still pondering the question, the captain of the Black Guards remained silent.

'Transfer Marie-Agnès,' she ordered. 'As soon and as quickly as possible. This message is not meant for Mère de Cernay, but for me. La Fargue knows that one of his letters would reach me. He wants me to lower my guard. He wants me to believe he is reduced to placing his faith in such a foolish enterprise. But our dear captain is not one to lose his head and shoot his musket into the dark. Rest assured that at this very moment he is up to something clever. Perhaps he is even planning Marie-Agnès' escape. Now that would be much more his style . . .'

'Would he dare?'

'Oh yes. Knowing the man as I do, I think he might even succeed.'

'So where do you want us to take the baronne de Vau-dreuil?'

'The Tour seems to me an appropriate place for her, from now on.'

D'Orsan hesitated a brief instant, but then bowed his head. 'As you command.'

Once she was alone, the Chatelaines' Mother Superior General went to the window, still thinking about La Fargue. She wondered what coup the old warhorse was preparing against her, thinking that he had outwitted her and regained the initiative.

She smiled.

Upon his arrival in rue des Francs-Bourgeois, Captain La Fargue found the d'Aubremont household in the midst of preparations to move. The custom was to travel with one's furnishings and, as the royal court would soon be leaving Paris, the master of the house was making ready to return to his country estate. This estate was not far from the Château de Saint-Germain, where the king retired for the season every year, away from the polluted atmosphere of the capital.

The marquis d'Aubremont received La Fargue in his private office, a pleasantly decorated room whose two windows with their small diamond-shaped panes looked out on the garden. The light shone through them, cut into crystalline patterns.

The two men exchanged a friendly handshake, before the marquis offered the captain a seat. He refused it.

'I can't stay,' he said.

D'Aubremont frowned.

'Does it have to do with our affair?'

'Yes. And more particularly, it concerns Agnès.'

'The baronne de Vaudreuil? Have you learned what has become of her?'

'We're almost certain that we know.'

La Fargue hesitated, looked towards the closed door, took hold of the marquis' elbow to draw him away from it, and said in a low voice:

'We think that Agnès is being held prisoner by the Sisters of Saint Georges, on the orders of Mère de Vaussambre. No doubt Agnès has discovered some secret. An important secret which the Chatelaines do not want revealed, and that somehow concerns your son . . . Be that as it may, Agnès lives and must be rescued.'

'I promised you my help, Étienne. The offer still stands.'

'That is precisely why I've come. Only a few days ago, I dissuaded you from using your rank to appeal to the king, did I not?'

'Yes, indeed. You convinced me to abandon the idea.'

'I was wrong.'

A short time later, upon leaving the Hôtel d'Aubremont, La Fargue met Saint-Lucq who was waiting for him in the shade of a porch. The half-blood was returning from the Temple neighbourhood, or the neighbourhood of the Chatelaines, as it was known.

'Well?' he asked.

'The marquis will help us,' La Fargue informed him. 'And on your side of things?'

'I've found a way.'

As the afternoon came to an end, Laincourt joined Marciac and Ballardieu at the Hôtel de l'Épervier. They were sitting in the shade beneath the chestnut tree, neither saying much. His hands clasped at the back of his neck, the Gascon was stretched out on the narrow bench, eyes closed, with a blade of grass in his mouth. As for Ballardieu, he was sprawled as much as one can be in a chair without falling out of it, with one arm passed over the back and one boot resting on a stool. He was getting slowly drunk on white wine. Three stoneware jugs were lying on the old bleached table, and Ballardieu was drinking from the mouth of a fourth while gazing moodily at some faraway point before him.

'Are you feeling all right?' Laincourt asked as he sat down.

The old soldier's features became animated.

'Yes, thank you.'

'I'm glad to hear it.'

'Oh, you needn't worry about me. I'm one of those people who are as right as rain after a good night's sleep.'

The truth was he was looking relatively well, with his beard now clean and trimmed, his eyes lively and his smile broad and sincere. And he still gave off an impression of strength and solidity.

'So,' he went on to say, 'it seems you're one of us, now.'

Laincourt lowered his eyes to the steel signet ring on his finger and said:

'So it seems . . .'

'I'm glad to hear it. And not simply because our ranks are thinning.'

'Thank you.'

'Almades' death. Leprat's departure . . . Do we even know why he left us?

Laincourt shrugged.

'He's gone back to the Musketeers,' announced Marciac, still lying on the bench with his eyes closed.

'That's not a good enough reason,' objected Ballardieu.

'He's sick with the ranse.'

'All the same. Besides, if the ranse doesn't stop him serving with the Musketeers . . .'

The Gascon had no counter to this argument, so the three men fell into silence. Until Marciac declared:

'I wish that Agnès were here.'

His two companions exchanged intrigued glances.

'Obviously. As do we all,' grumbled Ballardieu, his anxiety stirring again.

'I wish that Agnès were here,' continued Marciac, 'so I could tell her how much I miss Gabrielle. Have I told you about Gabrielle, Laincourt?'

Ballardieu rolled his eyes skywards.

The beautiful Gabrielle ran a brothel in rue Grenouillère. She was Marciac's one and only true love, despite his numerous other amorous adventures.

'I believe,' replied Laincourt, 'that your female conquests

must be the only people who do not hear you talk about your mistress.'

Ballardieu was unable to restrain an amused hiccup.

Marciac rose up on an elbow and turning to the young man, enquired:

'Are you mocking me?'

'A little, yes.'

The Gascon appeared to weigh up the pros and cons, the pertinence of the mockery and its humour. And, being a good sport, he stretched out again on his back and asked:

'Have we received so much as a single reply to all those messages that emptied our war chest?'

'No word, I believe, has yet come back from the Gaget Messenger Service. And Saint-Lucq, who could best answer you on this point, seems to have disappeared.'

'You'll have to get used to the sudden and mysterious absences of our dear Saint-Lucq. That's his style . . . But sending all those letters out like bottles tossed into the sea, they're not La Fargue's usual style. It's a positively clumsy effort on his part.'

'What else could we do? We cannot attempt to free Agnès by force. Even if we succeeded, Mère de Vaussambre would complain to the king and have us arrested. And I doubt the cardinal would come to our defence, when he has forbidden us from incurring the Chatelaines' displeasure . . . Moreover, even if this is a point of law that might be disputed, it's possible that the baronne de Vaudreuil—'

'You might as well call her Agnès.'

'—it's possible that Agnès is being held for entirely legitimate reasons.'

'Pardon?' Ballardieu exclaimed.

'The Sisters of Saint Georges have the right to administer high, middle and low justice within their fiefdoms and domains,' Laincourt reminded him. 'This affair falls under their jurisdiction, before which . . . before which Agnès would have to answer several accusations.'

'Would you by any chance be a man of law?' the old soldier asked in a suspicious tone.

Lawyers suffered from a bad reputation. They were viewed as masters at splitting hairs to prolong legal proceedings and multiply the number of documents required in order to earn as much money as possible from their clients. And their reputation was, by and large, well deserved.

'I almost became one . . . But the case remains: if we act openly against the Sisters of Saint Georges, we will be dragged before their courts of justice, not those of the king.'

'Nevertheless,' decreed Marciac, 'these letters will achieve nothing other than alarming La Vaussambre.'

'Perhaps that was their purpose . . .'

'One rarely gains anything by kicking an anthill.'

'Except for ants up the breeches,' declared Ballardieu who, at the mere thought, suddenly discovered an itch in an awkward place.

La Fargue's arrival interrupted these serious deliberations.

Straddling a chair turned back to front, the captain accepted the jug that Ballardieu offered him and emptied it in three gulps. Then he wiped his mouth on the back of his sleeve, smoothed his closely trimmed beard and, for a few seconds, looked gravely at the three men who all waited expectantly for him to speak.

'I have a plan,' he said at last. 'But you will need to trust me.'

'For your eyes, madame,' he said in his gentle voice. 'It's only for your eyes.'

The two gaolers had behaved in their usual manner, the one holding the torch remaining at the door while the other entered the cell. This time, however, they did not bring her a meal. So Agnès had recoiled when the man had leaned over her.

'For your eyes, madame. It's only for your eyes.'

Despite her weakened state, she had stiffened. But she had allowed the gaoler to tie a blindfold over her eyes. He had helped her to stand and guided her out of the cell, then through a series of corridors, stairways, and doors that she could not see.

She finally understood when she emerged into the open air, and full sunlight, on a high terrace within the abbey of Mont-Saint-Michel. The cloth was thin. She could almost see right through it, in the hot, dazzling clarity of a glorious day. The blindfold was intended to prevent the light from hurting her eyes, after the long period she had spent in darkness.

'Thank you,' she murmured to the gaoler.

She immediately regretted those two words that managed to pass through the barriers of her lips and her resistance.

'Goodbye, madame.'

Other hands seized her, hands that were more brutal, belonging to a soldier. Her wrists were tied together before her. Forced to advance, she had to struggle against an instinct-ive urge to turn back in distress to her gaoler, who – she imagined – was watching her move away, like a helpless and miserable lover observing the departure of his beloved. She regained her self-control, guessing that the men leading her away were Black Guards. But where were they taking her? And why?

She heard the wyverns before she could make out their silhouettes. The winged reptiles waited peacefully. She was put on the back of one of them, occupying the second seat of a double saddle. She knew that these saddles had leather handles for the passenger and, having found them by fum-bling blindly before her, she gripped them firmly while her feet were placed in the stirrups. A man mounted in front of her and took up the reins.

'Hold on tight,' he said.

And then the wyvern was flying.

After enduring the deep and stifling darkness of her cell, Agnès at first abandoned herself to a kind of happy exhilara-tion as they moved through the air, rocked by the slow beats of the wyvern's wings. Then the time started to seem unexpect-edly long and, prompted by curiosity, she lifted the blindfold to her brow. The guard who was directing their wyvern saw as much when he glanced over his shoulder, but said nothing. She thought about trying something against him, but finally rejected the idea. The man wasn't armed, but there were three other wyverns escorting them, all of them ridden by members of the Black Guards with swords at their sides, and more importantly, a pair of pistols apiece in their saddle holsters.

So Agnès bided her time and lost herself in contemplation of the landscape beneath them. They were proceeding westward.

Perhaps towards Paris.

They flew until evening, when they landed in the courtyard of a large fortified abbey belonging to the Chatelaines. Although she was kept under constant watch, Agnès was allowed to wash, change her clothing, and eat. She did not refuse the meal offered to her, aware that her situation was changing and that she might soon need her strength. She forced herself not to devour her food too quickly and was careful to water her wine, out of a fear of making herself sick. No one said a word to her and she asked no questions even though there were some that were burning her lips.

The following morning, after a good night's sleep in a real bed and another light meal eaten in the deserted refectory, Agnès once again had her wrists bound and was forced to climb into a heavy wagon that resembled a large strongbox. It was in fact exactly that: a solid box made of sturdy oak covered in iron plating and mounted on wheels, used for transporting valuables. It was entered from the rear, after bending double to pass through a reinforced door equipped with two locks and a small sliding hatch. Inside, there was an iron chest riveted to the floor against the rear wall.

Agnès sat on the chest, her back to the direction of travel and facing the door that was closed upon her, plunging her into darkness. She heard keys being turned in each lock, then saw the hatch open and remain so, no doubt to allow some air and light to enter. Then the driver's whip cracked and the wagon set into motion, escorted by five guards on horseback.

A short while later, the convoy was advancing along a dusty road at a fast trot, in the harsh light of an already scorching sun.

Antoine Leprat, the chevalier d'Orgueil, was having lunch alone in a modest inn near the Hôtel de Tréville, in rue du

Pot-de-Fer. Some birds – whose fat fell in yellow drops – were cooking on a spit in the fireplace, while various soups and stews simmered beneath the lids of small black pots arranged along its outer edge. There were several tables standing before the hearth. Two rather elderly sisters, both widows, ran the establishment, cooking and serving the dishes. The atmosphere was quiet and cosy, and the clientele was mostly composed of regulars. The wine cellar was mediocre but the food was rather good. The light, as well as the noise from outside, was heavily filtered.

'May I sit down?'

Leprat lifted his nose from his plate to discover, to his pleasure, a gentleman of some forty years of age, whose handsome appearance and calm bearing indicated – without any possibility of error – that this was a great nobleman. Yet no one knew his true name, only the *nom de guerre* under which he wore the blue cape of the King's Musketeers.

'Athos!' Leprat exclaimed joyfully as he rose.

They exchanged a warm handshake and sat down facing one another.

'It's . . . quiet in here,' said Athos, taking in the humble nature of their surroundings with a steady gaze.

Leprat smiled.

'There are more charming places in Paris, and even in the faubourg Saint-Germain itself, I grant you that. But as you said, it's quiet here . . . So how did you know where to find me? I only ever come here on my own.'

Rather than reply, Athos waited for the chevalier to guess, with a faint smile on his lips, and it did not take Leprat long.

'D'Artagnan,' he concluded.

'What can I say? He may have become a lieutenant, but d'Artagnan has not changed. And he's always been intensely curious. He has to know everything. Secrets have the same effect on him as those red capes the Spaniards – one can only wonder why – like to wave in front of bulls. And you can be sure that when he saw you slipping away at noon and in the evenings, that Gascon devil couldn't resist the temptation to follow you. You must not hold it against him.'

64

'I don't hold it against him; besides, my habit of coming here is no great secret.'

A second glass and a new jug of cool wine were brought to the table. However, it was not one of the two sisters who served them, but Grimaud, Athos' lackey, who had been trained by the musketeer to express himself solely by means of signs and monosyllables . . . and to anticipate his master's desires.

The silent, zealous and discreet domestic then went to wait, well away from the table.

'Your habit of coming here is no great secret,' Athos said. 'But it is no mystery, either, to anyone familiar with His Majesty's Musketeers . . . You've been given the cold shoulder since your return, haven't you?'

Leprat looked at the other man, noting that he had only just returned from several days' leave of absence and already seemed to know everything. Again, no doubt from d'Artagnan. Nevertheless, the information was accurate: the company had not extended a particularly warm welcome to the chevalier d'Orgueil, despite a few brave demonstrations of friendship, and despite the trust that Tréville had clearly manifested in welcoming him back.

'I have the ranse, Athos. What else could I expect?'

'Obviously, the illness from which you suffer does not help your case. And some will now portray you as a monster they prefer to despise rather than fear. Even today, there are many who consider the ranse to be a mark of infamy. That's just how things are. You'll have to make the best of it or become a hermit . . .'

Athos had spoken in a kind, firm, steady voice, looking straight into Leprat's eyes, as if he were a doctor announcing an irrefutable and terrible diagnosis to a patient, putting aside his feelings in order to expose matters plainly, although not without compassion.

But he had not finished.

'Nevertheless, your ranse is not the main cause of your current unpopularity.' Leprat gave him a puzzled look, until the other man explained. 'Do you realise that lately you've had a tendency to don and then remove your cape? Now, most of the King's Musketeers do not care about your disease, but they cannot abide someone who rejoins their ranks by default.'

'But I haven't—' Leprat started to protest.

Athos cut him short by lifting a hand in a sign of appeasement.

'I know that. But, nonetheless, that is the impression you give. So, follow my advice and be patient. Show them that you are a musketeer and have no intention of renouncing your commission any time soon. I take it you are decided on this point?'

'I am.'

'And are you really through with the company of monsieur de La Fargue?'

'Yes.'

'Well then. Wear the musketeer's cape proudly and serve faithfully. Time will not heal your disease, but it will let you demonstrate your loyalty. And above all else, avoid getting into any quarrels that certain people may try to pick with you.'

Leprat met Athos' gaze and realised the gentleman had not given him this last piece of advice by chance.

The armoured wagon carrying Agnès arrived in Paris at the end of the afternoon.

Still surrounded by the mounted escort of Black Guards, it passed through the Temple city gate, followed the street bearing the same name, and turned left to cross the drawbridge that straddled the last vestiges of a moat around the Enclos du Temple, the Chatelaines' headquarters. It advanced a little further and finally drew up before the lofty Tour du Temple.

Removed from the darkness and the stifling heat of the sealed wagon, Agnès, with her wrists still bound, staggered slightly as she set foot on the ground. But the baronne de Vaudreuil's pride immediately gained the upper hand and, with a brusque shrug of her shoulders, she freed herself from the hands that intended to support her. Squinting painfully in the bright light, she lifted her eyes to gaze upon the tower that was to be her new prison. This massive keep was one of the most secure places in the capital; so secure, in fact, that the kings of France had once deposited their treasure there. Agnès wondered if she should feel flattered to be locked up within it now.

The guards urged her forward.

Not knowing whether she would see the sun again, Agnès took in her surroundings as far as she could, gazing towards the houses neighbouring the Enclos, beyond the gardens and the crenelated wall. Some slaters were repairing the roof of one house, and a worker, no doubt intrigued by the strange-looking wagon that had just arrived, was looking in their direction. Standing, he removed his hat and wiped his brow with a red handkerchief before returning to his labour.

It was Ballardieu.

3

It was the last evening before his departure for Saint-Germain and the king wanted to spend it with the queen, along with some gentlemen from his suite. The royal couple's apartments adjoined one another on the first floor of the Louvre. Louis XIII's quarters occupied the aptly-named Pavillon du Roi, while Anne d'Autriche's were located in the southern wing of the palace; the wing overlooking the Seine. They were separated by a single door. Yet the king's visits were rare. Did this visit mean that His Majesty desired a rapprochement with his long-neglected spouse? There were those who wanted to believe it, and even some who started to dream of an heir to the French throne.

What drew particular comment, however, was the presence of Mère Thérèse de Vaussambre that evening, the Mother Superior General of the Sisters of Saint Georges. To be sure, it was not the first time that Anne d'Autriche and Mère de Vaussambre had met. But previously they had simply come into contact with each other during official ceremonies, where they were both constrained and protected by the rules of protocol. They had never exchanged more than three words unless they were obliged to and, until now, La Vaussambre had never even crossed the threshold of the queen's ante-chamber. It was common knowledge that Anne detested the Chatelaines to the point that she kept them all at a distance, even the sisters charged with her protection. This hatred had sprung from the horrid examinations the Sisters of Saint Georges had subjected her to when, newly wed, she had joined her husband in France. She had been fourteen years old at the time.

Anne d'Autriche owed her name to her mother, Marguerite d'Autriche-Styrie, the archduchess of Austria and the princess of Styria. But she was also a Spanish *infanta*, born with the name Ana Maria Mauricia, daughter of King Felipe III of Spain. And Spain was known to be particularly susceptible to the dragons' influence. So much so that, in Spain, they did not hide their true nature and some of them were even part of the high aristocracy, occupying eminent positions within the Spanish state. So it had been necessary to ensure that the future queen of France was free of all contagion, the ranse being the very least of the possible dangers that the Chatelaines dreaded. Hence the rituals they had employed to examine, throughout an entire night, the body and soul of a terrified and humiliated adolescent girl who never would forget the ordeal.

On this evening in July 1633, however, the queen made a special effort to welcome Mère de Vaussambre, which pleased the king. Only a very few knew she was paying for a mistake which, even now, remained the deepest of secrets: fearing she was sterile, Anne had turned to magic for a cure and had fallen under the spell of one of the Black Claw, a secret society of malevolent dragons. Nothing of the affair had been divulged, the main protagonists being either dead or constrained to silence . . . hence the astonishment amongst those who saw Anne d'Autriche holding out her hand to the Mother Superior General and addressing her in a kindly fashion, even if her words had clearly been rehearsed. Much repeated and discussed afterwards, these words and smiles did not fool many people. But the words were not important: the key point lay in the queen demonstrating her submission to Louis XIII, who did not linger long thereafter.

As for Mère de Vaussambre and the Chatelaines, they had won an astonishing victory.

La Fargue waited for dusk before going to the Louvre. He and Ballardieu kept their horses to a walk as they crossed the Pont Neuf and then followed the École quay, before turning into the narrow rue d'Autriche. The captain did not utter a word throughout the journey. He was worried, but still maintained the calm of a great general on the eve of battle, aware that what was about to play out – or was, perhaps, already being played out – no longer depended on him.

To be sure, the messages carried by monsieur Gaget's dragonnets had produced the desired effect: making Mère de Vaussambre bring Agnès to her headquarters in Paris. Meanwhile, the marquis d'Aubremont had agreed to provoke a major confrontation, even if it meant losing some of the king's esteem. But for the rest, La Fargue was forced to rely on the talents of his Blades, on the pride of La Vaussambre, and on luck. His plan was risky. He knew it and had not hidden the fact from anyone. Nevertheless, he felt responsible.

And rightly so.

For if this went wrong, then although he himself would not be spared, others would be the first to pay the price.

Night was falling as they landed nimbly at the foot of the wall. Saint-Lucq went first, followed by Laincourt and Marciac, the latter coiling the rope and hooking the grapple onto his belt after they had climbed the high crenelated barrier. They were in the main garden of the Enclos du Temple. With a gloved finger, the half-blood pointed to the three sentries who were patrolling the grounds, muskets on their shoulders, then indicated the door set in the inner wall, which they needed to pass to reach the Grande Tour. Laincourt and Marciac nodded.

Thanks to his dragon eyes, Saint-Lucq could see better than the others in the dark. He went first. Bent over, they reached the door in long silent strides, hugging first the outer wall, then the inner one. They huddled for a moment behind a hedge, holding their breath, but the sentry passed without spotting them, his regular steps gradually moving away from them. The door was locked, as they had anticipated, so while Saint-Lucq kept watch, Laincourt brought forth some fine tools in a leather case and, with Marciac looking on in admiration, he proceeded to attack the lock. It soon gave way. The three passed through and hurriedly shut the door behind them: another guard was approaching.

The Grande Tour du Temple was a solid square keep, flanked by round turrets at each corner, and measuring fifty metres tall. The structure was capped by a pyramidal roof surrounded by a terrace walkway. More slender and lower in height, a secondary building – the Petite Tour – was attached to the northern façade. To enter the Grande Tour it was first necessary to cross the ground floor of the Petite, where two members of the Black Guards were standing watch by the door.

The guards were quite astonished to see Marciac coming towards them, and especially to see him smiling as if it were the most natural thing in the world. This momentary distraction sufficed, before both guards felt the barrel of a pistol pressed to their temples, one to the right and the other to the left. As Saint-Lucq and Laincourt held them at gunpoint the Gascon disarmed them, throwing their swords and muskets aside, but keeping their pistols.

'If you call out, who will answer?'

'The porter.'

'Then call him.'

The man shook his head.

'Please,' Marciac insisted, jamming the the barrel of the guard's own pistol into the man's nostril, to painful effect.

Standing on tiptoe, the guard rapped three times on the door.

After few seconds, someone asked:

'What is it?'

'It's me,' replied the guard. 'Louvet. Open up.'

'But—'

'Open up!'

The door opened a fraction and Marciac forced his way through, quickly subduing the porter while Saint-Luc and Marciac followed, shoving the two guards before them. The ground floor of the Petite Tour was dark and silent. Frightened, the porter was eager to tell them that the prisoner who had arrived earlier that day could be found in the basement of the Grande Tour. He went on to explain that she had been treated very well, but that did not save him from being knocked unconscious with a pistol butt. As soon as they were securely bound and gagged, the two guards were subjected to a similar fate.

'And now?' Laincourt enquired.

Marciac gave him the pistols taken from the enemy and instructed him:

'You guard the door. We'll go find Agnès.'

The young man nodded.

'Don't take too long. Time is short.'

Upon leaving the queen's apartments, the Mother Superior General of the Sisters of Saint Georges found the captain of her Black Guards in the Louvre courtyard. He immediately summoned the white coach that was waiting nearby, and Mère de Vaussambre watched her team draw up in the torchlight with a thin smile of contained satisfaction, knowing that the sight attracted surprised and envious gazes from those observing the scene. Entering the Louvre in a carriage was a rare privilege, and the fact that the king had granted it to her was a public mark of his esteem. After the welcome the queen had given her, this evening was her moment of triumph. All that was left was her admittance to the Council, and the Order of the Sisters of Saint Georges would be fully restored to its former glory. And that would happen soon.

'The baronne de Vaudreuil arrived today,' the comte d'Orsan informed her discreetly.

'Without mishap?'

'None, mother superior.'

'That's very good news. I will speak to her tomorrow and I have no doubt I can bring her back to her senses. She cannot remain deaf to the call of her destiny much longer.'

Drawn by four horses, the coach came to a halt before them. A footman jumped down to open the passenger door, while another pulled the steps down. The captain of the Black Guards presented his arm and, with his support, the Chatelaines' Mother Superior General climbed into the cabin. Then, d'Orsan having closed the door, she settled herself as comfortably as possible, closed her eyes and waited to be rocked by the movements of the coach.

In order to leave the central courtyard of this former medieval fortress that had become the Louvre, one needed to traverse an archway measuring a dozen metres in length. It ran through the eastern wing of the palace and, passing between two round towers, opened onto a drawbridge that crossed the moat. Beyond that, there was an imposing fortified gate – known as the Bourbon gate – which defended the access from rue d'Autriche. The passage was narrow, particularly dark beneath the archway, and perilous as it crossed the moat, where carriages always ran the risk of tipping over the side.

The coachman advanced at a walk. The archway filled with the echoes of hooves striking the pavement, after which the team passed beneath the raised portcullis and started over the small drawbridge. That was where a Swiss mercenary sergeant, breathless from the chase, caught up with the coach and stopped it.

'Halt!' he ordered. 'In the name of the king!'

The Tour du Temple's ground floor consisted of a great hall that gave access to a spiral staircase housed in one of the corner turrets and smaller rooms located in the three other turrets. There were a few lamps burning dimly in the silent darkness of the hall, as well as in the stairwell that Saint-Lucq and Marciac descended quietly, swords in hand. They knew the general layout of the floors above, but had no idea what to expect below. They only knew that Agnès was being held prisoner down there somewhere.

After opening a door at the bottom with only the slightest of creaks, they discovered a large chamber that resembled a cloister. Bordering a flagstone gallery, a series of columns surrounded a square space with a sunken dirt floor six steps down and a vaulted ceiling whose fan of arching curves was supported by a central pillar. The gallery was plunged into darkness, but some oil lamps shed a weak light in the middle of the room, where they could make out a table, a rack, chains and shackles, a suspended cage, and various instruments of torture.

Without consultation, Marciac and Saint-Lucq split up, the first taking the gallery to the right, and the second the one on the left. Soon, the Gascon froze and listened carefully. He seemed to hear . . . was that snoring? He turned round, seeking Saint-Lucq, but could not see the half-blood. So, alone, he approached a small door and pressed his ear to its surface. Yes, the snores were coming from within. Loud snores, the kind that only a man stupefied by drink could produce without waking himself up.

Marciac's sense of curiosity was too strong to resist.

Softly, carefully, he opened the door.

In a narrow, stinking cubby-hole, a forgotten candle was on the point of consuming itself in a saucer placed on the floor. Its flickering glow barely revealed a human form lying entwined in a blanket upon a straw mattress pressed against the wall. But it was also just enough to perceive the gleam from a ring of keys that hung from a nail near the sleeper, as well as an iron bar similar to those used by torturers to break the limbs of the poor wretches who were condemned to the Catherine wheel.

Marciac only had eyes for the keys. They had to be the prison cell keys, since the man snoring like a bear could only be the gaoler. Neither he nor Saint-Lucq had Laincourt's skill in picking locks. If they wanted to open the door to Agnès' cell quietly, they would need this set of keys.

The Gascon held his breath and entered the cubby-hole on tiptoe.

The clicking of the chain alerted him, but he perceived his danger too late and barely had time to raise his arm for protection when a syle leapt for his throat from a shadowy corner. As large and as agile as a cat, the black salamander closed its jaws on Marciac's hand. He threw it off by reflex, its sharp teeth tearing away a strip of his skin. The syle struck the wall and fell, tangling itself up in the chain attached to its neck. But it was already spinning around to attack again when the Gascon planted his rapier in its skull.

Marciac had no time to ponder who would be mad enough to keep a syle on a leash. The snoring behind him had ceased, and he turned slowly towards the now-empty mattress. His injured hand forgotten, his gaze shifted upward with growing dread to see a colossal drac, massively built, whose enormous muscles were flexing beneath his black shiny scales.

Strangely fascinated, the Gascon gulped in awe.

He had never seen a drac like this, and it wasn't his size that made him so extraordinary. Nor the yellow, pointed fangs, wet with thick saliva. Nor the sharp claws on his powerful hands. Nor even the bestial glow in his reptilian eyes.

This drac had two heads.

That explains why the snoring was so loud, Marciac couldn't help thinking.

'Uhh . . . friends?' he ventured.

The monster emitted a dull roar.

Recalled by the king just as she was about to leave the Louvre, Mère de Vaussambre was forced to abandon her coach on the drawbridge, which the coachman had already started to cross, making it impossible for him to either turn around or to back up. Leaving her captain in charge, she followed the Swiss sergeant who had been sent after her and was soon admitted into His Majesty's apartments.

Louis XIII was waiting for her with Cardinal Richelieu and a dignified gentleman whom she recognised as the marquis d'Aubremont. The cardinal was standing slightly to the rear, while the king and the marquis sat next to one another and were conversing in front of an empty chair when the Mother Superior General entered, more puzzled by her summons than worried. Louis XIII invited her to sit and apologised for having recalled her in this fashion, without respect for etiquette and at such a late hour.

'Sire, I am at Your Majesty's service,' said Mère de Vaussambre occupying the armchair provided for her.

She greeted d'Aubremont with a nod of her head, and he responded in the same manner. Then she met Richelieu's gaze, without being able to read any clues at all in his eyes.

But the king was speaking:

'I have called you before me to quickly clear up an affair which is of little consequence, but which I should like to see settled before my departure for Saint-Germain. The marquis d'Aubremont, whom you know, is one of my friends. It seems he harbours some anxiety concerning a person dear to him, someone he believes you hold prisoner.'

She turned to the marquis and, without betraying any emotion, waited.

'I'm concerned about the baronne de Vaudreuil,' he explained in a cold tone of voice.

La Vaussambre withstood his accusing glare without blinking.

So that's what it was about: with no other recourse, La Fargue had turned to his friend d'Aubremont and persuaded him to appeal to the king.

'Really?' she said.

'Do you know her?' asked Louis XIII.

'Yes, Sire. I know her. She was one of our most promising novices, but she turned away from her divine calling to enter the cardinal's service.'

Richelieu leaned over the king's shoulder and whispered in his ear:

'Agnès de Vaudreuil is one of those who, under the command of Captain La Fargue, recently served you so well, Sire.'

Louis XIII nodded.

'Mother superior,' d'Aubremont resumed, 'I have a report that says the baronne de Vaudreuil is being held against her will in a cell at Mont-Saint-Michel. Is that true?'

'No, monsieur. That is not true.'

It wasn't a lie, since Agnès was now held in the Tour du Temple. La Fargue, once again, was a step behind her.

The Superior General's nerve troubled the marquis.

'Neither there, nor in any of your other gaols?' he insisted.

'Nor in any other,' replied Mère de Vaussambre with bland assurance.

She even permitted herself to display a hint of a benevolent but saddened smile, as if to apologise for being unable to assist him, despite her willingness to do so.

Marciac burst through the small door as if he had been shot out of a cannon. He crashed into a column and fell heavily to the flagstones. Grimacing from the excruciating pain in his back, he tried to get up but failed. He lost consciousness just as he saw the drac ducking both heads beneath the lintel to emerge from his lair.

Armed with the hefty iron bar that he kept by his bed, the colossus straightened up and contemplated the Gascon, who was still breathing. Then his attention was drawn by another intruder. Saint-Lucq was advancing sideways towards him, prudently but resolutely, his rapier pointed in a straight line from its tip to his shoulder, the axis of his gaze matching that of his blade. The half-blood halted before he came into range of the iron bar. Without lowering his guard, he took three steps to one side, drawing the drac away from Marciac.

And then waited.

The monster growled and struck.

Saint-Lucq evaded the attack, then a second and a third. There was no question of parrying or even deflecting a blow from that iron bar. They were delivered with such vigour that they could easily break his sword or tear it from his grasp. Concentrating, the half-blood leapt, stepped aside, and ducked, barely managing to avoid the bar as it slashed through the air. He was waiting for the drac to tire, but he was the one growing exhausted.

Beating a retreat, Saint-Lucq left the gallery and backed into the central space of the chamber, where the equipment and instruments of torture were laid out. The colossus followed him. The half-blood attempted to take advantage of the furnishings, but if the drac was too stupid to develop a strategy or predict the dodges and ruses of his adversary, his strength and speed more than made up for the shortcomings of his bestial intelligence. Nothing could stand against him. He overturned effortlessly the torture table, swept aside a heavy brazier with the back of his hand, and struck a powerful blow

77

at the suspended cage, which began to swing slowly back and forth. The movement temporarily distracted him from his blind fury.

Saint-Lucq chose that moment to risk it all and lunged, forgetting any notion of caution. He scored a hit, but the point of his sword simply skidded across the black scales. Even worse, as he lurched forward, an enormous fist closed around his exposed wrist, and it felt as though the drac was about to rip his arm off. Lifted from the floor by a prodigious strength, he flew towards a wall and struck it with full force. The impact knocked the wind out of him, and he dropped his rapier. His legs gave way beneath him. He tried to stand up, leaning clumsily against the stone wall. As if in a drunken stupor, he watched the drac approach out of the corner of his eye, then raise the iron bar and prepare to strike a blow that would smash the half-blood's skull. Turning to one side to disguise what his right hand was doing, Saint-Lucq seized the dagger tucked inside his boot. Perhaps he still had a chance. One. But no more than that. He waited until the last moment and made a desperate leap. The iron bar whistled past him, just before he plunged the dagger into the drac's scaly flank. And again. And again.

The drac moaned, staggered and dropped his weapon which bounced with a clear ringing tone on the flagstones . . .

. . . and then he closed his clawed hands around the half-blood's throat.

Saint-Lucq gurgled. His feet left the ground. He risked less choking to death than having his neck broken and his windpipe crushed by the fists strangling him. He stiffened his neck muscles as best he could, thrashed his legs and seized those powerful wrists, seeking to loosen their grip. He scrabbled for any hold, any weak point, any hope.

In vain.

Then a steel grapple dropped between the drac's two heads, hung for a moment against its chest, and abruptly began to be pulled up. It was the tool the Blades had used to climb over the outer wall of the Enclos du Temple, the one that Marciac had placed on his belt. The one whose rope Marciac now held.

The grapple caught in the V between the two thick necks and the Gascon, giving it a swift jerk, drove the metal hooks into the creature's throats on either side. Black blood spurted from the wounds. Releasing Saint-Lucq, the colossus tried to pull the grapple free. But Marciac had braced himself at the other end of the rope and the hooks worked themselves in deeper. The drac was pulled backwards but it refused to fall. The Gascon pulled harder, groaning as the hand bitten by the syle throbbed with pain, but he didn't give up. He heaved again, arching his back, grimacing, his soles slipping on the flagstones until the monster toppled over backward and the grapple was torn from the scaly flesh, ripping bloody shreds with it as it came loose with a sound like a chicken carcass being torn apart, when the bones and cartilage suddenly separate. A double sticky spray accompanied it.

The reptilian colossus died quickly, on his back, and the silence that returned to the devastated chamber seemed like a roar to the ears of the two breathless men.

'Are you all right?' asked Marciac after a moment.

Saint-Lucq, sitting with his back against the torture table, still needed time to recover.

'I'm all right,' he lied in a hoarse voice. He pointed with a shaky index finger. 'Over there. The . . . The door to the cells. I found it just before . . . Go look for Agnès?'

The Gascon nodded, advanced a few steps, then changed his mind and went to take the keys to the gaol cells from the two-headed drac's cubby-hole.

After all, they had earned them.

From a window in one of the older sections of the Louvre, La Fargue looked out towards the Enclos and, under the pale, bluish glow of the stars, had little difficulty in distinguishing the imposing silhouette of the Tour du Temple.

It was visible from almost anywhere in Paris and could be easily located after nightfall, thanks to the light that shone from its pyramidal roof. The light came from a big lantern containing a 'solaire', an alchemical stone that was also known as 'Bohemian stone', because only Bohemian alchemists knew its secret. The solaires – whose invention was fairly recent – shone like the brightest of flames and had only one drawback: their fabrication was both onerous and dangerous. The one in the Tour du Temple was white and, like others in Paris, it served to guide wyverns in flight. A blue one shone from the Louvre, a red one from the Palais-Cardinal and, soon, there would be a yellow one to indicate the Gaget Messenger Service.

His eyes fixed on the Chatelaines' distant beacon, the captain of the Blades waited, patient and alone.

Finally, he heard Ballardieu's footsteps approaching.

'The marquis d'Aubremont has just left the king, captain. He gave me this for you.'

'And Mère de Vaussambre?'

'The king has retained her.'

Without turning away from the window, La Fargue took the note that Ballardieu held out to him, unfolded it, and read its contents.

'She denied it,' he said, lifting his head.

And, gazing back towards the Tour du Temple, he crumpled the paper in his fist and added gravely:

'Now we can only hope they succeed.'

In the tower basement, the door that Saint-Lucq had indicated opened onto a narrow staircase, at the bottom of which Marciac found a small square room and four doors.

'Agnès?' he called. 'Agnès, are you there?'

'Nicolas? Is that you?'

'At your service, baronne.'

Thanks to the gaoler's keys, he opened the door from behind which Agnès had answered him, and freed the young woman.

They immediately embraced.

'God's blood, Nicolas! Am I happy to see you . . .'

'And I, you!'

'No doubt that explains why one of your hands is creeping dangerously close to my buttocks . . .'

'Sorry. Force of habit.'

'It's still moving down, Marciac . . .'

'The little rascal . . .'

Agnès thought it preferable to step away from the Gascon before she was obliged to break a few fingers, which would have spoiled their reunion.

'So, I did see Ballardieu on that rooftop this afternoon!'

'It was him.'

'I thought I was going mad. I believed he was dead, did you know that?'

'He's quite lively.' And showing her the way out, he added: 'Let's be off, baronne. We're not out of this yet, and time is running short.'

'You didn't come here on your own, did you?' asked Agnès as she followed him up the stairs.

'No. Laincourt and Saint-Lucq are with me.'

They found the half-blood back in the torture chamber and, as she passed, the baronne de Vaudreuil noticed the body of the two-headed drac lying in a pool of black blood.

'I see you met the master of ceremonies down here.'

'He gave us the most deplorable welcome,' replied Marciac.

They were quick to rejoin Laincourt, who, in the darkness of the ground floor, was standing with his back to the wall by the entrance. The young man had left the door ajar and was keeping an eye out for any signs of movement outside, a pistol in either hand.

He smiled upon observing that Agnès de Vaudreuil seemed to be in good health, although her face looked drawn.

'I'm delighted to see you again, madame.'

'Thank you,' she replied. 'Likewise.'

He also noticed the sorry state in which the fight with the drac had left the other two, but made no comment.

'The sentries have discovered that the little door in the garden was no longer locked,' he announced. 'You should go. The alarm will soon be sounded.'

'You're not coming?' exclaimed Agnès in surprise as she saw him step back to let them pass.

'I'll meet you where we left the horses, don't worry.'

Saint-Lucq went out first, and then he signalled Marciac and Agnès to follow him.

Laincourt closed the door behind them. He waited for long

enough to be sure they hadn't been spotted or forced to make a hurried retreat back inside the tower. Now on his own, he moved off and took the spiral staircase that rose up through one of the keep's corner turrets.

From his vantage point within the Louvre, La Fargue could not make out what took place at the summit of the Tour du Temple. Therefore he did not see Laincourt surprise and stun a sentry on the walkway. Nor see him catch the guard as he fell. Nor spread a great piece of red cloth over the lantern housing the Chatelaines' dazzling white solaire.

What he saw was the beacon at the Enclos suddenly turn red.

Like most strongholds, the Enclos was conceived to prevent invasion, rather than escapes. Having crept past several sentries unseen, Saint-Lucq, Agnès and Marciac climbed on top of a building that leaned against the outer wall and, with the help of the Gascon's bloody grapple, they soon made it to the other side. The last to straddle the crenelated rampart, Saint-Lucq looked up at the top of the Tour du Temple and saw the light of the beacon turn red: La Fargue would now know that Agnès was free.

The alarm sounded shortly thereafter, just as they rejoined André in a darkened backyard, where the Blades' groom had been waiting with their horses. There were shouts at first. Then shots were fired and the tocsin began to sound inside the Enclos.

'We have to go,' whispered Saint-Lucq.

'What about Laincourt?' Marciac protested in a low voice. 'We just abandon him?'

'That blasted tocsin will wake the entire neighbourhood, and it won't take the Black Guards much longer to send out patrols.'

'Laincourt is one of us!'

'He knew the risks.'

'We don't abandon our own, Saint-Lucq.'

'Yes we do, when the success of the mission demands it.'

'That's enough!' interjected Agnès, stopping herself from raising her voice. 'Laincourt is resourceful. He can still—'

'If he's being pursued, and if he has any brains,' the half-blood interrupted, 'this is the last place he will go. He'd be leading the whole pack straight to us.'

'Let's give him another moment,' the young woman said stubbornly.

Saint-Lucq cursed.

More detonations were heard. Curt orders were given, although their exact nature remained indistinct. But it was clear that a manhunt was under way.

'Well spoken,' murmured Marciac to Agnès. 'But all the same, you should not stay. It's too dangerous. I'll wait for Laincourt. You three should go. Laincourt and I will find you later.'

'Out of the question.'

'You don't have a choice, Agnès. Saint-Lucq is right: Laincourt knew the risks. So did we. And if we all agreed to run them, it was to liberate you. So don't let yourself be recaptured now.'

Agnès de Vaudreuil fell silent. Marciac was right, although it cost her to admit it.

She nodded sadly.

'All right,' she said. But . . .'

She didn't finish, but grinned instead as she saw Laincourt arrive with his sword in his fist, running at a steady jog and not looking particularly worried.

'What?' he asked, when he saw them all staring at him.

The king detained Mère de Vaussambre for a short while after the departure of the marquis d'Aubremont. He was courteous and attentive, seeking to end their interview on a more pleas-ant note than the climate of suspicion in which it had begun. Louis XIII had too great a need of the Chatelaines' support to risk alienating their Mother Superior General. Although she had not been forced to answer any accusations this evening, d'Aubremont's questions had put her in an uncomfortable position, despite the king's claim that it was 'an affair of little consequence'.

Mère de Vaussambre was not duped by this.

La Fargue had tried to compromise her and d'Aubremont knew perfectly well where matters stood. And Richelieu? Did he have any part in this? No. The trap was too crude, too clumsy, to be the cardinal's work. But what had La Fargue hoped to gain? That, in the king's presence, she would not dare deny she held the baronne de Vaudreuil prisoner?

She only understood when her coach brought her back to the Enclos.

She found the former Templar fortress in a state of upheaval, the tocsin pealing and lights at all the windows, her guards on a war footing, and even patrols out searching the surrounding streets. Men had infiltrated the Enclos. They had freed Agnès from the Tour du Temple and taken her away, leaving a dead body and several mistreated sentries behind. They had not worn masks, and one of them had been a halfblood.

'Saint-Lucq!' exclaimed the comte d'Orsan. 'It must have been the Blades.'

'A brilliant deduction,' said Mère de Vaussambre in a bitter tone.

'Mother superior, one word from you and I'll have them all arrested before dawn. Starting with La Fargue.'

'And on what grounds?'

'But mother superior!' the captain of the Black Guards protested in astonishment. 'Isn't it obvious?'

La Vaussambre remained silent.

She was in no mood to tell d'Orsan that she had lied to the king, exactly as La Fargue had known she would and had wanted her to do. How could she now accuse the Blades of liberating by force a prisoner she had just denied holding? She knew La Fargue. She knew that he would let matters rest, as long as she did the same.

Pale and simmering with frustrated rage, she ordered the tocsin silenced and the beacon restored to its original whiteness.

'And find a satisfactory explanation for all this uproar.'

La Fargue and Ballardieu left the Louvre on horseback and found the others waiting for them, also on horseback, in front of the Pont Neuf. There were smiles all around. Agnès and Marciac, above all. But Laincourt too, and even Saint-Lucq had a smirk on his face. They were relieved and happy. They were victorious.

Eyes shining with pride, their captain saluted them with a slight nod, while Ballardieu, beaming, gave the young woman a huge wink.

Reunited once more, they felt no need to say anything.

'Let's go home,' La Fargue said.

4

The dragon seated in front of the mirror had the appearance of an elegant gentleman with fine features and blond hair. He was unusually pale, his reptilian eyes shining with a dark lustre as he spoke. The mirror did not return his own image, but that of the individual he was addressing: an old red dragon whose massive scaly head, adorned with a triple bony crest, shone from the reflective surface and shimmered in the dim light. Located in Madrid, this other dragon also had a human form. But the ensorcelled mirrors revealed the true nature of those who used them.

'Do you think killing the Alchemist was a mistake?' the red dragon was asking.

'I don't know, Heresiarch.'

'I've already heard complaints . . . But the Alchemist knew the price he would have to pay. Could we have allowed him to fall into the Chatelaines' hands and taken the risk he might reveal our secrets to them under torture?'

'Certainly not. Yet—'

'The Heir can still see the light of day,' the Heresiarch continued without listening. 'Nothing can be allowed to prevent that! Nothing must impede our work!'

In front of his mirror, the gentleman remained silent. He waited until the red dragon regained his composure and then said:

'I am loyal and devoted to you, Heresiarch. However, the masters of the Grand Lodge are growing impatient. Our adversaries constantly draw attention to all the efforts and the fortunes the Black Claw has already devoted to our Grand Design. And they have no difficulty in finding willing ears to listen to them. For the moment, I have managed to minimise the extent of our failure, but—'

'It was the Alchemist's failure, and his alone!'

'Nevertheless. The Black Claw is now demanding results.'

'And it shall have them.'

'When?'

'Very soon.'

The Arcana

1

The day after her escape Agnès wanted to visit Almades' grave. And since she was determined to go there on her own, Ballardieu was forced to follow her to the cemetery discreetly, and to watch over her from a distance.

He knew she was grieving and he suffered as a result. Indeed, everything she felt affected him. He shared her joys and her sorrows, her doubts and her pleasures, her angers and her regrets. He could not be happy if she wasn't, and it had been that way between them ever since she was entrusted to his care, soon after her birth, by a man who was totally indifferent to the fate of his only daughter.

Ballardieu slipped behind a funeral monument when he saw Agnès walking back through the small cemetery. He heard her footsteps pass and waited for her to reach the gates before emerging from his hiding-place. But he held off for too long. Not seeing her anywhere, he cursed and had to hurry, panicked by the thought that he had no idea whether she had turned right or left in the street. He came out of the graveyard almost at a run and then halted, heart beating fast, desperately seeking a glimpse of the young baronne among the crowd thronging the city pavement.

'You just couldn't help yourself, could you?'

He managed not to jump in surprise and, composing an impassive expression on his face, turned with all the dignity of a prelate.

Arms crossed, one ankle placed in front of the other, Agnès was leaning against the cemetery wall. She was dressed like a squire, wearing boots, breeches, and a red leather corset over a white shirt, with a sword at her side. Her outfit drew glances from passers-by in the street, but she paid no heed. Bare-headed, with her long black braid draped over one shoulder, she was gazing fixedly at him.

'Excuse me?' he managed in reply.

'You couldn't help following me,' she said, drawing closer.

The old soldier, growing red-faced in the heat, feigned shock.

'Who, me?' he protested.

'What? You're going to deny it . . . ? You deny being here, at this very minute?'

He barely hesitated before answering.

'I don't deny the fact, I deny the intention. I wasn't actually following you. I was simply going to the same place as you, that's all.'

'And that's all,' mimicked the baronne de Vaudreuil. 'So what were you doing over there behind that big vault?'

'I . . . I was taking a piss.'

'In a cemetery?'

'Best place for it, doesn't bother anyone.'

She stared at him. Waiting. A trickle of sweat ran down Ballardieu's upper lip and he became aware of a wisp of hair stuck to his forehead.

'All right!' he exclaimed, suddenly stretching his arms wide in surrender. 'I was following you . . . ! So what? Can you blame me for worrying?'

'Worrying?' asked Agnès in surprise. 'Why?'

He looked warily around at the bystanders in the street and bent over to whisper in her ear:

'All of you seem to believe, and you in particular, that Mère de Vaussambre is going to accept her defeat with all the graciousness in the world. But I say she has not abandoned the idea of doing you an evil turn . . . *Ergo*, I'm watching over you.'

' "*Ergo*"?'

'*Ergo*. It means—'

'I know what it means,' Agnès laughed merrily. 'But I didn't know you spoke Latin . . . Very well, you old beast, you win. Watch over me as much as you please.'

'You won't even notice me, girl.'

'It would be the first time that ever happened.'

Shaking her head in amused disbelief, Agnès turned back to the cemetery, and as her gaze drifted towards the site of Almades' grave, hidden from her view, her smile slowly faded. Ballardieu became grim-faced as well.

'So it was a dragon that did this?' said the young woman after a moment.

'Yes,' replied Ballardieu, looking in the same direction. 'And if Almades hadn't been there, we would be grieving for La Fargue instead.'

Agnès' eyes narrowed.

'But there was another dragon there, in the room with them. The Alchemist.'

'So . . . ?'

'So . . . when did dragons start killing each other?'

In the inn on the rue du Pot-de-Fer where he had become a regular, Leprat had eaten his noonday meal alone. He was now moodily sipping *eau-de-vie* and was absently rolling a pair of dice as he kept an eye on the door. He was waiting for Athos, who was supposed to join him here when he came off duty. They would then make their way to the Louvre together, and from there the Musketeers would escort the king to his château at Saint-Germain.

It had only been a few days since Athos had advised Leprat to be patient over the cold, and even sullenly hostile, manner in which the other musketeers had greeted his return to their ranks. According to Athos, the main reproach against him was fickleness, for having doffed and donned his cape too many times. So now he had to demonstrate his loyalty. If he avoided getting into any quarrels then time would smooth over the rest. He just needed to keep his head down for the time being.

Athos was right, for the most part. But Leprat was also aware that the other musketeers looked at him differently as news of his illness spread. The ranse was eating away at both his flesh and his soul. In the long run, decades in some cases, its victims were slowly and irremediably transformed into grotesque, pathetic creatures, whose deformed bodies and tortured minds clung hopelessly to the last shreds of their humanity. But one of the disease's first symptoms was that at least some of the afflicted's acquaintances began to treat them like monsters as soon as they learned of the illness, long before that final stage was reached, and saw nothing but the inevitable and abject fall from grace. From that point on, sufferers ceased to be themselves and became merely diseased.

Became ranse-ed . . .

Antoine Leprat, the chevalier d'Orgueil, had known he had the ranse for several years now yet he had never thought of himself in those terms, as being diseased, not as long as he had kept it a secret. Now the looks he received every day reminded him of his condition and reduced him to being just that: diseased. And it wasn't just looks; there were the conversations that stopped dead when he approached, embarrassed faces, the slight gestures of recoil, and all the other more-or-less disguised, and more-or-less involuntary, signals of discomfort that were made in his presence.

His thoughts slightly befuddled, Leprat saw that his jug of *eau-de vie* was empty.

Already?

He was thinking of calling for another when the door opened. It was not Athos, but two other musketeers Leprat recognised, although neither was wearing their cape: Broussière and Sardent. The two men noticed him in turn and Broussière seemed to want to go elsewhere, but his companion obviously disagreed.

They sat down at a table.

Of the pair, Leprat was better acquainted with Broussière, Sardent having joined the King's Musketeers recently. He had never had any cause for complaint regarding the first man, but the second was one of those who were treating him badly, and doing so with increasingly boldness. Until now, following Athos' advice, Leprat had not responded to any of his cutting remarks and crude allusions. But it was becoming difficult for him not to hear them and understand the hurt they intended. Why had Sardent been behaving this way? Perhaps his spiteful hatred towards the diseased was born of fear, as was frequently the case. Perhaps he hoped, by denigrating a famous musketeer, to demonstrate that he was a better recruit to the King's guard. He was the younger son of a great lord with aspirations of adding glory to his name.

Leprat did not care to know the reasons behind the other man's animosity. But today, helped by his over-indulgence of alcohol, he was in no mood to tolerate it any longer. He knew, without the shadow of a doubt, that things would turn out badly if he stayed.

And yet he did.

The two musketeers had ordered drinks. As soon as they were served, Sardent called the girl back and asked in a loud voice:

'Is the crockery washed thoroughly, here?'

He pretended not to see Leprat giving him a black look. But Broussière noticed and seemed worried.

'Of course, monsieur. I assure you.'

The wench had started moving away to attend to other customers when Sardent asked:

'Is that truly the case?'

She turned round, looking uncertain.

'I . . . I can assure you that it is, monsieur.'

'That's enough, said Leprat in a cold tone of voice.

'Now, Sardent,' Broussière said in an appeasing tone, 'there's no need—'

'Because, you see,' his companion continued, undeterred, 'there are some people whose glasses you really wouldn't want to drink from . . .'

'I beg your pardon, monsieur?'

Leprat, livid, was on the verge of rising from his seat and only just managed to contain his anger. With a wave of his hand, Broussière dismissed the girl, who left with a shrug of her shoulders. Sardent seemed to have let the matter drop . . . when he pointed to the brim of his glass and asked:

'Is that not a trace of the ranse I see there?'

The mere mention of the disease provoked shudders of disgust among the other customers, some of whom instinctively leaned back away from their tables. Leprat stood up suddenly, and Broussière did the same as he saw the former Blade approaching with a furious step. Sardent detected the murderous gleam in the chevalier d'Orgueil's eye too late and Broussière moved to put himself between them, placing a hand on Leprat's chest.

'Leprat, please—'

But Broussière didn't complete his sentence. A sharp blow from Leprat's forehead broke his nose and made him tumble over backwards. Leprat continued to advance on Sardent. He had already unsheathed his famous white rapier. His gaze was that of a man who had decided to pin his adversary to the wall, rather than cross swords with him according to the rules.

'MESSIEURS!'

Leprat wasn't listening.

Sardent was scrambling to his feet and trying to draw his sword at the same time. But all he managed was to trip over his own scabbard and he lost his balance, falling among the suddenly deserted chairs behind him with a heavy crash. With the point of his ivory blade, Leprat pricked the other man's throat and forced him to stay on the floor.

Still simmering with a barely mastered rage, Leprat felt a hand calmly but firmly close about his wrist. It was Athos, who had just arrived and whose imperious call, 'Messieurs', had gone unheard.

'Get a hold on yourself, Leprat,' the gentleman said quietly.

With the air of a man waking from a bad dream, Leprat took two steps back and lowered his sword. Sardent stood up, while Broussière, his nose bleeding, struggled to rise. Athos' eyes ordered the pair to go, and they hastened to obey.

'This matter won't end here, will it?' asked Leprat.

'No, my friend, I'm afraid it will not.'

Sent out to gather news in the Temple neighbourhood, Marciac returned to the Hôtel de l'Épervier in the early afternoon. He found La Fargue and the others out in the garden, beneath the chestnut tree, sitting around the old table where they had just finished lunch. The Gascon's first act was to empty a glass of white wine. Then, drinking again and filching titbits from the dishes before Naïs cleared them away he recounted, between mouthfuls, how the Sisters of Saint Georges had managed to explain the previous night's commotion.

'The tocsin woke everyone in the vicinity. Not to mention the shots fired at Laincourt and the patrols sent out into the streets looking for us . . .'

He broke off his report to save two slices of *tarte aux prunes* from being returned to the kitchen, by swiftly placing them safely out of reach from Naïs, and her unassuming but formidable domestic efficiency.

'Go to the cellar and fill these wine jugs instead,' Agnès suggested to her gently.

'Yes,' said the Gascon. 'Go and do that instead.'

'Well?' Laincourt insisted. 'What was their explanation?'

'Dracs. Apparently some dracs tried to invade the Enclos last night. And the Black Guards, as one might expect, displayed their unceasing vigilance, bravely drove the intruders out, and then carried out a sweep of the nearby streets to make sure the danger had been entirely eliminated.'

'And why would these dracs have been trying to enter the Enclos in the middle of the night?'

Marciac shrugged.

'That remains a mystery. However, the Chatelaines are exhibiting four scaly corpses as evidence, one of them a colossus with two heads which is causing quite a sensation. People are packed shoulder-to-shoulder all the way to rue du Temple for the chance to see it.'

'I'd like to go and see it myself,' Ballardieu said in Agnès' ear.

The baronne preferred not to reply.

'I can understand the two-headed drac,' observed Saint-Lucq, 'But where did the other three come from?'

'I don't know,' Marciac confessed.

Nor did the problem seem to interest him much.

'Perhaps the Chatelaines were holding them in some

dungeon or other,' suggested Laincourt. 'And did away with the poor creatures to support their story.'

'Then again, there are plenty of dracs to be found in Les Écailles,' said the baronne de Vaudreuil.

Les Écailles, or 'The Scales', was the drac neighbourhood built on Ile Notre-Dame, which would later be re-named Ile Saint-Louis.

'The important thing to note here is that the Chatelaines are lying,' decreed La Fargue, as Naïs returned from the cellar with full wine jugs.

Having finished the prune tart, Marciac held out his plate to the young servant girl with a smile and a faint bow of the head. Shy Naïs took it and fled. Agnès, amused, gave the Gascon a swift elbow in the ribs as punishment for teasing the girl.

'If they're lying,' continued the Blades' captain, 'it's because they want the whole affair to end here and the truth never to come out. So we won't have to answer any accusations, as I thought. Mère de Vaussambre has too much to lose in a scandal . . .'

'But we still don't know why she was keeping you a prisoner,' said Saint-Lucq, turning to Agnès.

The previous night, after they were reunited, Agnès had told the Blades everything from the moment she set foot inside the abbey at Mont-Saint-Michel to her capture on the wyverns' flight platform. She had been there on a mission to find the son of the marquis d'Aubremont, François Reynault d'Ombreuse. A lieutenant serving in the Black Guards, he had disappeared after taking part in a clandestine expedition to Alsace. What had become of him? Was he alive or dead? Wounded? Ill? And if he was well, why did he send no word?

This was what the baronne de Vaudreuil had hoped to learn thanks to Sœur Béatrice d'Aussaint, the White Wolf who had led the expedition to Alsace, and who had been held in secret at the Chatelaines' abbey fortress on the mount.

Nothing, however, had prepared Agnès for what she actually discovered.

Still suffering from her ordeal, Sœur Béatrice had not told her how, with the support of a detachment of Black Guards under the command of François d'Ombreuse, she had tracked and almost vanquished a dragon belonging to the Arcana lodge. But she had warned Agnès of an incredible danger, when she shared a nightmarish vision of a great black dragon burning Paris to the ground. The White Wolves of the Saint Georges Order often had the gift of prescience, and the young baronne de Vaudreuil had not doubted the coming disaster was true, or that there was an urgent need to take action. Unfortunately, no further light was shed on the danger by the sister's confused ramblings afterwards, her strength exhausted. Thus there were still too many unanswered questions: Who was this dragon? Where did it come from? Why was it going to attack Paris?

And above all: when?

Her gaze becoming pained and thoughtful, Agnès returned to the crux of the matter, the vision she had seen on that fateful night:

'I saw a black dragon attacking Paris and reducing the Louvre to ashes,' she said. 'That's why the Chatelaines were holding me. They don't want me to divulge this secret, one that for her part Sœur Béatrice wanted me to learn at all costs.'

'But they couldn't have held you forever!' Marciac objected.

'They could have detained Agnès long enough,' Saint-Lucq declared coldly. 'Until the secret no longer had any importance. Or until Agnès agreed to hold her tongue about it.'

'Mère de Vaussambre has not yet given up on the idea of my taking the veil,' stressed the baronne de Vaudreuil.

'She's convinced that your destiny lies with the Sisters of Saint Georges,' said La Fargue.

'My destiny lies wherever I want it to.'

'There is one thing I don't understand,' confessed Laincourt, who was following his own train of thought. 'If your vision is prophetic—'

'It is,' affirmed Agnès. 'If nothing is done, then what I saw that night will come to pass.'

'In that case, why are the Chatelaines remaining silent? Why are they keeping this terrible prophecy a secret? Are they hiding something else, something even worse than the danger threatening Paris?'

'That's what we need to find out,' La Fargue declared.

A surprised silence followed this statement.

'Us?' Marciac finally asked. 'Why us?'

'Because someone needs to and no one else will. And because I have decided that we should.'

The Gascon felt that this last reason trumped all the others.

'So be it,' he replied.

'I have no scruples about going through the Chatelaines' dirty linen,' said Saint-Lucq. 'But the cardinal may see things in an entirely different light, under the circumstances . . .'

'The Chatelaines are powerful,' added Laincourt. 'Right now, they are in favour with the king, the Parlement, and the people, while the cardinal is more criticised than ever. Like Saint-Lucq, I doubt His Eminence will approve of our initiative.'

'That's true,' acknowledged the Blades' captain. 'That's why we won't tell him about it.'

Among his other names, both true and false, he was called the Gentleman after one of the twenty-two figures forming the Major Arcana of the Shadows Tarot. It was a tradition of the lodge to which he was proud to belong, a lodge so secret it was wreathed in a legendary aura even within the Black Claw. Like an unmentionable curse, the Arcana lodge inspired awe in those who believed in its existence and, in the remainder, an uneasy, superstitious respect. Even the powerful masters of the Grand Lodge in Madrid hesitated to call it to account for its plans, when it knew of them. As for its members, they obeyed no one but their leader: the Heresiarch.

Seated in a walnut armchair covered in Genoa velvet, The Gentleman was meditating in front of a mirror that stood on a table placed against a wall, between two large silver candelabra. His wrist lay limply on an armrest, his fingers grasping the rim of a glass filled with a golden liqueur which he swirled slowly, wrapped up in his thoughts. His blond hair was still damp from his evening bath, and he wore nothing but a pair of breeches and a shirt made of fine cloth that he had quickly pulled on over his wet skin. Tall and slim, he looked thirty years old. His features were delicate, almost feminine, and imbued with a strange, perverse charm. He was handsome, but there was something disturbing about the thrill he provoked in others.

The last rays of a flamboyant sunset still filtered through the curtains. They made the dust particles shine in the quiet dimness of his reading study, and gave an amber and purple sheen to the varnished furnishings, the lustrous woodwork, the rich tapestries, and the expensive book bindings. Stirring gently, the liquid gold in the Gentleman's glass gave off reddish shimmering glints, along with a heady fragrance.

The Enchantress came into the room.

Seeing her willowy figure approach in the mirror, the Gentleman smiled without turning round and caught her eye. She was almost naked, only wearing a pair of white stockings secured by crimson velvet ribbons. Her self-assurance and shamelessness were enough to clothe her. She was also smiling as she came towards him, slowly, splendid and sensual; the heavy curls of her mahogany-coloured hair falling to the dark areolas of her breasts. She slept or lazed about most of the day, and would only come out at night to partake in the cruel debaucheries that were her principal source of entertainment. She was of the Arcana lodge, like the Gentleman, and like him she belonged to the younger generation of dragons – the 'last-born' – for whom the outward appearance of humanity had become more natural than the draconic form.

The Enchantress leaned over the back of the armchair to kiss the Gentleman on the cheek, then came round the chair to face him, gripped the table behind her with both hands, and hopped up to sit nimbly on its edge in front of the mirror framed by the twin candelabra. A mischievous gleam in her eyes, she wormed one silk-sheathed foot between the Gentleman's knees and let it slither upwards to his groin.

He allowed her to do so without protest.

'So, what news?' she asked playfully as she started to caress him.

'I spoke with the Heresiarch last night. The Grand Lodge is growing impatient. It is anxious to see results.'

'And when was it ever otherwise?'

'Indeed. But the stakes are greater now. Our allies have become scarce, and silent. Our enemies, on the other hand, grow in numbers and speak ever more loudly. They are scoring easy points by saying that our endeavours are too costly and don't lead to anything.'

'And what do they know of our endeavours?' the Enchantress scoffed.

'Nothing. Precisely.'

'They're imbeciles. They will soon be jostling one another for the crumbs of our glory.'

'Right now, they are a nuisance which might hinder us. Who knows where their boldness may lead them?'

The Enchantress did not answer, but she did remove her foot. She stretched her hand out for the Gentleman's glass, took a deep swallow of the delicious liqueur and said:

'Don't drink too much of this nectar. You know the harm it can do.'

It was golden henbane liqueur, a popular drug amongst the idle rich. For dragons, it was the drink of choice. They relished it and sometimes indulged to the point of excess, especially the last-born. In their case, golden henbane woke long-buried instincts. It helped them reclaim their fundamental essence and, under its influence, those who struggled to assume even intermediate draconic forms were able to achieve complete metamorphoses. But there was a heavy price to pay for it. With habituation, heavier and more frequent doses became necessary, doses which could weaken, and even poison them. Numerous last-born had destroyed themselves in this manner.

Setting the glass down, the Enchantress slipped down from the table and, looking deep into his eyes, joined him on the armchair, straddling his thighs so that she knelt over him.

'But it's not those old lizards of the Black Claw who worry you, is it?' she asked him.

'No.'

'Then what is it, little brother?'

She slipped her hand between them and started to unbutton his breeches.

'The Heresiarch is not gauging the situation accurately,' he explained. 'Killing the Alchemist without consulting anyone was reckless. And waking the Primordial to achieve it was an even greater folly . . . It's as if the Heresiarch was . . . blinded by his Grand Design. He worries me and I don't know how to make him see reason.'

'Is such a thing even possible?'

'I hope so,' replied the Gentleman as he felt expert fingers slide into his breeches. 'But even the prospect of an Assembly doesn't seem to perturb him.'

'An Assembly? Who called for one?'

'The Master-at-Arms. But I suspect the Protectress was behind it. I'm convinced she is forming an opposition to the Heresiarch.'

'Meaning, against us. If the Heresiarch falls, your disgrace will follow and so will mine . . .'

'What are you trying to tell me?'

'Nothing.'

And as the Enchantress' fingers squeezed him gently but firmly, the Gentleman no longer felt a need to discuss it.

'Very well,' he said. 'But we will soon have to answer before the Arcana Assembly.'

'The Alchemist sealed his own fate,' the Enchantress reminded him.

Drawing him toward her, she made him slip his hips forward. He slumped slightly in the armchair.

'We will need to take action,' she said.

'Take action? What do you mean?'

'Later,' she murmured in his ear.

She lifted herself and eased him inside her, before abruptly sinking down upon him and arching her back with a single, great shudder.

Late that night, La Fargue joined Agnès in the stable where, unable to sleep, she was tending to her favourite horse by the lantern light. Seeing the captain enter from the corner of her eye, she continued to brush Courage, and said:

'Thank God, I did not choose him for the ride to Mont-Saint-Michel! I would have lost him . . .'

La Fargue sat on a stool.

'How are you, Agnès?' he asked gravely

The young woman stopped brushing the horse for a moment . . .

. . . and then resumed, with calm, steady strokes.

'I wasn't the one who almost lost an eye,' she said in a tone she had meant to be light.

La Fargue smiled.

He would have liked to reply that he no longer noticed the patch he was wearing, but his left eye still hurt and could not bear bright light.

'I know you too well, Agnès. There's something you're not telling us . . .'

She made no reply, but continued to brush the animal.

'If you don't want to talk about it, that's fine,' he continued. 'I just want you to know that I'm always ready to listen . . . But . . .' he hesitated. 'You were well treated, weren't you?'

'By the Chatelaines? As well as one can be, locked up in a pitch-dark cell . . . The most unbearable thing was thinking that Ballardieu was dead. And that it was my fault.'

Understanding, the old gentleman nodded.

'So what's bothering you now?'

'Apart from a dragon destroying Paris?'

'Yes, apart from that.'

Agnès put down the brush and, smoothing Courage's neck, admitted:

'I can't help thinking about what Sœur Béatrice told me. Or rather, what she tried to tell me . . . I keep trying to remember her exact words, but they were so disjointed and confused . . .'

And since La Fargue, by remaining silent and attentive,

encouraged her to continue, the young baronne said, with a distant look in her eyes:

'She said something about the arcana . . . And an heir . . . And she mentioned the Alchemist of the Shadows.'

'The Alchemist? Are you quite sure?'

Agnès shrugged.

'I wouldn't swear to that, but I have had time to ponder the whole matter. And I believe that Sœur Béatrice's expedition in Alsace was a mission to eliminate a dragon. She was a White Wolf, after all. And she had a detachment of the Black Guards accompanying her . . . Furthermore, only combat with a dragon could have caused the terrible state she was in. I think that even the vision she shared with me must have come from her confrontation with a dragon in Alsace . . .'

'And this dragon would have been the Alchemist?'

'Yes.'

'So that's why Sœur Béatrice wanted to warn you about him. Since she could not have known that we had captured him, she must have believed the queen was still in danger.'

'That's what I thought, yes.'

'But you no longer think so now?'

'I don't know,' replied Agnès, sounding annoyed with herself. 'I no longer know what to think.'

La Fargue stood up and, placing his hands on the young woman's shoulders, he waited until she looked him in the eyes before saying:

'The Alchemist is dead, Agnès.'

Uncertain, she gently freed herself from his grasp.

'I know, captain . . . And yet . . . And yet something tells me we're still not finished with him.'

2

Seated in his coach, which moved along the street at a slow crawl, with cushions wedged beneath his feet and behind his back, Cardinal Richelieu said:

'I'm hesitant.'

'I'll lead the negotiations myself,' replied Père Joseph. 'And if nothing comes of them, we will still be able to renounce the whole matter.'

'At risk of displeasing the Pope.'

'Indeed,' the Capuchin monk recognised.

Aged about fifty, he wore a plain grey habit and sandals, with a simple rope serving as a belt. He had long been the cardinal's closest advisor, his 'Grey Eminence', a figure who always operated in the shadows.

'Are we quite certain, at least, that we have squeezed everything we can out of this man?' enquired Richelieu. 'After all, he hasn't been in our hands for very long . . .'

'I believe we have, yes.'

'Has he been put to the question?'

'Yes, monseigneur. He's been tortured several times. By the Chatelaines, and on occasion even in my presence.'

The cardinal lowered his eyes to look at Petit-Ami who was curled up asleep on his knees, seemingly undisturbed by the jolting coach journey. He was fond of this dragonnet, a gift from the king. Its scarlet colour made it a rarity, but the price which His Majesty's chief minister attached to the little reptile went far beyond that.

'I would prefer to know why the Pope is so keen that we transfer this man to his custody.'

'No doubt to learn the same information that he gave us.'

'And what are we to receive in return for our prisoner?'

'Very little. But as we are in debt to Rome . . .'

The two men exchanged a long glance, before Richelieu finally asked:

'Where is the transfer to take place?'

'At the Château de Mareuil-sur-Ay.'

'Understood. You will arrange everything . . . But make sure that the game is worth the candle. And also see to it that the Sisters of Saint Georges don't get wind of this too soon. They might want to keep the marquis de Gagnière for themselves.'

That morning Antoine Leprat, chevalier d'Orgueil, paid particular attention to his appearance.

Freshly shaved, his moustache and goatee carefully smoothed, he put on a clean shirt and stockings, followed by a pair of breeches and a doublet still warm from his landlady's iron. He had polished his boots the previous evening. Nevertheless, he examined them again before putting them on, stamping his heels to make sure they fit snugly. He adjusted his baldric and added his white rapier, verifying that the sword hung at the correct height at his right hip and slid easily in and out of the scabbard. Finally, after a last glance at the handsome blue cape spread across his bed, he went out, shutting the door to his modest room where he had left everything tidy and clean behind him.

Having donned his felt hat while descending the stairs, he found Athos waiting for him below, in rue Cocatrix, at the appointed time. They saluted one another gravely before going to fetch their horses from the nearest stables. It was the start of a fine day, but neither of them was in any mood to take pleasure from it. The thought did occur to Leprat, nevertheless, that he would need to be careful to keep the sun at his back.

A quarter of an hour later, he and Athos left the Ile de la Cité by the Petit Pont.

'I would like to thank you for being at my side, Athos.'

'I am your second.'

'Precisely.'

As Leprat had expected, his violent altercation with Broussière and Sardent had not been the end of the matter. That was hardly surprising. He had broken the first man's nose and had almost impaled the second without any ado, acting in the heat of the rage Sardent had provoked. The affair was too serious to be settled in any other way but a duel and it had been decided that Leprat would confront Sardent first and then Broussière as soon as possible afterwards. The details of the first encounter were promptly agreed. It would need to take place quickly, as the more time passed the greater the risk news would leak out. Duelling was forbidden by the very royal edicts which the King's Musketeers, above all, were charged with upholding. To be sure, the king was willing to forgive them many trespasses, especially if they were at the expense of the Cardinal's Guards. But Captain Tréville could not tolerate his musketeers quarrelling and cutting one another to pieces. He would forbid the duel if he learned of it, which would leave Leprat and Sardent no alternative but to disobey him and bear the consequences. So it was best if they took their chance right away.

On the Left Bank, Leprat and Athos soon turned onto rue Galande. They crossed Place Maubert and then took rue Saint-Victor as far as the city gate of the same name. Out in the faubourg, they rode alongside the walls of Saint-Victor abbey, then those of the Royal Garden of Medicinal Plants, a vast domain which was just starting to emerge from the ground and behind which the duellists had agreed to face one another.

'There they are,' said Athos.

Indeed, Sardent, accompanied by Broussière, who would act as his second and whose nose was decorated with a large bandage, was just arriving from the faubourg Saint-Jacques by way of rue d'Orléans. They were also on horseback. Athos and Broussière saluted one another, but the other two men exchanged neither a word nor even a glance. While Sardent seemed furious, Leprat did not let his feelings show. Detouring around the site of what would one day become the famous

Jardin des Plantes, the four horsemen approached the appointed place. It seemed ideal: flat, unobstructed, and sheltered from indiscreet gazes . . .

If it were not for the fact that there was already someone there.

Seated on a large rock, the man had placed his hat upon his knee. He was wearing the King's Musketeers' blue cape with silver braiding, and was whistling as he fiddled with his horse's bridle.

His horse, tethered and placid, waited nearby.

'So?' asked d'Artagnan without raising his eyes from his task. 'Out for a ride? I like this spot very much, myself. It's peaceful here. Just right for thinking matters through . . .'

Completing his repair of the bridle, he donned his felt hat, stood up, and with an innocent smile but eyes full of gravity, he added in a casual tone:

'Unfortunately, it seems that we all had the same idea of retiring here this morning. Since I arrived first, I could insist that I stay and so oblige you to go elsewhere. But that might give you the idea that I was pulling rank, when I do like to be an amenable fellow. So, what do you say: shall we all agree to give up our present plans?'

La Fargue found Saint-Lucq helping Agnès practise her fencing skills in the main hall, watched closely by Ballardieu. Laincourt and Marciac were also present. The Gascon, who had spent most of the previous night drinking and gambling, was asleep on a chair tilted dangerously backward, his feet crossed on a window ledge. Laincourt was reading the latest issue of the *Gazette*, which was entirely devoted to an account of the dragon's attack on Le Châtelet.

Drenched in sweat, the baronne de Vaudreuil did not spare her efforts. Although she felt a need to spend her energy, she also needed to become accustomed to wielding her new sword. It was a little longer and heavier than the one she had been carrying for years, which the Sisters of Saint Georges had taken from her. And while this new one was excellently made, it was nonetheless a heavier rapier that soon tired her arm.

At the end of an exchange, Agnès suddenly lunged. Saint-Lucq parried, started a riposte but feinted and delivered a particularly treacherous thrust. Taught by the best masters, the baronne de Vaudreuil did not fall into his trap. Her counterattack was immediate and Saint-Lucq would have lost an eye had it not been for his reflexes and composure. The two fencers backed away from one another and saluted.

'Bravo!' exclaimed La Fargue.

Ballardieu wanted to applaud, a feat somewhat complicated by the paper cone filled with small cream pastries that he held in one hand, while eating with the other.

'Thank you,' said Agnès.

Putting down her sword, she reached for a towel to wipe her face, neck, and throat. She was breathless but satisfied, as if she had just had a good meal. The exercise had done wonders for her.

Saint-Lucq re-sheathed his weapon in silence.

'I have decided to trust your intuition, Agnès,' La Fargue announced. And for the others' benefit, he explained, 'Agnès thinks that we're not finished with the Alchemist yet.'

His mouth full, Ballardieu opened his eyes wide and raised an index finger to make an objection. The young woman cut him short:

'Yes, Ballardieu, I know the Alchemist is dead.'

Interested by the discussion, Laincourt closed his copy of the *Gazette*. Marciac was still asleep on his precariously balanced chair, a slight smile playing on his lips in the warmth of the sunlight streaming through the window panes. Ballardieu lowered his finger.

'But I have reasons to believe he remains one of the keys to the mystery before us,' continued Agnès.

'Reasons?' Saint-Lucq enquired.

'All right,' she conceded. 'It's more a feeling, an intuition.'

'That might be enough,' conceded the half-blood with an ease that astonished Laincourt.

'Nevertheless,' said Ballardieu after swallowing, 'the Alchemist is dead so it will be difficult to ask him . . . If only we still had La Donna in our hands!'

La Donna was an Italian adventuress who rented out her services, always excellent, as a conspirator, a spy, and a seductress. The Blades had crossed paths with her recently, when she had offered to sell to France valuable information about a plot threatening the Crown. Indirectly, this information had led to the capture of the Alchemist. But La Donna never lost sight of her own interests. Faithful to her reputation for duplicity, she had used the Blades to her own advantage before reclaiming her freedom with complete impunity thanks to the intervention of a powerful protector: Pope Urban VIII.

'Forget La Donna,' said La Fargue. 'When we arrested him, the Alchemist was serving madame de Chevreuse as her master of magic. So we know he had gained her trust, as well as the queen's. He was passing himself off as . . .'

He searched for the name.

'Charles Mauduit,' supplied Laincourt. 'Who actually exists, as it happens. Or at least, he used to.'

'Who was he?' asked Agnès.

'An itinerant philosopher and mage. The books he occasionally published were well regarded in certain expert circles. But he was known mostly through his writings, and only to the few.'

'In short,' said Saint-Lucq, 'this master of magic had a name, but no face. That made him the ideal victim, considering the Alchemist's projects. You can rest assured that the real Mauduit is dead.'

'Let us return to the Alchemist and La Chevreuse,' said La Fargue. 'Willingly or not, the duchesse was an accomplice of the man she took to be Mauduit. No doubt she knows something about him that could be of interest to us. Moreover, he could not have emerged out of the blue and, overnight, become the master of magic in one of France's greatest households. How did he introduce himself into her entourage? More to the point, who introduced him?'

The question hung in the air without a response and, excepting Marciac, all present agreed that it deserved an answer.

'Do you think the duchesse would receive you?' the captain of the Blades asked, turning to Laincourt.

The cardinal's former spy pondered the matter briefly.

'Yes,' he replied.

'Perfect. Pay her a visit and question her closely. Be skilful about it, because there is nothing we can offer her to encourage her good will. Marciac will go with you.'

The Gascon opened an eye on hearing his name spoken.

Marciac and Laincourt waited until early afternoon before going to see the duchesse de Chevreuse, as a lady of her station never received anyone before midday. They reached the faubourg Saint-Germain via the Pont Rouge, which involved paying a toll but saved them from making a long detour across the Pont Neuf and its crowds. On the Right Bank, they followed the Seine upstream before taking one of the large archways through the Grande Galerie, a long building running parallel to the river and linking the Louvre to the Tuileries palace. They travelled on foot, without fear for their boots and breeches as the scorching sun that turned Paris into a stinking oven had at least turned the perpetual muck in the streets into a hard, dry crust.

Along the way, Laincourt asked his companion in a conversational tone:

'This morning, when Agnès admitted she merely had an intuition that we should look more closely at the Alchemist, it seemed enough to convince you all . . .'

Marciac smiled.

'That's because we've learned to trust Agnès' intuitions. You will too, you'll see.'

'Really?'

'Agnès . . . You know she almost joined the Chatelaines? She would have become one of their White Wolves if she had taken the veil. That was not by chance, and . . . and well, it left her with a trace of something.'

'How is that?'

With a vague twitch of his lips, the Gascon searched for words.

'Something . . . Something inexplicable . . .'

Laincourt knew when innocent questions started to sound like an interrogation. He did not persist.

The Grande Galerie to the south and the rue Saint-Honoré to the north marked the boundaries of an old neighbourhood of narrow, miserable streets that were a blot on the landscape surrounding the Louvre. Yet it was here, in rue Saint-Thomas-du-Louvre, that the magnificent Hôtel de Chevreuse stood, the scene of elegant society parties only a few days earlier, before the mistress of the household's disgrace.

Upon their arrival, Marciac and Laincourt discovered the monumental gate to the mansion's grounds under siege. In front, a noisy throng of men and women were jostling one another and hindering traffic in the street, which only aggravated the disorder. Standing firm and impassive before them, a unit of the Cardinal's Guards in their scarlet capes prevented anyone from entering, despite protests and raised fists, while an officer tried in vain to make himself heard. Finally giving up, he ordered his men to clear the space while the great carved doors shuddered, began to open, and then spread wide. Those assembled thought they were finally being granted admittance. The uproar subsided as they retreated before the guards who enlarged their semi-circle, although elbows were out, each member of the crowd trying not to let anyone else get in front of them. But despite their hopes there was still no question of anyone entering the premises.

Slowly, ponderously, a tarasque appeared, harnessed to a train of two wagons loaded with bundles, chests, and furniture. Two handlers armed with pikes were leading the enormous, armoured reptile which, on its six short legs, turned left onto rue Saint-Thomas-du-Louvre, moving towards rue Saint-Honoré. Some lackeys escorted the convoy.

Marciac and Laincourt did not wait to see how the doors would be closed again. Some intrepid individuals were already trying sidle into the courtyard of the Hôtel de Chevreuse, where more guards were standing watch. They knew Parisians and their propensity to revolt. The heat was not helping to soothe tempers and the situation risked turning into a bloody riot if the crowd decided to attack the armed troops.

'Meeting the duchess is not going to be easy,' the Gascon observed.

Laincourt had frequented the Hôtel de Chevreuse recently. He was thus familiar with its layout, and said:

'Behind there is a large garden that stretches to the rue Saint-Nicaise. The garden wall has a small door that—'

'Do you really believe that it isn't guarded? Or that we will find it open?'

'No. You're right.'

'Let's start by finding out what this is all about, shall we?'

They took a table in a tavern close by, near a window that allowed them to watch the street and the approaches to the besieged gate.

'So what is happening at the Hôtel de Chevreuse?' asked Marciac.

The tavern was dirty, stank and only served a vile plonk. But the tavern keeper was willing enough to talk to them.

They thus learned that the king had, that very morning during his Council, pronounced the banishment of madame de Chevreuse for once more taking part in a plot against Cardinal Richelieu. Not a very distant banishment, however, since she would be assigned to residence in Touraine, at her Château de Couzières. But the news had alarmed her numerous suppliers, to some of whom the duchesse owed fortunes, and they had come seeking their money. Unhappily, except for those with special authorisations, the king had forbidden all visits to madame de Chevreuse, a measure she was probably thankful for at present.

For Laincourt and Marciac, these were ill tidings.

'There can be no doubt that the duchesse is under close watch,' said the Gascon. 'We won't be able to climb over the wall and go see her . . .'

'And time presses. She will soon be on her way to Couzières.'

'Perhaps it would be easier to reach her there, away from all the spies swarming around her in Paris.'

'Perhaps,' said Laincourt, who turned to look out the window.

It was then that he saw a spectre that had been haunting him more or less frequently, that of the hurdy-gurdy player who had been Laincourt's contact when he was still a spy for Cardinal Richelieu. Carrying his antique musical instrument on a bandolier, the old man was standing on the corner of the street and, with his finger, he was pointing at Jules Bertaud who was just leaving Hôtel de Chevreuse. Bertaud was the bookseller specialising in esoteric works who had shown a fondness for Laincourt, to the point of treating him like a favourite nephew, if not a son. Dressed in a long sleeveless vest and a crooked cap, the man was walking along, leafing through a notebook, and looking totally absorbed in whatever he was reading.

'Wait for me,' Laincourt said, abandoning Marciac at the tavern table.

Outside, he recalled his old spy reflexes and first made sure that the man he was about to greet was not being followed. Once he was convinced of that fact, he discreetly quickened his pace and caught up with Bertaud near the church of Saint-Thomas-du-Louvre which, dedicated to Saint Thomas of Canterbury, had given its name to the street. After greeting him, Laincourt drew the bookseller into the smaller rue Doyenné, on the pretext of seeking shade.

'But whatever are you doing round here?' asked Bertaud in friendly surprise.

Taking him by the elbow, the other man moved him even further away from prying eyes.

'I was going to ask you the same question, Jules.'

Bertaud frowned, looking to right and left.

'What's going on?' he asked.

'Everything's fine. No need to worry.'

The bookseller, however, was not so easily fooled.

'But it's not by accident if I cross your path near the Hôtel de Chevreuse, is it?'

'No. What were you doing in there?'

'Is it important?'

'Perhaps.'

Bertaud shrugged.

'Madame de Chevreuse desires to dispose of the books in her magic study. She has charged me with drawing up an inventory and organising the sale. There. No mystery in that.'

Those books had probably been gathered together for the most part by the Alchemist when he was calling himself Charles Mauduit and serving the duchesse de Chevreuse as her magic master. But Laincourt wished to pursue another point, and asked:

'So you have permission to come and go at the Hôtel de Chevreuse?'

'Yes.'

'Would you be able to deliver a message to the duchesse?'

Leprat, wearing his cape and with his white rapier at his side, had been waiting in monsieur de Tréville's small antechamber for more than hour. In his mansion on rue du Vieux-Colombier, the captain of the King's Musketeers had arranged two antechambers that communicated with his office by means of a different door. The 'large antechamber' was for ordinary visitors and petitioners. The 'small' was for the others.

Leprat stood at the window and passed the time by observing the preparations being made by the musketeers in the courtyard. Each of them was checking his equipment, polishing his boots, saddling his horse, having his sword sharpened on the whetstone of a passing blade grinder, making provision of victuals, greeting his friends, kissing his mistress, and accepting the gift of a ribbon or perfumed handkerchief from her. The company was making ready to depart. That evening the king would sleep at the Château de Saint-Germain and, as was proper, his Musketeers were to accompany him.

Antoine Leprat did not know where he would be sleeping. On the other hand, he had a very good idea why Tréville had summoned him: it could only be about his quarrel with Sardent.

A secretary, finally, ushered him into the captain's office. As was often the case when he had a difficult decision to make, the captain had his back to the room and was looking out the window. Old Tréville had fought at Henri IV's side before serving Louis XIII. He was a man of action who had trouble remaining seated for very long; it always made him feel he had ants crawling up and down his legs.

Leprat stood to attention and waited in silence, his hat in his hand. Although he knew he was risking dismissal, he was already preparing to refuse to offer his apologies. He would to Broussière, perhaps, because the man had unjustly fallen victim to Leprat's wrath. But not to Sardent, who had insulted him. Indeed, the affair with Sardent would inevitably be settled by a duel. By arriving first at the botanical gardens that morning, d'Artagnan had only delayed the coming confrontation between the two men, as the rules of honour dictated.

'A brawl,' said the captain after a moment. 'In an inn. Between three of my musketeers . . .' He suddenly turned round and looked Leprat in the eye. 'That's the behaviour of a common sword-for-hire and not of a gentleman, of a musketeer . . . And yet . . . And yet, I know the respect that you bear for your cape . . .'

Shaking his head with the air of a man saddened but determined to lay down the law, Tréville sat down at his desk.

'I know that this affair can only be settled by a duel of honour. I know that, but cannot allow it. You understand, don't you?'

Leprat nodded, still silent. He frowned, however. Was Tréville unaware that Sardent and he had been ready to fight a few hours earlier, in faubourg Saint-Victor?

'Moreover, if you fight this duel and win,' the old man continued, 'a friend of Sardent will pick a quarrel with you for vengeance's sake. And if you win that duel . . . Well, in short, you will wind up dead, and before you do, you will have killed or maimed half my company . . . That, too, I cannot allow.'

Once again, Leprat nodded without saying a word.

It was certain: Tréville knew nothing of his aborted duel. D'Artagnan had kept the matter secret, which was just like him. By preventing the duel from taking place through his presence, and by pretending not to be aware of anything, the clever lieutenant had acted in accordance with his rank without having to assert his authority. His ruse, moreover, relieved him of having to make a report: a way of protecting his brothers-in-arms from repercussions.

'Because it so happens,' Tréville continued, 'that I hold half my company as dear to me as I hold the entirety of your person . . .'

At this, Leprat cocked an eyebrow. Could Tréville know more than he let on? Had he chosen to save appearances in order to avoid having to take radical disciplinary measures?

Leprat hesitated, and then ventured:

'Th . . . Thank you.'

'You're welcome. So, to preserve both your person and my company, I am separating the one from the other. Monsieur le chevalier d'Orgueil, you will depart this evening on a special escort mission.'

The Illuminator arrived in Paris by the Saint-Antoine gate, beneath a blazing sun that obliged him to keep his eyes squinted.

Tall and massively built, with a large belly, he was riding a bay horse and leading a mule loaded with his baggage. He had a beret decorated with a pheasant feather on his head and a pair of worn-out, shapeless boots on his feet. His body was clothed in a dusty blue outfit. His shirt was sweat-stained beneath his open doublet, and an abundance of hair as thick and black as that of his beard emerged from his gaping collar. He was perspiring profusely. A powerful musky smell emanated from him and his breath came in muffled rasps. A *schiavone* hung at his side, a sturdy sword with a straight blade whose guard enveloped the entire hand and joined with the pommel. This Italian weapon was traditionally employed by the Dalmatian Guards of the Venetian Republic.

Leaving the crowded rue Saint-Antoine, the Illuminator took rue Saint-Paul as far as the Seine, which he followed downstream to Les Écailles.

The Scales.

Having been left in a wild state for years, the island had been adopted by the dracs who made it into their home: a damp and rotting maze of huts on stilts, rickety walkways, and dark lanes. By day, Notre-Dame-des-Écailles was a miserable village from whose depths rose a foul, marshy stink. But once night fell, Les Écailles became the beating heart of a violent, primitive culture which expressed itself by torchlight, in a moist air rich with spicy scents, and to the rhythm of sinister drums celebrating ancient rituals or punctuating warrior chants, lascivious dances, and blood-curdling tales. Here, only tribal laws and traditions held sway.

Except in the presence of a dragon.

After passing over the wooden bridge that linked Paris to Les Écailles, the Illuminator sold his mule and hired two drac slaves to carry his baggage. The trader did not negotiate with him. Usually one to drive a hard bargain, the old drac did not even dare look the Illuminator in the eye: he knew a dragon when he saw one, particularly when the dragon in question was projecting its aura of power, as the Illuminator never failed to do when in the presence of inferiors. This aura was sometimes strong enough to provoke uneasiness in humans; to a drac it was like a painful wave that resonated in the very depths of their being and woke fearful and servile instincts in them, the instincts of a race that had now been freed, but nonetheless one that had been created by the Ancestral Dragons and had been mercilessly oppressed by them.

Followed by his slaves for the day, the Illuminator rode through Les Écailles, conscious of the wary and sometimes hateful looks he attracted. He felt scorn for such reactions and pretended not to see them, but relished provoking them all the same. Proceeding at a walk and looking contemptuously down at the drac settlement, he soon crossed over a narrow canal that isolated one end of Ile Notre-Dame and delineated a closed paved quarter where a decadent community of last-born dragons had established itself. There were lurid rumours about the goings-on in this ghetto, whose mysterious dwellings were defended by sinister-looking walls and massive black doors.

At the end of a hemmed-in lane, the Illuminator arrived before one of these doors. Beneath a stone arch overhung with scarlet ivy, it presented two thick rectangular panels whose dark wood, large square-headed nails and solid iron fittings indicated their great age. The door opened slowly at his approach, revealing the courtyard of an elegant house.

The Hôtel des Arcanes, headquarters of the Arcana lodge.

There, on the bottom steps of the porch, the Gentleman awaited with a smile.

'Welcome,' he called.

Without answering, the Illuminator dismounted and exchanged a greeting with the master of the household which was far from enthusiastic. Ignoring this, the Gentleman said:

'I cannot disguise my pleasure at seeing you again, my brother.'

'It was lucky that I was in Lorraine,' replied the other dragon. 'When will the Assembly take place?'

'Soon.' And seeing the drac slaves waiting, the Gentleman asked: 'What's all this?'

'My baggage. The slaves are hired. Someone will come fetch them tomorrow.'

'Ah!' said the Gentleman in a slightly disconcerted tone. 'Have you eaten?'

'Not much.'

'Then come, I have a light meal prepared.'

On entering, the dragons passed three household servants who, pale-faced and glassy-eyed, were on their way to tend to the Illuminator's baggage, slaves, and horse.

While the Illuminator ate heartily but without showing either satisfaction or displeasure, the Gentleman kept him company, sipping a glass of golden henbane. They were alone in the luxuriously furnished salon of the Hôtel des Arcanes and spoke little: the Illuminator, when eating, obviously wanted to do just that. Once he felt full, he dismissed the lackey serving him, drank a last swallow of wine, wiped his fingers on the tablecloth, and smoothed his slightly greasy beard.

'Now it's my turn to ask,' he said, pointing a finger at the departing lackey.

This servant, too, was mute, pale-faced, with an absent look and slow gestures.

'The Enchantress' latest whim,' explained the Gentleman. 'She finds it more elegant to have human domestics. But don't ask me the secret of the potion she has them drink . . .'

'Is she here?'

'The Enchantress? Of course . . . She will be joining us for supper.'

A silence ensued between the two dragons. Their gazes crossed and locked on one another.

'The Heresiarch sent me,' the Illuminator finally said.

'Good.'

'He has charged me with a mission.'

'And that is?'

'If the Heresiarch wants you to know—'

'—the Heresiarch will tell me. Very well.'

The Gentleman did not insist.

With regard to the Heresiarch, the Illuminator displayed the loyalty of a guard dog. Whatever the Heresiarch wanted, the Illuminator would do. Without discussion, or even much thought.

'Is there anything you need?' the Gentleman asked coldly.

'Gold.'

'You shall have it. Besides that?'

'Nothing else for the moment.'

'In that case . . .'

He rose and was about to withdraw, when the Illuminator said, in a slightly raised voice, as if concluding a discussion with a final argument:

'What the Heresiarch has done, he has done for the good of the Arcana. The Alchemist's death was necessary. He had failed and was about to fall into the Chatelaines' hands. As if it were not enough that he had already allowed himself to be duped by that . . . by that Italian woman!' The dragon sounded aggrieved at the memory but quickly recovered his calm. 'No matter. But regarding the Alchemist, time was short and the Heresiarch had to act urgently. Necessity knows no law.'

And as the Gentleman continued to gaze at him without speaking, he finally asked:

'Will you support the Heresiarch at the next Arcana Assembly?'

'Does the Heresiarch doubt it?'

'If our adversaries carry the day, it may bring the Burning Sword down upon us . . .'

'Have I ever wavered?' replied the Gentleman with confidence as he turned on his heel and walked away.

But once the Illuminator could no longer see it, his expression became one of concern.

Upon their return to the Hôtel de l'Épervier, Marciac and Laincourt reported their findings to La Fargue and Saint-Lucq.

'It was only a matter of time before the king ordered madame de Chevreuse's banishment,' commented the Blades' captain. 'But when one knows how close she came to delivering the queen to the Black Claw, one can't help but think that a retreat to her château at Couzières is not such a cruel punishment . . . Nevertheless, it does not make our business any easier.'

'When must the duchesse leave Paris?' enquired Saint-Lucq.

'Very soon,' Marciac informed him.

'And for the moment, the Cardinal's Guards are keeping a close watch on her mansion, from which she is forbidden to leave . . .'

'Yes. And it's impossible to enter without the proper authorisation.'

'No visits?'

'None.'

'Letters?'

'All subject to censorship by the cardinal.'

La Fargue grimaced in annoyance.

Agnès made an entrance, returning from a long ride, while Ballardieu remained in the stable helping André with the horses.

'What's going on?' she asked.

Marciac brought her up to date.

'Argh!' she said in frustration when she knew as much as others.

'But Arnaud may have a solution,' the Gascon added.

'I know someone who is free to come and go as he pleases at the Hôtel de Chevreuse,' explained Laincourt. 'His name is Jules Bertaud, a bookseller and a friend of mine.'

'And what is this bookseller doing at the duchesse's home?' asked La Fargue.

'He is arranging for the disposal of the library in her magic study.'

'Would he agree to be our messenger?'

'I asked him and he said yes.'

'Is the man trustworthy?' Agnès wanted to know.

'I believe so.'

La Fargue scratched at his beard while he thought.

'I would prefer you to be certain,' he said.

'Bertaud is a bookseller,' retorted Laincourt. 'He is not a spy. I've known him for a long time, but I cannot answer for him absolutely.'

The old captain shrugged: the only other solution was to ask Cardinal Richelieu for a safe-conduct.

'Beggars can't be choosers . . .' he conceded finally.

'Even so, there is still a problem,' Agnès pointed out. And seeing the others looking at her blankly, she hastened to explain: 'I may be wrong, but I doubt that the duchesse de Chevreuse is able to say a word or take a step in her home without the cardinal learning of it immediately. She is most certainly being watched, discreetly but efficiently, day and night. And I would not be the least bit surprised to discover this Bertaud fellow is also being spied on.'

'You're right,' said La Fargue. Then, addressing everyone, he declared: 'We can't simply entrust this bookseller with a letter. We need to find a way he can deliver a message to the duchesse without compromising ourselves or alerting the Palais-Cardinal.'

Laincourt nodded:

'I'll think of something,' he promised.

The Bastille was built during the second half of the fourteenth century to reinforce the eastern defences of Paris. Standing by the Saint-Antoine gate, this massive fortress overlooked a bastion extending into the neighbouring faubourg. Surrounded by a large moat filled by waters drawn from the Seine, it comprised eight round towers which each had a name, such as the Tour de la Chapelle or the Tour du Puits. The towers were connected by walls as tall as they were, protecting a courtyard which was only accessible via a drawbridge which was lowered to connect with a fixed bridge across the moat. And reaching this bridge entailed traversing two outer courtyards. The first was the Cour de l'Avancée, which could be entered freely from rue Saint-Antoine and the Arsenal gardens, and contained the garrison's barracks and stables. The second outer courtyard was smaller and guarded by a gate. The Bastille governor's house was located here.

The Bastille had lost its military role during Henri IV's reign. The royal treasury was guarded there for a time. Then Richelieu rebuilt its cellars and the floors of all eight towers for use as a prison. It was a State prison, however, which meant that one could only be sent there by an order of the king, signed and sealed, known as a *lettre de cachet*. The prisoners locked away there were divided into two categories: illustrious and influential figures; and the secret enemies of France. Provided they had means, the members of the first group enjoyed fairly comfortable conditions of incarceration. The second group, in contrast, were condemned to long and anonymous solitude, without hope of a trial or a pardon.

The Masque de Fer, or the Man in the Iron Mask, was one of them.

But others preceded him.

*

In the courtyard of the Bastille, Leprat and the fifteen horse-men under his command waited patiently. Leprat was the only one to dismount, by the wagon that would convey the prisoner they were escorting. All of them were drawn from the King's Musketeers and wore the blue cape with silver braiding. They did not speak and remained in line in their saddles, grim and watchful, the butt of their muskets resting on their thighs.

Occasionally a horse became restless, but was quickly reined in.

Although it was still early evening, night had already settled within the high walls. The courtyard was silent and deserted, plunged into darkness as if crushed by the mass of grey stones surrounding it. Keys had been turned in all the locks until the following morning. All the bolts had been shot, the chains secured, and the doors shut tight. Sent back to their solitude, the prisoners knew that the gaolers would not answer their calls. The sentries who weren't patrolling the walls and towers fought with boredom in their guard-rooms, sitting around tables rolling dice. A strange tranquillity, an anxious calm, had invaded the sinister fortress. Time seemed to be standing still, which was only too true for some of the poor wretches shut away there.

Leprat did not know the identity of the prisoner he was waiting for.

He only knew that he was to accompany him to the Château de Mareuil-sur-Ay, not far from Épernay and the border with Lorraine. There, after some diplomatic negoti-ations, the man would be discreetly placed in the custody of a representative of Pope Urban VIII. Perhaps he was a Church spy that His Holiness was determined to reclaim. Perhaps he was a traitor or a fugitive criminal. Perhaps he was even an agent of a foreign power, for whom Rome was acting as an intermediary. Be that as it may, the prisoner was the object of an obscure transaction taking place at the highest level. And what would France receive in return? Another prisoner? Documents? Information? Unless the king was merely seek-ing the good graces of the Pope on the eve of a war with Lorraine – another Catholic power.

Such exchanges were not uncommon.

Indeed, based on his experience in the Cardinal's Blades, Leprat had not been overly surprised when Captain Tréville had given him his orders. And, immediately understanding what was likely to be involved, he had refrained from asking too many questions. All that he needed was information. pertinent to the success of his mission. As for the rest, he preferred not to know. He had no desire to be mixed up in intrigue and politics. A musketeer again, he only wanted to serve the king with honour, fulfilling his vocation as a soldier.

Behind an officer, a unit of arquebusiers filed out from the Tour du Puits in an orderly manner. They surrounded a man dressed in boots, breeches, and a shirt, whose wrists were shackled and whose face was hidden by a mask made of leather and riveted iron, with three rectangular holes, a large one for the mouth and two smaller ones for the eyes. He seemed to be young, and was of medium height with a slender, graceful build. His blond hair fell to his shoulders. He had the bearing of proud, refined man who had no weapons left to oppose his captors with but his pride and his scorn. He halted at the same time as his guards and waited, his head held high and his back straight.

The officer stepped forward, saluted Leprat, and took a sheaf of papers from the musketeer which he studied closely. As he did, Leprat observed and considered the prisoner. His silhouette seemed vaguely familiar, but it was the mask that intrigued him most. It was an exceptional precaution and Leprat was curious why it was necessary. Of course, it was meant to prevent the prisoner from being recognised. But why?

After declaring himself satisfied, the officer refolded the documents and returned them to Leprat. Then he ordered the prisoner to be placed in the wagon.

No doubt because they had seen more than one docile man rebel at the last moment, the solders were somewhat brusque with the prisoner who, when he was shoved, reacted as if he had received a hot poker to the shoulder and spun round. An arquebusier was already lifting his weapon, but Leprat leapt forward and interposed himself before a blow from the butt could be struck.

'This prisoner is mine,' he said. 'And he will be well treated.'

This intervention caused an angry stir among the soldiers, before their officer reminded them of their discipline.

'Thank you, monsieur,' said the prisoner.

That voice!

Squinting, Leprat suddenly recognised the eyes visible through openings cut into the mask. And he was even less likely to forget the eyes than he was the voice of a man who had coldly fired a pistol ball at his heart. Leprat remained dumbfounded while the soldiers placed the prisoner in the hitched wagon.

He realised someone was speaking to him.

'These two are for the irons,' the officer was saying, handing him a ring of small keys. 'And this one is for the mask.'

The prisoner's mask was held closed by a lock located at the rear of the skull.

Distracted, Leprat nodded as he pocketed the key ring.

'Any particular instructions?' he asked out of habit.

'None that you don't already know. But be careful, monsieur.'

'Why?'

'This prisoner, now entrusted to your care, has twice been the object of assassination attempts while under my guard. First by dagger, and then by poison. The dagger wounded one of my soldiers and the poison killed a gaoler.'

'Who wielded the dagger?'

'A madman who hung himself with his own belt before he could be interrogated. As for the poison . . .'

'I understand. Thank you, monsieur.'

'You're welcome. Good luck.'

Leprat climbed back into his saddle, placed five of his musketeers in front of the wagon, and ten behind it. Then he stood in his stirrups and, when he signalled their departure, the great courtyard rang with a loud din of hooves, creaking axles, and iron-bound wheels grinding into the paving stones.

The prisoner hidden behind the mask of leather and iron was the marquis de Gagnière, a cold and implacable killer.

Leprat had suffered the sad privilege of crossing his path recently, while on a secret mission for the king. Gagnière had laid a trap for him that a lone man had no chance of escaping, and had left him for dead after – without batting an eyelash – shooting him with a pistol at close range. Luckily, Leprat was left-handed. The ball had lodged itself in the thick leather of his baldric, which happened to fall across his chest from left to right. Shortly after that, the Cardinal's Blades had been recalled to service and confronted the Black Claw, in the person of a certain vicomtesse de Malicorne . . . and it had eventually come to light that Gagnière was her henchman. The vicomtesse had escaped. The sinister marquis had been captured and delivered to the cardinal's justice.

For Antoine Leprat to find himself escorting the marquis de Gagnière was a curious twist of fate. To crown it all, there was the possibility that he might have to risk his life to protect the man. To protect him from the Black Claw, no less! For there was little doubt the Black Claw were behind the attempts on Gagnière's life, either to punish him or to ensure his silence. Did he hide important secrets?

Leprat was only sure of one thing: the Black Claw would never give up. And there were forty-five leagues between Paris and their destination, which they would travel in a little under four days if they maintained a decent pace. The journey offered plenty of occasions for ambushes and attacks along the way.

With Leprat riding at the head, the wagon and its escort left Paris by the Saint-Antoine gate and galloped off into the night along a grey and powdery road.

When night fell, Marciac accompanied Agnès to the door of her bedchamber. They slept on the same floor of the Hôtel de l'Épervier and each had brought their own light. The Gascon, however, had no intention of retiring to his bed straight away.

'Really?' he insisted. 'Are you sure you won't come out with me to La Sovange's club?'

Madame de Sovange maintained, on rue de l'Arbalète in faubourg Saint-Jacques, a gaming house frequented by the very best society.

And by Marciac.

'No, Nicolas. Although it's sweet of you to ask.'

'I promise we'll come home early.'

'It's already late.'

'I bow to your wishes . . . But promise me that . . .'

'Soon, yes. I promise you I will.'

'Cross your heart?'

'Cross my heart. But if you want my opinion, you look like a man who needs a good night's sleep.'

The Gascon shrugged his shoulders and looked away, like a young boy caught doing something naughty.

'Sleep eludes me,' he confessed. 'I can't close my eyes without seeing Almades.'

'I know. It's the same for me.'

Marciac forced himself to smile.

'If someone had told me that I would miss his grim face so much . . . But to the Devil with this sadness!'

Pulling himself together, he opened Agnès' door for her, stepped aside to let her pass and ushered her inside with a bow and a flourish.

'Madame.'

'Thank you.'

She went in, placed her candle on a small table, and turned around to face the Gascon who remained on the threshold.

'Tell me, Nicolas . . .'

'Yes?'

'Do you know why Leprat left us?'

'Not exactly, no. He gave the captain an explanation, but I wasn't there.'

'And La Fargue, how did he take the news?'

'In his usual manner,' replied Marciac with a shrug. 'With cries, tears, and sobs. Afterwards, he wrote a poem recounting his sorrow . . .'

Agnès stifled a laugh but remained concerned.

'And you?' she asked. 'Did you speak with him?'

'With Leprat? No.'

'Do you think he would like it if I paid him a visit?'

'Perhaps. But you'll need to wait a bit. Or else go to Saint-Germain,' added Marciac. And seeing Agnès frown, he explained: 'The king has retired there, so the King's Musketeers went with him . . .'

'Oh yes, that's right . . . Well, good night, Nicolas.'

'Good night, baronne.'

Marciac closed the door and went away.

Feeling tired, Agnès undressed and freshened up. Then, turning her back to the mirror, she twisted her neck to examine the mark decorating her left shoulder. It was an old mark whose outlines had only become sharper over time. Now there could be no doubt that it was a rune or, more precisely, two runes entwined together to form one. The first signified 'dragon' and the second 'death'.

With her finger, Agnès de Vaudreuil brushed this mark which had seemed to waken recently and whose meaning she knew, although she couldn't admit it to herself. As she got into bed, she prayed for a dreamless sleep, only to have the vision of the great black dragon destroying Paris return once more to haunt her.

Upon arriving in the neighbourhood of Place Maubert that morning, Laincourt found Jules Bertaud's bookshop closed. That was hardly surprising; the bookseller rarely opened for business before noon. But his regular customers knew they could always knock on the door and peer through the shop's large front window. Bertaud was usually working in the storeroom or in some secluded corner of his shop. He would glance out and, seeing a favoured client, gesture for them to come round to the courtyard in the rear.

It was not Bertaud, however, who answered Laincourt's knock on this hot morning in July 1633, but his daughter. And rather than make him come through the courtyard, she hastened to open the door and usher him in. Clotilde was a pretty brunette with green eyes. Sixteen years old, she was totally devoted to her father and deeply in love with Arnaud de Laincourt, a fact that Laincourt alone was unaware of.

'Good morning, Clotilde. Is your father in? Could he receive me?'

'I will call him right away, monsieur.'

Thanking her with a polite smile, Laincourt began to wander distractedly about the shop, examining one book, leafing through another, without seeing that Clotilde had hesitated before leaving him, no doubt searching for something to say, before finally withdrawing reluctantly, cursing herself for being so dim-witted.

Bertaud soon came down from the first floor, where he and his daughter lived. He had his hat in his hand and the busy air of a man caught just as he making ready to go out.

'Good morning, Arnaud. You almost missed me: I was just on my way to the Hôtel de Chevreuse.'

'That's precisely what I've come to see you about. Can we talk?'

The bookseller caught Laincourt's meaning and brought him into the storeroom where no one could see or hear them. The room was dark and filled with the smell of dust and old paper.

'Yesterday,' said Laincourt in a low voice, 'I asked if you would undertake to transmit a message to the duchesse de Chevreuse. You replied yes, but I want you to know that I don't consider you bound by your answer. So, listen to me closely. I need to meet madame de Chevreuse. I must speak to her about a matter of which, unfortunately, I can tell you nothing. It must be done in greatest secret and I need to arrange a rendezvous with her. That's why I must go through you, given that you have access to the Hôtel de Chevreuse.'

'I say to you again, Arnaud, that I am willing to render you this service.'

'Don't answer just yet.'

'Are you plotting against the king?'

'No.'

'Against monsieur le cardinal?'

'No.'

'And are you acting for the common good?'

'I believe so.'

'Then that is enough for me. What must I do?'

Laincourt hesitated, and then pulled out a small book of poetry from his doublet.

'Here. Give this to madame de Chevreuse.'

'Is that all?'

'No. You must tell her: "Madame, here is the volume you spoke to me about, which I had in my shop".'

'But there was never any question of such a thing between madame de Chevreuse and me!'

'Precisely. That's how she will realise the particular worth of this book.'

'Will she accept it?'

'Without question. But if she does not, pretend that you wanted to offer it to her as a token of your admiration, but did not know how to phrase your compliment . . . But I assure you, madame de Chevreuse will take the book.'

'And after that?'

'After that, act just as you normally would. Go about your ordinary business and come home when you are finished. Neither sooner nor later than usual.'

'I don't wait for a reply?'

'Don't wait for anything. Don't change any of your habits. It's possible they are watching you.'

'"They"?' asked the bookseller in a worried tone.

'The cardinal's men.'

This reply disturbed Bertaud.

'But I thought you . . .'

'The matter is complicated,' Laincourt said evasively. 'Would you prefer to renounce this? I would understand if you did.'

'No! . . . So I just come home as if nothing were out of the ordinary?'

'Yes. If she wishes to, the duchesse will have transmitted her reply to you before then. It will either be "Yes" or "No".'

'And where will you and I meet?'

'Nowhere. If madame de Chevreuse replies yes, ask Clotilde

to wash the shop windows this evening. If no, make sure she does nothing of the sort . . . Have you understood?'

'I think so, yes.'

'Perfect.'

After leaving Bertaud's shop, Laincourt met the hurdy-gurdy player who was waiting for him and proceeded to walk along beside him.

Everything will go well, boy. The duchesse de Chevreuse will find the note you slipped inside the cover of the book and she will be at the rendezvous this evening.

That's not what worries me.

You're thinking of Bertaud.

I've compromised him. If they discover he—

There is still time for you to go back, recover the book from Bertaud and ask him to forget this whole affair. Will you do that?

No.

Well then, silence your remorse.

At the Hôtel des Arcanes, the Enchantress joined the Gentleman in the study where he kept – behind glass, set in racks, or placed on display stands – his collection of rapiers. He possessed several dozen, all of them forged by the best craftsmen of Europe. Each was worth a fortune, but that was not the main thing. Although he did not refuse to wear them, or to wield them, the Gentleman simply enjoyed the company of these lethal masterpieces. When he was preoccupied with something he spent hours, sometimes whole nights, admiring them and maintaining them in perfect condition. He would recall the memories attached to them, cherishing in particular those blades that had already taken a life, and promising the others they would shed blood soon enough.

'It seems the Heresiarch is suspicious of you,' said the Enchantress.

'Yes.'

'That's new.'

'I think the Heresiarch is suspicious of everyone right now,' the Gentleman declared calmly as he rubbed the blue steel of a sharp blade with an oiled cloth. 'His Grand Design has never been so close to being accomplished.'

'Or to failure.'

'Or, indeed, to failure.'

The Enchantress slowly walked around the study, pausing before one blade, running her fingertips down another. Wearing a crimson robe, she was beautiful and bewitching, her mahogany hair caressing her pale shoulders.

'The Illuminator gave me a letter from the Heresiarch.'

'A letter from the Heresiarch? Addressed to you?'

'To me rather than to you, that's right. Which is also something new, isn't it?'

The Gentleman rose to put away the rapier whose blade he had just been cleaning. He placed it within a long chest which he closed. For a moment he remained still, reflecting, before turning back to the Enchantress.

'And what was the subject of this letter?'

The Enchantress fixed her eyes resolutely on those of her lover.

'The Heresiarch thinks that the Arcana need new blood. He asked me to admit an initiate. In my own name.'

'An initiate. As if this were the time for initiations! And who does he want you to initiate?'

'The vicomtesse de Malicorne.'

For an instant, the Gentleman thought he had misheard.

'The vicomtesse . . . de Malicorne? Are you jesting?'

The vicomtesse de Malicorne was also a dragon. And although she did not belong to the Arcana, she had been one of the Black Claw's best agents in Paris. Daring and ambitious, she had come very close to establishing a Black Claw lodge in France, something the Sisters of Saint Georges had always managed to prevent. But it was not the Chatelaines who had thwarted her, it was the Cardinal's Blades. She had failed and had emerged broken from the ordeal. Struck by the after-effects of a powerful ritual that had been brutally interrupted, she was no longer even capable of assuming the appearance that she had long made her own, that of an adorable young blonde woman.

'But she is nothing!' protested the Gentleman. 'I know the Alchemist met with her recently. She was downcast, reduced to the state of an old woman deluding herself with dreams of one day recovering her power . . . The Alchemist said she was finished.'

'He was mistaken. The vicomtesse de Malicorne can recover her strength and vitality. She can do so thanks to me, and that is what the Heresiarch wishes.'

The Gentleman gave the Enchantress a long look.

'Yes,' he said at last. 'I know you can manage it . . . But even so? Why does the Heresiarch want us to initiate Malicorne now? I'm starting to think he's losing his mind . . .'

Drawing closer, the Enchantress displayed a superior smile, the smile of someone about to deliver a major revelation.

'Do you know why the Alchemist went to see La Malicorne after her failure?'

'To put his mind at rest, I suppose. To make sure she—'

'No,' the Enchantress interrupted. 'He went to her at the Heresiarch's behest. He was worried about her . . .'

'What?'

'La Malicorne came very close to establishing the first ever lodge of the Black Claw in France. You can imagine what sort of feat that would have been, can't you? But do you believe she came so close on her own? And why was the Black Claw willing to entrust her with the Sphère d'Âme that was so essential to her plan? La Malicorne was capable and trustworthy, true enough. But to go from that to having the old masters agree to entrust her with one of their precious Sphères d'Âme?'

'No doubt in their eyes, the game was worth the candle,' the Gentleman suggested.

'And now La Malicorne has failed, now she has lost everything, now she has lost her allies but still knows numerous secrets, how is it that the Black Claw has not had her assassinated?'

'Do you mean to say . . . ?'

'Yes. She is under the Heresiarch's protection. But he is

doing things as he always does, and as he has always fostered her projects in the past: in secret.'

'But why?'

'You make me laugh!'

'The Heresiarch and La Mal—?' He cut himself short, shaking his head. 'No. That isn't like him. The Heresiarch has never been one to give way to passion.'

'The Inferiors say that the flesh is weak. That applies to us, too . . . Happily so. How boring things would be if we were the same cold creatures as our ancestors!'

The Enchantress gave a burst of merry laughter.

After which, regaining a straight face, she said, almost tenderly:

'But rest assured. The Heresiarch did not forget strategy when he took La Malicorne under his wing . . . Answer me this: would the old masters of the Black Claw have ever permitted one of us, one of the Arcana, to attempt to found a lodge in France?'

'Certainly not! If one of us had succeeded, we would have won far too much prestige and influence.'

'And if it had been one of the Heresiarch's protégés?'

'No. For the same reasons; they would have been destined to become one of us.'

'But by secretly favouring La Malicorne, the Heresiarch was disguising his progress. If she had succeeded, no one could have prevented her from joining the Arcana, and certainly not the old lizards in Madrid. It would have been a *fait accompli*. They'd be furious, certainly. But powerless to stop it.'

The Gentleman nodded slowly, looking thoughtful, an admiring smile on his lips.

'Clever. Very clever, even . . . Which is much more like our old serpent of a Heresiarch.'

'And his plan offered the final advantage of not compromising the Arcana if La Malicorne failed. Which is indeed what happened . . .'

'So you believe that by resuscitating La Malicorne and admitting her to the Arcana . . .'

'. . . we will accomplish what the Heresiarch wants to do,

but which he cannot. If he openly comes to the vicomtesse's rescue, the Black Claw will learn of it and realise what he has been doing all along.'

'Do you really believe the Heresiarch still feels something for La Malicorne?'

'If you ask, then you've forgotten that he continues to protect her. He must, since she is alive. Besides, can we afford to displease the Heresiarch in this matter? He wants his sweetheart? Well then, let's offer her to him.'

The Gentleman silently reflected on this.

The Enchantress, however, knew she had already won the argument. Pressing herself to him, she presented him with a little note folded in quarters and, in his ear, she said:

'She goes by the name madame de Chantegrelle and she is pining away in a convent in the faubourg Saint-Jacques, whose address is written here. I know you can find the words to convince her . . .'

Night was falling when Marciac returned to the Hôtel de l'Épervier with the news they had all been waiting for.

'The bookseller's daughter washed the shop windows,' he announced to the Blades gathered in the fencing room.

'So the duchesse de Chevreuse has agreed to my rendez-vous,' said Laincourt.

'I don't understand it,' confessed Agnès pouring a glass of wine for the Gascon. 'Or not entirely . . . If I were her, and had almost handed the queen to the Black Claw, I would be relieved to be merely banished from the royal court. I certainly wouldn't risk giving the king the slightest motive to regret his clemency.'

'That's because you're not the duchesse de Chevreuse . . . She has the taste, a true passion, for intrigue. Not to mention that boredom is probably gnawing away at her.'

'But now she knows who you really are! She knows you serve the cardinal . . .'

'Precisely,' said La Fargue. He was straddling a chair, his forearms resting flat across its back. 'That detail must have particularly piqued the duchesse's curiosity. Because she must guess that it is not by the cardinal's order that Laincourt wants to see her. If his approach was of an ordinary nature, why surround it with such secrecy? Why try to elude the spies swarming about the Hôtel de Chevreuse? Isn't he supposed to be serving the same master as they are?'

'So the duchesse has already realised that we are acting without the cardinal's knowledge,' said Marciac.

'Yes.'

'That's hardly very reassuring.'

'More than that, it's dangerous,' declared Saint-Lucq.

As was his custom, he remained slightly apart from the rest of the group, sitting in profile in the recess of one of the windows looking out at the unkempt garden with its old table and chestnut tree.

'Dangerous?' enquired Ballardieu.

'Saint-Lucq is wary of a trap,' Agnès explained to him. 'Am I right?'

The half-blood, who had been carefully cleaning his spectacles, nodded.

'La Chevreuse might want to offer the king a token of her loyalty by betraying you, Laincourt. She might pretend to agree to meet you in order to give you up to His Majesty's officers.'

Because he was a former spy and had some experience in such matters, Laincourt was forced to admit that this hypothesis was plausible.

'Yes,' he said. 'It's possible.'

'Betraying you is even doubly in the duchesse's interest,' La Fargue added. 'For the reason that Saint-Lucq has just given us, first of all. But, secondly, because the rendezvous you have proposed could easily be a ruse of Richelieu's to test her loyalty. She is too sharp-witted not to have thought of it. And so the duchesse has every reason to ensure your ruin . . .'

'I am betting that madame de Chevreuse will not resist the temptation of hearing me out,' said Laincourt. 'Furthermore, I think she even feels a certain degree of affection for me.'

'It's too risky,' decreed Saint-Lucq. 'I'll go with you.'

'No. It will depend entirely on madame de Chevreuse's

goodwill whether she answers my questions or not. We need her, whereas she has nothing to gain from helping us. I doubt that she will be well disposed towards us if she senses that we are wary of her . . .'

'That is a valid point,' admitted La Fargue gravely.

'You are taking the risk of placing yourself, alone, in the wolf's jaws, Arnaud,' said Agnès, trying to make him see sense.

'I know. But it is a risk that I must take if we are to have any chance of succeeding. Don't forget that it is not just a question of me, or of us. The only trail likely to lead us to the dragon that attacked Le Châtelet passes through the Hôtel de Chevreuse.'

'Nevertheless, be very careful, Laincourt,' La Fargue instructed him. 'You will need to elude the Cardinal's Guards, and you more than any of us know their worth.'

The tavern was located in the depths of Les Écailles, on the Ile Notre-Dame. Daylight never penetrated here and the air was stagnant and moist beneath the low beams of a ceiling blackened by the smoke from the oil lamps. The dracs who gathered in this place were of the very worst sort. Thieves, mercenaries and assassins came here to amuse themselves, drink and to seek work or opportunities for plunder.

The Illuminator abruptly released his aura as he pushed through the door.

A silence immediately fell in the large hall, which, at this hour of the evening, was packed. All eyes turned toward the dragon. Some were fearful; most were wary and hostile; a few were violently hateful. Then interest in him subsided and conversations resumed as the Illuminator, his heavy *schiavone* at his side, diminished his aura and advanced with a tranquil step.

He approached a red drac who was dining alone, eating a thick fish soup. Tall and thin, the drac was dressed as a hired swordsman, wearing an old leather doublet over a filthy shirt whose collar gaped wide open, revealing his scaly chest.

Behind him, a muscular black drac stood motionless with his arms crossed.

The red drac did not look up from his bowl as the Illuminator halted before him and threw a heavy purse on the table.

'Departure in one hour,' announced the dragon.

The drac nodded, without even pausing over his meal.

Laincourt left the Hôtel de l'Épervier on his own.

A short time later, Captain La Fargue came out in turn, but took a different route into Paris, as a magnificent summer sunset stretched across the darkening sky, the last layers of purple, red, and orange light swathing the horizon and making the scattered clouds glow.

3

After a light supper, the duchesse de Chevreuse announced that she wished to enjoy the tranquillity and cooler air of the evening, at her ease. She thus refused to be accompanied during her stroll and walked off across the large terrace on her own. Despite the tall torches that burned here and there, darkness reigned in the immense garden that, at the rear of the Hôtel de Chevreuse, stretched as far as the rue Saint-Nicaise, between the Hôtel de Rambouillet on the right and the more modest dwellings on the left. The silence was soothing in this elegant island of nature. And the air was sweet, the Parisian stink relieved by a welcome breeze.

As if weary, the duchesse sat down on a bench sheltered by the branches of a handsome elm tree, near a torch stuck in the ground. With a wave of her hand she drove off an imaginary insect, which allowed her to cast a glance over her shoulder. No one had followed her and no one seemed to be watching her from the terrace. Then she opened the volume of poetry that she had been given that afternoon by Bertaud and pretended to read.

Ten minutes later, as the bell of the Saint-Thomas church was striking the half-hour, madame de Chevreuse closed her book and took on the pensive look of someone thinking about what they had just read. While doing so, she counted to five in her head, beating the time with her index finger against the cover of the book.

After which, she pretended to resume reading.

It was the signal that all was well. Almost immediately, Laincourt emerged from the shadows. But he stayed well back, visible only to the duchesse.

'Good evening, madame.'

'Good evening, monsieur de Laincourt,' replied madame de Chevreuse, without raising her eyes from her book.

He could observe her at leisure and was once again surprised by her beauty. The duchesse de Chevreuse was reputed to be one of the most beautiful women in Europe and Laincourt did not doubt the truth of this, as he admired, in the warm, lively torchlight, the perfection of her profile, her milky complexion, the shine of her tawny hair, and the roundness of her throat.

Laincourt collected his wits, convinced that the duchesse was well aware of the effect she was having on him.

'I want to thank you for agreeing to this rendezvous, madame.'

'To be frank, I almost doubted that you would come. You must know the risks you are courting here.'

'Have you thought about laying a trap for me?'

She turned a page.

'I thought about it, yes. However, playing the role of an auxiliary of the cardinal's police would be more than I could bear. You guessed as much, didn't you?'

As Laincourt made no reply, the duchesse continued:

'This bookseller, monsieur Bertaud, what is he to you, exactly?'

'A friend.'

'His hand trembled quite a bit when he handed me this book. And his voiced wavered as well. I doubt that this escaped the notice of madame de Luret, who informs the cardinal when she is not reading books aloud to me. She is also quite friendly with a certain monsieur de Brussand, whose handsome air won her over.'

'Brussand? He is here?'

'Do you know him?' the duchesse asked in surprise. But then memory returned to her. 'Ah, but it's true. I forgot that you wore that cursed red cape once yourself . . . Well, monsieur de Brussand commands the guards that watch over my house and my person. Is he a friend, too?'

'He was,' Laincourt replied.

He couldn't help thinking of the look old Brussand had given him when he, Laincourt, had been accused of spying on and betraying the cardinal. He had worn the red cape of the Cardinal's Guards at the time, and the false accusations were intended to help unmask the real traitors. But Laincourt had never had the opportunity to establish the complete truth with his friend.

Once again, he found himself needing to collect his wits.

'What did you do with the note that I slipped into the book?' he asked.

'Don't worry, I burnt it as soon as I read it. Nonetheless, in future, choose your messengers more carefully.'

'Considering the urgency, I hardly had the liberty of choice. Tomorrow, you are leaving for—'

'—for Couzières, yes. Thank you so much for reminding me . . . Have you come to see me about madame de Saint-Avold?'

The question caught Laincourt unprepared.

'No,' he said.

'Aude has returned to Lorraine, did you know?' said the duchesse in a conversational tone. 'But I have a means of sending her letters. I would be happy to make sure she received one from you, if you like . . .'

Laincourt admired the ease with which madame de Chevreuse had just offered him an opportunity to compromise himself.

'No, madame. I thank you.'

'Are you no longer in love? No, monsieur. Do not protest, it's useless. Believe me, I know how to recognise love.'

'Madame, I am here on a matter of importance.'

The duchesse sighed and turned a page with a weary finger.

'Very well. I am listening.'

Laincourt explained that the Blades were investigating Charles Mauduit. The so-called Mauduit must have lied to her, at least by omission, as she had not known he was a dragon. Similarly, she was unaware he had perished during the attack on Le Châtelet.

She did, however, sense that something was amiss.

'What are you hiding from me, monsieur?'

'Pardon, madame?'

'You must be hiding something from me since, if this were only about Charles Mauduit, you would not be acting without the knowledge and perhaps even against the will of the cardinal . . .'

'By way of circumstances about which I can say nothing, madame, this affair also concerns the Sisters of Saint Georges. The cardinal is not in a position to offend them and so we feared that he would forbid us from pursuing this path.'

'So it concerns the Chatelaines. Why didn't you say so sooner?'

Evidently, the duchesse de Chevreuse shared the queen's notorious loathing for the Chatelaines. Laincourt had not known this and took careful note of it.

'Madame, you must tell me everything you know about your former master of magic.'

'What can I say? Of course I did not know he served the Black Claw . . .' The duchesse lifted her head and gazed off into the darkness. 'People had spoken highly of his knowledge. And he appeared to enjoy a certain measure of prestige among his peers. I thought he would be a suitable member of my household . . .' For the first time, she turned toward Laincourt. 'You know, I do not have much liking for magic. A little divination on occasion, but nothing more . . . It was the queen's despair, at finding herself unable to conceive, which finally convinced me that perhaps a ritual . . .'

'I wager that Mauduit suggested it to you.'

'Yes, probably.' Mme de Chevreuse pretended to resume reading. 'But he was skilful enough to make it seem I thought of it. And later, I served this monster's plans with all the willingness in the world, persuading the queen to have recourse to sorcery to enable her to become a mother.'

She spoke feelingly. Her friendship for the queen had been real and she sincerely reproached herself for what had happened.

Or what had almost happened . . .

And then Laincourt understood why the duchesse showed

no signs of any rancour against the Cardinal's Blades, or against himself. Because although their intervention had brought about her disgrace, they had saved the queen.

'Do you remember who recommended Mauduit to you?'

'Of course, but it will be of no help to you. Because she was burnt alive in the fire that destroyed her home.'

Knowing the Black Claw, this news hardly astonished Laincourt. Nevertheless, to put his mind at rest, he asked:

'Her name?'

'The vicomtesse de Malicorne.'

Laincourt fell silent, dumbfounded. Before joining the Blades, his last mission as the cardinal's spy had been to foil the vicomtesse de Malicorne's plans.

'Monsieur?' enquired madame de Chevreuse nervously.

But someone was coming.

With a simple backward step, Laincourt retreated calmly into the shadows. A lady companion of the duchesse arrived, bearing a shawl and saying the air was growing chilly. It was madame de Luret, whom the duchesse greeted rather harshly. The woman stammered an apology and quickly withdrew.

Laincourt reappeared.

'No doubt she heard us,' he said.

'Yes. This shawl was a poor pretext. You'd better go.'

Madame de Chevreuse stood up.

'One last question, madame. Were you close to the vicomtesse de Malicorne?'

'Yes. She was a friend. But she remained aloof from intrigues. If you had been acquainted with her, you would know what a charming person she was . . . Goodbye, monsieur.'

'Goodbye, madame.'

Laincourt let the duchesse leave in the direction of the terrace and the mansion, and waited long enough to spy movements in the garden. He saw a red cape passing in one place, and then a second one elsewhere.

The Cardinal's Guards were already searching for him.

Laincourt knew he was doomed if he remained where he was. So he started to make good his escape, with silent, supple steps, staying within the shadows. He wanted to flee, of course. But above all, he did not want to be seen or heard. Because if he managed to depart undetected, the duchesse could lie with relative ease. No, she had been alone. And she wasn't talking to anyone, but reading aloud. Isn't that what one does, with poetry? If he was spotted, however, others would be held accountable. Madame de Chevreuse, first of all. And perhaps Bertaud, too, who seemed to have aroused the suspicions of that cursed madame de Luret.

The Cardinal's Guards were carrying out an organised search of the garden. They tightened the noose around him, using lanterns to shed light, watching and listening for the slightest movement, the slightest sound, and they had no hesitation in hacking at the undergrowth with their swords. Fortunately, having been a member of the Guards, Laincourt knew them and knew what to expect. It was futile to hope that a simple diversion would attract all of them to the same spot: two or three would go and see, but the others would keep their positions.

He would have to be cleverer than that.

At the end of a garden path, Laincourt took time to observe and think. He estimated he had only two or three minutes before the trap closed around him. He needed to find a solution.

The pond, murmured the hurdy-gurdy player in his ear.

Of course!

Within the park, there was a large ornamental pond filled with colourful fish that the duchesse liked to admire and feed on occasion. As far as Laincourt could remember, this pond was fairly deep, deep enough that a man could hide within its dark waters. If he reached it first, he could dive in and evade the red capes coming towards him. After that, climbing the wall and jumping down into rue Saint-Nicaise would be child's play.

Laincourt hurried, hunched over, gripping his sword's scabbard in one hand and holding the brim of his hat with the other. At the corner of a well-kept flowerbed, for a moment he thought all was lost, as he held his breath and waited for a guard without a lantern to walk by. He had almost run straight into the man, but was now starting to believe that chance smiled upon him . . .

. . . until he arrived at the pond.

Which was empty.

No doubt because the duchesse was leaving, the pond had been drained for cleaning. The young man cursed. But more guards were approaching. He had to turn tail now and find another way out. They would be on him soon, very soon.

'Don't move!'

Given in a calm voice, the order had surprised Laincourt just as he was reversing course.

He froze.

'Turn round, monsieur.'

Having recognised the voice that spoke, Laincourt obeyed, but lowered his head so that, in the darkness, his face remained perfectly hidden by his hat. Because the guard who held him at bay, threatening him with a pistol, was Brussand. Brussand who had taken him under his wing when he had first joined the Cardinal's Guards. Brussand who had been so proud of Laincourt's promotion to the rank of ensign. Brussand who had felt that he had lost a son when Laincourt had been forced to give up his red cape under troubling circumstances.

'Come forward into the moonlight, monsieur. And take off your hat. I want to see who I'm arresting.'

Laincourt hesitated.

'Come forward, monsieur!'

But Laincourt could not allow himself to be taken captive, or unmasked. Either way, the Blades would be compromised and would have to explain what they were doing to the cardinal. It was bad enough for the cardinal's men to know madame de Chevreuse had met someone at night in her garden, against the express orders of the king.

But what could he do?

Kill a friend? Kill an innocent man?

'Step forward, or I'll shoot!'

Brussand. Out of all the guards present, it had to be old Brussand . . .

Laincourt sighed and took one step forward.

'Your hat, now, take—'

The guard was unable to finish his command: Saint-Lucq had come up from behind and knocked him out cold.

'Quickly,' said the half-blood. 'This way.'

It was unwise to venture out on Pont Neuf after sunset. Unpleasant encounters were frequent and there was every likelihood of being robbed, or even of winding up in the Seine more dead than alive. That night, however, a man on the Left Bank started over the bridge without a trace of fear. His name was Étienne-Louis de La Fargue, he seemed to be in a hurry, and he had the look of someone it would be foolish to trifle with. An intimidating Pappenheimer sword hung at his side.

The captain was heading for the famous Bronze Wyvern, which stood at the very tip of the Ile de la Cité, facing Place Dauphine. Going round the imposing marble pedestal, he entered the thick darkness beneath the spread wings of the statue, which depicted a wyvern saddled and harnessed for war, but riderless. There he found the person who had requested this last-minute rendezvous, leaning on the railing overlooking the black waters of the Seine.

'What is it?' asked La Fargue grumpily. 'I don't have much time.'

The other straightened up and turned round.

He was an elegant gentleman, dressed in a grey outfit beneath a black coat and wearing a felt hat with a plume. A handsome man, he seemed to be about thirty years in age but his hair was the colour of slate. His eyes were the same pale grey as his outfit, the irises ringed by a dark border.

He bore a grave expression.

'The Seven are concerned,' announced the chevalier de Valombre.

At least, that was how he had introduced himself at their first meeting. La Fargue knew nothing of him, other than the fact that he was a dragon and that he also served the Guardians.

Also known as the Seven.

'And why are they concerned?

'Dragons are gathering in Paris.'

'To what end?'

'We don't know.'

'What do you know of the dragon that attacked Le Châtelet?'

'We know that it was a primordial.'

'What's that?'

'An ancient, primitive dragon. An archaic representative of what the draconic race was at the dawn of time . . . They are dangerous and savage creatures with a bestial intelligence ruled entirely by the violence of their instincts.'

'So, it was a primordial that killed Almades.'

'You can be sure that the primordial at Le Châtelet has a master who commands it. Or even several masters.'

'Such as the dragons who are now gathering in Paris?'

'We believe so.'

La Fargue nodded, and then asked:

'What do you want from me?'

Laincourt and Saint-Lucq arrived together at the Hôtel de l'Épervier. Ballardieu was sitting on the steps to the kitchen, drinking a glass of wine.

'Where is the captain?' Laincourt asked him.

'Gone out.'

'Gone out? Since when?' Saint-Lucq wanted to know.

'Less than an hour,' replied Ballardieu.

'And gone where?'

'A mystery.'

'And the others?'

'Agnès is resting. Marciac is in the fencing room.'

Laincourt and Saint-Lucq joined the Gascon inside. He had been drinking and, dishevelled, his feet crossed on the table, he was still drinking now, joylessly, alone in the dim light. His appearance astonished Laincourt. Saint-Lucq, although he never commented on it, knew of the sudden bouts of melancholy to which Marciac was sometimes victim.

'Do you know where the captain went?' the half-blood asked.

The Gascon displayed a dull-witted surprise.

'He's not here?'

Saint-Lucq cursed and walked away. Laincourt remained behind, feeling the need for a drink himself.

'So, your rendezvous with madame de Chevreuse?' Marciac enquired.

'It almost went horribly wrong,' the young man confessed. 'The alarm was raised. I could have been caught.'

'But Saint-Lucq intervened, as if out of nowhere. And he saved your neck.'

'Yes.'

'He loves doing that.'

Marciac finally noticed how shaken Laincourt looked.

'Come on, pull yourself together . . . Here, have a drink.' He filled two glasses to the brim. 'What's bothering you?'

'There will be an investigation at the Hôtel de Chevreuse.'

'No doubt. But I don't suppose it will be the first time for the duchesse . . .'

'It's not her that I'm worried about.'

'Bertaud?' the Gascon guessed.

'Yes. If they discover his part in this affair . . .'

Marciac sighed. He reckoned that he had drunk enough, put down his glass, took his feet off the table, and leaned towards Laincourt, his elbows resting on his thighs.

'Listen, my friend. Believe me, I understand you. But you're seriously mistaken if you think you can arrange a sanctuary for yourself. We all bear the burden of the intrigues we get mixed up in, and there is no way to spare those who are near and dear to us from the consequences, either. Worse, sometimes we have a duty to make use of those we love to further our aims. That can be done without their knowledge. It can be done with their willingness or not. And yes, it can lead to them being harmed. But nothing, nothing must ever prevent us from doing it . . . If that idea is unbearable to you, distance yourself from those you love once and for all. Isolate yourself. Be like Saint-Lucq . . . Or follow Leprat and leave the Blades.'

'And you? You're not Saint-Lucq, nor Leprat, as far as I know . . .'

The Gascon's face grew cloudy.

'Me? I am Marciac. I distract myself with wine, gaming, and women to forget the harm I do to those I lack the courage to leave. Choose one or another of my vices. It doesn't matter which because you will end up with all three if you follow me down the path of weakness . . .'

Just as he was delivering those words, Saint-Lucq returned, looking worried.

'La Fargue is nowhere to be found. I spoke to André: all the horses are in the stable, so he left on foot. And Guibot swears he received no letter or visit . . . It's as if he left the house suddenly, for no reason at all . . .'

'The captain is not a choirboy,' remarked Marciac as he rose to stretch. 'And he's quite capable of defending himself in Paris, even at night. Why are you getting so worked up?'

The half-blood did not answer him.

He could not find an explanation for La Fargue's absence. The captain should have been there on Laincourt's return, waiting for the result of the secret interview with madame de Chevreuse. His absence could mean only one of two things: either La Fargue was guilty of neglecting his duties by absenting himself on some frivolous errand, or he had been obliged to go out because a serious matter had arisen. Saint-Lucq could not believe the first hypothesis was true. So there was good reason to be alarmed, which Marciac would have understood if he wasn't Marciac.

Laincourt, in contrast, was also starting to wonder what was going on.

'Perhaps Agnès knows,' he suggested.

'Knows what?' asked La Fargue as he came bustling in, Ballardieu at his heels.

His arrival provoked an awkward silence, which the

captain did not seem to notice. But he carefully avoided Saint-Lucq's gaze as he straddled a chair and immediately asked Laincourt for his report.

The young man complied and when his account was finished, the captain of the Blades concluded:

'So, it was thanks to the vicomtesse de Malicorne that the Alchemist became the magic master of the duchesse de Chevreuse . . .'

'Yes,' said Laincourt.

'And she was the one who wanted to create a Black Claw lodge in France, wasn't she? And whose flight was assisted by the chevalier de Gagnière, on that famous night when we defeated her?'

'Yes, captain.'

'Do we know what became of her?'

'No. But it is unlikely that she still lives, because the Black Claw is rarely merciful towards those who fail. And even if she is alive . . .'

Laincourt did not think it useful to end his sentence.

'So we find ourselves at a dead end,' La Fargue said, sounding discouraged.

'I'm not so sure,' replied Marciac. 'There's still Gagnière, whom Saint-Lucq took prisoner. He must know a lot, as the vicomtesse's right arm. Let's find out which gaol he's rotting in and interrogate him.'

The idea was a good one, but they were all aware of the obstacle before them.

'We can't do any of that without the cardinal's approval,' said La Fargue. 'We can go no further without his knowledge.'

Agnès awoke a little before dawn, with a throbbing shoulder and her mind still haunted by the vision that troubled her sleep. She sat up in bed, looked towards the open window and the night sky that was becoming pale in the east, behind the Saint-Germain-des-Prés abbey bell-tower. She sighed, before getting up and, her back turned three-quarters to the mirror, examining her shoulder again. She knew what she was going

152

to see. The elegant lines of her mark that had been pulsing with a red glow in time with her heartbeat were now growing fainter, and the pain was beginning to fade. Soon, the two entwined runes would regain their normal appearance.

Agnès straightened her shirt and went over to the window, leaning on the sill.

Looking off into the distance, her expression was grim.

She had dreamed again of the great black dragon blasting Paris, and it had such a sharp clarity that she had felt the heat of the blazes on her face, the odour of burning wood and hot ashes had invaded in her nostrils, and it seemed her ears were still ringing from the terrible noise: the roaring flames, the crash of collapsing buildings, the screams of the victims, the cavernous bellowing of the dragon. The image of that black dragon had etched itself on her mind. She only needed to close her eyelids in order to see it again, immense and powerful, triumphant in the sky of a tormented Paris, its body covered with shining obsidian scales and its brow decorated . . .

. . . with a sparkling jewel?

Agnès abruptly opened her eyes again.

She had been the vicomtesse de Malicorne and she had lacked for nothing: neither youth, nor beauty, nor wealth. And now she was madame de Chantegrelle, an old woman, a pious lady who had retired to a convent in the faubourg Saint-Jacques, resting from the last labours of an over-long life. Which was equal to saying she wasn't much of anything.

That morning, she had gone out to take a few steps in the convent's garden when she received word of a visitor. Shortly after, she met an elegant gentleman for the first time, with blond hair, regular features, and a disturbing charm. They sat side-by-side upon a stone bench and, as soon as they were alone, the stranger briefly unleashed his aura. Madame de Chantegrelle felt a delicious, electrifying thrill run through her. So he, like her, was a dragon. But a powerful and vigorous dragon, one who was not prisoner of an aging, puny body and a miserable existence.

'Who are you?' she asked.

'I am the Gentleman. I should say, rather, I am "The Gentleman Lover", since that is the full name of my arcanum. But let's content ourselves with the Gentleman. I belong to the same lodge as the Alchemist.'

'The lodge of the Arcana. So it really exists.'

'Did you doubt it?'

'Yes.'

'Soon we will have all the time we need to set you straight on that score, madame.'

'What do you want from me?'

'I have come to ask you to join us.'

'You're mocking me.'

'Not at all.'

Then the Gentleman spoke and the former vicomtesse de Malicorne listened, weighing each sentence, each word, lending an attentive ear to each intonation, each inflexion of his voice, and searching for the slightest sign of deceit or duplicity in her visitor's face. But the gentleman knew how to please and how to persuade. And she could not help being tempted by what he proposed: to reclaim what she had once been and join the Arcana lodge.

'Why choose me?' she finally asked.

'We have been observing you for a long time, madame. And, in contrast to the Black Claw, we prefer to consider what you have accomplished and what you might still succeed in accomplishing.'

'Then let us speak of the Black Claw, as you mention it. What will they say if they learn—'

'Whatever they like. The Arcana lodge is free to initiate whoever it chooses. Besides, we don't pay much heed to the old masters in Madrid . . .'

'But don't you see what I've become?'

'We have the remedy for that.'

She shot the Gentleman a look that was alight with hope and ambition.

'Truly?' she asked.

He answered her with a gentle smile full of confidence; and they spoke some more.

This time, however, madame de Chantegrelle listened little and thought much. She quickly came to the obvious decision. If she was lacking in physical and magical strength ever since the aborted ritual had nearly killed her, she had lost none of her mental acuity. She was in no position to make any demands of the Arcana, but she was resolved to set one condition.

'If I am in the state and the situation that you see before you,' she said, 'it is by the fault of a handful of men and a woman. So I should like to know: if I join you, will I have my revenge?'

And being a person who appreciated audacity, the Gentleman smiled.

'Madame, I can promise you that.'

Marciac and Laincourt accompanied La Fargue to the Palais-Cardinal. They arrived just as Richelieu was preparing to join the king at the Château de Saint-Germain and as, in the great courtyard, sixty guards in red capes, already mounted and arrayed in parade order, were waiting for the departure of His Eminence's coach. The cardinal had in fact already taken his place inside the vehicle and the Blades' captain had a difficult time gaining permission to speak with him at the coach door.

Remaining a short distance away, the other Blades also waited patiently, the Gascon holding La Fargue's horse by the bridle, while Laincourt inspected the aligned guards. He saw with satisfaction that Brussand was among them and that he seemed to be in good form, even if a bandage that no doubt constricted his skull could be glimpsed underneath his hat. From where they were standing, Marciac and Laincourt could not hear anything of what La Fargue, hat in hand, was saying to Cardinal Richelieu. But the old captain seemed to be arguing as firmly as possible. Of the cardinal, they could only see a thin, motionless hand resting upon the coach door.

'This is taking a long time,' said Marciac.

'La Fargue does not have a strong hand to play,' Laincourt pointed out.

Indeed, the conversation dragged on, forcing all those in the courtyard to endure the scorching sun. The Cardinal's Guards appeared stoical enough but their horses, standing in ranks, started to grow nervous. Impatient hooves struck the paving stones. Some mounts whinnied and shied. Otherwise, a strange silence reigned. Everyone wondered what was going on, what had delayed a departure they had believed to be imminent.

Finally, La Fargue came away from the coach with its magnificent coats-of-arms, and replaced his hat on his head. An officer gave an order. Trumpets sounded and a first squad of guards took the lead, followed by His Eminence's coach which ponderously set off, and then the rest of the escort. The procession left the courtyard and was soon travelling along rue Saint-Honoré, in the direction of the gate bearing the same name.

The great courtyard of the Palais-Cardinal suddenly appeared quite deserted.

With a stern face and a hurried step, La Fargue rejoined Marciac and Laincourt.

'We should make haste,' he said, climbing into the saddle.

Less than an hour later, Agnès was watching as La Fargue, Laincourt and Marciac carried out their final preparations in the courtyard of the Hôtel de l'Épervier: making sure their horses were properly saddled, tightening a strap here, adjusting a bit there, patting a neck and, finally, mounting their steeds. André was helping them, always observing their mounts with an expert and vaguely critical eye. On the small step that marked the threshold of her kitchen, Naïs also looked on with a worried air. Old Guibot stood beneath the archway, where he had just opened the carriage gates and was now holding one of the two massive rectangular doors.

Once all three men were ready to depart, they each saluted Agnès: La Fargue with a nod of the head, Laincourt with a sign of the hand, and Marciac with a wink. Then they left, filling the courtyard briefly with the clatter of hooves on paving stones. In rue Saint-Guillaume, they came across Ballardieu who gaped in surprise as he saw them pass by at a full trot and hastened to return to the Blades' mansion. Hobbling on his wooden leg, Guibot was already closing the gate.

Ballardieu joined Agnès in the main hall. Dressed in her usual fashion as a squire, her waist cinched by her thick corset of scarlet leather, the young baronne de Vaudreuil was pulling on fencing gloves.

'What's going on?' Ballardieu demanded to know. 'I just saw the captain and the others who—'

'Who were leaving, yes.'

'Where are they going in such a rush?'

'The cardinal was willing to allow La Fargue to meet Gagnière,' she explained. 'The problem is that Gagnière, under close guard, is en route to a secluded château near Auxerre where he will be handed over to a representative of the Pope.'

'Handed over?'

'Delivered, if you prefer. Exchanged, perhaps. Or sold. Don't ask me what Rome wants with Gagnière.'

Agnès whipped the air with her rapier, and, looking satisfied, practised a few lunges.

'Why aren't we part of the expedition?' asked Ballardieu in a sulky tone.

'Because La Fargue has no need of us. And also because I am retained by matters here in Paris . . .'

The old soldier suddenly noticed the sword that Agnès was wielding.

'Hey!' he exclaimed. 'That's your rapier!'

'None other!' enthused the young woman, saluting him as if they were about to engage in a duel.

And as if to provide final proof of her claim, she released the blade of the stiletto lodged in the grip of her weapon.

'How is that possible?'

'It was delivered this morning by one of the Chatelaines' Black Guards.'

'From Mère de Vaussambre?'

'Who else? Besides, along with my sword there was a letter written by her hand.'

'And what did it say, this letter?'

The blood in the vat was fuming. It gave off powerful, acrid, nauseating scents. Carved into the floor's stone slabs, complex pentacles gave off a red glow, as if traced by incandescent wires. Black candles burned at their points, although the melted wax ran scarlet. The air vibrated with a deep and powerful presence.

The vicomtesse de Malicorne stood naked before the vat.

Soon, the elderly madame de Chantegrelle would be no more than a detestable memory, and so would this weak, shrivelled body with its flabby flesh and spindly limbs. Even the vicomtesse de Malicorne would be forgotten. Because while she would emerge from this rebirth just as young and beautiful as before, she would also be stronger, animated by a determination that nothing and no one could shake. For now, however, she was still an old woman who waited trembling amid the intoxicating vapours, her back tense, almost arched, her chin lifted, and her eyes closed.

The Enchantress also had her eyes closed.

Kneeling on the other side of the basin built into the floor, she chanted in a low voice, absorbed in her work. Warm blood ran from her slit wrists, as if endowed with a life of its own, slipping across the stone slabs to join the darker pool that already filled the vat. A spectral form emanated from the Enchantress, which could only be detected in the shadow on the wall behind her: that of a dragon whose power, still constrained, seemed to resonate from the bowels of the earth.

The vicomtesse knew that the crucial moment had arrived.

She took one step forward, plunged a foot into the blood, and struggled to contain a moan of pleasure at the burning sensation which, like a tongue of inner fire, filled her entire being.

4

Advancing at a trot in the middle of the countryside, still several leagues from the Château de Mareuil-sur-Ay, the small column of musketeers escorting their prisoner came across a coach sitting still at the side of the road. Leprat, riding at the front, saw it first. He immediately raised a hand, ordering his fifteen musketeers and the sealed wagon they escorted to come to a halt behind him. The dust settled slowly in their wake, without a breath of wind to disperse it.

Squinting beneath the brim of his hat, Leprat studied their surroundings, pressing both hands against the pommel of his saddle, his shoulders hunched slightly forward. The journey had proceeded, until now, without incident despite his fears. After three days, he had even begun to imagine that the Black Claw had renounced any intention to do the marquis de Gagnière an evil turn, or that it remained ignorant of the fact that he was being transferred, or how, or where. But that was no reason to abandon all precautions.

A musketeer joined Leprat and drew up his mount alongside him. It was Durieux, a gentleman of thirty years with a sharp eye and an austere face who spoke little and displayed a disconcertingly deadpan sense of humour. He always had good advice. Leprat had made him his second-in-command.

'Your opinion, Durieux?' he asked.

The musketeer took time to observe the scene in his turn.

'The terrain is hardly favourable for an ambush,' he replied. 'But the ruse may lie therein.'

They were not far from the town of Épernay. The road was crossing a charming corner of the Champagne countryside, green and peaceful. The weather was superb. In the distance they could see a sheepfold, but other than the coach there was no sign of a living soul.

'I'll go and see,' announced Leprat.

'Is that very wise?'

'Keep your eyes open and take command if necessary.'

'Never fear. If you should meet some misadventure, I'll make sure that someone other than Sardent writes your funeral eulogy.'

Leprat spurred his horse forward, smiling broadly at Durieux's jest, and crossed the distance to the coach at a full trot. He identified one individual as the coachman and, inside the vehicle, he could make out a shadow with whom a gentleman, leaning on the passenger door, one boot on the footboard and hat in his hand, was making conversation. The musketeer slowed and approached at a walk. Seeing him, the gentleman covered his head and advanced with a friendly smile. He was young, richly dressed, and attractive, moving with a supple grace.

'Hello there!' he hailed, raising his arm.

Leprat halted his horse, but kept one hand close to the pistols tucked into his saddle holsters. He did it with a perfectly natural air, as the gentleman gave no signs of hostility or wariness, but there were cases of murderers with even more innocent-looking faces. The true danger, moreover, could lie within the coach.

'I am Leprat, King's Musketeer. Is there a problem, monsieur?'

'A broken wheel, monsieur,' replied the other man with a strong Italian accent.

He stepped aside to point to the coach, whose left rear wheel was indeed broken. It was a very common accident, given the poor state of French roads.

'I've sent my man ahead on my horse to the next relay station,' the Italian continued to say, 'but we've been waiting two hours for him and the wretch has still not returned.'

'I fear that I cannot be of great assistance to you.'

'We are accompanying a lady of quality, monsieur. And I see that a harnessed vehicle follows you. If you could offer this lady a seat as far as the next village, one of us will remain here with the coach, while the two others could follow you.'

'This wagon, whose escort I command, is in no way suitable for a person of quality. Moreover, the only available place is next to the coachman. Even were there no question of decorum, the discomfort would be great. The sun, the dust, the jolts— '

'—are all inconveniences that I shall put up with, monsieur Leprat,' said a clear, feminine voice. 'You must remember that I am not one to be deterred by mere trifles. And furthermore, I have the feeling that we are going to the same place . . .'

Leprat then watched as a ravishing young red-headed woman descended from the coach.

A spy, a courtesan, and a schemer. Her name was Alessandra di Santi.

Otherwise known as La Donna.

Bois-Noir

The Gentleman, sitting in an armchair, was talking to the red dragon whose massive, scaly head, adorned with a set of three bony ridges, could be seen in the mirror, glimmering slightly in the dimness.

'Everything will be ready,' he promised in a grave, concerned tone.

'Good,' the Heresiarch replied with a tone of authority. 'And since that settles the final details for the next Assembly, I would like to touch on another subject with you.'

The Gentleman was immediately on edge, but he tried not to show it. Was this about La Malicorne? It would soon be two whole days and nights that the Enchantress had spent performing the ritual intended to restore the former vicomtesse's power and magnificence. She was working here, secretly, in the crypt below the Hôtel des Arcanes. Could the Heresiarch already have learned of this?

'La Donna is in France,' the red dragon announced.

The news caught the Gentleman unprepared. He needed a few seconds to gather his wits and understand what the Heresiarch was talking about.

'La Donna? But didn't the Black Claw promise to rid us of her?'

'That's what they promised, indeed. And they failed . . . So I have decided we will resolve this problem ourselves. The bitch deceived the Alchemist. She stole secrets from him that allowed Cardinal Richelieu to foil our plans. It's high time she paid the price for it!'

The Gentleman did not reply. He waited and the Heresiarch continued:

'Right now, La Donna can be found at a château in Champagne where she is taking part in the transfer of a prisoner that France holds and that Rome wants. The prisoner himself is of little consequence . . . But an opportunity like this will not present itself again any time soon. The Illuminator is already in place, and has recruited a band of drac warriors. The small number of musketeers guarding the château will not be enough to oppose them. The whole matter will be settled tonight.'

'What do you expect of me?'

'Very little. I want you to prepare the Tour de Bois-Noir for the Illuminator's return, with his dracs. They will hold La Donna in the tower for as long as necessary.'

'Just hold her?' asked the Gentleman in surprise. 'Why?'

The Heresiarch did not reply.

He waited, silent and inscrutable, until the other dragon bowed to his will.

'It shall be done, Heresiarch.'

'I am counting on it. Goodbye, Gentleman.'

'Goodbye.'

The cell door opened and Leprat, ducking his head, stepped inside. His hand on the pommel of his white rapier, he straightened up without removing his hat and allowed the musketeer posted in the corridor outside to shut the door. Low-ceilinged and damp, but clean, the gaol cell was furnished with a narrow bed, a small table, and a stool, all standing on a bare dirt floor. A bucket sat in the corner, there for the prisoner's bodily needs. The only light came from a small semi-circular opening in the wall.

'I understand you wish to speak to me,' declared Leprat.

The man he had escorted from the Bastille was sitting on the bed reading, his back against the cell wall. The leather and iron mask was still locked around his face. The prisoner closed his book and stood up politely for his visitor. There was elegance in both his gesture and in his general bearing. The marquis de Gagnière was a man of refinement and courtesy, but he was also a cold monster.

'Indeed, monsieur. I wanted to thank you for allowing me reading material.'

Leprat accepted the thanks with a curt nod of the head.

'Anything else?' he enquired.

Arms crossed, the prisoner observed the musketeer from head to foot and seemed to think.

Then he said:

'You know who I am, don't you?'

'Yes.'

'In fact, you recognised me from the moment I was entrusted to your keeping, in the courtyard of the Bastille. By my eyes, probably. And perhaps from my posture. Unless it was my voice . . .'

Leprat did not reply and watched Gagnière take a step to lean against the table.

'Do you remember your last words to me, that night in rue Saint-Denis?' asked the prisoner. 'You had just eliminated my henchmen. You were exhausted, wounded, defeated, while I aimed my pistol at you from horseback . . .'

'I told you a man of honour would dismount and draw his sword.'

'And what did I do? I shot you in the heart and left you for dead.'

Leprat nodded silently.

He had seen himself die in the service of the king, that terrible night in rue Saint-Denis.

'So you know what kind of man I am,' Gagnière continued. 'And, knowing it, you have given me no reason to complain of you during the course of our journey, while I was in your power. Another man, no doubt, would not have mistreated me – not strictly speaking. But I doubt that he would have spared me all sorts of humiliations. With you, there has been none of that.'

'I was not entrusted with the care of a man who tried to murder me in cold blood. Nor was I entrusted with the marquis de Gagnière. I was entrusted with a prisoner, and with the mission of protecting him and conducting him to a specific place. You might just as well be any other man.'

'And if we are attacked, you will defend me even at risk to your own life?'

'Yes.'

'Without regret?'

'I did not say that.'

'Do you know that the Black Claw has already tried to assassinate me, twice?'

'I know it.'

'And despite everything, you will persist in—'

'Yes.'

The prisoner took the time to appreciate this response, which he knew to be frank and firm.

Finally, he said:

'You are decidedly a most admirable man, monsieur le chevalier d'Orgueil.'

Leprat rejoined Durieux a little later, as the daylight was fading. The musketeers had arrived at Château de Mareuil-sur-Ay less than two hours earlier, where the final negotiations concerning Gagnière were to take place. They finished installing themselves and securing the stronghold, whose defence they were responsible for during the talks. Men in royal blue capes were already posted at the gate and on the ramparts.

In the courtyard, Durieux was explaining to the three stalwart fellows who usually stood guard over the château that, for the time being, they could put away their halberds, breastplates, and the single arquebus they shared. Leprat waited for him to finish, noting the skilful and courteous way he dealt with them. He could have invoked the authority his rank and his cape conferred on him, but he preferred diplomacy instead.

The halberdiers withdrew, looking satisfied.

'What did the prisoner want?' asked Durieux.

'To warn me of a danger, I think,' replied Leprat.

'Here?' Together they looked around the setting they found themselves in. 'We were much more vulnerable on the road.'

'I'm well aware of that. And yet . . .'

'Yes, I sense it, too. There's something in the air, isn't there?'

Worried, both men fell silent.

The Château de Mareuil had been built during the Middle Ages. It comprised three massive towers joined by high walls, surrounding a triangular courtyard with a keep at its heart. It was a property that had reverted to the Crown in the absence of legal heirs. A widow had previously made it her refuge, building a Renaissance-style pavilion next to one of the ramparts, which was now pierced with windows. On her death, the château had not been completely abandoned. As it was to the east of Épernay, in a wooded corner of the country-side filled with game, it had become a very convenient hunting lodge for its present owner; an old gentleman who enjoyed the king's favour. It also had the advantage of being secluded, and a full day's horseback journey from the border with Lorraine . . .

'We've finished setting up our quarters in the old keep,' Durieux announced after a moment. 'We had to do some tidying up, but we should be comfortable there. The horses are in the stable and the first watches have been posted.'

'Very good. The domestic servants?'

'People from the village. Most of them go home at night and return in the morning. They will provide a more than ad-equate service for us musketeers, but we also have to think of our guest who, as a lady of quality—' Durieux broke off when he saw Leprat's half-smile. 'What did I say that was funny?'

'Nothing.'

Leprat turned towards the Renaissance building, where Alessandra di Santi and the gentleman who accompanied her had elected to lodge, making themselves at home in the apartments belonging to the master of the château and his wife. The gentleman occupied the first, where weapons, trophies, and hunting scenes abounded. La Donna resided in the second, which was pleasantly furnished and decorated.

'Have no fear,' Leprat added with another quirk of his lips. 'I assure you that this lady can manage far more rigorous conditions than the ones she finds here.'

169

From a window, La Donna was inspecting the young village girls who had come to offer their services at the château. She pointed at two with her index finger and bid them come upstairs. The disappointed candidates turned away. Leprat knew who he was dealing with and had no doubt that Alessandra had selected the two prettiest and liveliest girls for her personal service. Seeing that he was looking in her direction she responded with a smile and a small wave of the hand. He replied more soberly with a pinch of his hat brim.

Durieux asked no questions.

Even so, Leprat deemed that he owed his fellow musketeer some explanations.

'I do not know who the gentleman escorting her is, but this Italian woman the Pope has sent us is an adventuress and a top-notch spy. I made her acquaintance under Captain La Fargue's command. She claimed to have knowledge of a plot and obtained the cardinal's protection in exchange for the details. As always, her motives were murky. Nevertheless, I must admit that the information she supplied turned out to be useful in a very grave affair – one I can tell you nothing about.'

Darkness was falling in the courtyard where lackeys, servants and musketeers came and went, all more or less busy.

'Is she dangerous?' asked Durieux.

'Very. Above all else, don't let yourself be taken in by that adorable face or her air of innocence. And be on your guard: she is one of those women who can't help trying to seduce men, who lives for the desire she arouses.'

From Leprat's cold manner, Durieux realised that he was speaking from experience. Then his attention was drawn by some of the village girls who had been rejected by La Donna, now standing near the château's gates and enduring – without too much resistance – the advances of two musketeers.

'Should we permit this?' he asked, indicating the joyful little group with his chin.

Leprat weighed up the pros and cons of intervening, but was not given the opportunity to reply. From the top of the château's towers, a musketeer shouted that riders were approaching at a full trot.

La Fargue, Laincourt, and Marciac arrived at Mareuil-sur-Ay in the evening. Covered in grime, they had ridden at a fast pace for two long days, over dusty roads in the blazing summer heat. They were exhausted, and had no idea if they were in time or already too late to speak with Gagnière. They were relieved when they saw the château's towers and its old walls, on top of which they spied blue capes with silver crosses.

'The King's Musketeers?' Marciac observed with surprise. 'I was expecting red capes.'

'The marquis de Gagnière is a prisoner of the king,' La Fargue noted.

A musketeer stopped them at the gate beneath the archway, beyond a drawbridge that crossed a brush-filled ditch and was rarely raised. La Fargue handed over their papers signed by the cardinal, without dismounting, and waited for the musketeer to examine them. Behind him, Marciac doffed his hat to wipe his brow.

'It's a relief to be here,' he whispered to Laincourt, who replied with an understanding smile.

'Captain?'

All eyes turned to the man who had just spoken: Leprat, who had come from the courtyard with Durieux. The musketeer on duty passed La Fargue's papers over to him, but Leprat merely glanced at them and asked:

'But what are you doing here?' And then, changing his mind: 'No, tell me later. You're a pitiful sight, all three of you, and by the look of things you've earned a rest.'

The riders were authorised to enter the château and could finally dismount in the courtyard. Leprat gave orders that their horses should be tended to and charged Durieux with finding them a place to spend the night. The old captain thanked him and, while removing his riding gloves, he caught a glimpse of a lady and gentleman at one of the windows. He did not know the gentleman, but the woman could only be Alessandra di Santi.

'Life is full of surprises, isn't it?' said Leprat watching him out of the corner of his eye. 'I'll explain everything later . . .'

The Blades spent a long while at the water trough refreshing themselves, before La Fargue and Laincourt followed Durieux into a dusty, vacant chamber within the keep where they would have to make do with straw mattresses for the night. Marciac had remained near the well, chatting with one of the pretty village girls that La Donna had engaged in her service.

Having taken the time to change his clothes, Laincourt found La Fargue and Leprat a little later in an agreeably cool room, seated at a table with a few jugs of wine. The Gascon had still not reappeared, which neither astonished nor worried anyone.

'I have informed Leprat of the essence of our affair,' the old captain announced as Laincourt entered.

While the young man took a seat and poured himself a glass of wine, the musketeer summed matters up:

'So, there's a mystery you wish to shed some light on, which has some connection to the death of the Alchemist. By investigating him, or rather the master of magic he claimed to be, you discovered that the vicomtesse de Malicorne recommended him to the duchesse de Chevreuse. La Malicorne disappeared after we foiled her plan to create a Black Claw lodge in France. So that only leaves her deputy, Gagnière . . .'

Over the rim of his glass, Laincourt shot an intrigued glance at La Fargue, who paid no attention to it. Leprat had made no allusion to the threat of a dragon destroying Paris. Was that because the Blades' captain had not told him anything about it?'

'That's right,' confirmed La Fargue. 'The cardinal has authorised us to speak with Gagnière, as long as doing so does not prevent or delay the negotiations over his fate. So we rode here post haste, in fear that these final discussions would be concluded before our arrival.'

'Those negotiations have not even commenced. Père Joseph will lead them for France and we do not expect him until tomorrow evening.'

'But La Donna is already here.'

'To be sure. But she is not here to negotiate on the Pope's behalf.'

'So what is her role?'

'To interrogate Gagnière in order to measure how much he really knows. After that, the Pope's negotiator, who will also be arriving tomorrow, will have a better idea of where he stands.'

La Fargue emptied his glass, leaned back pensively, and then gave a bleak smile.

'When one thinks,' he said, 'that less than a month ago it was La Donna answering monsieur Laffemas' questions in Le Châtelet. And now here she is, posing questions to a Black Claw agent . . .'

Leprat shrugged and said:

'My responsibilities here are limited to the prisoner's security. If you wish to speak with him, you will need to go through La Donna. At least until His Holiness' negotiator arrives.'

'I would prefer not to wait until tomorrow.'

The musketeer did not know what to reply.

'Perhaps that won't be necessary,' said Laincourt.

The two others turned toward him.

'How's that?' asked La Fargue.

'The gentleman with La Donna. I know him.'

'Signor Valerio Licini?' Leprat asked in surprise.

'That is indeed his name. A scion of one of the finest aristocratic families of Rome. But he is better known as Père Farrio.'

'A priest?' asked La Fargue.

'A Jesuit. He and I have crossed paths in the past. He is an agent of the Pope and I am prepared to wager that he also is the negotiator we are waiting for.'

'Might he also have recognised you?' the Blades' captain enquired.

'I don't know.'

'But why play this farce?' the musketeer wanted to know.

'It can be useful for a negotiator to test the waters first, to smell the air, perhaps hear things we might not have said in front of him if we knew his true identity . . . But I'm only guessing. It is not impossible to suppose that the motives of Père Farrio and La Donna are even more devious than that . . .'

Upon those words, Marciac entered the room.

Perhaps slightly more dishevelled than usual, he was in an excellent mood and had a wisp of straw in his tangled hair.

'I just ran into Durieux,' he announced. 'La Donna has invited us to sup with her this evening.'

Armed with heavy rapiers, daggers, and pistols, the dracs stood ready in the clearing, beneath the starry sky. Assassins, brigands, and mercenaries, they obeyed the orders of one of their own, who went by the name of Keress Karn. Most of them weren't much taller than him, but all of them were more heavily built than this red drac with sinewy muscles and the reflexes of a snake. Aka'rn, a colossal but silent black drac, acted as Karn's personal bodyguard.

Intelligent and devoid of any scruples, quick to be cruel, Keress Karn exercised exclusive authority over his band. He never explained his orders and they were never questioned. His cutthroats displayed a mixture of admiration and superstitious dread towards him. Indeed, who but Karn could have persuaded them to place themselves in a dragon's service? For a drac, it was like voluntarily returning to enslavement and asking for the lash. But not a single one had challenged his decision, nor had any of them balked, later, at riding behind this dragon whose aura was so powerful that they felt, to their great shame, a servile chord vibrate in the depths of their beings. The dragon even insisted on being called 'master'. He did not mingle with them and spoke only to Karn, who was not in the least intimidated by the dragon's brutal and contemptuous manner. The red drac then relayed his instructions to the rest of the band.

The last directive they received had been to dismount here, in this clearing.

And to make ready for combat.

So they had hitched their horses, furbished their weapons and checked their equipment as they listened to Karn explain that they would be attacking a nearby château and abducting a woman they would find there. Following those instructions, they had shared a frugal meal, eaten cold, without making a fire. Then some had addressed hurried prayers to the gods or to their ancestors, whose spirits would accompany them into battle. It was not a question of asking for protection, only of inviting an illustrious forebear to witness – perhaps – their death in combat so that glory would accrue to their lineage.

The Illuminator had, of course, observed these rituals with disdain, sitting apart from the dracs and snorting pointedly at them, when he wasn't snickering into his beard. Then he stood up, stepped forward and waited until all eyes were focused on him. In the middle of the clearing he planted the broad blade of his *schiavone* in the ground beside him and undressed completely.

He kneeled.

Was he now going to pray?

The dracs stirred, intrigued, but Kress Karn restored order and silence with a single word. He had already guessed what the dragon was about to do, having just before seen him discreetly drain a small bottle of golden henbane liqueur.

Looking rapt, eyes closed, the Illuminator began breathing more and more noisily. Then it was as if he was struck by a sharp pain. Without opening his eyes, he arched his back and suddenly grimaced. The pain seemed to go on and forced a moan between the Illuminator's clenched jaws. Soon, he was unable to contain the brusque movements of his shoulders and arms. He stood up, his brow covered in sweat, looking clumsy and shaky as his naked body changed and became covered in scarlet scales. He grew several inches in height and stifled a scream. He gained twenty pounds of muscle at the price of terrible pain. Bony growths sprouted from his suddenly knobbly spine and razor-sharp claws emerged at the tips of his rigid fingers. His face stretched forward into a snout and a pair of bestial jaws, while his eyes, turned yellow, were now divided by vertical slits.

Finally, the Illuminator – or the creature he had become – settled into his new state.

It was not a complete metamorphosis. The dragon had not

recovered its primal form, only one of the intermediate variants. But the creature that turned towards the dracs subjugated them with its air of strength, brutality, and savagery. It stared at them for a long while, as its powerful shoulders rose and fell in time with its deep, hoarse breaths and threads of thick slaver dripped from its fangs.

The dragon seized the *schiavone* planted in the ground and brandished it.

'Let's go,' it said in a cavernous voice.

Night had already fallen when, at the appointed hour, La Fargue and Laincourt crossed the Château de Mareuil courtyard heading for the signora di Santi's quarters.

'I'm still not sure this is a good idea,' said the old captain. 'After all, it was not so long ago that La Donna duped us and left us to be killed, as I hope I do not need to remind you.'

'No, captain. But we want to speak to Gagnière, which we can only do with the agreement of the Pope's representative. And we will certainly not obtain that if the signora advises against it.'

'Not to mention the fact that she probably knows more about the Alchemist than Gagnière does himself,' added La Fargue grudgingly.

'Quite true. This invitation to dine with her is an open hand La Donna is extending to you.'

'A hand, yes. Or another trap . . .'

They found Marciac and Laincourt waiting on the front steps and entered with them.

In the 'hall' of the Renaissance-style pavilion, everything was almost ready. Numerous candles were burning in holders on the walls, between the paintings and the stuffed hunting trophies, and La Donna's two village girls had just finished setting all the dishes on the table, as custom dictated, before the meal was served. Considering the place and the circumstances, La Donna had managed to prepare quite a feast: meats, pâtés, hams, cheese, fruits, creams and jams lay spread in abundance.

Embellished by several bottles of wine, this vision delighted Marciac but only aggravated La Fargue's suspicions.

'Who are they trying to dazzle here?' he grumbled.

Meanwhile Laincourt wondered what horn of plenty had supplied all this food. He told himself La Donna must have brought these victuals in her carriage and sacrificed most of her stocks to make a strong impression on her guests.

But to what end?

Alessandra di Santi soon arrived, entering on the arm of the gentleman Laincourt had identified as a Jesuit agent of Rome. Dressed and coiffed according to the latest fashion, La Donna was superb. She wore a blue satin dress that highlighted her red hair and pale complexion, and was smiling and radiant, as if enchanted to be receiving long-lost friends. Signor Licini was no less elegant, nor less courteous.

Leprat took charge of the introductions. La Donna greeted each of the Blades with a charming word and extended her hand, last of all, to La Fargue. Then, after glancing at her escort who was exchanging amiable remarks with Marciac, she whispered to the captain:

'It is Providence that sends you. We need to speak together alone, later.'

It was said in a single breath, after which Alessandra regained her smile and invited her guests to take their places around the table.

A gracious and playful hostess, she wanted La Fargue to sit on her right and Valerio Licini on her left. Then she proposed a toast, 'In honour of the captain, whose merits are never appreciated enough.' A glass of wine was filled, in which a piece of toasted bread was placed to soak. The glass was passed from hand to hand so that each guest could take a sip and, according to custom, when it was La Fargue's turn, as the one being toasted he was supposed to finish the wine and swallow the bread, cheered on by the others.

As the glass went round the table, Laincourt watched Licini.

He wondered if the Jesuit priest had recognised him as well, and had realised that his identity was no longer a secret. On meeting the cardinal's former spy's gaze, the Pope's agent removed any ambiguity by giving him a complicit nod of the head.

Laincourt concluded that they knew where they stood with one another, but was not given the chance to pursue his train of thought.

'To arms!'

The château's gate was blown away by the deafening explosion of an enormous powder charge. Spat out through the archway, a cloud of dust and debris invaded the courtyard. Fused grenades had followed and gone off, adding to the confusion.

'To arms! To arms!'

Rapiers in their fists, La Fargue and the others burst from the building where La Donna and Licini were quartered, just as the first musketeers reached the courtyard. The poor devils who had been caught in the initial explosion were staggering around in a daze, some of them wounded. But no one had time to go to their aid: sinister silhouettes were swiftly making their way through the smoke, bent on attack.

'Draaaaacs!'

While combat was engaged with Karn's band of mercenaries, La Fargue held back from the fray, trying to take stock of the situation. He looked around, wondering why the sentries had not raised an alarm prior to the explosion. His eyes lifted at the precise instant when the Illuminator leapt down from the ramparts and he tracked the path of the dragon's fall. The creature landed heavily but without harm in the middle of the courtyard before straightening with a roar. It brandished the massive *schiavone*, a detail that struck the captain.

'Leprat!' he yelled over the noise of the battle. 'Look to your prisoner! We'll take care of this monster!'

Leprat had already spotted a red drac who appeared to be directing the assault. But he nodded to the captain, renouncing his target. As La Fargue, Laincourt and Marciac deployed themselves around the scaly colossus, he ordered:

'Durieux, with me! Musketeers, stand firm!'

And he left at a run, with Durieux at his heels.

He was leaving his brothers-in-arms to fight against two-to-one odds and the Blades facing a monstrous adversary that looked capable of breaking a man's spine over its knee. But he had no choice. His first duty was to protect Gagnière, and the dracs were here to either set him free or to kill him. The Black Claw must have instigated this attack. But why would they choose to take the château by force when it would have been easier to attack the musketeers between Paris and Mareuil? Had they lacked the time to set up an ambush along the road?

Gagnière was locked up in the basement of one of the corner towers. Leprat and Durieux had to go round the big central keep to reach it, ignoring the cries and the smoke from the courtyard. They ran into a drac who was pulling his blade out of the body of an unarmed stable boy. Without halting, Leprat laid the murderer out with a blow from the guard of his ivory rapier, leaving Durieux to finish him off with his sword as he passed. The tower door was ajar. Leprat's mighty kick slammed it wide open against the wall, surprising a drac inside who turned, pistol in hand. The gun went off and Leprat felt the ball brush by him as he charged forward and hit the drac in the shoulder, almost lifting the reptilian from the ground. The musketeer brutally shoved him into the wall and stepped back. The drac had no time to recover: Durieux fired a pistol ball into the middle of his brow. The two musketeers exchanged a glance. They made a good team.

The room suddenly shook from another explosion.

A powder charge had detonated in the ditch at the foot of the tower, a good third of which collapsed outwards in a cascade of stones, wood, and ancient dust. The rest of the shattered structure groaned, creaked, and tottered danger-ously before falling in on itself. Leprat and Durieux barely had time to fling themselves back outside before the cellar was engulfed in rubble and a thick cloud of debris.

In the courtyard, the battle continued.

Three musketeers were lying in a pool of blood amongst a dozen drac bodies. Most of their comrades were wounded and only a few blue-caped figures were still fighting, but they did not concede an inch of ground. A short distance from the general mêlée, La Fargue, Laincourt, and Marciac stood against the Illuminator. They harried the dragon, attacking it from the right and left, forcing it to turn back and forth in response, always retreating before its blows to allow another to take it from behind. They had quickly realised that they could not accomplish much against this powerful and cunning creature whose scales deflected most of their sword strokes. It was a lesson they learned at great expense to themselves. The *schiavone* had sliced into Marciac's arm, while Laincourt had recklessly exposed himself to the monster's claws, which had ripped through his doublet and shirt, leaving a row of bloody stripes across his chest. As for La Fargue, with his vision restricted by his eye patch, he'd been too slow to see a reverse blow by the dragon's fist that had struck him in the temple and left him senseless for a moment. It was only a matter of time before one or another of the trio committed an even graver mistake.

A fatal one.

Covered in dust and still staggering from the aftereffects of the explosion, Leprat and Durieux were rejoining the fight when the blast of a horn resounded in the night, at some distance from the château. Immediately, the dracs broke off combat and retired in good order. The scaly monster seemed to hesitate, considering its exhausted opponents. Then with three mighty bounds it was at the top of the ramparts and, after a last backward glance, it disappeared off into the night.

Within the devastated château, those who were still standing struggled to understand what had just transpired. Then the reality of their situation set in and they rushed to the aid of their fallen comrades. Leaving Durieux to see to the most urgent cases, Leprat went to confer with the Blades:

'God's blood!' he exclaimed. 'For a moment I thought . . . Are you wounded?'

'Nothing serious,' asserted La Fargue.

The two others nodded or confirmed the same with reassuring expressions as they re-sheathed their weapons.

'Gagnière?' Marciac enquired.

'Dead . . . . But what just happened here?'

Leprat turned to give an incredulous glance around the

courtyard that had been transformed into a battlefield and at the ruins of the collapsed tower.

'The Black Claw,' La Fargue said. 'Obviously, they were prepared to do anything to prevent Gagnière from being handed over to the Pope.'

Leprat nodded, thinking that although the Black Claw had been forced to employ a sizeable force to achieve its aim, their third attempt on Gagnière's life had succeeded.

'I don't know, captain,' Laincourt objected. 'The dracs managed to place the mine that brought down the tower without being seen. Why would they attack us, rather than simply set it off and kill Gagnière? Why this assault? Why all these risks and useless deaths?'

La Fargue stared at Laincourt for a long moment in silence.

Then he cursed and ran for the pavilion where La Donna had been lodging.

'What now?' wondered Marciac, following Laincourt and Leprat as they raced after the captain.

'It was a diversion!' shouted the musketeer. 'A bloody diversion!'

The Renaissance-style pavilion was filled with an ominous silence.

They found Valerio Licini's lackey lying on his stomach in a puddle of his own blood at the bottom of the great stairway.

'Dead,' said Leprat, turning him over.

The poor wretch's throat was slit.

Sword in hand and bleeding along one side, Licini himself lay across the last flight of steps before the first floor.

'He's still alive,' Laincourt pronounced after leaning down to inspect him.

They called out, conducted a rapid search of the premises, and discovered the two village girls hiding in a cubby-hole. But La Donna had vanished.

The outer wall had been pierced with windows on this side of the Château de Mareuil. One of them stood wide open to the night, next to an overturned table, torn curtains, and a single woman's shoe.

'MERDE!' swore La Fargue, driving his fist into the wall.

2

It took a day for Cardinal Richelieu to learn of the attack on Château de Mareuil and the terrible price its defenders had paid. It took two for La Fargue, Laincourt, and Marciac to return to Paris and, on the third day, the captain of the Blades was summoned to the Palais-Cardinal. That morning, it was Rochefort who bade him enter the antechamber where Richelieu waited for him, dressed as a cavalier. The cardinal had taken advantage of a hunting expedition organised at Saint-Germain by the king to come back to the capital in secret, riding full out. At forty-eight years of age and despite his precarious health, Armand-Jean du Plessis, cardinal de Richelieu, was still an accomplished horseman. His boots were dusty and he held a slender cravache in his gloved hands.

La Fargue presented himself, hat in hand, saluting the cardinal with a bow and then waiting in silence. The cardinal was standing, facing the window.

'In a few weeks,' he said, 'the king will enter Lorraine at the head of his armies. There will be some last-minute negotiations but nothing will hinder His Majesty's inexorable march towards Nancy. The capital of Lorraine will undergo a siege and, very soon, the duc Charles IV will have no choice but to capitulate . . . This intervention has legitimate motives, not least of which is to force the duc de Lorraine to respect both the spirit and the letter of the treaties he signs with the king of France and then seems to . . . forget about later on. The European powers will condemn us for this invasion but do nothing to impede it. To be sure, some will accuse France of wishing to annex Lorraine in order to gain a door onto the Holy Roman Empire in Germany, and they are not entirely mistaken . . .' The cardinal turned away from the window to catch La Fargue's eye. 'As you can see, the future is already written. And if God wills, only a few cannon will need to be fired in the execution of this necessary operation.'

A flagon of wine with a glass, a plate of biscuits and a plate of grapes stood on a tray. Richelieu took off one of his gloves in order to detach a grape from its bunch, started to bring it to his mouth, then changed his mind and put it back down.

'The only real difficulty,' he continued, 'stems from the fact that Lorraine is Catholic. And the Pope does not look at all kindly on one Catholic state making war on another, when there are so many Protestant states to make war on instead. In France, the Catholic party that hates me says as much in all its tracts, just as they oppose France being allied with the Protestant republic of the United Provinces of Holland against Spain . . .'

The cardinal fell silent for a moment, thinking to himself.

'The king will need the benevolent neutrality of the Pope when he occupies Lorraine. That is why France has been trying so hard not to displease Rome recently, and has even sought ways to please her. The marquis de Gagnière was an opportunity to do just that. Now he is dead, which is unfortunate. Even more serious is that signor Licini, otherwise known as Père Farrio, one of Rome's most zealous agents, has suffered a sword thrust through his body. Graver still, La Donna has been abducted. And all of this occurred in France, under the very noses of a full detachment of the King's Musketeers.'

'Four of those musketeers perished during this mission, monseigneur, and most of the others were wounded. The attack also took the lives of several innocent victims among the château's personnel.'

Richelieu stared at La Fargue.

Was the captain insidiously reproaching with him with only considering the diplomatic implications of this affair, while ignoring the human toll?

There was a knock at the door and Charpentier, the cardinal's old and faithful secretary, appeared.

183

'It's time, monseigneur,' he said.

'Already? Very well. Accompany me, captain.'

And leading La Fargue as he strode through the Palais-Cardinal, he asked:

'This creature that you and your Blades confronted, was it a dragon?'

'Yes, monseigneur. No doubt a last-born, as it was incapable of a complete metamorphosis.'

'Thank God. Are you one of those who believe the Black Claw instigated this attack?'

They descended a small spiral staircase which brought them to the ground floor.

'Who else, monseigneur? The Black Claw had an account to settle with La Donna after the affair with the Alchemist. Moreover, since she often serves the Pope, she must know secrets likely to be of considerable interest to the Grand Lodge.'

They arrived at a brisk walk in a courtyard where several gentlemen, including the comte de Rochefort, were waiting in their saddles.

'I am convinced that Gagnière's death was not the main objective of the attack,' added La Fargue. 'The Black Claw were really after La Donna.'

'I want you to find her,' said Richelieu, halting to pull his glove back on. 'It is only a matter of days before the Pope, through his ambassador, complains about this to the king. I want to be able to reply that signora di Santi is safe.'

'Monseigneur,' replied the captain of the Blades with a tense jaw, 'there is a more formidable danger than the Pope's displeasure now threatening Paris . . .'

'A danger that you affirmed had something to do with the Alchemist of the Shadows, wasn't that the one?'

'Yes.'

'Well, who knows more about the Alchemist than La Donna?'

'But who is to say whether she is still in France, monseigneur? Who is to say she is even still alive?'

'Find out.'

'How?'

Leaning towards La Fargue, the cardinal replied in a low voice:

'It is high time that your loyalty to the Seven be rewarded, don't you think? Ask them. They'll know.'

Without waiting for a reply, he joined the other riders and mounted his horse with the help of a lackey who held the stirrup for him. Then he added, just before spurring his mount forward:

'Indeed, you may be pleasantly surprised by the amount of good will that your contacts are prepared to demonstrate in this affair. Do not fail me, captain.'

And then the riders quickly filed out of the courtyard in the wake of Cardinal Richelieu.

In the garden of the Hôtel des Arcanes, the Gentleman was exercising with his sword beneath the shady vault of an arbour over which black rosebushes climbed. He practised alone, in his shirtsleeves, his hair gathered back with a leather thong.

The Enchantress observed him for a moment, admiring his feline grace and the lethal elegance of his movements. Then she approached and picked up, one after another, the three spare rapiers that the Gentleman had brought and left on a bench, comparing their weight and other qualities. He watched her do so, a half-smile on his lips. She finally chose the lightest and best-balanced of the trio. After whipping the air with the blade to loosen her wrist, she went to join the Gentleman in the shadow of the black roses.

They exchanged a fencing salute and crossed swords.

The Enchantress knew how to fight and did not seem overly hampered by her dress, lifting the heavy skirt with her left hand. She executed a series of cuts and thrusts, parried, and soon found her rhythm, gaining in boldness while the Gentlemen preserved his sang-froid and prevented their exchange from ever becoming too heated. The Enchantress soon realised that he was holding back. Without warning, she attacked with greater speed and vigour, taking the Gentleman by surprise and giving him no time to recover. She feinted and suddenly slapped him across the face with the back of her hand.

He broke off combat, retreated, and touched his bleeding lip with his fingertips, addressing an admiring and amused glance at the Enchantress. She raised her eyebrows at him in mocking defiance and placed herself *en garde*.

The duel resumed, this time in earnest.

Now, just as the Enchantress had wished, the Gentleman held nothing back. He dominated her with art, with science. He imposed his rhythm and his strength, forcing her to give way step by step. Delighted, she sensed his gaining the upper hand, knew he dominated her, handling her as he pleased. He was virile, powerful, and implacable. And when he was finished with her, he disarmed her, giving her wrist a sharp twist as he did that caused her to cry out briefly in pain. She found herself shivering with her back to the wall, under threat, completely vulnerable to the steel point that brushed against her heaving bosom pearled with sweat.

'If you kill me now, you'll never receive the gift I have in store for you . . .'

The Gentleman smiled and withdrew his sword.

'A gift?'

'Come.'

She took him by the hand and led him into the mansion.

He followed her, intrigued, and played along as she eluded him by darting up a staircase, waited for him to appear, provoked him, and then eluded him again. He saw that she was drawing him towards their bedchamber and started to realise what she had prepared for him.

'Really?' he said with a faint smile.

In his eye, there was the uncertain, happy gleam of someone who has guessed what has been offered to him just by seeing the package. Retreating before him, the Enchantress plucked a tarot card from her bodice and twirled it teasingly. He glimpsed a major arcanum card, but which one? He wasn't allowed the chance to see.

Reaching the end of the corridor, the Enchantress passed her hands behind her to open the door at her back. Following the movement, she entered and stepped aside, one arm pointing towards what lay within.

Towards the bed.

It was a splendid bed, immense, solid, made of black sculpted wood from whose canopy hung scarlet curtains attached to the columns by leather laces that often found other uses. And there, on the white sheets, a naked young blonde woman was waiting for him. She had a juvenile beauty with an adorable face, a milky velvet complexion, a slender waist and perfect curves.

She smiled, gazing at the Gentleman without uttering a word.

He remained still but was already carried away by his desire. He could not tear his eyes from her.

'Forget madame de Chantegrelle,' the Enchantress whispered in his ear. She embraced him from behind. 'Forget the vicomtesse de Malicorne.' She showed him the tarot card she had teased him with a few instants before. 'And bid fair welcome to—'

'—the "Demoiselle in the Tower",' finished the Gentleman, having recognised the major arcanum in question.

He advanced, climbed on to the bed and lay down beside the Demoiselle who offered herself to him, and he kissed her while the Enchantress unlaced her dress and joined them.

At the Hôtel de l'Épervier, the Blades conversed as they waited for La Fargue to return from Palais-Cardinal when, guided by a blushing Naïs, Leprat joined them in the garden. He was warmly welcomed, particularly by Agnès and Ballardieu who not seen him since their departure for Mont-Saint-Michel. He seemed slightly intimidated. Perhaps it was the house, where he felt less at ease now that he had reclaimed the blue King's Musketeers cape for good. But the others treated him like a lifelong comrade and even Saint-Lucq greeted him with a nod and a faint smile.

So Leprat let Ballardieu seat him forcefully on a stool beneath the chestnut tree and was happy to clink the glass of wine that Marciac served him with those of all the Blades present. Laincourt busied himself with slicing sausage for everyone and they begged Naïs to bring more wine, bread and butter, and the remains of the ham they had started to eat the previous day.

It was almost noon.

'Firstly, what are you doing here?' the Gascon asked gaily. 'And without your cape, no less! Aren't Tréville's Musketeers at Saint-Germain, with the king?'

'Indeed. But I have been granted a leave of absence, like all those of us who were at Mareuil . . . Well, at least . . . like all those who survived . . .'

'That Durieux gave me the impression of being an excellent fellow,' noted Laincourt.

'He is,' affirmed Leprat.

'Were you close to any of the musketeers who perished there?' Agnès enquired gently.

'To some, yes.'

'How many died?'

'Six. Five fell in the battle and I learned this morning that a sixth succumbed to his wounds in the night . . . We weren't prepared,' explained Leprat, who was feeling a need to confide. 'Not for what we confronted there, in any case . . .'

'There were thirty dracs,' Laincourt explained. 'They were organised and determined, showing no mercy. They had well-made weapons and powder charges. And they knew how to fight . . . How could we have been prepared for that?'

'Not to mention the dragon,' added Marciac.

'All that just to kill Gagnière?' asked Ballardieu in surprise.

'To abduct La Donna,' corrected Agnès.

'Are we really sure about that?' objected Saint-Lucq as he leaned across the table to snag a slice of ham with the point of his dagger. 'Couldn't all of this be a ruse, more of La Donna's stagecraft? It would be just like her.'

'To be sure,' admitted Marciac. 'But why would she?'

'To escape from the Pope's supervision. To recover her freedom. To cover her tracks while she took flight . . .'

'But where would she have found thirty-odd dracs to do her bidding?' asked Agnès. 'And a dragon to command them?'

'You're right,' conceded the half-blood. 'So we must believe that, if she lives, La Donna is a prisoner of the Black Claw. I don't envy her fate . . .'

La Fargue returned a little while later, after Leprat had already left to pay his respects to the family of the dead musketeer.

'Well?' enquired Marciac.

'We must find La Donna.'

'We must?'

'By order of the cardinal.'

'How will we even start?' Agnès asked.

La Fargue hesitated.

'I'll know soon,' he said, trying to ignore Saint-Lucq's penetrating glace. 'For now, get some rest, all of you.'

They spent the afternoon in a state of torpor. Saint-Lucq went out without saying where he was going, as usual. The others remained in the dimness and quiet of the Hôtel de l'Épervier, taking shelter from the summer heat. La Fargue, Laincourt, and Marciac had been riding almost without pause for four days, and had fought hard at the Château de Mareuil. Their short night of sleep since their return had not allowed them to recover from their fatigue or their wounds, as light as the latter might be. They isolated themselves to rest, aware that they might need all of their strength again soon.

In the fencing room, Agnès read and Ballardieu dozed, until La Fargue, too worried to remain still for long without something to do, came and joined them. He sat down with a sigh and took off his patch so that he could massage his damaged eye.

'Guibot told me you received a letter from the Chatelaines' Mother Superior General,' he declared.

'Guibot talks too much.'

'He didn't mean any harm by it. It occurred to him when I asked if anything had happened here during my absence.'

'In fact, I received a first letter from La Vaussambre before your departure. And as I didn't reply to it, a second letter arrived yesterday.'

'Can you tell me what they said?'

'I can. La Vaussambre wants to see me.'

'Did she say why?'

'No.'

'But you have an idea.'

'Yes.'

'You can't keep avoiding this forever, Agnès.'

Ballardieu, who was listening, frowned and anxiously watched the young baronne de Vaudreuil. Closing the treatise on fencing she had been reading – a gift from Almades which he had annotated in his own hand – she stood up and left, saying:

'I'm going to rest a while.'

La Fargue crossed glances with the old soldier.

'When will she understand?' he asked.

Ballardieu shrugged, looking distressed.

At the end of the day, Marciac was finishing a game of patience on his bed when Guibot came to warn him that he had a visitor.

'And who would that be?'

'The vicomte d'Orvand, monsieur,' replied the old concierge.

Glad to have an excuse to be up and about, Marciac pulled on his boots, decided to do without his doublet, unhooked his rapier as he was leaving the chamber, and hastened downstairs. He was making some final adjustments to his baldric when he joined d'Orvand in the courtyard and greeted him with a broad smile.

'Good afternoon, vicomte. How are you?'

D'Orvand was like a big brother to Marciac. He worried about the Gascon, reproached him repeatedly over all the scrapes he got himself into, and then never took long to forgive him. He had often offered him room and board, paid off certain of his debts, and once had even lent him a sword when Marciac had pawned his and needed to fight a duel. While he would never stop loving him, he despaired of ever seeing

Marciac become reasonable. Perhaps he even secretly envied the Gascon's carefree attitude.

'Good afternoon, Nicolas. You look tired.'

'Not at all. So what brings you here? What do you say we go round to visit madame de Sovange? We could wager a little of your money . . .'

'Another evening. Right now, there is someone who needs to speak to you.'

'Ah?'

'Follow me, would you? My carriage is waiting outside.'

The vicomte's coach did indeed stand in the street in front of the Hôtel de l'Épervier. D'Orvand opened the passenger door and invited Marciac to embark first.

'Where are we going?' asked the Gascon.

'Nowhere.'

Intrigued, he climbed into the vehicle and found himself sitting opposite Gabrielle.

His Gabrielle.

An elegant woman, she had as much poise as she did beauty, with strawberry-blonde hair, deep blue eyes, and a calm gaze. She intimidated most men but Marciac was not one of them. He loved her completely and sincerely. In his eyes, other women didn't count, or counted very little. And never for long, in any case.

'She didn't want to come,' said d'Orvand taking a place inside the coach. 'I had to convince her to come to you for help.'

'What's happened?' asked the Gascon in alarm. 'Are you in trouble?'

'Yes,' replied Gabrielle, before correcting herself. 'Well, actually, no, it's not about me.'

Perplexed, Marciac turned to the vicomte.

'One of the . . . one of Gabrielle's protégées has disappeared,' explained d'Orvand.

Gabrielle directed a brothel located in rue Grenouillère, called *The Little Frogs*. The protégées to which the vicomte bashfully alluded were the female residents of the house.

'Who are we talking about?' Marciac enquired.

'Manon,' replied Gabrielle.

The Gascon nodded. Young, pretty, blonde, and plump: he knew perfectly well who Manon was.

'And?' he prompted.

From time to time, Gabrielle allowed her 'frogs' to take part in special evening parties at the homes of rich clients. They had heard nothing from Manon since she had gone to one of these parties.

'Didn't she have a guardian angel?' asked Marciac.

He knew that Gabrielle made sure that her protégées never went out without a bodyguard to accompany them.

'Of course she did, but . . .'

'But what?'

'What Gabrielle is reluctant to tell you,' interjected d'Orvand, 'is that she has lost most of her associates and backers of late. And even some of her best clients . . .'

'"Of late!" You mean since Rochefort has been making difficulties for her!' exclaimed the Gascon, gritting his teeth in anger. 'Gabrielle? Am I wrong?'

'I haven't come here to complain,' she retorted.

Recently, Gabrielle had rendered the Blades a service by providing refuge to a young girl being hunted by the Black Claw. This young girl was La Fargue's secret, hidden daughter, and the captain had been quick to find her another sanctuary. But this service had been enough for Rochefort to take an interest in *The Little Frogs* and to put pressure on Gabrielle in a variety of ways, including intimidation, in the hope of extracting information from her.

'But you must allow Nicolas to help you,' the vicomte insisted. 'He has experience in these matters and you know you can trust him completely . . .'

Gabrielle nodded, took a deep breath, found the courage to look Marciac in the eyes, and confessed:

'I had no choice. I resorted to Mortaigne.'

Upon hearing this name, the Gascon went rigid and pale.

A quarter of an hour later, Marciac watched the vicomte d'Orvand's coach drive away down rue Saint-Guillaume, then turn into rue des Saints-Pères. Worried, he went to find La Fargue in the small office next to the fencing room.

'Captain?' he called, as he knocked on the door left ajar.

'Come in.'

'May I sit down?'

'Please. What's the matter, Marciac?'

The Gascon reported everything he had just learned. La Fargue listened to him without interruption, and then asked:

'You and this Mortaigne, you know one another, am I right?'

'We've been associated in the past.'

'And that's all there is to it?' insisted the captain, directing a penetrating gaze at Marciac.

'No,' admitted the Gascon. 'Gabrielle was his mistress once.'

'Ah . . . But let's return to the present affair. What did he say about it? Surely he's not claiming this Manon vanished into thin air, is he?'

'According to him, the girl used this evening party to escape Gabrielle's supervision and run away with a beau.'

'But Gabrielle doesn't keep her girls against their will.'

'Indeed not.'

'So Mortaigne is lying. What kind of man is he?'

'A scoundrel. There are worse scoundrels than he, but he is a scoundrel nonetheless.'

With his feet on his desk, La Fargue gazed towards the window that looked out over the garden, now being invaded by the evening shadows. He thought for a moment, and then asked:

'Who organised the party? Who was receiving the guests at their home? Who paid for it?'

'Gabrielle did not want to tell me. Perhaps she doesn't know.'

The captain addressed him a faint cynical smile.

'I rather think she knows perfectly well who it is, and that it is a person of some importance. A person who wants their name to go unmentioned and who pays well for that privilege . . . Moreover, Gabrielle no doubt fears your provoking a disaster by going to see this man and hanging him by his feet until he tells you whatever you want to know. You have to admit it's the sort of thing you'd do . . .'

Marciac shrugged.

'Shaking the tree is not the worst way of making fruit fall out,' he said sulkily.

'But some trees are better left unshaken, and Gabrielle knows this full well.' La Fargue scratched his beard pensively. 'So what are you planning to do?'

The Gascon had already thought about the question.

'If you don't need me, I'll go talk to Mortaigne tomorrow.'

'All right. But be careful. And assure Gabrielle that we will provide all the help we can. I've not forgotten that I am in her debt.'

'Thank you, captain.'

After supper, La Fargue waited until night had fallen before going up to his bedchamber. He locked the door, put the lit candle down, and brought a small casket out of his nearly empty clothing chest. Sitting down at his table, he opened the casket with a small key that never left his person, gently lifted the lid and removed an object wrapped in cloth. It was a precious silver mirror, which he unwrapped and placed before him, next to the candle. Its flame trembled, disturbed by a breath of air from a half-open window.

And then he waited.

At the first stroke of the bell tolling the hour, La Fargue closed his eyes and, with a rapt expression, recited a ritual formula in an ancient tongue that he had learned by heart. The surface of the mirror rippled, and then it no longer showed his reflection in the dim light.

The translucent image of a white dragon's head appeared, the contours and edges of the image sparkling slightly.

'Good evening, master.'

'Good evening, captain. What is it?'

'I require your aid, at the request of the cardinal.'

'Cardinal Richelieu knows full well that the Seven do not respond to requests. What is this about?'

'La Donna had been taken by the Black Claw. I have received the order to save her, but I . . .'

'When?! When did this happen?'

'Two days ago, in Champagne. It was at the Château de Mareuil where La Donna was carrying out—'

'—a mission for the Pope, yes,' concluded the dragon.

Then, as if to himself, in a voice that combined anger and regret:

'And yet we told her not to intervene . . .'

'I beg your pardon?'

'It was far too dangerous for her to reappear so soon. But she refused to listen to us . . .'

'I don't understand,' La Fargue said, with a troubled air.

The dragon fell silent, reflecting, and finally decided to explain:

'La Donna serves us, just as you serve us.'

The old captain froze.

'Since when?' he asked.

'What does that matter? The cardinal is correct in this instance: it's absolutely necessary that she be saved. Go to the regular rendezvous tomorrow. Valombre will tell you what to do.'

The dragon's head faded and the mirror soon recovered its ordinary appearance.

La Fargue remained still, mulling over what he had just learned. So, he and La Donna sometimes served the same masters, the same cause. But whereas the rest of the time he devoted himself to serving the king of France, she hired out her talents as a spy and a schemer to the highest bidder.

. . . to the highest bidder? Really?

If she were truly the greedy adventuress that people claimed, the Guardians would not call on her services. So he had to believe that the beautiful and dangerous Italian had a moral code, after all . . .

La Fargue thought he saw a movement out of the corner of his eye.

Calmly, he turned towards the half-open window, saw nothing alarming, but got up anyway to check.

Had he imagined it?

Taking care to stand well back, he opened the window wide and craned his neck to look outside.

Nothing.

He stepped forward, leaned out, listened and looked in both directions along the deserted rue Saint-Guillaume, in search of a movement, a sound, a clue.

In vain.

La Fargue was forced to accept the evidence of his senses, but his instinct rarely deceived him. Was he simply tired? Possibly. Nevertheless, he felt a nagging doubt as he closed the window.

Clinging to a ledge just above, Saint-Lucq waited a moment before hauling himself up silently to the roof.

He had seen and heard everything.

In the most elegant and comfortable chamber of the Hôtel des Arcanes, the Gentleman, the Enchantress and the Demoiselle drowsed, naked and sated, among the sheets in disarray on the black wooden bed. The Gentleman lay on his stomach and had his back to the two entwined women. The morning light seeped through the open windows, along with the distant, soothing murmur of Paris. It was already warm outside. The remains of a fine supper, served on expensive crockery, were spread upon a table draped in red cloth.

Preceded by the pounding of his heavy tread, the Illuminator entered without knocking or waiting to be announced. He was filthy and unkempt, sweating profusely, and he reeked of the stable. He marched straight for the food, picked items from the dishes almost at random and ate them, drank, and then continued to stuff himself noisily. Although this intrusion left the Gentleman indifferent, the Enchantress did nothing to hide her exasperation. The Demoiselle was the only one to show signs of a reflexive modesty. But she caught herself before she drew a sheet over her body.

'So?' asked the Gentleman, sitting on the edge of the bed.

'The expedition was a success,' announced the Illuminator between two fat mouthfuls.

'La Donna?'

'In our custody at Bois-Noir. What are we going to do with her?'

The Gentleman shrugged.

'Sell her to the highest bidder. Or offer her to the Black Claw. The Heresiarch will decide.'

The Enchantress embraced him from behind and murmured:

'I'd so much like to amuse myself with her . . .'

'We'll see, my dear,' replied the Gentleman, turning to kiss her.

Having drunk from the neck of a flagon, the Illuminator wiped his mouth with the back of a sleeve and belched.

'Who's this?' he asked, pointing with his chin at the former vicomtesse de Malicorne.

Drawing apart from the Gentleman, the Enchantress pivoted on her knees and said:

'May I present the Demoiselle. She is henceforth one of us, or will be soon, exactly as the Heresiarch desires . . .'

The Illuminator examined the newcomer for a long moment, then snorted in disdain and turned heel.

'I'll be at Bois-Noir,' he said as he left the chamber without closing the door.

The Gentleman gave a burst of laughter and fell back on the bed, arms spread.

Both furious and taken aback, the Demoiselle stammered:

'Wh— who was . . . that brute?'

'That was the Illuminator,' replied the Enchantress, getting up to put on a vaporous garment. 'You will get to know him, but it may take some time for you to appreciate him – if you ever do.'

'He's useful,' added the Gentleman, rising in turn. He approached the table, in search of food that had not been pawed by the Illuminator. 'By the way,' he continued in a conversational tone, 'the Enchantress tells me that you have some projects of your own in mind, is that right?'

The Demoiselle rolled onto her side and propped her head on her elbow.

'I was thinking of gathering some of my former followers. I had assembled many of the servile Black Claw worshippers around me. Some of them were influential, and not all of them have been rounded up by Cardinal Richelieu's men.'

'That's probably a good idea. What do you say?' the Gentleman asked the Enchantress.

The Enchantress was dressing her hair in front of a mirror.

'It's just as well that the idea pleases you,' she replied. 'Because the Demoiselle and I have already started to put it into effect . . .'

That morning, master Guibot went to find Agnès de Vaudreuil in the fencing room, where she was practising her fencing with Ballardieu.

'Madame, someone has brought a letter for you.'

Breaking off her assault, the young woman turned towards the concierge.

And waited.

'Well?'

'Oh!' exclaimed Guibot, realising the misunderstanding. 'The bearer has instructions to deliver the letter to you in person. He asked to wait in the courtyard.'

Agnès sighed, giving the old man a curt look. Then she tossed her rapier to Ballardieu, snatched a towel as she passed and, intrigued, went to see who it was.

There was indeed a man in the courtyard. Turning his back to the front steps of the main building, he stroked his horse's mane. He wore the uniform of the Black Guards, the elite company charged with the security of the Sisters of Saint Georges.

Agnès frowned: one of the Black Guards; that surely meant another letter from the Chatelaine's Mother Superior General. But the young woman's expression went from one of wariness to incredulity and joy when the messenger turned around.

It was François Reynault d'Ombreuse, the son of the marquis d'Aubremont and younger brother of Bretteville, whom Agnès had loved in secret.

'François?' she exclaimed. 'François, is it really you?'

She fell into his arms.

'By God!' he responded. 'And who else would it be?'

A tall, handsome man, wearing his sword with an elegant air and natural poise, he was displaying a broad smile. His eyes shone, as did those of the fiery baronne, who, drawing apart from him, gave him a hard punch on the shoulder.

'Do you know how worried we all were? Your father, above all. We've been searching for you high and low, and with those cursed Chatelaines—'

'I'm well,' said Reynault. 'And I'm here. I haven't disappeared. But I was away on a mission, after which I was assigned as a guard at Mont-Saint-Michel.'

'At Mont-Saint-Michel? Recently? You mean—'

'That I was there when you so distinguished yourself, yes!'

She remembered then the astonishing kindness with which her gaoler had treated her at the abbey on the mount, and suddenly she understood whom she owed it to.

'Come,' she said. 'Come in. I'm sure the captain will be delighted to see—'

'No, Agnès,' Reynault interrupted her. 'I must leave again at once. You know these are grave times . . .'

'Ah,' said Agnès, her smile vanishing. 'So this is what brings you here . . . There is no letter, is there?'

'No. I wanted to be sure of seeing you . . . You must agree to speak with the Mother Superior General, Agnès. Please.'

The young woman reflected. Then she sighed in resignation.

'So be it. I will go this afternoon . . . But only on one condition.'

'Which is?'

'Send your father news, or allow me to.'

'I'll do that. I promise you.'

Reynault remounted his horse and Agnès watched him ride off through the carriage gate. Turning round, she saw Ballardieu standing on the front steps.

The old soldier was smiling at her tenderly.

Paris was home to a dozen courts of miracles, the enclosed areas where the communities of beggars, criminals and other marginal elements would congregate under the authority of a single chief. The most famous of these courts was on rue Neuve-Saint-Sauveur, located behind the Filles-Dieu convent and ruled by the legendary Grand Coësre. There were also the Cour Brisset, the Cour Sainte-Catherine, the Cour Jussienne, the Cour du roi François, and other more or less populated and fearsome places.

Among them, the Cour-aux-Chiens was a well of shadows and stinks, surrounded by miserable façades to which clung a tangle of rickety galleries and rotting stairways. A noisy, turbulent life thrived in the dirty and polluted air. Down below, children played, ran around, appeared and disappeared through dark alleys, the soles of their clogs stamping through the unsanitary muck. Beneath browning canvas cloths, in which the remains of past downpours of rain slowly stagnated, tables flanked by stools were occupied by men condemned to a precarious, roving existence: unemployed workers, lackeys without a master, soldiers without a billet. They drained cups of sour wine and waited to be joined by women who would urge them to drink more before dragging them away to the sordid cubby-holes where they performed their services. Some of these women did not even make the effort to come back down and instead stood at the railings above, having quickly swiped between their thighs, calling out to whoever would listen: naming their prices, boasting of their talents and mocking those who hesitated. Others, more weary or resigned, simply waited. And when no one came, they chattered amongst themselves and watched over their boisterous off-spring from the heights.

At a window situated on the first floor of one of the buildings overlooking the courtyard, Marciac also observed the brats amusing themselves. Perfectly indifferent to the misery surrounding them, they charged forward with joyful cries to assault their imaginary enemies. The Gascon, behind his dark spectacles, counted nine of them entering an unlit passage in single file, by order of age and size. A snot-faced blond boy armed with a wooden sword led the charge, while a tiny girl wearing rags trotted at the rear, always out-distanced but nevertheless happy to be part of the game. A woman shouted that they were to stay within sight. In vain.

'Monsieur?' asked a timid voice.

Marciac turned his head toward the very young girl who, with lowered eyes, presented him with a glass of wine. Wearing a patched dress that was fraying at the sleeves, she was thin and pale, perhaps ill, certainly fearful. Everything about her expressed the submissiveness of a broken soul.

The Gascon took the glass without saying a word.

The girl went away. She left the door to the corridor open, and Marciac saw a drunken man struggling to retie his breeches. A dishevelled prostitute was holding him by his vest.

'You haven't paid!' she cried.

The man tried to free himself with a shove of his shoulder, but the woman wouldn't let go.

'You're not going anywhere until you've paid!'

'I did pay!'

'Not enough! Twenty deniers have never made a sol!'

With a nasty back-handed blow, the drunkard struck the prostitute in the face. She fell backward and hit the wall with her skull, bleeding from the mouth.

'There's your account paid in full.'

Then the man saw Marciac observing him.

'And you? Got anything to say?' he spat.

The Gascon gave him a disdainful look and turned back to the window.

The drunkard moved off as the woman picked herself up from the floor and insulted him, furious. Sipping his wine, Marciac waited to see him come out in the courtyard below. There, three men armed with clubs caught up with him, hit him without warning from behind, and continued to bludgeon him, egged on by the cheated prostitute. Finally, they emptied his pockets and left him bloodied on a pile of rubbish. The Gascon recognised one of the brutes: a certain Tranchelard, whom he was surprised to see here. Outside, no one did anything to stop him delivering a last blow to his dying victim.

'Sorry to have kept you waiting.'

Marciac turned to the man who had just entered the room

and was walking toward him with a smile on his face. Caught short, Marciac accepted his warm and friendly accolade before the other man released him and declared:

'I'm happy to see you again. It's been a long time, hasn't it?'

Without waiting for a reply, Mortaigne went to fill two glasses from the bottle placed on a table.

'Here's to our meeting again,' he said, handing one glass to Marciac.

Dark-haired, his chin marked by a scar that did not detract from his charm, Mortaigne seemed to be in good health but had put on weight, as far as the Gascon could judge. He was dressed as a hired swordsman, wearing a heavy leather doublet, with a dagger tucked into his right boot. His sword and baldric hung from the back of a chair.

He seemed sincerely glad to see Marciac.

'How are you?' he asked. 'I heard that you had some problems with La Rabier.'

'That matter was settled.'

'Good. She's a mean woman, that one. It's not wise to be indebted to her for long.' Mortaigne lifted his glass and drained it in one gulp, while Marciac contented himself with a mouthful. 'So . . . to what do I owe the pleasure of your visit?'

'I'm looking for one of Gabrielle's girls who has gone missing.'

Mortaigne's expression grew cloudy.

'Ah,' he said. 'Manon, is it?'

'Yes. What really happened that night? Do you know?'

'Gabrielle is making a whole story about it, but there's no real mystery . . .'

At that instant, Tranchelard and his companions went past in the corridor, bantering cheerfully with one another. Mortaigne could not see them, but he heard their voices.

'Is that Tranchelard?' he enquired.

'Yes.'

'Call him over, will you?'

'No.'

Mortaigne stared at the Gascon and then hailed his hench-man in a loud voice:

'Tranchelard!'

Coming back the way he came, the man in question ap-peared in the doorway. Tall, with long, greasy hair and a surly look, he still held the club he had just employed on the drunkard. The weapon's studs were spattered with blood and hair.

'*Patron?*'

'Did you kill him?'

'Maybe.'

'If he doesn't crawl out of here before then, dump him in the Seine when night falls.'

'Right you are.'

'That evening, Tranchelard was the one keeping an eye on things,' explained Mortaigne. Then he addressed the hench-man again: 'Marciac is a friend of mine. Tell him what hap-pened, the night that girl from *The Little Frogs* scarpered off.'

'After supper, she went up to a bedroom with a young gentleman. And in the morning, they had both disappeared. The bed wasn't even messed up.'

Tranchelard said no more.

'And that's all?' prompted the Gascon.

'Well . . . yes.'

Mortaigne thanked Tranchelard, who left.

'You see?' he said. 'There's no mystery. A young man falls for a pretty whore and carries her off, convinced that their love will overcome all obstacles. It will last until the twit discovers how much he misses his paternal allowance . . .'

The two men exchanged a long glance without blinking and Marciac recognised the gleam of a challenge in Mor-taigne's eye. The master of the Cour-aux-Chiens seemed to be saying to him: 'You've heard what I have to say. Now, either call me a liar or accept my word.'

'I'll be seeing you very soon,' Marciac promised as he left.

Mère de Vaussambre received Agnès in the large cloister of the Enclos du Temple. She waited for the baronne alone, seated on a stone bench. She did not get up, but she did close her breviary when the young woman joined her.

'Welcome, Marie-Agnès.'

'Mother superior.'

'Will you sit with me for a moment?'

Agnès sat down, ill at ease, as the Chatelaines' leader was quick to perceive.

'Calm yourself, my dear. You're in no danger here.'

'Not even in danger of being thrown into a cell in your tower keep? I seem to recall having had that experience recently . . .'

'You secretly infiltrated our sacred abbey on Mont-Saint-Michel,' retorted Mère de Vaussambre in a tone of gentle reproach. 'And rather than lay down your weapons when the alarm was raised, you had no hesitation in crossing swords with the Black Guards . . . Did you really believe that would go unpunished?'

Agnès was at loss for a reply.

'But let us forget all that, Marie-Agnès. Stop seeing me as an enemy and accept the peace offer I am making.'

'What's happened, mother superior? Why this change of heart?'

'I have never been hostile towards you, and neither have the Sisters of Saint Georges. Quite the reverse.'

'Then why do I have the feeling that you dislike me? You have never accepted the fact that I renounced taking my vows, mother superior.'

The Superior General of the Chatelaines was silent for a moment, and then suggested:

'Let's walk a little.'

They slowly paced along the lanes of the cloister.

'Your mark has awoken, hasn't it?'

'Yes, it has.'

'Don't you see that as a sign?'

'I won't take the veil, mother superior.'

'And how about your nights?'

Agnès refused to answer.

'All of the White Wolves bear the dragon's rune,' continued Mère de Vaussambre. 'But yours is different.'

'How do you know that?'

As if weary, the Superior General sighed.

'The Good Lord has singled you out, Marie-Agnès. And with each passing day, I pray you will come to understand that before it is too late. A terrible ordeal awaits you, and it is only the first, the one that will reveal if you are worthy of this destiny you so obstinately turn your back on. The destiny that you will be forbidden to fail . . .'

Agnès halted, forcing the Superior General to do likewise and turn round.

'Why me?'

'It is the Good Lord's will, Marie-Agnès.'

'I don't believe a word of it.'

'This dragon haunting your sleep, you will have to confront it soon. Do you think you will manage that on your own?'

The young woman was shaken by what she saw in Mère de Vaussambre's gaze.

She turned away.

'It's not fair,' she said.

'No, it's not . . . But this dragon is a primordial. A primitive and savage creature, extremely brutal, which certain parties have succeeded in turning into a formidable weapon. If no one opposes it, it will destroy Paris and plunge the kingdom into a storm that will devastate it. There will be misery, famine, and war.'

'Who knows about this?'

'The Chatelaines.'

'And no one else?'

'For now.'

'Why keep it a secret?'

'Because it hides another secret. One even the king does not know; one on which the fate of the entire world hangs.'

The young baronne waited.

In vain.

'No, Marie-Agnès,' the Superior General said to her with a

resigned smile. 'I cannot confide that secret to you now . . . But before you leave, grant me the boon of a favour.'

'Which is?' asked Agnès in a defensive tone.

'Speak with our new mother superior of the White Wolves. She will know how to persuade you and I think you will be glad to learn that she has recovered from her ordeal.'

Then, looking in the direction indicated by Mère de Vaussambre, Agnès recognised Sœur – or rather – Mère Béatrice d'Aussaint, who waited, smiling, with her sword at her side.

The last time they had seen one another, the Chatelaine had lain delirious on a narrow bed in the abbey at Mont-Saint-Michel.

That evening, Marciac went to rue Grenouillère. Making a cautious approach, he discreetly observed the surroundings. Not so long ago, men in the pay of Rochefort had been keeping watch over *The Little Frogs*. The Gascon had put one of them out of action, but he did not know whether his message has been received. The only sure result of his initiative had been to greatly displease Gabrielle, who knew how matters stood and – quite understandably – preferred he left Cardinal Richelieu's henchmen, as abject as some of them were, alone. Hence their most recent dispute, and their most recent separation.

Marciac did not see anyone or anything out of the ordinary, except that shutters had been recently added to the brothel's windows. He did not try knocking on the door. He went around to the back and climbed over the wall into the garden, where he found Gabrielle sitting at a small table in the shade, busy with her correspondence.

'You do know we have a door,' she said, glancing up at the Gascon. Unmoved by his appearance, she did not pause in her writing. 'We even have a porter to open it for you.'

'And how is he, dear old Thibault?'

'You can ask him when you leave. By way of the door.'

Marciac sat down on a low wall and removed his hat, fluffing his blond hair which was tangled and shiny with sweat.

'I went to see Mortaigne,' he announced.

Gabrielle put her quill down and straightened her shoulders.

'And?'

'That evening, it was a certain Tranchelard who was "keeping an eye on things", as Mortaigne put it. You know him?'

'No.'

'I thought perhaps you might have heard of him. Tranchelard enjoys a degree of renown, along with some of the other unscrupulous brutes of his type. But the last I heard, he was still part of the court of miracles in rue Saint-Sauveur. I didn't know he'd left the Grand Coësre's service. And I'm wondering why.'

'Passing from the King of the Beggars' service to that of the master of the Cour-aux-Chiens does not seem like a promotion to me . . .'

'Well put.'

'Do you think that Tranchelard might be involved in Manon's disappearance?'

'Yes.'

'And Mortaigne?'

'It's possible. I can't say for certain.'

Marciac put his felt hat back on and adjusted it to the proper angle.

'Do you believe Manon . . . Do you think she's still alive?' asked Gabrielle suddenly, with a vibrant emotion in her voice.

Her distress, which she allowed herself to reveal for the first time, moved Marciac deeply. He went to crouch beside her, took her hands tenderly, and looked up, seeking her gaze.

'The truth,' he said, 'the truth is that I don't know. Not for certain.'

'It will soon be three days and three nights, Nicolas . . .'

'Even so, we can't . . .'

On the verge of tears, but in a voice ringing with anger, she interrupted:

'If you only knew how much I blame myself!'

'It's not your fault, Gabrielle.'

'But why did I decide to rely on Mortaigne?'

'It wasn't such a bad decision. And you couldn't know Mortaigne would delegate the duty to Tranchelard.'

Gabrielle rose and drew away from Marciac.

'You're trying to excuse me,' she accused, turning her back on him.

He stood up. Embarrassed, not knowing what to say, he scratched the stubble on his cheeks and neck.

Finally, after a moment of silence, Gabrielle turned and, regaining control of herself, said:

'We can expect no help at all from Mortaigne, if I've understood you correctly.'

'No, I'm afraid not.'

'So, what do you intend to do?'

'It's time you told me who hosted this party, Gabrielle.'

'Go to the usual rendezvous point tomorrow. Valombre will tell you what to do,' the white dragon in the mirror had said.

Saint-Lucq was hiding in a porch on rue Saint-Guillaume when La Fargue came out of the Hôtel de l'Épervier, just before midnight, alone. Invisible and silent, the half-blood watched him walk away and waited until he turned into the rue des Saints-Pères before following him.

The captain walked quickly to the Seine, where he turned right on the Malaquais quay. That could only mean one thing: he intended to enter Paris via the Nesle gate. All of the capital's gates being closed at this hour, La Fargue would have to use his permanent pass signed by Cardinal Richelieu. Like all the Blades, Saint-Lucq carried a similar document. But he couldn't pass through the Nesle gate at the same time as La Fargue, nor could he afford to wait for the guards to re-open the gate for him . . .

Saint-Lucq pondered the situation for a moment, made his decision and then did not hesitate.

Retracing his steps back up rue des Saints-Pères, he quickly turned away from the river, went past the Saint-Germain-des-Prés abbey and finally presented himself at the Buci gate. His pass worked its magic, allowing the half-blood swift access to rue Dauphine. Breathing hard, for a moment Saint-Lucq thought he had lost La Fargue. But he stayed calm and spotted his captain just as La Fargue ventured out onto Pont Neuf.

The stalking resumed, more delicate than ever, as La Fargue was careful to watch for anyone tailing him and the deserted Pont Neuf offered a clear view behind. Saint-Lucq could count on the darkness as an ally, however. And his dragon eyes could see far. He gave La Fargue a long lead, wondering whether the captain would continue across the Seine or turn into Place Dauphine. But in the event, he did neither. After a last glance around him, he disappeared behind the Bronze Wyvern's pedestal, at the tip of the Ile de la Cité.

So here was La Fargue's rendezvous point with this Valombre the white dragon had spoken of. A 'regular' rendezvous, which made the half-blood wonder when these meetings had started. Who had started them. And why. He could not bring himself to admit that his captain was a traitor . . . but he was determined to get to the bottom of all this.

Midnight tolled.

Ten minutes passed without anyone turning up. Either Valombre was late or he had arrived at the meeting point first. He and La Fargue must be in the midst of their discussion. Nevertheless, Saint-Lucq rejected the idea of approaching the statue to eavesdrop on them. Too risky. So he waited.

At last, La Fargue reappeared and, in a great hurry, travelled back the way he had come. No doubt he was returning to the Hôtel de l'Épervier. The half-blood tracked him with his eyes but did not move. Almost immediately, another gentleman wearing a felt hat and a black coat emerged from behind the Bronze Wyvern.

Surely this was Valombre.

And he was a quarry worth following.

La Fargue made haste to rejoin the other Blades. Valombre had told him where La Donna was probably being held prisoner, without being able to give definite assurances of this or guarantee she would remain there for long. So they needed to act tonight, and address any doubts or questions afterwards.

At the Hôtel de l'Épervier, the captain ordered André to saddle the horses and summoned the others to the bottom of the main stairway. Agnès and Ballardieu arrived, and then Laincourt and Marciac almost immediately after.

'So?' asked the young baronne. 'How do matters stand?'

La Fargue had refused, of course, to let anyone accompany him to his rendezvous. He had, however, announced before leaving that he might return with news concerning La Donna.

'We know where she is,' he said now. 'She's being held in an old tower, a place called "Bois-Noir".'

'I know it,' indicated Marciac. 'It's on the Seine, not far upstream from Paris.'

'Is the information reliable?' enquired Laincourt.

'As reliable as we can hope to get.'

'And where does it come from?'

La Fargue had no idea how the Guardians had discovered where La Donna was being kept. To crown it all, he could not even tell the others who had given him this piece of intelligence.

'From one of the cardinal's agents,' he lied.

But Agnès had other concerns:

'Is Alessandra still held captive by the dracs who abducted her?'

'Yes, definitely.'

There was a moment's silence, broken by Marciac after he had done the sums:

'There were about thirty of them before they attacked us, and they left ten bodies on the ground. That leaves twenty dracs, well armed and well trained. Even without counting the dragon who commanded them, that's a lot to take on.'

'There are only five of us,' Ballardieu pointed out.

'Saint-Lucq isn't here?' asked La Fargue in surprise.

'No, captain.'

'Where is he?'

'No idea,' Marciac confessed.

The Blade's captain cursed. But there was no time for that, either.

'We can't wait to see if he shows up. Make your preparations. I want to be on the move in less than an hour.'

The others hesitated for a brief instant and then nodded; whatever their reservations none of them would question their captain or his authority. Only Agnès spoke up with a suggestion:

'At the very least, allow me to fetch Leprat, captain. We'll need his sword.'

'All right. But don't take too long.'

'And I'm going to need my bag of tricks,' muttered Ballardieu.

Laincourt heard him and frowned, but understood a short while later when he saw the old soldier return with a heavy pouch full of fused grenades slung over his shoulder on a bandolier. Agnès had already mounted the first horse that André had finished saddling and called out:

'Meet us at La Tournelle gate.'

Then she dug her spurs in and left the courtyard at a gallop.

La Fargue watched her leave, still thinking about Saint-Lucq. Worried about their mission, he already sensed that the half-blood's lethal efficiency was going to be sorely missed.

After his rendezvous with La Fargue, Valombre did not leave the Ile de la Cité. He crossed the Pont Neuf, then took the Grand-Cours-d'Eau quay. His path took him alongside the dark, high walls of the Palais de Justice until he reached rue de la Barillerie, which stretched from the Pont au Change bridge to the north to Pont Saint-Michel to the south. Beyond this street lay a twisted maze of medieval streets and alleys, which Valombre entered at a brisk pace, forcing Saint-Lucq to reduce the distance separating them or risk losing sight of his quarry. The half-blood was resolved to discover exactly where the captain's secret contact was going. But his anxiety increased the closer Valombre came to the so-called Cloister neighbourhood of Notre-Dame.

The Cloister occupied the eastern end of Ile de la Cité, in the shadow of Notre-Dame cathedral. A legacy of the Middle Ages, it consisted of three streets and about forty small houses owned and occupied – in principle – by the cathedral's canons. A wall surrounded it and the area inside was only accessible through three gates. Lacking any taverns or shops, this tiny neighbourhood was much envied for its tranquillity and some of the canons had realised the profits they could make if they allowed their dwellings to be let. This practice had become firmly established and, under Louis XIII, the Cloister had more secular than religious residents.

Was this Valombre's destination?

For Saint-Lucq, the question was answered when he saw the man present himself at the gate in rue de Colombe. One minute later, the man passed through the wall into the Cloister where visitors were rare and intruders were immediately suspect.

The half-blood winced in frustration.

Should he take the risk of following the mysterious gentleman inside the Cloister? He realised this was his only opportunity to find out what La Fargue was hiding, and duly located a spot where he could climb the enclosure unseen. He landed in a garden, went over a first low dividing wall between properties, then a second, and spotted Valombre just before the man disappeared at the end of rue Chanoinesse. Saint-Lucq ran silently alongside the houses' façades but arrived at the street corner too late: the place was deserted.

Breathless but still focused on the hunt, the half-blood searched the darkness with his dragon eyes, pricked up his ears, and searched for any glow in the windows around him.

Not a trace.

He cursed – and failed to see the blow that knocked him out cold.

Of the stronghold of Bois-Noir, nothing remained but an old stone bridge, a circular wall still in fairly good shape, some ruins that had been reduced almost to ground level, and a partially collapsed keep whose bevelled silhouette was outlined against a paling sky only an hour before dawn. These isolated, long-abandoned remains stood on top of a steep hill overlooking the Seine. They could be reached by road or via a footpath. Narrow and treacherous, this footpath wound towards the riverbank in a series of switchbacks, ending at a floating landing stage where a boat was moored, with dracs already busy on board. The road climbed the far slope in a large loop leading to the old bridge, which crossed a ditch filled with brush. Down below, where the road began, a temporary enclosure had been erected to hold twenty horses grazing next to a stream. Some dracs were also camped there, but the majority of the band were within the ruins, where La Donna was almost certainly being held.

La Fargue, Laincourt, Leprat, and Marciac approached the château on the same slope as the road, but ascended by a shorter, more direct route in great silent strides, taking advantage of the darkness and only halting behind cover to catch their breaths, measure the distance travelled, and inspect the surrounding area.

'It will be daybreak soon,' murmured Leprat as he joined La Fargue behind a large rock.

The captain nodded gravely.

They had ridden flat out from Paris, with only a brief delay to scout out the terrain and evaluate the enemy's forces, but now they were running out of time. Once the sun rose, the dracs would be up and about, too.

La Fargue risked a glance up the hill. They had almost reached the foot of the walls, which had sentries posted along the top. There were some breaches by which they could pass. But to reach them would require a perilous climb.

Behind them, Laincourt and Marciac waited.

'Captain.'

La Fargue turned toward Leprat and saw that he was pointing to the landing, down below, lit by lanterns. They enjoyed a good view of the boat and the handful of dracs who were completing preparations for an imminent departure. There was a man on the landing as well: bearded and massive, with an impressive *schiavone* at his side.

'He's the dragon,' said Leprat. 'The one who attacked us in Mareuil.'

La Fargue nodded again.

'If we act quickly and effectively,' he replied, 'he might not have time to reach the château, after the alarm has been raised . . .'

'Let's hope so.'

'There are four dracs with him. We saw three more guarding the horses at the bottom of the road. So that leaves twelve or thirteen up here.'

'It gives us a chance.'

'Then let's go!'

The four men resumed their silent ascent.

'I see three,' whispered Agnès.

'So do I,' said Ballardieu. 'Two near the fire and another one, over there.'

They lay flat on the grass and were spying on the dracs charged with guarding the horses. One was seated and smoking a pipe near the dying campfire, while the second, lying still, seemed to be asleep. The third one, apart from the others, was supposed to be guarding the horses, but was in fact watching the preparations going on aboard the boat moored at the landing.

'You take care of the sentry, girl?'

'Understood. Be careful.'

'As always.'

They separated, Ballardieu heading toward the fire and Agnès making a wider detour. She went round the enclosure stealthily, taking pains not to disturb the horses, and approached the drac from behind. He had not moved and continued to gaze in the direction of the lantern-lit pontoon. She was upon in him two quick strides, clamping one hand against his mouth and stabbing him three times in the kidneys. The drac gave a stifled moan and slowly slumped, held up by the young woman.

The drac smoking a short distance away didn't notice a thing. Tired from the night watch, he was bored and sucked on his pipe, his gaze absent. A noise made him turn three quarters round, just before a pouch heavily loaded with grenades struck him beneath the chin, snapping his neck.

Killed instantly, he fell backwards as the leather bag continued its trajectory at the end of the bandolier that Ballardieu wielded with art. Its next victim was the drac who had been dozing on a blanket and who only had time to rise up on his elbows. He, too, collapsed, his temple shattered.

Satisfied, Ballardieu admired his work before collecting the first drac's pipe and blowing on the tobacco that was still burning in the bowl. Agnès and he had almost completed their mission. Their task now was to free the horses and prevent any pursuit when they fled with La Donna. In passing, the old soldier noticed that there were four blankets around the campfire.

He raised an eyebrow.

Why four?

Agnès was finishing laying out the body of the sentry she had killed when the fourth drac came out of the grove, where he had been detained by a nasty bout of the runs. Shocked, they stared at one another for a brief second.

Then it was a matter of who reacted first.

The drac had a pistol at his belt.

So did the corpse the young baronne was leaning over.

The pistol shot caught them by surprise, coming when they had already infiltrated the ruins. Leprat was silently finishing off a guard on the ramparts; Marciac was dragging a body behind a low wall; Laincourt was sneaking up on a drac who had his back turned to him; and La Fargue was progressing towards the keep, a pistol in one hand and his solid Pappenheimer in the other.

Everything suddenly accelerated.

Senses abruptly alert, the last sentry standing spotted the intruders and raised the alarm. The dracs who were sleeping woke with a start and realised they were under attack. There was an immediate stir of activity. Shouts were raised. Shots rang out and, taking advantage of what little remained of the element of surprise, the Blades hurried to do as much damage as possible.

La Fargue raced towards the keep and eliminated the drac

at the entrance with a pistol ball fired right into his mouth before kicking in the worm-eaten door. Inside, sacks and kegs were deposited in a large room from which rose a spiral staircase. La Donna was almost certainly being held on the first floor, the storeys above either no longer existing or partially destroyed.

The old captain dashed towards the steps, but was forced to beat a retreat as a huge black drac came down them, rapier in his fist. La Fargue recognised the drac even as he placed himself *en garde*: he had seen him at Mareuil, fighting beside the red drac who had led the attack. The black drac stared at the captain in return, and no doubt recognised him as well.

Combat commenced and La Fargue quickly took the measure of his formidable opponent. The drac was fast, powerful, and he knew how to fence. Right from the start, the two adversaries threw all of their strength and skill into the battle. The drac because his brutal nature drove him to it and the captain because he knew time was against him. Their blades crossed and clashed violently in a series of attacks, ripostes, and counterattacks. Neither was prepared to give way. Neither could press home an advantage.

Not until La Fargue made a mistake.

Tripping, he clumsily parried a twisting attack that tore his sword from his hand. He fell on his back, rolled to the right and then to the left to avoid two thrusts that would otherwise have pinned him to the floor, then caught the drac's ankles in a scissor movement of his legs. The reptilian tumbled, allowing La Fargue time to stand up and seize with both hands a keg, which he heaved at his opponent. It struck the drac on the brow and broke open, spilling the gunpowder within. Seeing this, the captain realised the kegs stored here were mines similar to those the dracs had employed in their assault on Château de Mareuil. But the black drac, stunned by the impact and blinded by the cloud of black powder, was already getting back up. La Fargue pounced on his Pappenheimer and, straightening, brandished it in both hands, blade forward . . .

. . . before planting it all the way to the hilt in his kneeling opponent's chest.

The drac slowly sagged and then lay down for good, arms outstretched, in a spreading pool of blood.

Out of breath, La Fargue gathered his wits before climbing to the floor above. He quickly found La Donna, who was a sorry sight to behold. She did not seem to have been beaten or particularly mistreated, but several days of captivity and fear had taken their toll. She was dirty and dishevelled, still wearing the dress in which she had been abducted. Frightened, she had her back to the wall. Her hands were bound and her eyes covered by a blindfold.

'It's me,' the captain announced.

'La . . . La Fargue?'

'Yes.'

A sudden sob shook her shoulders. La Fargue freed her of her bonds and her blindfold. Still afraid but with a gaze full of gratitude, she pressed herself against him, trembling and fragile. She thanked him in a soft whisper:

'Grazie . . . Molte grazie . . .'

'Later.' He pried her away from him. 'Can you walk? Run?'

'Yes.'

'Then follow me.'

He was already moving, dragging La Donna by the hand, when an idea came to him.

The lantern burning in the room was no longer the sole source of light, as the first glow of dawn entered through a tall embrasure oriented towards the rising sun. La Fargue approached the opening and cast a glance down below. The embrasure overlooked the steeper side of the hill, the side where the dracs at the landing had been struggling up the footpath since hearing the alarm. Led by the Illuminator, they would soon pass just beneath the keep.

'Let's go,' La Fargue said. 'Take the lantern.'

In the courtyard, among the ruins of the Château de Bois-Noir, Leprat, Laincourt, and Marciac faced odds of two or three to one. The musketeer and the cardinal's former spy were fighting back-to-back in the middle of a circle of dracs, while the Gascon was defending the top of a flight of steps.

La Fargue and La Donna left the keep at a run.

'DOWN!' yelled the captain.

He immediately pushed the young woman to the ground behind a low wall and shielded her with his body. The others were caught short by the explosion of the powder charges stored in the tower. The detonation was enormous, violent, and deafening. It projected stones that whistled past like cannon balls while a cloud of dust and dirt engulfed the ruins. What remained of the keep tipped into thin air and fell in an avalanche of stone, wood, and rubble that swept down and carried away the dracs climbing the steep footpath. Their screams were inaudible from above.

La Fargue was the first to pick himself up.

His ears buzzing, he saw a powdery landscape on which a rain of debris, some of it aflame, was still falling. He helped La Donna to stand. Men and dracs were also struggling to their feet around them, dazed, staggering, and no longer in any state to fight. Their gestures were slow and uncertain.

'ANY INJURIES?' shouted La Fargue.

Leprat and Laincourt shook their heads. Marciac waved a hand. He, too, was unhurt, or at least as unhurt as one could hope for. Two riders suddenly burst into the courtyard: Agnès and Ballardieu arriving, leading mounts for the others. As the dracs were beginning to recover their wits, they made haste. La Donna mounted behind Le Fargue and the Blades spurred their horses. As a final stroke, Ballardieu covered their escape with two grenades, which he tossed over his shoulder as they left the château.

The whole band galloped down the wide looping road to the bottom of the hill. There, La Fargue ordered a brief halt, out of range of any musket fire. The expedition had almost been a disaster, but they were all still alive and La Donna had been rescued.

'Is everyone all right?' the captain asked, concerned.

They reassured him, with the exception of Marciac who was

trying to unblock his left ear by slapping the right with his palm . . .

. . . and Agnès, who was looking back in the direction of the ruins.

Dressed in the tattered remains of an outfit of clothing, a scaly creature stood at the top of the sole remaining turret. It leapt from its perch and came charging down towards the Blades.

They immediately set off again at a gallop.

The dragon had somehow survived the explosion and the keep's collapse. Worse still, anger, fear, and the threat of death had triggered its uncontrolled metamorphosis into a monster even more bestial than the one the Blades had faced at Mareuil. It was now bigger, more powerful and more compact, with arms so long that its clawed hands touched the ground when it bent its knees. Its shoulders were enormous and its spine bent into a hump where it met a neck that was as short as it was wide.

The creature came hurtling straight down the slope, taking the most direct route, then followed the road in hot pursuit of the riders. It did not run, but rather progressed by bounds with the help of its arms and legs, its body gathering itself in when it touched the ground and stretching into the air with each forward push. Its speed was extraordinary and the Blades, even at a full gallop, were losing their lead.

Agnès and Ballardieu were at the back of the column.

Without slowing down, the old soldier slid the pouch on his bandolier against his belly. He plucked out a grenade and lit the fuse from the bowl of his pipe, before letting the device fall behind him. He repeated this operation twice, but the grenades rebounded willy-nilly when they hit the earth. Only the third remained on the road, and it exploded well before the dragon reached the spot.

Ballardieu realised that he wasn't going to accomplish anything that way.

He also realised they were lost if he did nothing.

'KEEP GOING!'

Pulling hard on the reins, Ballardieu forced his mount to

rear and pivot on its hind legs. Before Agnès could react, he raced away in the opposite direction. Without thinking, she turned back as well.

Ballardieu galloped full tilt towards the dragon, which, its eyes sparkling with a savage rage, also sped up. They met just beyond the bridge that crossed over a dry riverbed. The old soldier lit a last fuse; the creature bounded for him. Their collision overturned the rider and his mount. The horse gave a whinny of pain as the two opponents rolled in the dust and tumbled down into the dry gulch, disappearing from Agnès' view. The monster was the first to rise. Foaming at the mouth, it looked about and saw Ballardieu clumsily trying to stagger away. Then the dragon saw that a strap was wrapped around its neck and felt a weight hanging between its shoulders.

Ballardieu's bag of tricks exploded and decapitated the dragon right in front of Agnès, who had jumped down from her horse and was running towards the creature, sword in her hand. She instinctively protected herself with an elbow and could not contain a grimace of disgust when she discovered what remained.

Then she turned to Ballardieu, who was standing but tottering as if drunk, with a bleeding brow and a dislocated shoulder. She realised they would not finish hearing the tale of the day when Ballardieu slayed a dragon. She gave a smile . . .

. . . which immediately vanished.

'Ballardieu!' she yelled, pointing her finger.

Still dazed, the old soldier looked down to see the last grenade at his feet, which had not exploded with the others. The burning fuse was just reaching its end.

The sound of the explosion drowned out Agnès' scream.

3

The riders arrived in the courtyard of the inn at a gallop. They immediately dismounted and, carrying their wounded, blood-soaked comrade, almost broke down the door in their rush to bring him inside.

'Make room!' shouted La Fargue.

He was holding Ballardieu up. Agnès, Marciac, and Leprat helped him. Together, they laid the old soldier out on the first table they saw. Laincourt and Alessandra followed them.

In the large common room, the customers had stood up and moved away from the newcomers. The innkeeper didn't know what to do, unable to tear his eyes away from the dying man, whose whole right side was one huge wound.

'Leprat,' La Fargue ordered, 'make sure there's no one following us.' The musketeer nodded and left. 'Marciac, what do you need?'

The Gascon had started to cut away the scraps of blackened clothing that were stuck to Ballardieu's raw wounds and burns.

'Water and linen. And lint for bandages.'

'Did you hear that?' La Fargue asked the innkeeper.

The man was slow to react, but he nodded and hurried off.

'And some straps!' shouted Marciac. 'Bindings, laces, anything like that!'

He needed something to make better tourniquets than the emergency ones he had already put in place.

Agnès was leaning over Ballardieu with tears in her eyes. She was whispering softly in his ear as she stroked his brow covered in dirt, sweat, and blood.

La Fargue turned to Laincourt and La Donna, and it was the captain rather than the man who spoke.

'Madame, you must leave now. You have to reach the Palais-Cardinal as soon as possible. Only then will you be safe.'

'But I can't leave you like this,' protested the beautiful spy. 'This man—'

'His name is Ballardieu.'

'It was while rescuing me that he—'

'The mission comes first, madame. Laincourt, if you please . . .'

The young man nodded and urged La Donna to turn away.

'Come madame. I will escort you.'

She started to follow him, pulled gently backward by the arm.

'Thank you,' she said. 'Thank you with all my heart . . .'

But the Blades did not care about her gratitude: one of their own was dying.

As Agnès continued to comfort Ballardieu, who probably could not hear her, Marciac murmured to La Fargue:

'I'll do my best. But he needs a surgeon.'

The captain nodded and asked those gathered in the common room:

'Is there a surgeon who lives near here?'

People shook their heads and the innkeeper, who was returning with a basin filled with the items requested by Marciac, replied:

'We are in the country, messieurs. The closest doctor lives in the faubourg Saint-Victor.'

'By the time one of us travels to Paris for a surgeon and returns,' La Fargue thought aloud, 'we could be there ourselves . . .'

'It's out of the question. Ballardieu can't ride a horse now. He's lost too much blood, it would kill him.'

'I have a cart,' offered one good fellow among those watching.

'Here.'

Squinting painfully, Saint-Lucq took the spectacles from the hand holding them out to him. He had just woken and was trying to adapt to the light. His dragon eyes saw better in the day when protected by the red lenses. The headache that had threatened to overwhelm him receded.

'Thank you.'

He found himself in the peaceful surroundings of a modest chamber, lying on a narrow bed. He was fully dressed, or almost; only his doublet was missing, hung on the back of a chair. His hat was on the table, beside his rapier in its scabbard, and his leather baldric.

The person who had returned his spectacles was sitting next to the bed.

Elegant, in his thirties, and with grey hair, it was the gentleman La Fargue had met in secret the previous night, and whom the half-blood had followed as far as the Cloister of Notre-Dame.

Before being knocked out.

'Where are we?'

'In my home, rue du Chapitre.'

The man saw the glance that Saint-Lucq gave his sword.

'You're not in any danger here,' he said. 'I'm not your enemy.'

'Then why did you attack me last night?'

'I did not know who you were. And after I found that out, I needed to seek advice.'

'Seek advice from whom?'

The man smiled.

'Very well,' allowed Saint-Lucq. 'Then: seek advice on what subject?'

'What should be done about you. And also, what I could reveal to you.'

Sitting up in the bed, the half-blood turned towards his host and leaned back against the wall.

'Who are you?' he asked.

'My name is Valombre.'

'That's only a name.'

'And I am a dragon.'

'That I can well believe. What do you have to do with Captain La Fargue?'

'He and I serve the same masters.'

'Explain that to me.'

'I can do that. But wouldn't you prefer to hear the truth from your captain?'

Saint-Lucq thought about it, probing the grey, tranquil eyes of the other man, and then said:

'Let's start with you.'

Marciac did everything he could to keep Ballardieu alive. Then the Blades transported the old soldier to Paris in the cart that had been so generously offered to them. Their patient was laid out on two superimposed mattresses, to protect him from jolts during the journey. Agnès sat nearby to comfort him, to reassure him that he would recover and that all would be well. La Fargue took the reins and the Gascon followed them on horseback. They had to halt twice on the road to tighten the tourniquets.

Upon their arrival at the Hôtel de l'Épervier, Leprat was waiting for them. He had gone ahead at a full gallop, and had found a surgeon whose services were often used by the King's Musketeers, the same doctor who had tended him when Gagnière had left him for dead in rue Saint-Denis. Ballardieu was carried into the kitchen, where he was laid out on the large oak table. Then the surgeon asked that they leave him with his patient so that he might examine him without disturbance. He had come with an assistant and had no need of anyone else. He would call if there was something they could do.

The others waited in the courtyard with Guibot, André, and sweet Naïs who was clutching her apron and flinching at the slightest sound, the smallest movement.

Finally, the surgeon came out, wiping his hands on an old rag.

'This man has already received care,' he said. 'Who ministered to him?'

'I did,' replied Marciac.

'Are you a doctor, monsieur?'

'No, but I came close to becoming one.'

'Be that as it may, if not for you, your friend would not be alive . . . Nevertheless, he is not yet out of danger. Far from it.'

'Can his leg be saved?' La Fargue asked.

'I fear not,' answered the surgeon.

At those words, Agnès turned away, seeming both upset

and furious. Leprat put an arm around her and drew her a few steps apart from the others.

'The leg is too badly damaged,' the surgeon continued with a grave face. 'It must be taken off. However . . . However, I fear your friend will not survive an amputation. He has already lost a considerable amount of blood. He is very weak. And no longer young.'

'I do not understand, monsieur,' said La Fargue. 'What do you advise?'

'The leg is lost. It must be cut off, but perhaps we might risk waiting for the patient to regain some strength before inflicting this ordeal upon him. But I stress the word "risk". For if we wait and the terrible wounds to his leg begin to spoil, your friend will certainly perish as a result.'

'So you are asking us to make a wager.'

'I am asking you to make a choice, for a friend who no longer has all his reason . . .'

Still and pale, Agnès saw the Blades' captain turn toward her.

'This decision belongs to you, Agnès,' said La Fargue. 'But if you do not want to make it, I will.'

The Gentleman dismounted in the ruins of Bois-Noir and held his horse by the bit. Without saying a word, he contemplated the smoking rubble, then the corpses that the survivors had aligned in front of a wall. There were no more than a handful of drac mercenaries still alive, and most of them were wounded. La Donna had escaped. And the Illuminator had vanished.

It was a disaster.

The Gentleman lifted his eyes towards the Enchantress who had remained in her saddle. They exchanged a long, serious, worried look, which was interrupted by the arrival of three riders.

It was Keress Karn and two of his soldiers. Filthy with dust and sweat, the red drac wore a bloody bandage on his right arm, just above the elbow.

'We found him,' the drac leader announced as he leapt down from his horse.

'Dead?' asked the Gentleman.

'Yes. In a dry riverbed, about half a league from here. We followed his tracks there.'

'Dead?' exclaimed the Enchantress in disbelief. 'The Illuminator is dead?'

Keress Karn deemed it useless to repeat himself. Besides, he considered it beneath him to answer a woman. He only spoke to the Gentleman.

Overcome by anger, the latter clenched his jaws tightly.

'Who?' he asked in a rasping voice. 'Who could have—'

'Their leader is called La Fargue,' explained the red drac. 'I recognised him. He was there at Château de Mareuil.'

'I want him to pay,' ordered the Gentleman. 'I want him to suffer, and I want him to die.'

The operation went well, and afterwards Ballardieu was carried up to his chamber. The surgeon said he was satisfied but remained cautious: he would not permit himself much hope unless his patient survived the night. He left some instructions and promised to return the following day. Then he left, taking the severed leg with him, while Naïs scrubbed the kitchen clean. The old soldier finally drifted into a deep sleep and the Blades had nothing to do but wait.

Because he knew he was of no further use to the patient and hated feeling impotent, Marciac washed, changed his clothes, and, after hastily ridding himself of the garments encrusted with Ballardieu's blood, left the Hôtel de l'Épervier while trying to persuade himself that he wasn't running away.

Besides, didn't he have other business to settle?

Exhausted but incapable of resting, he followed rue Sainte-Marguerite which ran some distance, then rue des Boucheries in the same direction, crossed through the old city wall by means of the Saint-Germain gate and ended up in the neighbourhood of rue de la Harpe. On rue Mignon, he found a taproom that was ideally located for his purposes. He stopped there, ordered a glass of *eau-de-vie* and, leaning on the counter, sipped while he kept watch on the house where Gabrielle told him the party had taken place, during which the young and pretty Manon had disappeared.

It was a big bourgeois dwelling with a solid-looking gate and a courtyard separating it from the street. Its owner was a rich and powerful man who led a discreet life. He was named Cousty, was a widower and for a long time had been the most feared judge sitting at Le Châtelet. He no longer presided there, but he was still very influential. Rumour had it that he was also mean and greedy. As proof of that, he only retained one old lackey in his service, and he beat him often.

Having finished his glass, Marciac suffered from a slight dizziness. Another man in his position would have recalled that he had not eaten since the previous day and taken remedy. Another man would have told himself that he needed to sleep and have gone home. But Marciac was Marciac, so he had another *eau-de-vie* while devising a plan. A voice inside him told him that his plan was most certainly a bad idea, but it was a voice that the Gascon seldom listened to, so that life would continue to offer him surprises. Alcohol, moreover, had a tendency to silence it.

Marciac drained a third glass and left to carry out a few errands in the neighbourhood.

Firstly, to find a pair of thick gloves.

And secondly, to buy some lamp oil.

Agnès finally fell asleep at Ballardieu's bedside.

When she reopened her eyes and straightened up in her armchair, night was falling, a candle was burning in the chamber, and the old soldier was gazing at her, his head turned to the side on his pillow.

His face was livid, with drawn features and eyes surrounded by black circles, but he smiled at her tenderly.

'Hello, girl,' he murmured in a voice still hoarse from his screams when the saw had bitten into the bone. 'So, we meet again . . .'

'You . . . You're awake? For how long?'

'No, don't fuss . . . You were sleeping so soundly I didn't have the heart to disturb you . . . And then, everything was . . . Everything was so peaceful . . .'

Agnès stared at him, incredulous, not knowing what to say,

her eyes both bright with joy and drowning in tears. Ballardieu was talking to her. Ballardieu wasn't dead. Ballardieu was there and always would be, exactly as he used to tell her when she was a small child, to reassure her.

'How is it,' he asked, 'that I'm feeling no pain?'

'You're full of golden henbane liqueur.'

'Henbane, hmm? . . . My word, it . . . it works wonders.'

'Leprat brought it. No doubt he takes it himself to soothe the pain of his ranse . . .'

'I'll need to . . . thank him.'

'I'll fetch him!' said the young and fiery baronne, jumping up. 'And the others! They're downstairs, waiting for—'

In her enthusiasm, she was almost at the door when Ballardieu stopped her.

'No, girl . . . No . . .' He raised a hand in her direction, but let it fall back on the sheet limply. 'Later, perhaps . . .'

Agnès understood and, feeling a little embarrassed, returned to his bedside.

However, instead of sitting in the armchair, she carefully sat on the bed by Ballardieu and took hold of his hand.

'I . . . I'm sorry,' she confessed, lowering her eyes.

'About this old leg?' he retorted, forcing a note of gaiety into his voice. But as Agnès would not smile, he became grave again. 'I have to believe Providence wanted me to finish my life on one leg rather than two. Of course, this is going to keep me out of some adventures, but that's not such a bad thing. I'm getting old, after all. Perhaps it's time I retired . . .'

'You?'

'Look at me, Agnès. What have I become?'

'An old beast who I love and who is still a long way from making his last trip to the stable . . .'

Moved by her words, Ballardieu smiled.

'Listen to me . . . I was a soldier, a man of the sword in your father's service. I imagined I would find glory, or perhaps fortune, on the fields of battle. Or perhaps none of that. Perhaps death. But I never imagined a different destiny from that of other warriors and hunters of fortune . . . And then your father entrusted you to my care. My life changed from the moment I laid eyes on you, but I didn't understand that to begin with, far from it. I even denied the obvious, when time passed and I became attached to you. And do you know when I finally understood?'

'No.'

'You were still very small. Perhaps four or five years old. You . . . You weren't even as tall as my sword.' Ballardieu's gaze became lost for a moment in the past. 'To make matters short . . . one day you disappeared. You simply disappeared . . . Of course, we searched for you. In the manor, first of all. Then all around, in the domain, and then even farther afield. You were not to be found, no matter how loudly we called. We beat the woodland. We sounded the pond and dragged the riverbed. All in vain. And I thought I was going to die. I stopped eating, and sleeping. And each time someone came by with news, I was torn between the hope that you were safe and the terror that they had discovered your little body lying lifeless somewhere . . . It was . . . It was a veritable torture . . . But I needed that torture to understand . . . or rather to admit to myself, that I loved you like the flesh of my flesh, and that my destiny was to protect you always.' Agnès, her eyes brimming with tears, was unable to wrench her gaze away from his. 'What I'm trying to tell you, girl . . . What I'm trying to tell you is that, sometimes, it takes us time to recognise the path that has been traced for us, and that only delays the inevitable . . . We all have a destiny, don't you see? A destiny that might be very different from the one we believe in or the one we want for ourselves. For some people, that destiny is modest. But for others, like you, it's . . . something immense . . .'

Now pensive, Agnès nodded slowly but turned her eyes away and did not answer.

'I think . . . I think I'm going to sleep for a while,' said the old soldier in a weak voice. 'You should do the same.'

The young woman stood up.

'But not in that armchair,' Ballardieu added. 'Not here . . . Go and rest in your bed.'

'The surgeon said we should watch over you.'

'Your chamber isn't far, Agnès.'

She hesitated, and then said:

'All right. But—'

'But what?'

'But I'm here, aren't I? How did your story end?'

Ballardieu managed a weary smile.

'Oh . . . you reappeared three days later, as suddenly as you had vanished. Marion found you: you were playing in the garden as if it were the most natural thing in the world. You were wearing the same clothes. You were clean and in good health. You were just a little thirsty, and we never found out—'

'I don't remember any of that.'

'Of course not. I told you: you were very little. A strange adventure, don't you think? And yet after that, you're surprised that I'm afraid to let you out of my sight . . .'

'Get some rest, you old beast.'

La Fargue dined alone in the garden.

Sitting at the table beneath the chestnut tree, he turned his back to the mansion and chewed without tasting his food, his gaze lost in the shadows. He was not hungry, but he knew that an empty sack could not stand upright. The darkness surrounding him was profound, barely relieved by the trembling flicker of the candle placed on the old table, which had attracted the attention of a moth.

Finally the captain realised he had company. He did not react with alarm and, still looking straight ahead, asked:

'How long have you been here?'

'Not long,' replied Saint-Lucq.

La Fargue knew that if he had become aware of the other's presence, it was because the half-blood wanted him to. Saint-Lucq, in more ways than one, belonged to the night.

'Are you spying on me?'

'I'm observing you. Who are the Guardians, captain?'

La Fargue became perfectly still, then pushed his plate away.

'I like to see who I'm talking to.'

'Very well.'

Without a sound, the half-blood dressed in black seemed to appear out of thin air. As was often the case, it was the scarlet disks of his spectacles, reflecting the light, that became visible first.

Saint-Lucq sat at the table, facing the old gentleman.

'Who are the Guardians, captain?'

'If you're asking me that question, you already know the answer.'

'I'm doing you a favour, captain.'

'A favour? You?'

'That of giving you a chance to explain yourself.'

'And since when do I answer to you?'

'Since I have served and fought and killed under your orders. Who are the Guardians?'

'They are one of the reasons why the human race has not been decimated, or enslaved, by the dragons. They operate in the shadows . . . and they watch over us. They are dragons, but they know that their time and that of their race, in this world, is drawing to a close. They believe they have no solution other than to live in accord with humans or hidden amongst them.'

'And you serve them.'

'Yes.'

'Since when?'

'Do you really not know? Valombre sent me a message about your meeting. I've been waiting for you, Saint-Lucq.'

'Since when?'

'It started five years ago. After La Rochelle.'

'Does the cardinal know?'

'He knows. He's always known. They often conceal their true intentions, but the Guardians are not the enemies of France. On the contrary, without them, the Chatelaines would not exist. You can't imagine the services they have rendered us in the past.'

'That doesn't matter to me. I want to know who I serve. I want to know who I kill for and who I might be killed for.'

Saint-Lucq stood up and walked away.

Motionless, La Fargue watched him disappear into the night, and then lowered his eyes to the table and the steel signet ring the half-blood had left there.

The Gentleman and the Enchantress returned home in the darkest hours of the night.

Having burned their dead in the ruins of Bois-Noir, they rode back to Paris at a slow walk, almost without speaking, followed by Keress Karn and the few armed dracs who had survived the Blades' attack. The Hôtel des Arcanes was brightly lit when they arrived. Surprised, they dismounted in the courtyard and exchanged puzzled, worried glances when they heard the sound of laughter coming from the garden.

They found the Demoiselle and the Heresiarch having supper together by torchlight.

The judge Cousty woke with a start when a hand gloved in thick leather was clapped over his mouth. Immediately, the man pinning him down poured a liquid on his face. It had an odour he recognised: naphta. He struggled as the lamp oil ran into his eyes and over his temples, drenching his hair and soaking his pillow. He inhaled a little of it, gagged, and almost vomited. But the hand stifling his cries was firm and the man continued to press down with all his weight. Frightened, Cousty thrashed in vain while the naphta continued to run.

When the goatskin flask was empty, Marciac threw it into a corner of the chamber and waited for the judge to calm down and submit to him. Only then did he relax his hold slightly, in order to signify to his victim that he was making the right decision. Cousty finally became still, with the sheets twisted around his naked legs. He rolled his immense, fearful eyes. His gasping breath lifted his bony chest and made greasy bubbles form at his nostrils. He squinted, trying to make out the Gascon's face in the light of the sole candle placed on a table beside the bed. He was certain he had extinguished that candle before going to sleep, as he did every night.

'I took care of your servant. So you and I are on our own, in effect. You can call out, but it will serve no purpose except to make me angry, because I hate it when people yell. Do you want me to be angry?'

The judge shook his head. The Gascon's breath stank of

alcohol and his eyes had that disturbed gleam that comes with drunkenness. Yet he seemed to be in control of himself, which made the situation even more worrying.

'That's just as well. Because otherwise, I will take that candle over there and bring the flame close to your face and hair that I've just soaked in naphta. And you know what will happen then, don't you?'

Cousty nodded slowly, convinced that he was at the mercy of a dangerous madman. Unable to move his head, his eyes strained toward the side when Marciac reached out with his free hand to seize the candlestick and brought it nearer. The judge's panic-stricken gaze tracked the movements of the flame.

'Now,' continued the Gascon, 'I am going to take my hand from your mouth. Will you be good?'

Still unable to tear his eyes away from the flame, the judge nodded. Then he breathed more freely, in both the literal and figurative sense, as Marciac withdrew his hand and moved the candle to a slightly safer distance.

The judge then recognised the Gascon's face in the light.

'I . . . I know you,' he said, out of sheer surprise.

Marciac looked at him with an extremely perplexed air.

'Firstly,' he replied, 'I strongly doubt that. Secondly, if it is true, telling me so would be an act of the greatest stupidity, don't you think? Because it might incite me to do you a very evil turn.' Cousty stayed silent. 'So let us return to the matter at hand. I am going to ask you questions and you will answer them. At the first refusal or the first lie, I will set fire to your head as if it were a big packet of tow. Have you understood me?'

Thoroughly frightened, the judge promised and he kept his word.

So much so that only few instants later, Marciac was pushing him out of the chamber and forcing him down the stairs.

'And now?' the Gascon demanded when they reached the bottom of the steps.

Cousty pointed to a recess in the entry hall, just beneath the stairs. Marciac brought him there and, without letting go, watched him press two stones at the same time on the bare wall.

A secret passage opened with a click.

'Who knows of this place?'

'No one.'

'No one. Really? Not even your lackey?'

The judge saw the slap to the back of his skull coming, but could do nothing to avoid it.

'My . . . My brothers!' he hastened to say. 'My brother acolytes know!'

'Your . . . ?' The Gascon considered the trembling, scrawny sixty-year-old man he held by the collar. Words failed him, which was rare. 'No, nothing. You go first.'

Steps spiralled downward. They descended them in the dark, before the judge opened the door to a vaulted chamber dimly lit by red solaire stones. Bare flagstones covered the floor. On the walls hung black drapes decorated with golden draconic runes, one of which was often repeated. Marciac recognised it because it featured on the banners flying over the ruins where, two months previously, the vicomtesse de Malicorne had summoned her followers to a grandiose ceremony which would have led, without the Blades' intervention, to the founding of the Black Claw's first lodge in France. It was the rune of the secret society.

Marciac shoved Cousty again, roughly. The judge tripped forward, fell down, and decided to remain on the floor. The Gascon examined the contents of the chamber slowly and carefully: the black candles waiting to be lit on their large candelabra, the diverse ritual objects, the fat grimoire on a lectern, the altar covered with a scarlet cloth.

Unmasked and vanquished, the vicomtesse de Malicorne had disappeared. More or less willing and zealous servants of the Black Claw, the supporters she had converted had been for the most part either arrested or dispersed. But it was thought that some had managed to slip through the net and that they continued to practise their 'religion', which was nothing other than a perverse cult obsessed with black draconic magic.

Cousty was evidently one of them.

'Where?' Marciac asked brusquely. 'Where is she?'

From the floor, the judge pointed a shaking finger towards the altar.

The Gascon frowned, then understood and hurried forward. He lifted up the cloth covering the altar, revealing a black wrought iron box whose sides were pierced with a few triangular holes. The box had a door with a latch. Marciac crouched down to open it and was struck by the sharp scent of urine before he made out the form of Manon, naked and trembling, her cheeks stained with tears and dirt, huddled at the bottom.

He reached out a hand to her.

'It's me, Manon. It's me. Marciac.'

Marciac had to use tender words and careful gestures to coax her out. Manon had recognised him, but the remnants of the terror provoked by everything she had been subjected to in this room, which had almost driven her mad, still gripped her and prevented her from trusting him. Finally, she rushed into the Gascon's arms and clung to him, bursting into sobs. He wanted to comfort her, but hesitated out of fear that the touch of male hands had become odious to her. He finally stretched out an arm to grab the altar cloth and wrapped it around her.

She let him.

'You,' Marciac said to Cousty over the young woman's shoulder. 'Into the box.'

Still kneeling on the floor, the judge took on a worried and incredulous expression.

'What? But . . .'

'Into that box. Now.'

'But I—'

'Don't make me force you in there.'

The Gascon's gaze was terrifying.

Defeated, humiliated, the judge obeyed and crawled into the wrought iron box on all fours. Marciac kicked the door closed and allowed the latch to fall into place of its own accord. Then he lifted Manon and carried her as one might carry a child, the young girl putting her arms around his neck and, soothed, resting her head against his chest.

In his cubby-hole, Cousty placed an eye against an air hole.

And seeing the Gascon leaving, he called out in a miserable voice:

'When will you come back to free me?'

'Did I say I was ever coming back?' retorted Marciac without turning round.

'But . . . But you must! My man doesn't know about this place! No one does! They can't even find the entrance!'

'And I imagine that you've made sure that no one can hear any screaming that goes on here, haven't you?'

'Mercy! You must come back! I'll . . . I'll die in here!'

'What a shame.'

Marciac continued to walk away at a slow but resolute pace.

'I KNOW WHO YOU ARE!' the judge shouted. 'I KNOW!'

'That doesn't worry me any more now than it did before . . .'

'I REMEMBER!' added Cousty in desperation. 'YOU WERE THERE, THAT NIGHT! YOU WERE WITH THOSE ONES WHO ATTACKED US, WHO STOPPED THE VICOMTESSE'S CEREMONY! I . . . I SAW YOU!'

Manon in his arms, the Gascon arrived at the small staircase.

'THE ENERGY OF THE DRAGON WAS DISPERSING! EVERYONE WANTED TO FLEE AND I WAS RUNNING TOWARD THE STABLE WHEN . . . IT WAS YOU!'

'So?'

'LET ME LIVE AND I'LL HELP YOU! I'LL TELL YOU EVERYTHING I KNOW ABOUT THE BLACK CLAW! I'LL TELL YOU EVERYTHING ABOUT ITS SECRET SUPPORTERS! EVERYTHING I KNOW ABOUT LA MALICORNE!'

His curiosity aroused, Marciac halted.

'La Malicorne? She disappeared without a trace . . . Goodbye, Cousty.'

'SHE HAS RETURNED! LA MALICORNE! SHE WANTS US TO CALL HER THE DEMOISELLE, BUT IT'S HER! LA MALICORNE HAS RETURNED!'

The judge believed all was lost and his voice broke down in sobs.

But Marciac was thinking.

4

Agnès had barely found the strength to remove her boots before she fell asleep. So she woke fully dressed and lying sideways on her bed. The first rays of the morning sun came in through the open window. Birds twittered and Paris was beginning to stir. Life started early in summer. It was only just past six o'clock.

The young baronne de Vaudreuil got up and stretched. Her sleep had been deep but was still haunted, as she had dreamed again of the great black dragon with a sparkling jewel upon its brow, and once again seen Paris disappear in the flames and the cries.

Worried, she leaned at her window. She closed her eyes.

Forced herself to breathe calmly.

The Hôtel de l'Épervier was waking, peacefully, along with the rest of the great city and its faubourgs.

André would soon be opening the stable doors, which always scraped at the end of their path before they touched the wall. Clip-clopping along, his wooden leg striking the courtyard paving stones, master Guibot would come out in his turn to open the gates for the first suppliers. The sound of Naïs' pretty voice could already be heard rising up the staircase: the timid servant hummed in the mornings when she thought no one was listening. La Fargue would soon be up too. It was also the hour when Marciac sometimes came home, when he had every chance – before, that is – of running into Almades who, having finished his morning exercises, would be performing his ablutions outside, barefoot and bare-chested, whatever the season. Laincourt was no doubt reading and God only knows what Saint-Lucq was doing.

And Ballardieu?

Ballardieu had just died in his sleep.

His exhausted heart had finally ceased to beat.

IV

The Primordial

Ballardieu had to be buried the day after his death. The heat prohibited any delay so his funeral was the simplest of ceremonies. It took place at a chapel, in the morning, after which the Blades carried the body to the cemetery under a dazzling sky and a white gold sun. They proceeded at a slow, steady pace, wearing their weapons, La Fargue and Laincourt on the right-hand side of the coffin, Leprat and Marciac on the left.

Agnès de Vaudreuil followed them, wearing black with scarlet gloves, a plume-less felt hat, boots, and her sword by her side. Guibot limped along heavily behind her. Next came Naïs, who sobbed and clutched a small casket against her, and André, who held the young woman by the waist and the elbow to help her walk. Even with the priest and the two choirboys leading the way, they did not make a large group. And those who moved out of the way for this meagre procession, those who watched it pass, those who doffed their hats and crossed themselves before resuming their lives without further disruption, would never know what kind of man Ballardieu had been.

After the priest left, La Fargue, Agnès, and the others gathered in the quiet of the cemetery, beneath the bored gaze of the gravediggers who waited in the shade and took turns drinking from the same bottle. All that remained was to lay the body to rest, which the Blades had decided to take charge of personally. When the moment came, Leprat, Laincourt, and Marciac watched for the sign from their captain, upon which all four set to work in silence. But as they slowly let the ropes slide and the coffin descended into the freshly dug grave, fragile Naïs broke down in sobs again. She gave a hoarse lament and, all strength deserting her, she sank to her knees and dropped her casket, which opened when it struck the ground. André helped the young servant to rise, drew her aside from the others, and did his best to comfort her. Guibot hurried to pick up the items scattered over the ground.

Naïs had felt more than friendship for Ballardieu.

At first intimidated by him, she had then been touched by the kindness and the awkwardness of this old soldier whose heart of gold could be discerned behind the cracks in his rough exterior. She had been drawn to him for precisely that reason, because he would be clumsy perhaps, but also tender and thoughtful. One night she had joined him in his chamber, slipping into his bed before taking off her shirt and snuggling up naked against him. At first, he hadn't known what to do. And since he didn't dare try anything, she had been forced to make the first move, murmuring in his ear:

'You'll be gentle, won't you?'

He was her first.

Naïs returned the following night and other nights thereafter. She offered herself to him and made love to him without saying a word, then fell asleep trustingly in his arms. She was always gone in the morning. He didn't understand it. But he respected her silence and kept the secret, although he wondered about it. Troubled, sometimes he felt guilty at the idea that he was taking advantage of her, of her youth and innocence. Did she love him? If so, she was making a mistake and would soon realise it. And what should he do in the meantime? He'd started to make her little gifts, things she would find in her chamber or on her pillow. It might be a comb, a ribbon, a brooch, or a small mirror that he had bought or won on the Pont Neuf, and usually poorly chosen because he always thought of Naïs as a child.

Nevertheless she cherished these few treasures that Guibot quickly gathered up in the cemetery and returned to her. She took the precious casket and pressed it tightly to her bosom again. Broken, docile, she let Guibot and André take her back to the Hôtel de l'Épervier.

Agnès had not even blinked when Naïs collapsed.

She stood up straight, her features pale and drawn, with dark circles under her eyes and pinched lips. She had not shed a tear or uttered more than three words since Ballardieu's passing. She had not slept, either. She was alone, prisoner of a pain that had ripped her soul from her body and slowly tore up her insides. Her gestures were slow and her gaze was distant. Everything seemed faraway, insignificant. The world no longer had colours or flavour for her. Nothing affected her except for her sense of emptiness and abandonment, except for the inner abyss on the verge of which her reason tottered.

The coffin rested inside the grave and Blades slowly backed away from it.

La Fargue saw that the gravediggers were growing impatient, indifferent to the suffering of mourners who all seemed the same to them. He waited, approached Agnès, and whispered to her:

'It's time.'

And when she did not respond, he insisted:

'It's time to go, Agnès.'

'You go,' she said in a rasping voice. 'I'm staying here.'

'These men need to do their job, Agnès. They're going—'

'I know what they're going to do!' the young baronne snapped. 'Let them go ahead, I'm not stopping them. But I'm staying here for a while longer.'

Embarrassed, La Fargue looked at the waiting gravediggers, with clogs on their feet and spades resting on their shoulders. He hesitated, then signalled to them to start work. But he remained at Agnès' side and took her arm. Consumed by an icy flame, she trembled and closed her eyes as she heard the first spadeful of earth strike the coffin lid.

When they returned from the cemetery, Agnès, still refusing to speak, immediately went upstairs to her room. Knowing she did not want to be comforted by anyone, the others went to the fencing room, where Guibot brought them wine.

'We had to put the girl to bed,' he said as he served La Fargue.

The Blades' captain nodded vaguely and waited for the

concierge to finish filling their glasses. Once Guibot left, he raised his.

'To Ballardieu,' he said.

'To Ballardieu,' repeated Leprat, Marciac, and Laincourt in chorus.

They clinked their glasses together and then La Fargue took a bottle with him out to the garden. Through the window, the others saw him sit at the table beneath the chestnut tree.

He, too, wanted to be alone.

Marciac sighed as he sprawled in an armchair, his feet crossed upon a stool. Laincourt also sat down, removed his hat and, leaning forward, hands upon his knees, he massaged his aching temples with his fingertips. Leprat remained propped against the mantelpiece of the fireplace.

A silence set in.

'I thought that Saint-Lucq would come,' Laincourt said at last.

'It's been three days since I last saw him,' replied the Gascon.

'If he'd been with us at Bois-Noir . . .'

' . . . Ballardieu might still be alive.'

'He was here the night when Ballardieu passed away,' Leprat told him. 'Guibot saw him talking to La Fargue in the garden.'

'And?'

'I don't know. The captain did not want to talk to me about their conversation.'

'Is Saint-Lucq still one of the Blades?' asked Laincourt with concern in his voice.

'The Blades!' snorted the Gascon. 'Or what's left of them . . .'

That earned him a black look from Leprat.

'What?' he said, raising his voice. 'You've put your cape back on, Saint-Lucq is nobody-knows-where with no sign of returning, and Almades and Ballardieu are dead. Count carefully: that just leaves Laincourt and me.'

'And Agnès,' corrected the musketeer.

'Agnès?' exclaimed Marciac, standing up. 'Do you know her then so little?' He pointed a finger at the ceiling. 'Do you know what she's doing up there, at this very moment? She's packing her bags!'

'You don't—'

The Gascon spread his arms and turned in a circle, as if calling on the whole world to be his witness.

'And who could blame her?' he asked. 'Don't tell me that you don't think that re-forming the Blades was a mistake.' And when Leprat didn't reply, he added bitterly: 'Gabrielle was right and I should have listened to her. Wasn't our first death enough? Did we have to bury Almades and Ballardieu, after Bretteville?'

'Marciac,' said Laincourt.

Marciac fell silent, turning round.

And saw Agnès.

'I'm leaving,' she announced. 'I . . . I won't be coming back.'

She turned on her heel and walked away.

'Agnès!' called Leprat, after a pause.

'Let her,' La Fargue said to him in a toneless voice. He stood in the doorway to the garden. 'Let her leave.'

The musketeer hesitated, cursed, and went after Agnès anyway.

He joined her in the courtyard, where she was already mounting her horse.

'Agnès!'

She looked at him patiently, both hands together on the pommel of her saddle.

But he couldn't find anything to say to her:

'Agnès, I . . .'

She gave him a sad, tender smile.

'Goodbye, Antoine. Take care of Nicolas, will you? And tell the captain that I don't blame him for anything.'

Then she turned her mount around, urged it forward slightly with her heels, and rode away at a slow jog.

Leprat stood alone in the courtyard for a moment, underneath the blazing sun. Finally, when he decided to go back inside, he passed La Fargue coming down the steps with a determined air.

'Where are you going, captain?'

The old gentleman did not stop.

'To speak with La Donna,' he replied. 'This comedy of secrets has lasted long enough.'

'But she's being held under guard at the Palais-Cardinal for her safety!' Leprat warned him as La Fargue crossed the courtyard. 'They won't let you anywhere near her!'

'Then they will have to kill me,' said the captain, without turning or slowing down.

In the park at the Palais-Cardinal, Alessandra was reading near the fountain. She was sitting in the shade, on a bench, and seemed completely oblivious to the presence of ten of the Cardinal's Guards who, stationed all around the park with rapiers at their sides and short muskets over the shoulders, watched over her. Charybdis and Scylla, her twin dragonnets, were drowsing to either side of the ravishing spy. They lifted their heads and gazed in the same direction moments before the first sounds of an argument attracted her attention.

On one of the garden paths, two sentries in red capes had stopped La Fargue. The discussion between them grew heated. Although the Blades' captain had privileged access to the Palais-Cardinal, in this case His Eminence's instructions had been quite explicit: no one was to see La Donna, not without an express order signed by the cardinal himself. But La Fargue would not hear of it. The altercation was starting to become a scuffle.

Alessandra rose with the intention of intervening before things degenerated:

'Messieurs!'

But the guards held her back and, deaf to her protests, they were quick to remove her from the possible threat, not handling her too gently in the process, which upset her dragonnets.

'Scylla! Charybdis! Be still!' La Donna ordered her small domestic reptiles.

They immediately obeyed her, ceasing to growl and flutter about as La Fargue was knocked out by the butt of a musket.

*

246

It did not take La Fargue long to come round, with a terrible headache.

He was lying on a bench, with La Donna applying a damp cloth to his brow.

'That was very stupid of you,' she said, when she saw that he had regained consciousness.

'I needed to speak with you.'

'All the same.'

'I achieved my goal, didn't I?'

'Because you planned to get your skull cracked open in order to see me?' she asked ironically.

La Fargue sat up and pressed the cool cloth to the back of his head.

'No,' he admitted reluctantly.

'They could have killed you.'

'Bah!' He looked around the elegant antechamber in which he found himself. 'Where are we?'

'We're still at the Palais-Cardinal,' replied the beautiful spy as she poured two glasses of white wine. 'In the chambers where I am staying . . . There was some talk of throwing you into a cell, but I prevailed upon monsieur de Neuvelle to entrust you to my custody instead, while they decide your fate. Nevertheless, you are officially under arrest on the grounds of attempting to stun one guard using the head of another. That was very bad behaviour.'

'Neuvelle?' enquired La Fargue, grimacing painfully.

'He is the young ensign commanding the detachment that is . . . that is holding me.'

'That is *protecting* you.'

'Yes. That, too.'

Alessandra returned to sit next to La Fargue and handed him a glass. Feeling suddenly tired, the old captain removed the damp cloth from his head, spread it across his thigh, took the glass, and thanked her.

'Really very stupid,' said La Donna by way of a toast.

They drank a sip of white wine together and then fell silent for a moment. Birdsong came through the open window, from the feathered creatures perched in the trees out in the park.

'We buried Ballardieu this morning,' La Fargue said, watching the yellow reflections of wine in the cut glass.

'I . . . I didn't know.'

'Less than three weeks after Almades . . .'

'I'm sorry. Sincerely.'

'They were good, brave men. Neither of them deserved to die as they did . . . And another may fall tomorrow. It could be Laincourt, Marciac, or Leprat. It could be me . . . Don't you think we've earned a few answers?' he concluded, locking his gaze on La Donna's.

Affected by his argument, she rose and went to the window.

Then she returned to La Fargue, stared at him a few seconds, and nodded curtly.

'Thank you, madame,' said the captain of the Blades, rising in his turn. 'Let's start with you, shall we? The Guardians told me you serve them, just as I do.'

'That's true.'

'But you also serve the Pope.'

'Just as you also serve the cardinal. However, I work on occasion for my own benefit, unlike you. But one needs to earn a living, doesn't one?'

La Fargue did not reply to that.

'If I remember correctly,' he continued, 'you once gave me a hint of your allegiance to the Seven . . .'

'That evening at La Renardière, yes. Before everything started to move so quickly.'

'You mean: before you almost got me killed, and my men along with me, at the hands of the dracs pursuing you.'

'I was desperate, captain. I absolutely needed someone to rid me of those dracs and, above all, their sorcerer. I used you, to be sure. But it was for the common good, believe me. At the time I had information that urgently needed to be transmitted to the Pope and the Guardians.' Looking nervous, Alessandra drained her glass. She gave herself time to recover her calm. 'Besides, I don't think I was totally ungrateful for your assistance. Without me, would you have captured the Alchemist?'

'Precisely! So who was the Alchemist, exactly? And what goal was he pursuing? I no longer believe his aim was simply to abduct the queen. I also no longer believe he was acting alone.'

The beautiful Italian lady looked at La Fargue for a long moment, during which she reflected. Then, her decision made, she asked:

'What do you know of the Arcana, captain?'

Caught unprepared, he had no reply. So she led him into the adjoining room.

'Come.'

La Fargue followed Alessandra into her chamber.

There was a large cage next to the four-poster bed. The dragonnets inside stirred as soon as they saw their mistress enter, but she did not pay them the least attention. Consequently, Charybdis and Scylla watched the Blades' captain with a jealous eye.

'Look,' said La Donna, pointing at a small round table.

There were a number of illustrated tarot cards on it, next to a quill and an inkwell. Most of the cards were annotated, covered in strange inscriptions, and sometimes they were even crossed out. La Fargue leaned forward to look at them. They were splendid and bore evocative names, but he did not recognise any of them.

'These twenty-two cards form the major arcana of a tarot deck,' explained Alessandra. 'This one is a draconic tarot, however.'

The captain's gaze continued to run over the cards.

The Weaver, he read. *The Gentleman Lover, the Protectress, the Blind Illuminator, the Astrologer* . . .

'This tarot is employed in sorcery.'

. . . *the Crowned Heresiarch, the Architect, the Forgetful Thief* . . .

'It is primarily used for divination, of course. But there is more to it than that.'

. . . *the Master-at-Arms, the Demoiselle in the Tower, the Assassin, the Immobile Pilgrim* . . .

'But there are other reasons why these arcana cards interest us. Or these "blades", as they are still sometimes called.'

. . . *the Alchemist of the Shadows!*

'What does this mean?' asked La Fargue, placing his index finger on this last card.

'The Arcana are a lodge within the Black Claw,' explained La Donna. 'All of them are dragons and each member takes his *nom de guerre* from one of the major arcanum of the draconic tarot. The Alchemist was one of them, as was the dragon who abducted me and whom you fought to rescue me.'

'And which one was he?'

'The Illuminator.'

'So, he was this one,' said the captain, pointing to the card of the Blind Illuminator on the table.

He noticed that it was crossed out.

'Yes,' replied Alessandra as La Fargue examined the spread cards again.

'If there are twenty-two major arcana, does that mean that—'

'—that the Arcana lodge has that many members? I think so. But truth be told, I don't really know. And even if there were only ten of them . . .'

'But who are they, exactly?'

'Most of them are last-born dragons. They are ambitious, capable, prudent, determined and quite formidable. They are a force apart from the other lodges of the Black Claw. I suppose they are accountable to the Grand Lodge, but they enjoy a great deal of freedom. In fact, I think they only really obey themselves.'

'That does not sound like the way the Black Claw usually operates.'

'That's true. But the Arcana are most likely protected by their successes.'

'What successes?'

'I know that the rich and powerful always take the credit. Nevertheless, it would seem that the Arcana have been involved to a greater or lesser extent in the worst tragedies and reverses France has suffered recently.'

'Such as the failure of the siege of La Rochelle,' said La Fargue bitterly.

'Yes. Or the assassination of King Henri.'

Flabbergasted, the old captain stared at La Donna. The notion that she might be jesting crossed his mind, but the beautiful Alessandra's face remained as if carved in marble.

'The Arcana are in great danger,' announced the Heresiarch turning away from the window in the Swords study. 'The old masters of the Black Claw, who have never loved us much, are no longer willing to tolerate us. Our enemies are strong and numerous. They seek to bring about our downfall within the next month . . .'

As the Gentleman said nothing in reply, he added:

'The Council of the Grand Lodge will make a decision on this soon, but through my spies I know the matter is already settled. Our lodge will be dissolved. And if we do not submit to their ruling we will be condemned and hunted down without hope of clemency.'

Dressed as a gentleman with taste but without ostentation, the master of the Arcana looked about fifty years in age. His features were bony and severe, with prominent cheekbones, hollow cheeks, and a thin straight nose. He had a perfectly trimmed moustache and goatee. And he exuded an air of confidence and authority.

'Is it really that serious?' asked the Gentleman.

'Yes,' affirmed the Heresiarch gravely.

'The Arcana have already survived a number of cabals. Why can't we foil this one?'

'We were united then. Today, the Protectress and the Master-at-Arms plot against me and divide us. Have they not tried to approach you?'

'No.'

'Really? Perhaps the Enchantress, then?'

'Do you doubt our loyalty, Heresiarch?' the Gentleman asked coldly, feeling anger rise within him.

The two dragons stared at each other.

Narrowing his eyes, the Heresiarch scrutinised the Gentleman, while the latter seemed to challenge him to elaborate on his suspicions. Neither of them blinked, and finally the Heresiarch said:

'No, no, of course not . . . But I know that the Protectress was meeting secretly with the Alchemist, and that she had won him over to her cause.'

'I doubt that very much. The Alchemist was loyal to you—'

The master of the Arcana cut him short with a gesture of annoyance, much as one would wave away a buzzing insect . . .

The Gentleman fell silent and waited. The Heresiarch's unexpected arrival had taken him by surprise and, since then, the behaviour of the leader of the Arcana had frequently been disconcerting. He was suspicious, sometimes irritable, and alternated between sudden silences and brusque manifestations of arrogance. At first, the Gentleman had only wished to see the signs of a great fatigue. Now he was beginning to revise his opinion, suspecting something far more serious. The Enchantress, on the other hand, had immediately evoked the image of a house where just a few cracks in the façade presage an imminent collapse.

The Heresiarch took down a rapier that was prominently displayed, examined it, and said:

'Splendid. Made in Toledo, wasn't it?'

'Yes.'

'The best.'

'It's the temper of Toledo blades that is so excellent,' replied the Gentleman as if by rote. 'But I prefer Bohemian blades.'

The master of the Arcana pulled a slight face and replaced the sword. He let a moment of silence pass and then said in an even voice:

'One must grant her this much, the Protectress has very ably and very patiently woven her web. That should come as no surprise, however. The cursed Gorgon has always been opposed to the Grand Design and she has long nourished the dream of deposing me and taking my place . . .'

The Gentleman nodded.

'She is in Madrid, did you know that?' continued the Heresiarch in a casual tone. 'At this very moment, the Protectress is in Madrid to court the old lizards in the Grand Lodge, trying to convince them that she is better able to lead the Arcana and that the Black Claw would have less reason to complain if—' He did not finish. 'And all of this on the pretext of saving the Arcana from an abyss I am about to push them into!' He gave a brief burst of laughter that did not fool the Gentleman. 'An abyss,' he repeated bitterly. 'But what would become of the Arcana if the Protectress led them? Hmm? What would become of them?'

The Heresiarch's gaze took on a strange fixed stare and he added almost in a whisper:

'I would almost prefer the abyss . . .'

Once again, the Gentleman kept silent.

The other dragon slowly returned from the limbo where his obsession had taken him.

'The Guardians are plotting against us,' he said. 'The Chatelaines are hunting us, the Black Claw is abandoning us, and some of our own are betraying us. There is no more time for intrigue: if we wish to live, we must take our enemies by surprise. Will you be at my side, Gentleman?'

'I will be.'

'And do you answer for the Enchantress?'

'As I do for myself.'

'Then I will have a task for you, soon.'

'And right now?'

'Right now, we must prepare our triumph. I have not renounced our Grand Design. It would have been accomplished long ago if not for these cursed Chatelaines, but I believe it is still possible to bring it to fulfilment before it is too late. And since a ruse did not work for the Alchemist, we will resort to more . . . radical methods.'

In the chambers that Alessandra occupied at the Palais-Cardinal, La Fargue tried to take stock of the beautiful Italian spy's revelations.

King Henri IV had been assassinated on 14 May 1610, the day after the coronation of Marie de Médicis as queen of France, just when he was preparing to go to war with Spain. He had been stabbed by a Catholic fanatic named Ravaillac and – even if the Black Claw had been suspected for a time – the investigation had concluded that it was the isolated act of a madman. But could it be that the Arcana had armed and guided Ravaillac's hand? Could it be that in doing so they had spared Spain from a conflict she was poorly prepared for, and all of Europe had been dreading? The queen had been notoriously opposed to this war, and it had also displeased the Pope. Upon becoming regent of France, after her husband's death, she had immediately renounced the project. In fact, negotiations had quickly resumed between the two countries, which ultimately led to marriage between the young Louis XIII and the Spanish *infanta*.

'Don't ask me for proof, captain,' said Alessandra as if she was following the thread of his thoughts. 'The Guardians only arrived at this conclusion after careful research and patient deductions. And a few extrapolations, it is true.'

'Who else knows?'

'Who else suspects the existence of the Arcana and their schemes, do you mean?'

'Yes.'

'The Guardians, first of all. The Pope and the Chatelaines. The cardinal, for a short while now.'

'And you.'

'And me. But before you reproach me for not telling you all this earlier, you should first know that my information is recent. Moreover, for everything that concerns the Arcana, I obey the Seven in every detail and they alone decide what I am permitted to reveal to anyone.'

'You just told me that cardinal has only known this for a short while.'

'It's true.'

'Did his knowledge come from the Guardians?'

'For the most part.'

'So, what made the Guardians decide to inform him? Why now, rather than yesterday or tomorrow?'

Alessandra reflected, admiring the old captain's sagacity.

'The Arcana have been devoted, for years, to an important project they call the "Grand Design". The Guardians know nothing – or at least feign to know nothing – of this Grand Design. Perhaps the Chatelaines know a little more . . . Be that

254

as it may, the Grand Design is on the point of being accomplished. My belief is that the Alchemist was working on it when you captured him. And I would add that I believe he was probably killed because of the things he could reveal about it.'

'Killed by one of his own?'

'Almost certainly.'

There was a knock on the door, the dragonnets became restless, and a servant announced monsieur de Neuvelle. The man himself soon appeared, wearing a red cape, his hat in his hand, and his fist curled around the pommel of his sword. He was a young gentleman, recently promoted to the rank of ensign, whom La Fargue did not recall ever having met.

He was not alone, however.

Rochefort, Cardinal Richelieu's henchman, accompanied him.

When Marciac arrived at *The Little Frogs*, Gabrielle and her charming lodgers were gardening. Contrary to his habit, he presented himself at the door and was led by Thibault into the coolest room in the house, where ordinarily these demoiselles waited for their messieurs. Through the window, the Gascon saw Manon trimming a rosebush, which seemed to amuse her and the others, who closely surrounded her and were laughing with her.

Informed of his visit, Gabrielle returned from the back of the garden, removing her gloves as she walked. But it was only once she had come inside that she untied the scarf holding in place the wide-brimmed hat, which protected her from the sun. The fierce summer heat had made her cheeks flush. She was slightly out of breath and a faint trace of perspiration beaded her brow. With a distracted air, she fixed the arrangement of her strawberry-blonde hair.

As soon as that was done, she embraced Marciac affectionately, and for once his hands did not wander anywhere.

He let himself fall into an armchair.

'We buried Ballardieu this morning,' he announced.

'My God, Nicolas! So soon?'

'The heat, Gabrielle. The damned heat.'

'But you should have warned me! I would have come. I . . .'

255

'It was better you stayed here, with Manon.'

Gabrielle turned towards the window and the cheerful young women who could be seen out in the garden. One of them was trying to catch a butterfly with her hat and provoking much mirth.

'How . . . How is Agnès?'

'Distraught,' Marciac said. 'Destroyed. She left the Blades.'

'I can understand that. And the others?'

The Gascon's only response was to shrug and scowl.

'And you?' insisted Gabrielle.

Marciac looked into her eyes with a pained gaze.

'Me? Me, I am weary.'

And to cut short any further expression of his feelings, he rose and went to the window.

'I have come for news of Manon,' he said.

Gabrielle joined him and, over the Gascon's shoulder, looked in same direction as he.

'She will get over her ordeal. We'll help her.'

'Good.'

'And Cousty?'

'He was taken in the middle of the night by people who do His Eminence's dirty work. We will never hear of him again.'

'So this story is over.'

'It will be when I've settled accounts with Tranchelard.'

'What do you mean?' asked Gabrielle, with the beginning of a note of alarm in her voice.

'Cousty confessed that he paid Tranchelard to look the other way, and to pretend that Manon had fled. He is as responsible as Cousty for the torment that girl was subjected to. He should pay for it.'

'No!'

Surprised, Marciac turned towards Gabrielle.

'What?'

'No, Nicolas. Enough blood has been shed!'

'Tranchelard is a scoundrel, Gabrielle. He should answer for his deeds!'

'No! There's been enough violence! . . . After you've dealt

with him, whose turn will it be next? Out of those who may want to avenge him? Mortaigne? The Grand Coësre?'

'But—'

'Promise me that you will not seek to harm Tranchelard!'

'Gab—'

'Promise, Nicolas! Promise!'

She had seized hold of Marciac and, with tears in her eyes, she gave him an imploring look so full of distress that it shamed him.

'Yes,' he hastened to assure her. 'Yes. I promise.'

'Truly?'

He nodded sincerely.

Then Gabrielle burst into tears and clung to him. In return he held her tightly in his arms, felt her trembling body, and inhaled her perfume.

'I promise,' he repeated, caressing her hair gently. 'I promise.'

'I have some money,' she whispered to him. 'And I've just bought a small estate in Touraine. We could live there happily if you wanted. Just you, and me, and the child I am carrying.'

Some sixty years old, Mère de Cernay had previously led the Sisters of Saint Georges. Supplanted by Mère de Vaussambre after a ferocious internal struggle, she was now the mother superior of a beautiful and prosperous abbey in Ile-de-France. She was living out her days peacefully there, without relinquishing, however, a certain degree of influence within the Order. She continued, in fact, to be widely respected and widely heeded. And consequently, closely watched.

The sun was setting when she joined Agnès, who was waiting for her near the ivy-covered dovecote where she had liked to retire during her novitiate with the Chatelaines. On her father's death, guardianship of the young baronne had been entrusted to a distant relative who had immediately given way to the temptation to lay hands on Agnès' inheritance by sending her off to the Sisters of Saint Georges, where an aunt and two or three cousins had already taken the veil. She had only recovered her wealth and her freedom several years later, on the eve of pronouncing her vows. But as fortuitous as her connection with the Order might have seemed at the time, this time spent with the Chatelaines would decide her destiny.

Mère de Cernay became concerned from the moment she saw Agnès wearing black. Then the young woman turned round and the mother superior saw her downcast expression and the tears flowing from her reddened eyes.

'My God, Marie-Agnès! What's wrong? What's happened?'

Sitting together beneath the ivy, Agnès and Mère de Cernay spoke.

Or rather Agnès spoke while Mère de Cernay listened and tried to comfort her. The young woman let herself open up and confided her feelings, releasing herself from the stranglehold of repressed pain. Without shame or modesty, she recounted all of her sorrows and doubts.

All of her anger, too.

A nearly full moon rose in the still bright sky, while sweet cooing drifted down from the dovecote. Torches were lit here and there in the great, peaceful abbey.

'Let us pray together,' the mother superior proposed at last, taking Agnès' hands. 'I know it may seem a feeble and ridiculous remedy, but it is often a real comfort.'

'No,' replied the young woman as she rose to her feet. 'No, I . . . I must go . . .'

'It's almost night. Where will you go?'

Agnès remained standing, hesitant and distressed, looking around as if the answers to her questions could be found under the ivy.

'You have felt the Call, haven't you?' asked Mère de Cernay.

Agnès gave a resigned sigh.

'Yes,' she confessed.

'Your mark?'

'Woken. Almost burning.'

'You know what that means . . .'

'What I have guessed is enough to frighten me.'

'You must not be afraid. No one should fear their destiny . . . It's Providence that sends you, Marie-Agnès.'

'A Providence that has killed Ballardieu so that there is nothing left to hold me in the secular world?' Agnès retorted aggressively.

The mother superior now rose in her turn.

'Come. Let's walk,' she said, taking the arm of this young woman who, even as a novice, had shown exceptional quality.

They were only a few steps away from the medicinal herb garden, whose paths they slowly paced.

'When I was the Superior General, the Chatelaines made a mistake,' revealed Mère de Cernay. 'An enormous mistake, and one for which I take full responsibility . . . Unfortunately, we discovered it too late, when there was no time to repair it. All we could do was to hide it. Since then, the Sisters of Saint Georges have done everything in their power to prevent their mistake leading to a tragedy . . .'

'What mistake, mother?'

'I can't tell you that because you are not a Chatelaine. But you should know you may be the one to undo it. The mark you bear signals a great destiny and . . .'

Agnès halted, obliging the mother superior to do the same and turn round to face her.

'No, mother. If I must take the veil, if I must pronounce my vows and become a Chatelaine, I deserve to know. I am so tired of secrets.'

Mère de Cernay gazed into her eyes and saw an unshakeable resolve there. She reflected for a moment longer, however, before saying:

'I suppose I should start at the beginning.'

'The beginning?'

'With the Arcana.'

On returning to the Hôtel de l'Épervier, La Fargue found Leprat waiting, who told him:

'Rochefort was here. He was looking for you.'

'I know. He found me at the Palais-Cardinal.'

'What did he want?'

'To inform me of our latest mission from the cardinal. Where are Laincourt and Marciac?'

'Laincourt is here. And there's Marciac coming back.'

The Gascon was indeed just arriving.

'I was with Gabrielle,' he announced as he joined the two others on the front steps. 'What's going on?'

'Let's go inside,' said La Fargue.

Shortly after, he addressed Leprat, Laincourt, and Marciac, gathered in the fencing room.

'As you know, Agnès has left. So has Saint-Lucq, who returned his signet ring to me. Only you two and myself remain. And you, Antoine, if you are willing to lend us a hand once again.'

'I am still on leave from the King's Musketeers,' said Leprat. 'As long as that lasts, you can count on me.'

Laincourt gave the musketeer a grateful nod and Marciac clapped a friendly hand on his shoulder.

'Thank you,' said La Fargue. 'But before you commit yourself to serving again, there are a few things you need to know.'

Then he sat and spoke in an even voice, his eyes sometimes lost in the distance, without any of the other three daring to interrupt this old gentleman who had never revealed his secrets to anyone before but was now making honourable amends. He told them how, five years earlier, after La Rochelle and the infamous disbanding of the Blades, the Guardians had approached him and persuaded him to join their service. He explained who they were and how they were trying to avoid a war between the human race and the dragons out of which no victor could emerge. He said they were known as the Seven because a council of seven dragons led them, but that the Guardians brought together numerous agents from both races – including La Donna – who operated in the shadows and were prepared to risk their lives for the common good. He confessed at last that when Richelieu had ordered him to re-form the Blades he had consulted the Guardians, and they had told him to reveal his secret to the cardinal alone. He had obeyed them, and now he sincerely regretted it.

'Sometimes honour lies in disobedience,' he concluded.

Silent and grim-faced, Laincourt, Marciac, and Leprat exchanged long glances. The Gascon realised he could speak for all three of them and asked:

'So? This new mission, what is it?'

'I believe that the Heresiarch is placing us in peril,' said the Gentleman in a worried tone.

From a window on the first floor of the Hôtel des Arcanes, he was watching the Heresiarch and the Demoiselle as they took advantage of the coolness of the evening to walk in the garden. Approaching him from behind, the Enchantress pressed herself against him and rested her chin on his shoulder.

'I think so, too,' she murmured.

'Sometimes he gives the impression he is losing his reason. He's obsessed with his Grand Design and he imagines that everyone is conspiring to bring about his downfall or that of the Arcana.'

'Which, for him, are one and the same thing.'

'I fear so. According to him, the Alchemist was betraying him in favour of the Protectress.'

'The Alchemist? That's nonsense.'

'Yet he believes it.'

'Do you know what that means?'

'That he distrusts everyone.'

'Everyone except the Demoiselle. But what else?'

The Gentleman nodded grimly before replying:

'That the Heresiarch may have killed the Alchemist out of personal motives and not because there was a danger he would reveal the Grand Design under torture . . . The Heresiarch may see clearly, however. Perhaps the Protectress does seek to supplant him. And perhaps the Black Claw has decided to dissolve our lodge.'

The Enchantress moved smoothly apart from the Gentleman.

'The masters of the Grand Lodge hate us due to their fear

and jealousy. I don't doubt for an instant that they might want our deaths . . . As for the Protectress, I don't know . . . She's not driven by ambition. So if she is plotting against the Heresiarch, it's because she's convinced that he's leading the Arcana to their doom . . .'

'The Heresiarch's plan is to deliver Paris to the Primordial's fury. That would help fulfil the Grand Design, but at what a price! The Protectress may also be right.'

'If the Heresiarch falls, you and I will not survive him. It is too late for us to turn away from him now.'

'So he has to succeed.'

'Or we need to find ourselves a way out while there's still time. What does he expect of us?'

The Gentleman looked away from the window.

'An emissary of the Black Claw is in Paris. The Heresiarch wants us to find him and kill him.'

'That's all?'

'Almost.'

'It's just as well. The less we have to do the better . . . And the Demoiselle?'

'He has given her full liberty to carry out her act of revenge. I don't know much more than that.'

'It doesn't matter.'

The Gentleman abruptly seized the Enchantress by the waist and pulled her against him.

'What do you have in mind?' he asked.

'I think we need to give the Heresiarch reasons to hope for a success. Besides, a burning city makes such a magnificent spectacle . . .'

Cardinal Richelieu was praying in the dim light of the chapel at the Château de Saint-Germain. He was alone, or at least he believed he was, until he sensed someone behind him. The exits were all guarded and no one should have been able to enter unannounced. Even so, he was not alarmed: he had been expecting the one person who was capable of eluding any security measures he might surround himself with.

Saint-Lucq was deliberately making his presence known.

He waited.

'If you were an assassin I'd be dead, wouldn't I?' asked Richelieu, rising from his prie-dieu after a last sign of the cross in the direction of the altar.

'I *am* an assassin, monseigneur.'

The cardinal turned towards the impassive half-blood and stared at him a long while.

'It has been brought to my attention that you have left Captain La Fargue's Blades,' he said. 'Is it true?'

'Yes, monseigneur. For reasons that are mine alone.'

'Those reasons matter very little to me. Do you wish to leave my service?'

'No.'

'That's fortunate, because I have great need of your talents.'

Returning to Paris in the morning, Agnès thought of paying a last visit to the Hôtel de l'Épervier, to make a proper farewell to La Fargue and the others. But she renounced this idea, afraid it would weaken her resolve, and crossed the Seine via Pont Neuf, remembering that it had been Ballardieu's favourite place in all the capital. She slowly crossed the sinister Place de Grève, made her way up the long rue du Temple and rode through the fortified gate of the Chatelaines' Enclos.

The Mother Superior General of the Sisters of Saint Georges was waiting for her.

2

Three days passed without the summer heat weakening to any degree.

At night, a little coolness relieved Paris, but the heat and the stink returned with the day, as soon as the first rays of sunlight ceased to skim caressingly over the roof-tiles and started to stab down obliquely onto the streets and courtyards encrusted with dried muck. Soon, in the absence of any wind, fresh excremental stenches mixed with the staler odours of urine and dirt. Mucky exhalations rose from ditches and trenches. The smell of blood and carrion haunted the abattoirs. Acid vapours escaped from the tanneries. All of these emanations were left to slowly cook together beneath the vault of the dazzling sky, in a furnace that exhausted men and beasts alike.

Three more days passed, until that Friday evening, in July 1633, when Paris burned.

The former mansion of the marquis d'Ancre was called the Hôtel des Ambassadeurs extraordinaires. It was the property of Louis XIII, who had resided there on occasion, and now reserved it for foreign diplomats visiting Paris. The custom was to host the envoys of foreign powers as royal guests for three days following their arrival in the capital. Magnificent-looking and sumptuously appointed, the Hôtel des Ambassadeurs was ideally suited for receiving guests of distinction, and their suites. It was located, moreover, in a pleasant neighbourhood on rue de Tournon in the faubourg Saint-Germain, only a stone's throw from the Luxembourg palace.

After a final inspection of the upper storeys, Captain La

Fargue joined Leprat in the entry hall at the bottom of the main stairway.

'The sentries?' he asked.

'All of them are in place and briefed.'

'The relief?'

'In three hours.'

'Marciac? Laincourt?'

'Marciac is combing the grounds again. Laincourt was recalled to the Hôtel de l'Épervier.'

'He was recalled?'

'By a visitor. He promised not to take long.'

'All right.'

La Fargue gazed about absently, like a man trying to think of anything he might have forgotten or left undone. This evening, these walls and gilt trimmings would play host to a secret meeting whose security Cardinal Richelieu had assigned the Blades to ensure. La Donna had arranged the details, acting as an intermediary; and the most difficult issue had been finding a meeting-place. The Hôtel des Ambassadeurs had finally been agreed upon, as it was easy to guard and anonymous coaches with drawn curtains coming and going there would not attract attention. Even so, it did have some drawbacks from the point of view of security. As the Blades had quickly realised, threats could come from the neighbouring rooftops but also from the park that stretched back as far as rue Garance. When night came, they would need to increase the patrols.

'It will soon be three o'clock,' said La Fargue. 'You might as well be off to the Palais-Cardinal now.'

'At your command,' Leprat replied. 'Until later, captain.'

The musketeer departed.

At the Palais-Cardinal, he would find La Donna and one of the two guests they expected this evening. Right now the man was meeting Richelieu, incognito. He was ostensibly an envoy from the king of Spain, but in fact he spoke for the Black Claw. Louis XIII's chief minister receiving a representative of this execrated secret society was less unusual than one might think: the Black Claw was an actor on the European diplomatic and political stage, and as such, most governments had contacts with it. On the other hand, the mission that the old dragons of the Grand Lodge had entrusted to their emissary was without precedent. He was here to deliver a warning to France: that a terrible danger threatened her, and that it was the work of a handful of renegades, not of the society as a whole. Powerless to stop them, the Black Claw was nevertheless disposed to offer tokens of its good faith and wished to agree in advance to a *status quo ante bellum* in case the worst should come to pass.

The meeting planned this evening was also one of those tokens.

Both houses being located in the faubourg Saint-Germain, it was not far from the Hôtel des Ambassadeurs to the Hôtel de l'Épervier. Nevertheless Laincourt arrived in a sweat and, without taking time to refresh himself, went to find Jules Bertaud who was nervously pacing back and forth in the fencing room, where Guibot had asked him to wait.

'Arnaud!' exclaimed the small bookseller. 'At last!'

'What's happened, Bertaud?' asked Laincourt. 'I'm very busy today and can't—'

'It's Clotilde!' Bertaud said, looking very agitated. 'She's disappeared!'

'What?'

'Disappeared! My daughter has disappeared, Arnaud! She's been abducted!'

'Calm down, Jules. Calm down,' said Laincourt in a soothing voice.

With measured gestures, he sat the bookseller down, poured him a glass of water and obliged him to drink it.

'There. Slowly . . . Now, breathe . . . That's it . . . Slowly . . .'

And when Bertaud was a little more settled, he said:

'Now, tell me everything. From the beginning.'

So the bookseller told him how Clotilde had failed to return from the market that morning. He had been at the Hôtel de Chevreuse, where he was finishing the inventory of the library in the duchesse's magic study. He had therefore not been immediately alarmed that his daughter was absent when he returned home. Then, finally wondering if she had taken to bed, oppressed by the heat, he had gone to her room and found a letter, addressed to Laincourt.

'I opened it,' said Bertaud, handing him the letter with a trembling hand. 'Forgive me.'

The cardinal's former spy took the unsealed letter, observed that it was addressed to him in an unfamiliar hand and carefully unfolded it. It was a blank sheet of thick paper, which held a lock of hair. Hair that could only belong to Clotilde. Laincourt did not have to ask the bookseller if he was sure: one look into the anxious father's eyes told him all he needed to know.

'She . . . She's been abducted, hasn't she?' asked Bertaud.

'Yes.'

'Do you think she is unharmed?'

'I believe so.'

'Is this my fault? If Clotilde has been abducted, is it my fault?'

'Your fault? Where did you get that idea?' asked Laincourt.

But he was in fact unsure whose fault it was that the innocent young Clotilde had been kidnapped.

'I agreed to deliver a note to the duchesse de Chevreuse for you. Perhaps someone found out. Perhaps they want—'

'No, Jules. No . . . This is something unrelated and you must not reproach yourself for it. Look. This letter is addressed to me. Therefore I am the one they are trying to send a message to . . .'

'But who? Who? And why? . . . Oh, Arnaud, what sort of calamitous adventure have you dragged us into?'

'Who? I don't know . . . As to why, whoever has taken Clotilde means to frighten us and to cloud our judgment. No doubt they wish to draw me into a trap. Soon they will send you another message. It will be this evening, or tomorrow at the latest . . .'

Laincourt remained absolutely unflappable as he said this. Inside, the spy had taken over and was coolly analysing the situation. Clotilde had been abducted. But in broad daylight and in the neighbourhood of Place Maubert she could not have been taken by force. Not without causing a commotion. So she must have gone quietly, probably following someone she knew and had no reason to suspect.

'Someone has almost certainly abused Clotilde's trust,' said Laincourt. 'So you need to listen to me and think hard. Has Clotilde met anyone new lately? Do you know if she has made a new friend?'

'No,' replied the bookseller, shaking his head. 'No.'

'Think. It could be a beau . . .'

'A beau? No!'

'Girls don't tell their fathers everything. But you might have sensed that—'

'No! There was nothing like that . . .' The bookseller's gaze grew distant for a brief moment, and then his face took on a glimmer of a suspicion. 'Unless . . .'

'What, Bertaud?'

'There was a woman, a new client of mine, but . . .'

'Who is she?'

'A young widow who recently moved into the neighbour-hood. An excellent new customer who showed a deep love of books and who seemed fond of Clotilde. Clotilde delivered books to her at home several times.'

'Her name?'

'Madame Chantegrelle. But really, Arnaud, I think you're mistaken if you think—'

'Describe her to me.'

Bertaud gathered his recollections.

'Young. Ravishing. Blonde. With sparkling blue eyes and an angelic expression. A sweet voice. An air of innocence . . . But why these questions?'

Laincourt did not reply. He wasn't even listening anymore, and had gone quite pale.

The bookseller had just described the vicomtesse de Malicorne.

Wearing a veil and dressed in the white robe of the Sisters of Saint Georges, Agnès was praying beneath the octagonal cupola of the Sainte-Marie-du-Temple church when a young sister approached her, timidly murmured a few words in her ear, and then left with soft footsteps. Sœur Marie-Agnès – she had pronounced her perpetual vows the previous day – finished her prayer. She crossed herself, stood up, and walked to the large cloister of the Enclos.

Mère Béatrice d'Aussaint was waiting for her there.

She, too, was wearing the Chatelaines' immaculate white robe. But she had a sword at her side and boots on her feet. And her robe had a tough inner lining and was slit on either side to allow riding. It revealed the cavalier's breeches she wore beneath. She also had a Latin cross and an heraldic dragon embroidered over her heart. She was dressed as a louve, a member of the Order's White Wolves, and had recently become their leader; mother superior of the Saint-Loup abbey.

Tall, beautiful, and dignified, Mère Béatrice was barely older than Agnès. The two young women exchanged a warm accolade.

'So you are one of us now, Agnès. Welcome.'

'Henceforth, it's Sœur Marie-Agnès, mother.'

'Quite right,' said Béatrice with a smile. 'Let's take a few steps together, my daughter.'

She took Agnès' arm and they walked for a moment in silence, beneath the shade of the cloister's gallery.

'I particularly wanted to greet you, Agnès. And to assure myself that you are ready.'

'It's a little late to worry about that, since that I've already taken my vows.'

'That makes you a Chatelaine. But you are not a louve. Not yet, even if you promise to become the very best of us . . .'

'Only the future will tell if that is true.'

'No. There can be no doubt about this . . .'

Agnès glanced at Mère Béatrice out of the corner of her eye and decided not to argue the point. They continued to walk with slow, even steps until the mother superior said:

'We're going to have to hasten your initiation, Agnès. You will undergo the Ordeal tonight. I have brought the Sphère d'Âme that is destined for you.'

Taken aback, the newly ordained Chatelaine halted.

'Tonight? Why so soon?'

'The truth is we have no choice in the matter. We have just learned that the Arcana have started to waken the Primordial. And you and I both know how they intend to use it. Tonight they will—'

'I'm not ready!'

'You are not as ready as you should be, but better prepared than you believe.'

'No! It's impossible! I'll never be able to—'

'There are things I know about you, Agnès, that not even you know. Trust me. You can do this.'

'It's too soon!'

'We're short of time, to be sure. But at least we know what to expect . . . Tonight, the Chatelaines will face the threat head-on. But they will all perish trying to vanquish the Primordial. They will die without you. We are still missing one louve, and that louve is you.'

Laincourt accompanied Bertaud back to his home and then went on to rue des Bernardins, where this madame Chante-grelle who so closely resembled the vicomtesse de Malicorne had acquired a house. Cautious by nature, he started by doing a little reconnaissance of the immediate area. The rue des Bernardins was close to the Place Maubert and to Bertaud's small bookshop. It was also located near the city gates of Saint-Victor and La Tournelle.

Practical if one wishes to leave Paris quickly, said the hurdy-gurdy player over Laincourt's shoulder.

The young man did not turn round and continued observing the street from the recess of a carriage gate.

You should have been on your guard from the instant Marciac discovered La Malicorne had returned. You should have known that she was planning to wreak revenge on you . . . After all, you're the one who unmasked her, just when she was about to create a Black Claw lodge in France.

A brave feat of mine that cost you your life.

Bah! You know what they say about making omelettes . . .

There's no guarantee this Chantegrelle widow is La Malicorne. There are other pretty blondes in the world. I could be mistaken.

You know very well that you're not . . . By the way, where is Maréchal?

Maréchal was the old man's dragonnet. One-eyed and utterly emaciated, it was a woeful creature to behold but the hurdy-gurdy player was very attached to it. When he died, Laincourt had inherited the reptile.

He's safe at the Hôtel de l'Épervier. I've entrusted him to master Guibot's tender care.

The young man focused his attention on the façade of the house that Bertaud had indicated to him. A ground floor and two upper storeys, with a sign representing a sleeping dragon hanging over the door. The dragon motif was very common in Paris. But knowing who was living there . . .

Laincourt wondered if La Malicorne had appreciated the irony.

The nearby Bernardins convent had given its name to the street. The chapel bell rang five times.

'God's blood!' Laincourt muttered. 'Five o'clock already.'

You're getting careless, Arnaud.

The hurdy-gurdy player's tone of voice was serious.

Retreating further into shadow, Laincourt turned towards the spectre and saw that the old beggar looked bruised and bloodied again, as he had been at the moment of his death. Lately, he had appeared to him with a dirty face, to be sure, but one that was intact.

Careless?

No one knows you're here.

Bertaud knows.

And will he go to the Blades if you're late returning?

As Laincourt did not say anything, the hurdy-gurdy player continued:

Anyway, what are you planning to do?

La Malicorne and her henchmen think they're at least one move ahead of me. According to their plans, I should be worrying myself sick while waiting for them to manifest their intentions.

271

They don't know that I've already started to track them down. They may even still be in that house . . .

I doubt that very much.

Let's go and see.

No, boy! You—

But Laincourt was already leaving his hiding-place.

He soon found a way to gain access to the so-called madame Chantegrelle's house, from the rear, and after making sure that no one was watching him, he nimbly climbed over a wall and landed in the overgrown garden. There, he drew his sword before peeping through a half-closed window, which he then opened wide.

Silent and tidy, with modest furnishings, the house seemed to be empty.

Laincourt crept in noiselessly and listened. Then he explored the ground floor on tip-toe, all of his senses on alert. A flight of stairs led to the upper storeys. He climbed it and, on the first floor, a door left ajar attracted his attention. He approached and thought he heard a muffled whimper behind it. Fearing the worst, he cautiously pushed the door all the way open.

Clotilde and the Demoiselle were sitting opposite one another at a prettily set table. The tablecloth was embroidered and the crockery was delicate. The pastries sitting on the plates looked delicious. A golden syrupy-looking wine shimmered in a decanter and in two small crystal glasses. Perfectly at her ease, the Demoiselle was nibbling on candied fruits which she plucked from the crust of a piece of cake with her fingertips. But Clotilde's cheeks were stained with dried tears. Her gaze full of distress, she was fighting back sobs and sat petrified on her chair, not daring to move. Shielded by the back of her seat, a drac mercenary stood behind her with a dagger blade against her throat.

'Congratulations,' said the woman who, in Laincourt's eyes, remained the vicomtesse de Malicorne. 'You came just as quickly as I hoped you would.'

Somewhere in secret, cavernous depths, a rudimentary consciousness awoke and a reptilian eye opened slightly. The

Primordial slowly came to life and eventually heard the call which had awoken it from a distance of many leagues. The jewel on its scaly brow released a burst of light when the Heresiarch projected his mind into that of the archaic dragon. The Primordial bellowed in response to the other's presence. Then, its feet clawing over stone, it slipped into the waters of an underground tunnel leading to a black lake from which it would emerge into the evening air, before flying towards Paris.

'Any news of Laincourt?' asked La Fargue.

'No,' replied Marciac.

Daylight was already fading.

On the front steps of the Hôtel des Ambassadeurs, the two men were waiting for Leprat to return from the Palais-Cardinal with La Donna and the representative of the Black Claw. It had been less than an hour since the latter's interview with Richelieu had come to a close. His arrival under close escort was imminent and torches had been lit in the courtyard of honour in front of the mansion. Everything was ready to receive both him and the person he would be meeting here in secret.

The sound of hooves striking the dried muck approached from rue de Tournon.

'Here they are,' said the captain of the Blades.

Mounted on a black horse, Leprat was the first to enter the courtyard. Three armed horsemen followed him, then a coach without coats-of-arms and six more riders. La Fargue did not know the identity of the Black Claw's envoy, but he had no trouble recognising the one-eyed man riding just behind Leprat and commanding the escort. Armed with a solid rapier, both his clothes and his hat were made of black leather. A patch – also made of black leather and decorated with small silver studs – masked his left eye, but failed to conceal a ranse stain that spread over his cheekbone and temple. His name was Savelda, one of those who carried out various sordid and violent tasks on behalf of the masters of the Grand Lodge.

La Fargue and the Gascon exchanged a glance.

The Blades had crossed paths with Savelda on several

occasions recently. In fact, the last time he had narrowly escaped capture by them in the gardens of the Château de Dampierre after he threatened the queen's life.

First to dismount, Leprat hastened to join La Fargue and Marciac on the front steps. His expression was grave.

'That's not the worst of it,' he announced.

And the Blades' captain understood what the musketeer meant when he saw who climbed from the coach and gallantly lent his arm to La Donna.

It was the comte de Pontevedra.

La Fargue turned pale and absently took the note that Leprat was holding out to him.

'What's this?' he asked.

'It's from His Eminence, captain.'

La Fargue broke the seal, ran his eyes over the letter and returned it open to the musketeer so he could read it before passing it to Marciac.

Monsieur le capitaine,
    Please do me the favour of forgetting the promise you made the comte de Pontevedra during your last conversation with him.
Richelieu

'What promise?' asked the Gascon.

'I promised I would kill him.'

With a face made of marble, La Fargue watched as Pontevedra climbed the steps and entered the brightly lit mansion, exchanging smiles and polite courtesies with Alessandra. Savelda followed three paces behind him.

If they were capable of vanquishing the dragons they hunted down and fought for the salvation of the kingdom of France, the White Wolves of Saint Georges did not owe their success solely to their courage and their piety, or even to the supernatural virtues of the draconite blades they wielded so boldly. They owed their success, above all, to the protection offered them by powerful entities. By departed dragons, in fact. Or rather, forgotten dragons who no longer had any physical existence but continued – sometimes for centuries – to haunt the spectral world.

Each louve associated her soul with that of a protective dragon, thanks to a ritual taught to the Chatelaines by the Guardians in the distant past. This ritual was dangerous and Agnès knew the risks she was taking when she let the heavy doors of the Hall of the Ordeal close behind her. Dressed only in a white vestment, her hair cut very short since she had pronounced her vows, she knelt in prayer on the bare flagstones. Candles were burning in the darkness. The silence was deep, and suitable for spiritual communion. Before her, on a small wooden stand, Agnès saw a globe that seemed to be filled with a black, shifting ink whose slow swirls drew in the eye like an abyss.

A Sphère d'Âme.

A strange irony. The last time she had seen a Sphère d'Âme, Agnès had destroyed it to disrupt a Black Claw ceremony. She'd witnessed the extraordinary power contained within. A power which she would now have to confront on her own before she could be accepted by it, because it was as much a matter of dominating this spectral dragon as of winning its respect. The Ordeal richly deserved its name. It had cost some candidates their lives. Others emerged with their spirit numbed and broken. Those who passed the test successfully did not speak of it, or only to other louves, who alone could understand.

Focused on her task, determined, Agnès plunged mentally into the tormented shadows of the Sphère d'Âme . . .

. . . and felt an immense presence invade the hall.

It was as if she could feel the shadows vibrating all the way down to the bowels of the earth.

The Ordeal had begun.

Night had fallen.

At the Hôtel des Ambassadeurs, La Fargue gazed out from the torchlit terrace at the dark flowerbeds and straight paths of the great garden, where patrols paced up and down with a steady step. Alone and unable to concentrate his thoughts on any single subject, he thought about the Arcana and their Grand Design, about Laincourt who seemed to have gone missing, about the secrets of the Guards, and about the strange manoeuvres of the Black Claw and the comte de Pontevedra.

Pontevedra . . .

He had borne the name Louveciennes, and he had been La Fargue's best friend. At the time he had been a gentleman of honour and of duty. Together they had performed many brave services for the French Crown, on the fields of battle and behind the scenes of great historical events. Together they had founded the Blades at Cardinal Richelieu's request. They had carefully recruited Almades, then Leprat and Bretteville, and Marciac almost immediately after. Very quickly, the Blades had registered their first successes and gained in boldness. Then Agnès and Ballardieu had joined their ranks.

Leaning on the terrace balustrade, La Fargue heard someone approaching behind him. He glanced over his shoulder and recognised the tall and elegant silhouette of the man now known as the comte de Pontevedra. He gave no reaction, and turned his eyes back to the garden. The other joined him without saying a word and set down two glasses and the bottle of wine which he had brought out with him. He filled the glasses and pushed one in front of the captain.

The old gentleman looked at it briefly and then away.

'Surely you jest,' he said coldly. 'I would kill you if I could.'

'Yes, but you cannot . . .'

Louveciennes' betrayal had been brutal and unexpected. It had occurred during the siege of La Rochelle, in the course of a mission that subsequently ended in an appalling fiasco and the death of Bretteville. It had been a terrible blow for La Fargue: after betraying the Blades, his friend, his brother-in-arms, had fled to Spain, where he had enjoyed a dazzling ascent in his fortunes, becoming the comte de Pontevedra.

'You must return to your chambers, monsieur l'ambassadeur,' said La Fargue. 'You will be much safer than you are out here.'

'It's stifling upstairs! And Savelda is here to watch my back.'

The one-eyed agent of the Black Claw was indeed standing nearby.

'As you will. You know I would be the last person to mourn if a pistol ball fired from a nearby roof were to pass through your throat.'

With these words, La Fargue turned round and took a few steps towards the mansion, but Pontevedra called out:

'How is Ana-Lucia?'

'My daughter is called Anne. And she is well.'

'Indeed? Are you quite certain of that?'

The Blades' captain scowled.

'What are you trying to say?'

The comte de Pontevedra approached him.

'Do you know what I'm doing here?'

'You are representing the Black Claw,' said La Fargue, displaying an expression of profound contempt. 'It's not enough that you betrayed your king. You also had to betray your race.'

'Really? Am I the only one here to serve dragons?' asked Pontevedra with cutting irony. When La Fargue made no reply, he added: 'And if we're giving out lessons on morality, let's not forget which one of us seduced the other's wife, shall we?'

They had loved the same woman, although La Fargue had resisted acting on his feelings with all his might, out of loyalty to his friend.

'We loved one another, but there was only that one night,' he replied. 'One night, which Oriane and I never forgave ourselves for. Besides, you were the one she joined in Spain. With Anne.'

The two men remained silent for a moment, both prisoners of painful shared memories. Then Pontevedra spoke to Savelda:

'Leave us.'

The order took the Spanish henchman by surprise:

'My lord, I—'

'Leave us!'

Savelda hesitated again, then bowed and retired.

Pontevedra took La Fargue by the elbow and led him a few steps away. Intrigued, the captain did not resist.

'Here,' said Pontevedra, removing a leather wallet from his silver-embroidered doublet. 'I wanted to give this to you, hand-to-hand.'

La Fargue took the wallet.

'What is it?' he asked warily.

'I have resources at my disposal you cannot imagine. I know that you entrusted your daughter to the Guardians to keep her away from the Black Claw and from Richelieu's curiosity. I also know the Guardians assure you that she is safe. That's not true, and this is proof . . . You see, I don't ask you to take my word on it.'

'You do well not to.'

The captain of the Blades slipped the wallet beneath his shirt, against his skin.

Shortly after, upon returning inside, La Fargue pondered matters as he watched the comte de Pontevedra climbing the main stairs towards his quarters. Then he joined Alessandra and Leprat on the steps leading to the front courtyard. Looking worried, La Donna was clutching a note a messenger had just delivered from the Palais-Cardinal.

'Well?' asked the old captain.

'No news,' said Alessandra. 'I want to believe, but I'm beginning to think that he will not come . . .'

The person they were still waiting for, the person that Pontevedra had come to meet in secret, was none other than Valombre. The Black Claw had asked to enter into contact with the Guardians under the aegis of Cardinal Richelieu. They had insisted on the urgency of this unprecedented meeting. But Pontevedra had not deigned to explain the reason for requesting it, which had in turn complicated matters for La Donna. The Guardians were exceedingly cautious. They did not like to proceed without knowing why.

'Valombre will come if the Seven permit him to,' said La Fargue.

A rider then came into the courtyard. It was Marciac, returning from the Hôtel de l'Épervier.

'Laincourt still hasn't turned up,' he said after jumping down from the saddle. 'And it's been a few hours since he left with his bookseller friend.'

'Bertaud,' Leprat reminded them.

'Yes, Bertaud. According to Guibot, the man was frantic with worry.'

'Laincourt has no doubt gone to assist him,' La Fargue reckoned. 'But didn't he tell anyone where he was going or what he was intending to do?'

'No.'

'That's not like him,' said Alessandra gravely.

She had met Laincourt in Madrid, when he had been spying on behalf of the cardinal. She knew his qualities and held him in high esteem.

'Perhaps the bookseller is at home,' said Marciac. 'He has a shop near Place Maubert, I believe. I could pay him a visit . . .'

La Fargue cursed.

One of his men was missing and he could do nothing about it, being retained here by a secret meeting which, it seemed, might not even take place! And to crown it all, one of the participants was an individual he hated, yet was duty-bound to protect!

The captain of the Blades forced himself to recover his calm. Fists on his hips, he took a deep breath and arched his back, his face lifting to see an enormous full moon in a deep blue sky.

A window shattered just above him, showering him with sparkling debris as Savelda's broken-limbed corpse crashed to the ground at the bottom of the steps.

After a brief instant of stupor, La Fargue, Leprat, and Marciac rushed inside the building. They unsheathed their rapiers and seized their pistols as they dashed up the main stairs. Broke down the door to Pontevedra's chambers. Crossed the antechamber in a bound. Burst into the adjoining room.

Seriously wounded, Pontevedra had dragged himself over

to the bed leaving a wide trail of blood in his wake. A drac was bent over him, preparing to finish him off with a sword thrust to the chest. A second one stood near the window by which they had entered and which Pontevedra had no doubt opened to take in the fresh night air. They were armed and dressed like mercenary swordsmen, but these were no ordinary dracs: they had leathery wings, ample and powerful enough to permit them to fly.

Surprised, the first drac leaped through the window and escaped. But the Blades did not allow the second any time to react. La Fargue opened fire, then Marciac and Leprat. One pistol ball hit the winged drac in the middle of the chest. The second pierced him in the neck, and the third put out an eye and tore away the back of his skull.

La Donna arrived, but was jostled aside by the sentries who had been guarding the doors and windows on the ground floor. The room rapidly filled with agitated people. The winged drac inside was already dead. A few musket shots fired from the window failed to hit his fleeing companion, now flying off into the distance. La Fargue raised his voice to restore order while the dying Pontevedra was laid out on his bed. The captain sent the sentries back to their posts, except for two who remained at the door. Leprat helped Marciac examine the wounds of the man who – in a former life – had been one of their own. Meanwhile, Alessandra studied the winged drac. Intrigued, she picked up his rapier, looked closely at it, turned suddenly pale and dropped the weapon.

'My God!'

She ran from the room.

Marciac had just stepped back from the bed and was wiping his hands with a cloth. There was nothing he could do to save Pontevedra, as the other two already understood. Surprised by the behaviour of La Donna, he hesitated as to whether he should go after her, and gave his captain a questioning look.

'Find her!' ordered La Fargue, just before the dying man gripped him by the collar with a blood-slicked hand.

The Gascon went.

*

In the front courtyard of the Hôtel des Ambassadeurs, there were horses waiting. Alessandra had already mounted one of them side-saddle when Marciac joined her.

'Where are you going?' he asked, seizing the animal by the bit.

'The rapier. It was made of draconite.'

Draconite was an alchemical stone dreaded by the dragons. It allowed in particular the fabrication of a steel that inflicted terrible wounds on them, but gave humans no more cause for fear than the ordinary variety.

'Don't you think it strange those dracs had draconite weapons?' continued La Donna. 'Why go to all that trouble, just to kill Pontevedra?'

At that point, realisation dawned on Marciac.

Although the Black Claw's envoy was not a dragon, Valombre was. Alessandra feared that the winged dracs had been sent to assassinate him, too. Perhaps they had already struck the Guardians' representative, which would explain his alarming lateness for the meeting.

La Donna forced Marciac to release her mount and left through the carriage gate at a fast trot.

'Wait!' yelled the Gascon, climbing onto a horse.

He took off in pursuit of her.

Coughing up blood, eyes already growing glassy, Pontevedra had seized La Fargue by the collar. His fist was firm but his arm was trembling when, stammering, he tried to draw the Blades' captain towards him. The old gentleman bent down, bringing his face close to that of his former friend.

'If you're hoping for a pardon . . .' he started.

'Not . . . Not a . . . pardon,' murmured the dying man in a barely audible voice. Without releasing La Fargue, he swallowed painfully and gathered his last remaining strength. 'The . . . queen . . . The queen . . . in . . . danger . . . The qu—'

He died with the words trapped in his throat.

La Fargue had to tug on his wrist to free himself from the

dead man's grasp. He stood up and turned to Leprat with a worried expression.

'What did he say?' asked the musketeer.

'He . . . He said that the queen was in danger.'

'What? In danger now?'

'I believe so, yes. But I don't know anything about it.'

'The queen is in Saint-Germain with the king and I don't—' Leprat corrected himself: 'No, I'm wrong. The queen is not in Saint-Germain. It's Friday.'

'So where is she?'

'She's here. In Paris.'

It was a black, massive creature, which advanced across the night sky with great, steady beats of its wings.

The Primordial was flying towards Paris, and it could see the first lights of the city in the distance before it, as well as the luminous blazes of the three powerful solaires. One – white – was at the top of Tour du Temple, in the Chatelaines' Enclos. Another – red – indicated the Palais-Cardinal. A third – blue – shone above the Louvre.

The dragon with the jewelled brow felt a strange emotion pervade it: in the Arcana's magic study, the Heresiarch had just smiled.

Laincourt emerged from unconciousness and grimaced in pain.

In the dim light, Clotilde was gently dabbing his battered face with a piece of cloth torn from her dress and dampened with a little stagnant water. She looked down at him with a smiling but exhausted face, her eyes reddened and her cheeks smeared with dirt. Long locks of hair had escaped her un-ravelling chignon.

Laincourt slowly returned to full awareness.

And remembered.

Contrary to appearances, the house on rue des Bernardins had not been empty. Not only had the Demoiselle been wait-ing for him while holding Clotilde prisoner, but there were numerous drac and human mercenaries hiding in the upper storeys.

Laincourt had been disarmed.

Then, at the Demoiselle's order and before Clotilde's eyes, he had been beaten. With fists at first. Then with boots, when he had fallen and curled into a ball on the floor. And the blows had continued thereafter, methodically administered with a cold cruelty, devoid of passion or fury, while Clotilde, in tears, had begged the dracs to stop and implored the Demoiselle, who alone had the power, to put an end to the torture.

Laincourt had finally fainted.

'Where are we?' he asked, in a thick voice.

Squinting, he sat up and discovered an empty cubby-hole, damp and dusty, faintly lit by the rays of a lantern coming through a gap beneath the door.

'I don't know,' replied Clotilde. 'When you lost consciousness, they locked you up inside a chest and then put me in another. I don't know where they took us, but I think we are still in Paris. It could be . . . It could be a cellar, don't you think?'

He nodded and then rose to his feet, unable to contain a moan of pain as he did.

'Monsieur Laincourt! You shouldn't get up! You—'

'It's all right, Clotilde. Those dracs knew what they were doing. They only wanted to make me suffer and to torment you, not to do any serious damage.'

'But why?'

'Out of cruelty. And I think you can call me Arnaud, Clotilde.'

But the explanation put forward by Laincourt left the girl mute with disbelief. He availed himself of her silence to examine the door: it was solid and double-locked. There was no other exit.

'Who are these people?' Clotilde finally asked. 'Why did they hurt you? What do they want from us, exactly? And why do they . . . ? That woman. She . . . She said that you were old friends . . .'

Laincourt suddenly became aware of the full degree of

young Clotilde's distress. He came back to sit down next to her, took her hands, and said:

'Everything that has happened to you is my fault, Clotilde. I am sorry for that.'

Then, because she was looking at him in utter incomprehension, he decided that she deserved to know. He told her that he was an agent of Cardinal Richelieu. He told her about the vicomtesse de Malicorne, what she had tried to do, and how he had foiled her plans. Lastly, he explained she was now called the 'Demoiselle', but was still seeking vengeance.

'And she abducted you to get to me, Clotilde,' he confessed.

But he lacked the courage to admit that he didn't know why she was still alive. The bait was of no interest once the prey had fallen into the trap. Clotilde no longer served any purpose . . .

. . . unless the Demoiselle was reserving some refined piece of cruelty for him.

The door suddenly opened. A drac and two men burst into the room. The first struck Laincourt in the face before he had time to react. The others seized Clotilde despite her screams of terror. Laincourt tried to defend her, but a kick from a boot to his belly cut off his breath. The men dragged the girl out by force and the drac slammed the door shut behind them. He locked it with a key as Laincourt got up, staggered over, and threw himself against it in vain. His brow pressed against the wood, he hammered on the solid panel with both fists, but could only hear Clotilde crying and calling out to him for help.

'No!' he shouted. 'No! TAKE ME! ME! TAKE ME!'

Alessandra had been serving the Guardians for several years now. She enjoyed their confidence and knew Valombre, their representative in Paris, quite well. She liked him, had a genuine affection for him. So there was a growing fear in the pit of her stomach as she rode towards the house where the dragon dwelled on the Ile de la Cité. Sensing her fear, Marciac watched her out of the corner of his eye as they rode. He had spurred his horse forward to catch up with her at the end of rue de Tournon and had been escorting her since, without really knowing what to expect.

Having crossed the Seine via Pont de l'Hôtel-Dieu, they passed in front of Notre-Dame cathedral and were astonished to see it lit up. Surmounted by the gallery of the kings of Israel and of Judah, the three portals of the western façade were open and gave them a glimpse of intense activity within, while Chatelaines and Black Guards were assembling on the forecourt. Marciac thought there were even some White Wolves among them.

'What's going on here?' he asked.

'I don't know,' replied La Donna.

But, like him, she feared the worst.

They entered the private little neighbourhood of the canons' Cloister, to which Alessandra had a gate key.

'Valombre entrusted me with it,' she explained before the Gascon could ask.

The dragon was lodged on rue du Chapitre, not far from the old footbridge that linked the Ile de la Cité with Ile Notre-Dame-des-Écailles: a vestige of the days – before the dracs moved in there – when the canons of the cathedral still laid claim to the neighbouring island. Marciac and Alessandra found the door to the house locked but, backing up a few paces, the Gascon noticed an open window on the first storey.

'Keep an eye out,' he said to La Donna as he handed her the reins to his horse.

Then he climbed the façade with ease and slipped inside.

Increasingly anxious, Alessandra kept watch as she waited for Marciac to appear again. In the nocturnal silence she heard the murmur of religious chants coming from Notre-Dame. And wasn't that a bell tolling in the distance? A bell, which others were now answering?

Marciac opened the front door for her.

'Come inside quickly,' he said.

Hitching the horses to a ring fixed to the wall, she followed the Gascon into the house. Silent and dark, it seemed deserted.

'Nobody upstairs,' Marciac announced in hushed voice.

They explored the ground floor by the glow of the

moonlight that entered through the windows. They wanted to remain discreet. They did not call out, they made no light, and they almost failed to notice the badly damaged wall panel. It looked as though someone had been kicking at it about half-way up. As if they were trying to break it down.

As if it was a door.

Alessandra and Marciac understood. Exchanging a glance, they began to examine the wooden panel, running their fingertips along the frame, fishing around and finally finding the places to push and determining the correct order in which to push them. All of this took some time, but La Donna, luckily, had experience in these matters. At last, the panel slid to one side and revealed an iron door which the Gascon opened cautiously, pistol in his fist. It concealed a staircase at the bottom of which they found Valombre, lying in a pool of his own blood, lit by the dying flame of an oil lamp.

In 1621, Queen Anne d'Autriche acquired a property in the faubourg Saint-Jacques where she decided to install a community of Benedictine nuns from the Bièvre valley. Three years later, the first stone of their new cloister was laid. Thus was born the Val-de-Grâce abbey, a place where the queen experienced a tranquillity she could never find at the Louvre, hidden far from the royal court and – so she believed, at least – Richelieu's spies. She went there often and liked to stay there on Fridays, taking her meals in the refectory and lodging in a modest two-room apartment. After the Dampierre affair, the king severely reduced the liberties he allowed his wife. But he was unable to force her to give up her weekly retreats to Val-de-Grâce, even though she used them to meet in secret with her friend the duchesse de Chevreuse and to send letters to Spain with the aid of the abbess, Mère de Saint-Étienne. None of this had escaped the cardinal's notice.

La Fargue and Leprat reached Val-de-Grâce at a full gallop. If the queen was there, she was in some kind of danger. At least that was what Pontevedra had claimed before he died.

'Louveciennes only told us the queen was under threat

when he was on the very brink of death,' observed Leprat as they rode. 'Why was that, do you suppose?'

'No doubt he knew the queen was in danger, but not how imminent that danger was.'

'And he finally understood when he fell to the two assassins?'

'I think so. He must have believed that if they were attacking him now, it meant that the plot against the queen was about to take place.'

'But attacking him is the same thing as attacking the Black Claw. Who would want that?'

The captain did not reply: they were arriving and slowed their mounts.

Val-de-Grâce offered an unusual spectacle at this hour of the night. Approaching at a walk, the riders discovered the abbey lit up and the gate open. In the courtyard, numerous soldiers belonging to the light cavalry company of Saint Georges – the celebrated Black Guards – were coming and going. All of them were wearing breastplates and most of them had swords in their hands. But they were moving calmly and efficiently, without shouts or excessive haste.

'No one may enter!'

La Fargue gave his name to the sentries at the gate, showed his pass signed by the cardinal, and announced that he had a message of the highest importance for the officer in charge.

'One moment,' said one of the guards after examining the document in the glow of a lantern.

He ran off.

'Black Guards?' murmured Leprat in surprise. 'What are they doing here? They're not assigned to watch over the queen.'

'I know. And yet . . .'

The sentry was speaking with an officer in the middle of the courtyard. The officer listened to him, before turning to beckon La Fargue and Leprat forward. They dismounted and walked towards him, leading their mounts by the bridle. It was only then they recognised François Reynault d'Ombreuse.

'What's happening here?' asked La Fargue after exchanging a frank handshake with the young officer.

'We have just repulsed an assault by winged dracs. There's no merit in it, we were expecting an attack.'

'Is the queen safe?' worried Leprat.

'The queen is not here. She's being kept in safety at another location, which I don't know. You have come to warn us of a danger threatening her, haven't you?'

'Yes,' said La Fargue. 'But you knew that already. How?'

'Thanks to information secretly transmitted to the Sisters of the Saint Georges. And you?'

The Blades' captain was about to answer when a cavernous bellow made the night tremble. Together, they turned to the north, towards the centre of Paris.

There they saw the Primordial, flying in slow circles in the sky and roaring.

With rage boiling in his belly, Laincourt had resigned himself to wait. He knew that he would only exhaust himself in vain by hammering away at the door of the cubby-hole where they had him locked up. It was also useless to shout, to call out, to insult his captors. He needed to save his meagre strength so he could act when the moment came. His tormentors had neglected to tie his hands. No doubt they believed him less dangerous than he really was, an error which he was counting on being able to turn to his advantage.

For now, the hardest thing was trying not to drive himself mad imagining what Clotilde was being subjected to. That was precisely the reason why the girl was still alive and why they had been locked up together. It was so they could tear her from him, reduce him to impotence, and leave him to torment himself. La Malicorne – she would never have any other name for Laincourt – knew how to torture souls . . .

The key turned in the heavy lock.

Sitting with his back to the cubby-hole wall, Laincourt seemed listless and defeated. Even close to being unconscious:

body limp, breathing slow, head hanging, and hair before his eyes. His left hand rested inertly on the floor, palm upwards, easily visible. He was hoping to divert attention from the right hand, which lay concealed beneath his thigh, gripping a shard of pottery he'd discovered in the dust. A feeble weapon that would only allow him to strike once, but which might just slice through a jugular vein.

As long as the intended victim came close enough. And bent over.

Laincourt waited, hearing the door open with a creak and someone come inside dragging . . . a sack?

'I would appreciate it if you lent me a hand,' said a familiar voice.

Flabbergasted, Laincourt opened his eyes and discovered Saint-Lucq, dragging the dead body of one of the guards who had been posted in the corridor.

'Saint-Lucq? But how did you—'

'There's another one,' said the half-blood.

Laincourt got up and, together, they laid a second body on top of the first inside the cubby-hole. One of them had his throat cut; the other had been stabbed in the heart. All done without the slightest noise.

'Hurry up,' said Saint-Lucq.

He had posted himself on the threshold and was glancing furtively into the corridor.

'But how did you manage to find me?' asked Laincourt as he stripped one body of its sword and baldric.

'The cardinal has charged me with eliminating La Malicorne's cult. That will be achieved by the time I've finished up here.'

'By eliminating—'

'Yes.'

Laincourt stopped fiddling with his scabbard.

'Clotilde is being held prisoner.'

'The bookseller's daughter. I know, yes.'

'We have to save her!'

Emotionless, Saint-Lucq turned the blank and hypnotic gaze of his scarlet spectacles towards Laincourt.

'I thought you might say something like that.'

He offered him one of his pistols.

Valombre still lived.

Lying motionless at the foot of his hidden staircase, he had moaned when Marciac had gently turned him over onto his back, then he had regained consciousness while the Gascon examined him.

'Don't move, monsieur. My name is Marciac and I serve Captain La Fargue.'

'I know who you are, monsieur.'

'Then you also know that I am something of a doctor.'

The dragon had a deep wound at his side whose edges seem to have been eaten by acid, a sure sign that it had been inflicted by a draconite blade. He also had a broken leg and a nasty bump on his forehead.

'You have broken your femur. But I am going to take care of this wound first, before you drain yourself of more blood.'

Alessandra came back with thread, a needle, a basin of water, and cloths which she had found upstairs in the house. They would need a stretcher to lift the wounded patient up to the ground floor above, but unable to do so right away, Marciac had decided to tend to the most urgent injuries on the spot. Afterwards, they'd see about the rest.

Grimacing with pain while the Gascon sutured his wound, Valombre explained that he had been surprised by two winged dracs in his chamber, that they had attacked him, but that he had been able to escape and close the secret passage behind him. Then he had lost consciousness at the top of the steps.

'What is this room?' asked Marciac.

They were in a small hexagonal chamber, empty and bare.

'A meditation study,' replied Valombre. 'A place which is indispensable if one wishes to keep control of . . .' He searched for the right words. 'If one wishes to keep control of the dragon.'

The Gascon nodded distractedly.

'Your would-be assassins could not linger, which certainly

290

saved your life,' said La Donna. 'They still had much else to do.'

And then she recounted how two winged dracs – the same two, no doubt – had assassinated Pontevedra at the Hôtel des Ambassadeurs, prompting them to come and see about him. 'So they dared,' said the dragon. 'The Arcana dared to strike at the Black Claw . . .'

'And at the Guardians.'

'Unfortunately, I'm afraid that they will dare do much worse before tomorrow, madame.'

'Did you hear that?' asked Marciac, cocking an ear.

The Primordial had first flown over Paris at a fairly low altitude, making circles and bellowing. Then, as the bells of the capital joined together to sound the tocsin, the Parisians surprised in their sleep had sought to comprehend what was going on before lifting alarmed gazes towards the great black dragon which flew over their heads again and again, describing great loops in the night sky but not doing more than bellowing occasionally, its black scales gleaming in the light of the moon and stars.

The uncertainty of the population, however, did not last.

It gave way to horror when the Primordial began to belch its destructive fire, pulverising rooftops and seeding immense blazes at random across the city.

Reynault d'Ombreuse and his detachment of light cavalry left Val-de-Grâce at a fast trot. Accompanied by La Fargue and Leprat, the Black Guards rode up rue du Faubourg-Saint-Jacques as the neighbourhood became agitated, and the residents' anxiety turned to fear. The dragon seemed to be sparing the faubourgs, but for how long? Should they wait, or try to go now? Save their lives, but leave their dwellings and worldly goods behind, perhaps to be pillaged in their absence?

Reynault had had the foresight to send one of his men ahead. The troops thus found the Saint-Jacques gate open to them, but were forced to slow down nevertheless. Within the city walls, the streets were thronged. Houses were burning and the roar of fires was mingled with cries and sobs, along with the deafening din of all the city's bells pealing out at once. People deserted their homes, taking whatever they could with them. Others fought the flames with the inadequate means were at hand, or tried to help their neighbours. Shouts advised the inhabitants to flee, to stay, to take refuge in the cellars, to go the churches to pray, or to run towards the banks of the Seine. Jostling became brawls. Some poor wretches were trampled. Leprat saw a woman, babe in arms, throw herself from a second-storey window of a house on fire.

They often had to force passage through the crowds.

Reynault, La Fargue, and the riders at the head of the column had no choice but to push their horses into the innocents they knocked down, the imperative being to reach Notre-Dame as quickly as possible. In this fashion, the detachment reached the Petit Châtelet, which guarded the bridge leading to the Ile de la Cité. As they were crossing the smaller arm of the Seine river, Leprat exclaimed:

'Look!'

In the sky, the Primordial was no longer alone.

Mounted on white wyverns, the White Wolves of Saint Georges surrounded it, harassing it, drawing its attention, dodging away, goading it again and again with their draconite blades. They were taking every risk to drive the creature mad. But at least it was sparing Paris as long as they kept it distracted. At least it was directing its incandescent spurts at them rather than at the city below.

Behind Reynault, the Black Guards were cheering them on.

'We need to hurry!' he ordered, breaking the mood. 'The sisters can only offer us a brief respite!'

The Ile de la Cité, too, had become a chaos of flames, cries, and terror. Making their way through the crush, Reynault and his men took rue Neuve-Notre-Dame which led straight to the cathedral and its beautiful twin towers. A row of three terraced houses was burning, and as the façades threatened to collapse into the street, the column urged their horses to pass by, braving the torrid swirls of hot coals and ash.

At last they reached the cathedral's narrow forecourt.

Men, women, children, and old people had gathered there. Seeking refuge in Notre-Dame, they had come up against a wall of Black Guards on horseback, who, impassive, with their swords at their sides and their musket butts resting on their thighs, held their mounts in place with a steady hand and would not let anyone approach the cathedral. Fear and anger on the one hand, and intransigence on the other, threatened to provoke a riot. Fists were being raised among the rancorous crowd. Two or three stones had already flown through the air.

Prudently, Reynault d'Ombreuse skirted the forecourt and led his troops alongside the cathedral to the southern entrance, or Saint-Étienne portal. This was also guarded, but as it was protected by the episcopal palace, the immediate area around it was relatively peaceful. La Fargue and Leprat dismounted with the rest of the column. They alone, however, followed Reynault inside.

Within Notre-Dame, there was a strange atmosphere of calm.

Thirty metres tall and ten spans long, the immense nave was deserted, as were the side aisles, the transept, and the crossing where four imposing pillars rose directly to the vault far above. The air seemed to be vibrating. The silence, in fact, was resonating softly with an incantation whispered with fervour by a group of kneeling Chatelaines in the choir, located behind the high altar. There was magic in their prayer. It gave off a power which set one's nerves on edge.

Discreet but vigilant sentinels, Black Guards were posted at the doors and in front the altar steps. Calling one of them over, Reynault charged the soldier with conducting Captain La Fargue before Mère d'Aussaint. But he requested that Leprat remain by his side: it was clear he would soon have need of an experienced officer.

The musketeer agreed to stay.

From the Grande Galerie, on the third storey of the magnificent western façade of Notre-Dame, Mère Béatrice d'Aussaint was watching her sisters who — as white-draped silhouettes atop white wyverns — were risking their lives to divert the

293

Primordial's wrath. Below her, the Ile de la Cité spread between the two arms of the Seine, whose dark slow waters merged, and flowed on between the two halves of Paris. A great clamour was rising from the streets and squares invaded by crowds. Blazes had broken out everywhere. They roared, wheezed, and crackled. Some of the buildings at the Saint-Germain abbey were burning. Tall flames were flickering from the windows of the oldest section of the Louvre.

'Did the cardinal send you?' she asked upon seeing La Fargue approach.

'The circumstances did, more like it.'

'Then it's divine Providence at work.'

Side by side, they lifted their eyes towards the Primordial and the white forms that were confronting it.

'The battle being waged by your louves is doomed to failure, mother.'

'They know that. But it's only a matter of gaining time.'

'Gaining time for what?'

'For the ritual the sisters are preparing inside . . . Oh my God!'

The great black dragon had just struck a Chatelaine with a fiery blast. Burning alive in her flaming robe, she plunged from her wyvern, a long silence accompanying her fall before she vanished in the black waters of the Seine.

On Ile Notre-Dame, joyful exclamations and war cries greeted the terrible spectacle of the living torch, which fell from the skies trailing a swathe of flames. The damp and rotting alleys of Les Écailles were full of excited dracs who, ever since the tocsin had sounded, had been following the Primordial's manoeuvres. They instinctively took its side against the Chatelaines and applauded this success.

Keress Karn broke off observing the aerial combat to keep an eye on his men who, at a street corner beneath an enormous lamp, were replacing one barrel with another. Their return was welcomed with acclamations, both from dracs who were already drunk but wanted to drink some more, and from new arrivals who had been drawn by the rumour of free drink.

The first barrel had been emptied in less than an hour. The second was immediately tapped and would not last long.

Karn knew that similar scenes were taking place here and there all across the stifling maze of Les Écailles. The Heresiarch had ordered him to provide a generous flow of drac wine and that's exactly what he was busy doing. The task itself was an easy one: dracs loved this mix of wine, *eau-de-vie* and golden henbane that intoxicated them after just a few glassfuls. But Karn needed to make sure that his own men didn't touch the stuff. Although most of his band was waiting out of harm's way to go into action, those he had entrusted with delivering the barrels were susceptible to temptation. Karn himself had to avoid breathing in the fumes from the irresistible brew. To his men, he explained that they needed to keep a cool head in readiness for the forthcoming combat that night.

It was the truth, but not the whole truth.

For Karn still mistrusted the mercenaries he had hired to replace those who had fallen at Bois-Noir. The new recruits knew how to fight and to obey orders, and had no fear of dying and even less of killing. They were true drac warriors. But how would they react if they knew? What would they do if they found out the Enchantress had poured a substance that induced madness into each of the barrels? Would they accept the idea of poisoning other dracs simply to achieve the aims of the Arcana?

As for the red drac leader, he couldn't care less.

The idea of Paris burning delighted him, and now he was eager to plunder the helpless city.

Long and spacious, the cellar featured rows of columns upholding elegant vaults. Large flagstones covered the floor and the lit candles placed in large candelabra cast tortuous shadows on the bare walls. Gathered before the altar, there were thirty people reciting an incantation in the old draconic tongue. All of them were masked and draped in scarlet cloaks. All of them carried a sword. They had secretly sworn allegiance to the Black Claw and, not content with having placed their names, their fortunes, and their influence at its service, they also worshipped it in a cult whose sinister rituals induced an unhealthy fascination in them that flattered their basest instincts.

The Demoiselle was leading the ceremony.

As she chanted the words that her acolytes repeated after her, she hardly resembled the charming young person that she ordinarily pretended to be. The features of her face had become sharper, more bony and hollowed. Her eyes shone with a cold and cruel sparkle. Her tangled blonde hair fell upon her bared bosom. She seemed taller and stronger. More mature, too. But that was nothing compared to another change: below her waist, her body had formed a thick scaly tail upon which she held herself upright.

With her arms spread and her head tilted backward she undulated slightly, abandoning herself to a pleasure which was enhanced by the vapours from the decoctions of henbane which were being heated in bowls filled with red-glowing coals, placed on either side of two long, crossed daggers upon the altar. Powerful fragrances rose into the air, thick and yellow. They affected the acolytes too, and had also plunged Clotilde into a hypnotic torpor. The girl was behind the Demoiselle, bound to a stone table that was inclined to expose her to the view of all present. She was naked, and her body had been shaved and covered in painted inscriptions, and her wrists and ankles were held by leather straps.

In her ecstatic trance, the Demoiselle did not see the flasks of naphtha flying towards the gathering. She did not see them fall, burst and splatter in all directions. She only opened her eyes when one acolyte, soaking and surprised, overturned a large candelabra as he stumbled, and then suddenly caught fire. The layer of oil in which the cult members found themselves suddenly floundering was set alight. Other acolytes began to go up in flames. There was panic. The human torches screamed and struggled while the others hastily stepped away, jostling one another. Some threw off their burning cloaks, slapped on their sleeves or breeches to put out fires, threw away smoking gloves, and rubbed at their scorched hair. Meanwhile those the fire had spared stared around them without comprehension, their minds still sluggish from the golden henbane.

Saint-Lucq approached with his sword in his fist, having left two dead bodies at the door behind him.

'TAKE HIM!' screamed the Demoiselle, pointing her finger.

Having entered by a second door, two mercenaries – a drac and a human – rushed forward to meet the half-blood. Very calm and still advancing, he parried the man's attack and pierced him in the chest, withdrawing his blade just in time to avoid an attack from the drac, whom he brought down with a knee to the groin before finishing him off with another blow to the chin.

Frenzied with rage, the Demoiselle roared as her face became more brutal and scales appeared on her shoulders and throat like armour plating. She seized the two sacrificial daggers placed before her and turned to the inclined stone table. And then she roared again in fury, a prominent ridge emerging in the middle of her brow. Laincourt had freed Clotilde. The girl was having trouble standing and clung to his neck, so he held her tightly against him with his left arm while he backed up and pointed a pistol at the Demoiselle, or rather at the creature she had become.

He opened fire.

Hit in the left shoulder, the Demoiselle reeled back, but then straightened up like a reed on her scaly tail and looked in stupor at the hissing wound. The pistol ball was made of draconite. Another detonation rang out. This time, the reptilian creature arched her spine, hit in the back by a second draconite projectile. She spun round and saw Saint-Lucq aiming at her with a smoking pistol.

'FLEE!' he yelled to Laincourt. Then, giving the Demoiselle a contemptuous look, he added: 'I'll take care of this bitch.'

Blackened corpses lay on the floor, emitting a faint sound of hot sizzling grease. Only a few scattered puddles of naphtha were still burning. Among the acolytes who had not fled the scene, some drew their swords and went to attack the half-blood. Very coolly, he reversed his pistol with a flick of the wrist and grasped it by the barrel. Then he smashed in a temple, slit a throat, and perforated a heart, eliminating his adversaries in three strokes of lethal precision. The bodies collapsed almost simultaneously. The last hit the ground just as Laincourt gave a last glance backward before disappearing with Clotilde.

Saint-Lucq caught his gaze and nodded.

Foaming from the mouth, the Demoiselle had gone completely berserk. Her jaws yawned open in an uncanny fashion as she screamed at the half-blood and unleashed the full power of her aura. Its impact drove away the last remaining acolytes, who fled in wide-eyed horror, and it even forced some of the mercenaries, who had just arrived hungry for a fight, to beat a hasty retreat.

Saint-Lucq remained where he was. The dragon blood that ran in his veins made him immune to the Demoiselle's influence. Impassive and unimpressed, he raised one eyebrow behind his red spectacles and placed himself *en garde*, his black rapier in his right hand, and his pistol held like a club in his left.

Armed with the two long ritual daggers, the Demoiselle came at Saint-Lucq, her serpentine tail writhing with a scraping noise across the flagstones. A terrible duel began between them. Blows were delivered, parried, deflected, and dodged faster than the eye could see. The steel blades clanked and clashed as if propelled by a life of their own. Concentrating fiercely, the half-blood knew the slightest error would be fatal and that, in addition to the daggers, he needed to be wary of the scaly tail that threatened to knock his legs out from under him. The two adversaries were equal in the swiftness of their reflexes. They seemed to be dancing rather than fighting. They circled one another, striking to right and left, immediately riposting, advancing and retreating, never holding anything back.

And it went on and on.

Finally, Saint-Lucq decided to risk his all. He was tiring. The sweat running into his eyes was hampering him. He had to act.

Lowering his guard, he struck with his pistol, and the blow

broke the Demoiselle's wrist, forcing her to drop one of the daggers. In doing so, he exposed his side. The reaction was immediate: with her second dagger, the creature lacerated his flank. But his trap was nevertheless in place. For anyone else but Saint-Lucq would have backed off at this point, but he did not.

Instead, he promptly riposted.

And planted his rapier to the hilt in the Demoiselle's belly.

The creature froze, gurgling, transfixed by pain and horror.

Pressed up to his enemy, Saint-Lucq also waited without moving. At last, as he felt the Demoiselle growing heavier and heavier against him, he slowly turned the blade running through the body, jerked it up sharply while holding on to his victim, and pushed the creature away as he backed off.

The Demoiselle remained standing for a moment, heaped entrails falling from the gaping wound in her abdomen and hitting the floor with a flaccid noise. Then she collapsed and, giving a long strident cry, convulsed frenetically until death finally had its way.

A final shiver ran through the scaly tail.

Saint-Lucq looked at the body before slipping his pistol into his belt. Then, rapier in one fist, holding his side with the other hand, he left.

Saint-Lucq escaped without encountering any more resistance and discovered a city in distress as fires ravaged its buildings and its frightened inhabitants sought to flee. Suffering more than he wanted to admit, he leaned against a wall. He was on rue Saint-Honoré, at the entrance to rue Gaillon. The hand pressed to his flank was sticky with blood.

'Saint-Lucq!'

It was Laincourt coming back for him.

Looking very pale, Saint-Lucq straightened up.

'The girl?' he asked.

'In safety. I entrusted her to the Capuchin monks on rue Saint-Honoré.'

'Good.'

'La Malicorne?'

'Dead.'

'You're wounded.'

'I can manage.'

'Let me see.'

'I can manage!' Then, settling down a little, the half-blood added: 'We need to get to Notre-Dame. That's where everything will be decided. And I'm willing to wager that's where La Fargue will be too.'

Laincourt nodded but watched the frantic scene in rue Saint-Honoré with a worried eye. A burning house nearby fell down, throwing up great incandescent plumes and prompting cries of terror. Men and beasts knocked into one another as they scrambled away from the raining debris. Saint-Lucq understood the reason for the young man's anxiety and, with his finger, he pointed to the Gaget Messenger Service's tower.

From the Hôtel des Arcanes, the Heresiarch strove to control the Primordial. He would have preferred to ignore the armed Chatelaines that were harassing them in the air, but the great black dragon wanted to finish off the unbearable white winged creatures. They attacked it and then flitted away, sometimes inflicting a brief, stinging pain that increased its anger. The Heresiarch could not do anything about this. He was seeing the world through the eyes of the Primordial. He guided it. But he could not act against its instincts. Indeed, he ran a great risk of losing himself within the primitive meanders of the Primordial's intelligence, of being taken over by its brutal emotions and primal impulses.

It was intoxicating to be nothing more than sheer, unbridled force.

Numerous louves had already perished. Others had been forced to retreat on wounded or exhausted wyverns. Only a few remained to divert the Primordial's fury. Without them, Paris would have been one immense inferno by now, but their sacrifice had only postponed the inevitable. They would not be able keep this up much longer.

There was a jolt.

A psychic blow struck the Heresiarch just as a searing pain blinded the Primordial. The mind of the Arcana's master tottered. Dazed, he needed a moment to recover and restore the link, but he managed it . . .

. . . just before another jolt shook him again.

A drop of blood ran from his nostril.

When the great tenor bell, called the *bourdon*, of Notre-Dame tolled for the second time, once again it seemed as if the Primordial had been hit full on by a cannon ball. Driven back by the impact of the sound, the giant dragon only regained mastery of its flight after some contortions and roars. The pain faded as the deep, low-pitched note of the enormous bell diminished in the night, but the Primordial did not repeat its original mistake: it remained a safe distance away from the cathedral.

In the streets of the capital, this small victory over the dragon was celebrated with cheers of joy. But beneath the tall archways of the Grande Galerie of Notre-Dame, La Fargue asked:

'What now? Because we won't be able to stave this monster off forever, will we?'

'No,' replied the White Wolves' mother superior without taking her eyes off the great black dragon as it soared in the distance. 'No, we won't.'

The Ordeal had come to an end and there was no more time for waiting and hoping.

'Open it,' said Mère Thérèse de Vaussambre in the silence of the crypt.

A massive door stood before her.

Solemn, two Chatelaines seized hold of the rings of the heavy twin panels, turned them, and then pulled.

Slowly the door opened, without a sound, and let the light enter within.

Standing, head bowed, Agnès de Vaudreuil held something against her chest, hidden in the shell of her hands.

'Are you a louve?' asked the Superior General of the Chatelaines.

As her sole response, Agnès lifted a grave face and extended her joined hands, revealing an empty and translucent Sphère d'Âme.

In Valombre's house, Marciac climbed the secret staircase wiping his brow and rejoined Alessandra, who was observing the sky from a window. He had carefully sutured the dragon's wound and placed a makeshift splint on his broken leg.

'Well?'

'I don't see the Primordial anymore,' replied La Donna. 'It seems as though the sound of the bell at Notre-Dame is forcing it to keep its distance.'

The bourdon of Notre-Dame was indeed continuing to toll in a slow but steady rhythm.

'We must have the Chatelaines to thank for that. This must be what they were preparing earlier,' added the Gascon.

He recalled that when Alessandra and he had passed in front of Notre-Dame on their way to Valombre's home, the cathedral had been lit up and occupied by the Sisters of Saint Georges.

'Except that the dragon had not yet shown itself,' objected the young woman. 'But since the Chatelaines were certainly not there by chance, they no doubt had good reasons to believe the Primordial would strike tonight. And they were preparing for it.'

'How could they have known?'

'As for that . . .'

La Donna shrugged her shoulders, pensive. Then she turned away from the window to look at Marciac. The moonlight shone on her pretty profile and scattered silver in her red hair.

'How is Valombre doing?'

'He's sleeping. Or has fainted again. In his state, it's more or less the same thing . . . But even though he's lost a lot of blood, he'll live. Of course, he'd be better off in his bed, but I don't feel strong enough to carry him up on my back . . . Be that as it may, if you hadn't been so concerned about him, he'd be dead by now.'

While Alessandra went down to be at the patient's side, Marciac went into the kitchen to search for something to drink and a moment of calm. He found an open bottle of wine that he drained in three gulps from the neck and was starting to feel a little more at ease when he heard cries, noises, and savage laughter outside.

Intrigued, he went to have a look out one of the windows, and swore.

Bands of dracs were leaving Les Écailles across the crude wooden bridges that linked their island to the two banks of Paris, but also over the rickety and almost forgotten footbridge that led to the canons' neighbourhood, at the end of the Ile de la Cité. And even on boats, some of which capsized and went adrift, carried off by the current.

They were drunk, excited by the fires, exasperated by the din of the tocsin, exalted by the spectacle offered to them by the great black dragon in the sky. Above all, most of them were plunged into a state of madness engendered by the Arcana's wine and the drug that the Enchantress had added to it, in accordance with the Heresiarch's plans. A temporary madness, true. But a madness that blinded them, woke their warrior spirit, and revived their taste for blood. They felt a need to kill and to destroy, carry out acts of violence and satisfy their vile impulses. They brandished weapons and torches, howled war cries, burst into peals of cruel laughter.

In the Cloister neighbourhood of Notre-Dame, the pillage of the first houses in rue du Chapitre began as Marciac looked out onto the street.

Alessandra had slipped a cushion beneath Valombre's head. Sitting on the floor by the dragon in the small secret room, she heard the Gascon running down the stairs and stood up, alarmed.

'What's going on?'

'We have to go. Come.'

'Why?'

'The dracs are attacking. They're arriving from Les Écailles and plundering the neighbourhood. It's a question of minutes before they break down the door.'

'The dracs are attacking? But that's impossible!'

'Well, you can tell them that in a minute. Come on.'

He tried to grab her hand, but she would not let him.

'We can't abandon Valombre here.'

'We don't have a choice, Alessandra.'

'I won't abandon him!'

'Alessandra!'

'I'm staying here!'

Marciac cursed but refrained from commenting on the stubbornness of women. He needed to think fast and well. Of course, he could lock all three of them in here and pray that the dracs did not find the hidden staircase. But if he and La Donna had found it, why shouldn't they? And even if the looters lacked the patience to find the mechanism for opening the passage, they still had the solution of breaking in. The winged dracs who had tried to assassinate Valombre were short of time and could not make too much noise for fear of alerting the neighbours. The dracs who were coming now could do as they pleased.

'All right,' the Gascon said resignedly. 'Stay here. I'll do what I can.'

'You are leaving us?'

'I must.'

He went back up to the ground floor after waving goodbye to Alessandra, closed the iron door first and then the sliding wooden panel.

Torchlight danced behind the window panes.

Bracing himself against a large and heavy cupboard in the corridor, Marciac succeeded in dislodging it, and then pushed it against the wall with the secret passage. There he had to turn it before putting it into place. The front door of the house was already shaking from the thuds of boots. Huffing and straining, he finished the job, but exhausted, he could only check the general effect achieved: Alessandra and Valombre should be safe as long as no one thought of moving the cupboard.

Marciac left through the rear garden just as the front door gave way.

He climbed over a wall, jumped down into an alley, and in rue Chanoinesse, saw people fleeing in the direction of Notre-Dame cathedral. Dracs were breaking down the doors of the last dwellings in rue de Chapitre. Bodies were being thrown through windows to crash bloody on the paving stones. Man, woman, child, or priest, no one was spared. It would soon be the turn of the small rue des Chantres.

Marciac knew that he could not do much, except to hurry stragglers along and urge as many people as possible to flee. But there were many residents huddled up in their dwellings out of fear of the Primordial, and who were completely unaware of the new danger that threatened them. So the Gascon knocked on doors and window panes, yelling vainly over the din from the bourdon of Notre-Dame and the thousand other bells of Paris that were sounding the tocsin. Enraged by his helplessness, he thought he glimpsed a movement through a window of a house, broke down the door with a great kick, entered, and called out, warning those inside of the great danger they were in.

A small door inched open beneath the stairway and a frightened man passed his head out through the gap.

'You must leave, monsieur!' Marciac told him. 'You are not safe here!'

'But . . .'

'Are you alone?'

'No. With my wife . . . and . . . and my children. In the cellar.'

'Then they must make haste or all of you will die!' the Gascon ordered. 'And me with you,' he muttered to himself.

When he returned, the man was carrying a three-year-old boy and held a little girl by the hand. His wife followed him. She was eight months with child and had difficulty walking, breathing heavily. Marciac helped her pass through the low door.

The sound of breaking glass came from the kitchen, on the garden side of the house.

'What was that?' asked the woman in alarm.

'Quickly!' said the Gascon in a low voice.

But the little girl screamed: a grey drac marauder had just entered the room.

'Flee!' shouted Marciac. 'To Notre-Dame! Go!'

And drawing his rapier, he placed himself *en garde* while the couple and their two children escaped out into the street.

The grey drac also unsheathed his sword, and was immediately joined by another drac – this one black – who already had a sword in his fist. They advanced. Marciac retreated, overturning a table back against a wall so that it would not hamper him. The black drac was chuckling uncontrollably and his eyes, in the dimness, shone with an insane glow. The grey drac had a slightly unsteady step, but nothing more. With a kick, Marciac slid a stool towards the black drac who easily avoided it and chuckled even harder. No luck. The two dracs spread out, with the intention of obliging their adversary to fight on two fronts. Seeing this, the Gascon started to look truly worried. His guard position began to waver and the grey drac sneered . . .

At least until Marciac reached his left hand behind his back, suddenly brandished a pistol and opened fire. The drac tumbled over backward, hit in the middle of the brow. Astonished, the black drac reacted too late: the Gascon had already lunged at full stretch and planted the point of his rapier in the invader's heart.

Withdrawing his sword and backing up, Marciac looked at the two corpses.

Not a very honourable way to fight, but it was effective.

Without giving it further thought, he came out on the threshold of the house and saw that Black Guards were taking up position in the street while others were protecting the survivors' flight, aiding those who had difficulty walking, carrying those who couldn't. They were just in time: dracs were arriving from rue Chanoinesse and were immediately routed by a volley of musket fire.

Marciac recognised the officer commanding the guards.

'Leprat!'

'Marciac!'

The two men exchanged greetings.

Reynault had entrusted Leprat with keeping watch at the northern entrance to the cathedral: the Cloister portal. Realising what was happening in the canons' neighbourhood, the musketeer had decided to go to the assistance of all those who could still be saved.

'Where is La Fargue?' asked the Gascon.

'At Notre-Dame.'

'What's going on there?'

'The Chatelaines are praying, thanks to which the bell of Notre-Dame is keeping the Primordial at bay. But don't ask me any more than that. I don't understand these matters myself . . . And La Donna?'

Marciac had no time to reply.

Other dracs were arriving, with Keress Karn at their head. Neither Leprat nor Marciac knew his name, but they recognised him as the red drac who had led the assault on the Château de Mareuil-sur-Ay, when Alessandra had been abducted.

That could not be a coincidence.

Leprat gave the order to retreat and the guards abandoned the small rue des Chantres, slowly, to allow the refugees time to reach the cathedral. But then the dracs charged and furious hand-to-hand combat broke out alongside Notre-Dame, the guards falling back in good order towards the Cloister portal, where the last fugitives from the canons' neighbourhood were now jostling their way inside. Disciplined, courageous, and fighting every inch of the way, the Black Guards formed an arc in front of the portal, which gradually tightened as the survivors entered the cathedral.

Then it was the turn of the wounded, of Marciac and the rest, to enter one by one.

Lastly, Leprat and a few others retreated together into the cathedral, just as the heavy doors of the portal were closed behind them.

The siege of Notre-Dame had begun.

Fanning the night air with great beats of their wings, two saddled wyverns were flying over Paris. Above them, the sky was immense, starry and peaceful, beneath the impassive eye of a beautiful round moon. Below them the city had been thrown into fear and panic, with scenes of violence, stampedes towards the city gates, and outbreaks of rioting all across the capital. Fires burned everywhere the dragon's breath had struck. And they were spreading, flames rising with a roar like greedy, furious monsters.

His bruised face caressed by the wind, Laincourt guided his wyvern, trying not to be overcome by emotion. Or rather, by all of the emotions that were thrashing about inside him: hatred, anger, fear, revolt. He held tightly to the reins of his anxious mount and followed Saint-Lucq who was flying ahead, just as he had followed him to the Gaget Messenger Services, where the half-blood had requisitioned the two wyverns. After a few heavy, lumbering steps in the courtyard, the reptiles had taken flight. They were now carrying the two men towards Notre-Dame, whose song reached through the clouds of smoke and set off a low vibration that stirred in their guts.

Stone-faced, Saint-Lucq did not take his eyes from the twin towers of the sacred citadel.

That's where everything will be decided, he had said to Laincourt.

Everything.

Looking livid and tense, his long hair floating over his shoulders, the half-blood held his wounded flank with one hand as the glow from the great blazes below were reflected in the red lenses of his spectacles.

La Fargue and Mère Béatrice d'Aussaint had climbed to the top of the south tower of Notre-Dame, the one housing the bourdon, which – slow, low-pitched and steady – continued to ring out its protective toll.

From this terrace, exposed to the winds sixty metres from the ground, they saw the drac bands that had left Les Écailles and were now engaged in wild pillaging, starting with the Saint-Paul quay on the Right Bank, La Tournelle quay on the Left Bank, and the nearby Cloister. The mother superior of the White Wolves had sent messengers to the Louvre, the Bastille, and the Arsenal, where troops were garrisoned, alerting them to the situation. But even those who were not already mobilised to fight the fires would not be able to intervene in time. At present, the dracs were encountering no resistance and could carry out their atrocities with complete impunity, terrorising a defenceless population. Already plundered, most of the Cloister neighbourhood had been set alight and the rest of the Ile de la Cité was now under threat. Under the orders of Reynault d'Ombreuse, the company of the Black Guards was preparing to defend Notre-Dame's western forecourt. The Cloister gate on the north side of the cathedral had already been subjected to an assault by the dracs.

'Nothing will have been spared us,' said Mère d'Aussaint. 'Just when we repelled the Primordial, the riot started in Les Écailles and now we have to defend Notre-Dame itself.'

The great black dragon passed in the distance: its wide circles still keeping it well away from the cathedral bell tower. But it had not given up.

On the contrary, it appeared to be waiting.

'These riots have started just in time to suit our enemies,' said La Fargue. 'I don't know how, but the Arcana are behind them. Moreover, the dracs who attacked the Cloister portal and continue to besiege it are all well-disciplined mercenaries who are obviously following orders.'

'Orders to interrupt, at any cost, the ritual taking place inside Notre-Dame. Without it, the bell will toll in vain.'

'I agree,' replied the Blades' captain turning round. 'Perhaps you should shift some of the guards defending the forecourt and . . . Look out!'

La Fargue leapt and pinned Mère d'Aussaint to the ground as a winged drac flew past, delivering a mighty sword stroke to the empty air. As they picked themselves up and unsheathed their own weapons, five dracs landed on the terrace and, rapiers already in fists, tucked in their leathery wings.

Back to back, La Fargue and the White Wolves' mother superior placed themselves *en garde*, waiting for the dracs to make their move.

'They want to reach the bell tower,' said the Chatelaine. 'If the bell ceases to toll—'

The winged dracs attacked.

Inside Notre-Dame, as the besieged Cloister portal was being closed, the Black Guards had been quick to lead the escapees across the transept, and then made them leave by the Saint-Étienne door to seek refuge in the adjoining episcopal palace. Some of them wanted to remain under the double protection of the cathedral and the Sisters of Saint Georges, but the guards were adamant: the tranquillity of the Chatelaines at prayer had to be preserved as much as possible. Kneeling in the choir behind the high altar, the sisters had been praying for hours, their murmur haunting the empty space of the immense nave. Their fervour was such that the air seemed to vibrate, as if traversed by echoes between the slow, grave peals of the bourdon. But they were growing exhausted, to the point that some had fainted and had to be carried away.

Nevertheless they were still managing to hold firm.

As long as they prayed and the bell of Notre-Dame continued to sound, the Primordial would be forced to keep its distance from Paris.

Joining Leprat near the Cloister portal, Marciac saw his friend succumb to a bout of weakness that he alone noticed. The musketeer's legs suddenly gave way beneath him and he had to lean on a pillar to disguise his weakness. His face was pale, however, and his jaws clenched as he tried not to grimace.

Marciac took Leprat by the elbow in a gesture that might seem merely friendly, but supported the musketeer's weight as he drew him aside, beneath the first arches of the ambulatory.

'What's wrong with you?' the Gascon asked in a low voice.

'Nothing. I . . . I'm just tired.'

'Pull the other one. It's the ranse, isn't it?'

Leprat sighed. Looked away. Nodded.

Marciac understood what was happening to his friend.

'It's the ritual, it's hostile to dragons,' he said. 'It threatens your ranse which is defending itself and eating away at you. It will kill you if you stay here!'

'And where do you suggest I go? To the Hôtel-Dieu hospital next door?

'No, Antoine, no one is asking you to—'

'At this hour, my place is here, Nicolas. Here, and nowhere else.'

Irritated, the Gascon turned away.

'Anyway,' added Leprat in a jesting tone, 'don't you think I have more to fear from a drac's sword than from the ranse, if I stay here? And so do you, by the way . . .'

Marciac did not reply.

They were near the Red portal, which owed its name to the colour of its panels. Much smaller than the Cloister portal, it gave the canons direct access to the choir. The Black Guards had barricaded it rather than defend it.

A wisp of smoke was rising from beneath it.

When he saw it, Marciac thought – too late – of the mines that had blown away the gates at Château de Mareuil.

'Down!' he yelled, pushing Leprat behind a pillar.

The blast threw the Gascon into the air.

He fell back heavily on the flagstones and, covered in dust and with blood dripping from his nostrils, he tried to get up. A high-pitched whistling filled his ears and the thump of his own heartbeat was deafening, but any sounds from outside his body were muffled. His vision was clouded and the ground beneath him seemed to sway and rock, making him dizzy. His legs like jelly, he stood with the help of a pillar and then almost slipped back to the ground. In a great blur, he saw armed dracs entering Notre-Dame through the demolished Red portal. He also recognised Leprat, advancing towards them. The mine's explosion had not spared the musketeer. His step was unsteady. He struggled to remain standing and drew his white rapier with a far too expansive gesture, like that of a drunken man. Combat was engaged as Black Guards came to the rescue. One of them jostled Marciac as he ran by.

The Gascon tripped and caught himself the best he could. The sounds of the fighting came to him from a distance, in a distorted form. For him, seconds stretched out in slow motion. He straightened, saw Leprat brandishing his sword with two hands in the midst of a confused mêlée, taking large swings with it. The musketeer was possessed by a warrior's fury. He had already taken several wounds without yielding ground and he continued to strike to the right, to the left, and to strike over and over again. Marciac wanted to come to his aid. He tried to unsheathe his rapier, took a step, then two, three, but was overcome by dizziness and fell to one knee. The immense lines of perspective within the cathedral danced, blurred, and separated above him.

Gathering his wits, he searched for Leprat . . .

And suddenly there was a great silence.

Suddenly his ears stopped buzzing and his heart stopped beating.

Suddenly icy terror stamped in his memory an image that would never leave him: Leprat had a blade planted up to the hilt in his belly and was vomiting up blood.

On the roof of the south tower, La Fargue and Mère Béatrice d'Aussaint had slain one winged drac apiece. Three remained, two of which joined forces against the captain of the Blades. Striking, parrying, riposting, at one corner of the terrace he defended the turret which housed the stairway leading to the belfry. They needed at all costs to prevent the dracs from reaching it and stopping the slow peals of the bourdon. Evading one clumsy cut, La Fargue passed beneath the guard of one of his adversaries and found the drac's chest. Then he broke off to avoid the thrust of the second drac, engaged his blade, pushed it away from the line of his body and – obeying old reflexes – projected the reptilian's body into thin air with a strong kick to the abdomen. But the creature simply deployed his wings and immediately returned to the fray, while La Fargue cursed. The drac had barely managed to set one foot back on the terrace, however, when he was struck by a pistol ball right in the middle of his forehead. It was a service rendered by the mother superior to the captain, just after she had disposed of the third drac she had been confronting alone.

'Quickly!' she said before dashing into the turret, smoking pistol in one hand and her rapier in the other.

Notre-Dame itself was under threat.

All up and down the front of the cathedral, Black Guards and louves were now desperately resisting the enemy: on the forecourt before the main façade's three portals; in the twin recesses of the gallery of the Virgin; beneath the archways of the Grande Galerie where a number of winged dracs had landed, and even on the walkway that ran across the top of the upper gallery, linking the two main towers.

La Fargue followed the mother superior and closed the door of the turret behind them, pushing the bolts home. Then they dashed down the narrow spiral staircase inside the tower housing Notre-Dame's enormous bourdon bell and the magnificent wooden frame from which it was suspended. At the bottom, a small door opened and a winged drac entered. Surprised, Mère d'Aussaint took a sword blow and backed away. La Fargue leapt to her rescue, split the drac's skull open, and pushed him back outside. But others were arriving just as the bourdon gave a deafening peal. The captain rushed towards them and forced them back along the Grande Galerie.

'Close the door!' he shouted to the leader of the White Wolves.

Mère d'Aussaint, one hand pressed over her wound, shut the door behind La Fargue, stranding him alone on the gallery. He was condemned to do or die, but the vital task now was to protect the bourdon.

Inside the cathedral, in the furious fighting between dracs and Black Guards near the remains of the Red portal, Marciac rushed towards Keress Karn as the red drac, with evil glee on his face, pulled his blade from Leprat's body. The Gascon struck with fearsome power, forcing Karn to parry and back away. But then the drac recovered and, while not managing to gain the upper hand, he ceased to retreat before the Blade's assault.

A bitter duel began.

Attacks were met with parries. Counters were followed by ripostes. The red drac knew how to fight and kept a cool head. His fencing was the kind learned on the battlefield: effective and without flourishes. Tense and focused, Marciac realised they were evenly matched. So he thought of Leprat and, careful not to let himself be blinded by anger, he drew renewed strength from the memory. His arm became the instrument of vengeance. His strokes were powerful, precise and formidable, and Karn started to grow worried. He wanted to call for help, but their confrontation had taken the two adversaries far up the ambulatory, away from the main mêlée. The red drac could do no more than defend himself. And while his moves became more and more frantic, but less and less accurate, the Gascon's never varied in their effectiveness.

At last, Marciac knew the moment had come.

Twisting Karn's blade with his own, he sent it flying away and, body stretched, he slipped the point of his sword beneath the disarmed drac's chin. Then he plunged his gaze into that of his vanquished enemy and, brusquely pushing his shoulder forward, sank two good inches of steel into the drac's throat. Keress Karn tossed his head backward and stumbled, his hand against his wound, unable to staunch the thick, heavy blood spurting out.

The Gascon watched him fall and die.

La Fargue rapidly took stock of the situation: it was not to his advantage. The dracs had taken control of the Grande Galerie and a handful of Black Guards were now retreating into the north tower. There was no one left on the side of the south tower, other than a few dead bodies and himself.

The captain of the Blades placed himself *en garde* with his back to the door, determined to sell his life dearly. He held the grip of his sword with both hands. Glared at the dracs approaching him. Took a deep breath.

And charged with a warlike scream.

He stunned the first drac with a violent blow, felled another by smashing the guard of his sword beneath his chin, brought his Pappenheimer down on a skull to the right, on a shoulder to the left, and into a belly straight ahead of him. He had taken his adversaries by surprise but their riposte was not long in coming. He was forced to parry various attacks by cut and thrust, received a wound to the arm which he did not feel in the heat of battle, followed by a blow to the head that left him stunned for an instant. He retreated, delivered two killing thrusts of his own, and then felt a pain in his thigh and a burning in his side. He withdrew again, still battling away, and felt his back bump into the tower door. At which point he knew that his moments were numbered. He squared up to his enemies, nevertheless, breathless but standing firm, his eyes sparkling and his face spattered with drops of blood.

Ready to meet his end.

Yet the dracs hesitated. The final stroke did not come.

The battle had turned in favour of the defenders inside Notre-Dame. The dracs sensed it and didn't know what to do. The fighting had already ceased out on the forecourt. Winged dracs were launching themselves into the air from the gallery of the Virgin as Black Guards arrived by way of the north tower. Pistol shots rang out, fired at the indecisive dracs in the Grande Galerie. This threat persuaded them that safety lay in flight and those who could jumped over the side and flew for safety. The others fell before pistol balls or to the swords of the guards who retook control of the gallery.

Victory seeming assured, La Fargue let himself slump down the door he had defended so well and sat on the ground, exhausted, his head bowed and his wrists resting on his raised knees.

Soon, someone approached him.

'Happy to see you again, captain.'

It was Laincourt, with a bruised face and a bloodied rapier in his fist. Even more surprising, Saint-Lucq was just behind him, busy turning over drac bodies and planting his sword in their hearts. Their borrowed wyverns had landed on the north tower of the cathedral and they had helped defend it until the counterattack came from the Saint Georges Guards.

Accepting the hand that the young man held out to him, La Fargue got up with a grim face.

'Are you wounded, captain?'

'Nothing serious. But you're a sorry sight, Laincourt.'

'La Malicorne did me an evil turn. If not for Saint-Lucq, I'd be either dead or praying I was, right now.'

La Fargue turned to the half-blood, who was gazing at him. They exchanged nods. The one said: *Thank you for being here.* And the other: *You're welcome.*

'What are your orders, captain?'

His answer was lost as the Primordial bellowed, suddenly very near.

Marciac returned to the Red portal and its corpse-strewn rubble. Having successfully defended the forecourt of Notre-Dame, Reynault had retreated back inside the cathedral. This allowed him to send a portion of his troops into the towers to retake the galleries, but also to send some of them to rescue those defending the Red portal. And so Karn's dracs were defeated and repelled. Nevertheless, the explosion of their mine and the subsequent assault had achieved the desired effect: interrupting the prayer of the Chatelaines gathered in the choir and ending the ritual that allowed the Notre-Dame bell to keep the Primordial at bay.

The defenders had won a bitter victory, then. And one which announced certain disaster.

But Marciac cared nothing for any of that.

Kneeling, he gently lifted Leprat's head and the musketeer opened his eyes slightly.

'It . . . It hurts less than . . . than it usually does,' he said in a weak, hoarse voice. 'That . . . That means it's serious doesn't it?'

The Gascon did not know what to reply.

Brushing the hair, now sticky with sweat and blood, out of his friend's eyes, he nodded and tried to smile.

'DRAGON!'

Not everyone had the reflex to dive for cover when the cry rang out.

Swooping between the twin towers of Notre-Dame, the Primordial belched fire over the Grande Galerie, taking the Black Guards by surprise. Many were set ablaze and men tumbled over the walls, screaming.

'Good God!' swore La Fargue. 'But how . . . ?'

He stood up and, incredulous, looked at the dragon now making a large loop above the Ile de la Cité. The bell still tolled, but did not seem to bother the giant creature. Evidently, the Chatelaines' magic was no longer working.

Which meant the cathedral was doomed.

'Inside!' ordered the captain of the Blades. 'Everybody inside, quickly!'

The Primordial was already coming back.

Taking their wounded with them, the guards retreated into the towers. La Fargue, Laincourt, and Saint-Lucq did the same, the half-blood closing the door at the very moment when, beating its wings slowly and hanging in the air before the Grande Galerie, the dragon sprayed it with a long incandescent burst that incinerated the dead bodies and ate into the stone like acid.

Its work done for now, the Primordial resumed its flight.

The last defenders of Notre-Dame assembled in the nave, around Mère Béatrice d'Aussaint. There were only twenty of them, including the Blades, and most of them were wounded. All of them were exhausted. They had fought, suffered, seen brothers-in-arms fall and they sensed that it had all been in vain.

They had no more doubts when the bell ceased to toll.

The Primordial was triumphant.

'We need to evacuate,' said La Fargue.

'Flee?' asked Reynault d'Ombreuse, offended by the idea.

'The Primordial is going to reduce this cathedral to ashes, and there is nothing you or I can do to prevent it.'

'The captain is right,' agreed the White Wolves' mother superior. 'We must be able to fight other battles.'

A makeshift bandage enveloped her wounded shoulder. She was pale and her features were drawn, but her gaze shone with a fierce determination. Very calmly, she thought and then said:

'We can reach the episcopal palace via the sacristy. It will keep us out of sight of the dragon.'

Reynault nodded and went to give the orders, while the mother superior took hold of La Fargue by the arm and confided:

'If you can, hold here. One hope remains.'

'I know, mother.'

Sure of its victory, the Primordial slowly circled Notre-Dame.

Intoxicated by its own power and restored liberty, it bellowed triumphantly. The Heresiarch no longer dominated it: it was as if he had been washed away, submerged by the simple and brutal emotions that guided the primitive dragon. It could indulge its primary instincts: to fly and to destroy.

The Primordial sent a few playful balls of fire that exploded across Paris, set fire to the windmills on Saint-Roch hill, and amused itself by burning the trees in the Tuileries park. But in the end, it returned to Notre-Dame. It gathered speed, aimed for the great rose-window that adorned the cathedral's main façade and, tucking its wings against its body, smashed through it in an explosion of multicoloured glass, to land heavily inside.

The Blades were waiting on the steps of the choir. La Fargue was in the middle and Laincourt, Saint-Lucq, Marciac, and even Leprat were at his sides, although Leprat, dying, could barely stand and gripped the Gascon's shoulder. They all had their rapiers in hand because they could not imagine, at this hour, perishing any other way.

Intrigued and wary, the enormous black dragon advanced with a slow, heavy step, its feet smashing the flagstones each time they struck the floor, its scaly tail lashing the rubble behind it.

It halted, stretched its neck out and lowered its head, decorated with its distinctive faceted jewel, to examine the five men closely.

The Blades did not make the slightest move.

In the silence, the Primordial's powerful breathing filled the devastated cathedral, sounding like a forge. It spent a long moment observing the pathetic creatures that were blocking its path and giving every appearance of defying it.

In a hoarse voice, it managed with difficulty:

'WH . . . WHY? . . . FU . . . TILE . . .'

'Because it is not given to everyone to choose the manner of their death, dragon,' replied La Fargue without blinking.

The idea that a being might sacrifice itself was perfectly foreign to the Primordial. It considered the five men standing before it, as if their attitude obliged it to ponder the necessity of killing them.

And suddenly the dragon turned round and moved away, with a waddle like that of a big lizard, climbed the cathedral's great organ — which it broke beneath its weight — and slithered back outside through the ruined rose-window.

Agnès stood alone on the forecourt littered with the bodies of dracs and men. She was armed and dressed as a White Wolf of Saint Georges: high beige boots whose upper folds covered her knees, lined riding breeches, a slit robe, a heavy belt that cinched her waist, ample sleeves, thick gloves, a wimple which framed her face in an oval, and a veil. She bore the cross and dragon of her order over her heart, but where the dragon was embroidered in black on the uniforms of other louves, hers was scarlet. She had drawn her sword, which she held point down, slightly apart from her body. The blade and the pommel of her sword were made of gleaming black draconite.

There she waited.

Behind her the small church of Saint-Christophe was burning.

The Primordial examined Agnès carefully without coming too near. It was uneasy. Recent experience had taught it to be wary of louves, but this one was different. It sensed an immense, extraordinary power inside her. A power that was perhaps superior to its own, although such power could not possibly inhabit a puny, frail body such as the one it saw before it.

It sensed the power of an Ancestral Dragon.

The great black dragon bellowed, and the louve did not react in the slightest.

And then it leapt.

Agnès immediately plunged forward in a roll as the dragon passed over her, and came up with her sword to slit its belly open. The draconite blade sliced cleanly through the scales and into the flesh beneath, which sputtered as if eaten by acid. Agnès stood and turned. The Primordial also spun round brusquely, with a powerful heave of its muscles. They stared at one another again, but now the louve had her back to the cathedral. The dragon was in pain. Furious, it crouched down, bellowed once more, and belched.

In a single movement, Agnès put one knee to the ground and turned her blade point down. Eyes closed, she was already praying when the flames reached her, and they parted around her like waves before the prow of a ship. The dragon per-severed, breathing out a river of screaming, turbulent flames. The air itself seemed to catch fire. The corpses around her were devoured by this furnace and turned to piles of ashes that were immediately swept away. The paving stones blackened, then glowed red with the heat, and shattered. The flames striking Notre-Dame's façade rolled over the stone and ex-ploded like the crash of fiery surf on a rocky shore.

But it was to no avail.

Exasperated and tired, the Primordial gave up. It ceased belching fire and watched the louve stand up unharmed, while the cathedral doors burned behind her. Agnès raised her eyes and looked deep into the terrifying and abysmal gaze of the archaic dragon.

It understood that she felt no fear and gave a long, mourn-ful growl.

'Now it's my turn,' said the louve.

Abruptly spreading her arms, she cried out words of power and the air vibrated and crackled around her.

Discharges of energy shot forth around her as a white form

detached itself from her body, a white form that grew and grew, becoming immense. She was liberating her spectral dragon, summoning its power. And it reared up and deployed its wings before the increasingly frightened, mesmerised Primordial. In a trance, her arms outstretched to either side and her head tilted back, Agnès began to levitate as sparks of light whirled around her, as gusts of wind whipped her sleeves and the flaps of her robe, as the night tore open and a low roar swelled in volume . . .

And this time it was the Ancestral Dragon who belched flame.

A white fire descended upon the Primordial and submerged it in a dazzling inferno. The black dragon struggled but could not escape the blast. In its violent contortions, it smashed in the façade of one of the houses bordering the forecourt, causing the building to collapse, and with a mighty swipe of its tail it completed the destruction of the Saint-Christophe church. It screamed and moaned, a prisoner of the torments inflicted upon it by the sacred fire. And suddenly it arched its back and remained still, for the brief second it took for the jewel on its brow to explode into pieces.

The Primordial's lifeless body collapsed with a final, heavy thud.

Alone in the magic study at the Hôtel des Arcanes, the Heresiarch slumped on his back, his gaze staring and wide, and his brow split by a deep wound. Black blood ran from his nostrils and ears as he breathed his last.

All was quiet and still again on the Notre-Dame forecourt.

Agnès re-sheathed her sword.

Then, turning away from the smoking body of the Primordial she entered the cathedral through the central portal whose doors had been completely consumed by the flames, crossed the silent, devastated nave with a calm step, and found La Fargue and the others beneath the cross of the transept.

Grave, silent and still, they had gathered around Leprat who lay dead on the steps to the choir.

3

With the dawn came a fine, fresh rain.

It did little to fight the fires, but it was as though a soothing balm had been applied to the wounds of Paris. The population wanted to see it as a sign, welcoming it with hope and gratitude. Having rung a sinister tocsin the entire night, some church bells celebrated the shower with more joyful chimes.

It was still raining when Agnès found La Fargue in the court-yard of the Hôtel de l'Épervier, which had been reduced to charred and smoking ruins. The captain stared at the wreck-age without really seeing it, but did not turn away when he heard Agnès approach on horseback and dismount.

'Naïs has turned in her apron,' he said tonelessly. 'André was seriously burned while saving the horses. And Guibot is dead, and buried somewhere underneath this rubble.'

The louve crossed herself.

'Paris is saved,' she said. 'Order will soon be restored in the city and we'll rebuild.'

'But the dead won't come back to life, will they?'

Agnès did not reply.

A silence settled over them.

La Fargue had not washed or changed his clothes since the night's battle. His clothing was encrusted with dirt and blood, and his face was smudged with soot. His head was bare and his wrinkles had deepened.

'What have you come to tell me, Agnès?' he asked.

'The truth. You deserve to know. The Blades have paid a heavy enough price for it . . .'

'I'm listening.'

'The Arcana's Grand Design was to seat a dragon on the throne of France. A dragon who would be born to the queen, thanks to a draconic seed planted within her, without her knowledge. They did it when she still the *infanta* of Spain, after she was promised to Louis XIII.'

'A draconic seed?'

'Her physician was a member of the Arcana. When she manifested the initial symptoms of the ranse, he performed various rituals which saved her. But he also used the opportunity to ensure that any children she carried would be transformed, becoming dragons.'

'This member of the Arcana, it was the Heresiarch.'

'Yes.'

'But weren't the Chatelaines supposed to prevent such things from happening? And besides, didn't they subject the queen to tests? Such scrupulous ones that she still nurses an enduring grudge against them?'

'Yes, indeed. But they failed to detect this seed, and when they finally realised their error, it was too late. They could not acknowledge their mistake without discrediting themselves. And what a scandal it would have created! What an insult to Spain! What a humiliation for France! It was lucky that the queen had not yet given birth to a child.'

'So the Chatelaines kept silent. And what else did they do, other than protect their secret?'

'Whatever they could . . .'

La Fargue frowned and then he understood.

'They encouraged the king's disenchantment with the queen?'

'They provoked it with certain powders.'

'And the queen's miscarriages?'

'Those children's births had to be prevented at all costs, captain. And each time, when they were examined, they revealed that the draconic transformation had begun . . .'

'The king, the queen, the cardinal, none of them know of this?'

'The cardinal knows.'

La Fargue kept silent, thinking, considering certain

323

mysteries in a new light. Such as the fertility ritual the Alchemist had wanted the queen to undergo, no doubt to counter the Chatelaines' manoeuvres and allow her to give birth to a child. And the assassination of Henri IV, which La Donna had told him was the Arcana's work: unlike his wife, the good king Henri had firmly opposed a marriage between his son and the *infanta* . . .

'And now?' asked the captain of the Blades. 'The Chatelaines can't deprive France of an heir forever . . . Are you going to bring about the repudiation of the queen?'

Agnès hesitated.

'We will find a solution. Perhaps we will have to be content with second-best.'

Second-best? La Fargue wondered.

Only to realise that he couldn't care less what their second-best solution was. There was almost nothing he could care about now . . . except, beneath his shirt, the leather wallet Pontevedra had given him. It contained documents about his daughter's disappearance who, to regain her freedom, had escaped the Guardians' surveillance and fled.

La Fargue had sworn to find her again.

'I have decided to move Ballardieu's body,' announced Agnès suddenly. 'I will dig him a grave at Vaudreuil, at the bottom of the garden, under a tree by the river. He liked to rest there.'

'That would please him,' said the captain. A memory came back to him. 'One day, when Ballardieu had been drinking . . .'

'Yes,' said the young woman ironically, but giving a sad smile. 'I remember that day . . .'

'One day, when he had been drinking,' continued La Fargue, 'Ballardieu told me he had spent the happiest years of his life at Vaudreuil, with you. Indeed, he made no mystery of the fact.'

Sœur Marie-Agnès de Vaudreuil nodded.

With a heavy heart and tears in her eyes, she turned to leave, leading her horse by the bridle.

'Goodbye, Agnès.'
'Goodbye, captain.'

The Gentleman and the Enchantress watched Paris from the heights of the village of Montmartre, seated on horseback and draped in large cloaks that protected them from the rain. Flames still danced here and there in the city, but mostly they could see thick columns of black smoke rising toward the low sky. After the riots, order had still not been completely restored in the capital. Refusing to lay down their weapons, the renegade dracs had built barricades which companies of the Gardes-Françaises were seizing and dismantling one by one. Drac corpses hung from every gallows in the city. And it would be unwise for those dracs remaining to leave Les Écailles for quite some time . . .

'Will we ever come back?' asked the Enchantress.

'I am sure of it.'

Laincourt brought Clotilde back home but did not stay to watch her tearful reunion with her father. As soon as the girl found refuge in her father's arms, he withdrew.

You'll miss them, won't you? said the hurdy-gurdy player walking beside of the young man.

Yes.

You can always write to them.

It would be best if they forgot all about me.

And me?

I know you're never going to leave me.

Having found La Donna and Valombre safe and sound, Marciac went to rue Grenouillère. A few houses had burned there and Gabrielle, with her frogs, was helping the owners recover anything that could be salvaged from the rubble.

Gabrielle abandoned her task when she saw the Gascon approaching. Smiling and almost crying, she walked towards him, then hurried and ran to throw herself in his arms, before breaking into gentle sobs.

'I love you,' she murmured, embracing him with all her might. 'Oh, how I love you . . .'

He smiled, exhausted but happy, and breathed in the fragrance of her hair.

'Tell me again about this estate in Touraine,' he said. 'And tell me again about this child you are carrying. I want to know what my life is going to be like.'

The next day the king returned to Paris by coach, so that he could show himself to his people and reassure them. On the way he asked:

'What was the name of that captain again?'

'La Fargue, Sire,' replied Cardinal Richelieu.

'We will have to reward him one day, won't we?'

'Yes, Sire.'

'La Fargue . . . La Fargue . . . I recall that my father had a great esteem and friendship for a La Fargue . . .'

'They are one and the same, Sire.'

And as the king said nothing more the cardinal imitated him, while reflecting on the ingratitude of princes.

Searching for his daughter, La Fargue, alone and penniless, embarked at Dieppe on 27 September 1633 aboard *La Bienfaisance*, bound for La Nouvelle-France. The adventures and events that marked his life in America remain to be told.

Marciac lived happily with Gabrielle until his heart failed him during a game of cards. He was seventy-nine years old and was teaching his granddaughter how to cheat.

A viewing was organised for Leprat at monsieur de Tréville's mansion in rue du Vieux-Colombier. For three days and three nights the King's Musketeers watched over his mortal remains. He was buried with full honours and still lies in his family's tomb at the Château d'Orgueil.

Laincourt disappeared on the road to Lorraine, and was never heard of again.

Nor was any more ever heard of Saint-Lucq.

As for Agnès . . .

4

On 5 September 1638, at the Château de Saint-Germain-en-Laye, Anne d'Autriche gave birth to twin boys in secret . . . twins who could in no way be considered identical.

Mère de Vaudreuil was immediately consulted.

'Which one?' asked Louis XIII, looking down at the two newborn babies in their swaddling clothes.

'This one,' replied the White Wolves' mother superior.

'I want him to live!' cried the queen from her bed. 'I will bear the sorrow of his being torn from me, but he must live!' she insisted between sobs.

'Madame, I have promised you this,' said the king gravely.

Shortly after, Mère de Vaudreuil galloped away into the night carrying the child.

And so the Masque de Fer was born . . .